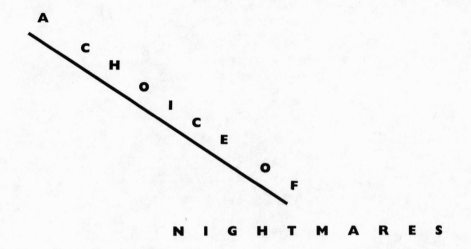

A CHOICE OF NIGHTMARES

A CHOICE OF NIGHTMARES

LYNN KOSTOFF

Crown Publishers, Inc.
New York

Published by Crown Publishers, Inc., 201 East 50th Street, New York, New York 10022. Member of the Crown Publishing Group.

CROWN is a trademark of Crown Publishers, Inc.

Manufactured in the United States of America

Library of Congress Cataloging-in-Publication Data

Kostoff, Lynn.
    A choice of nightmares / by Lynn Kostoff. — 1st ed.
        p.   cm.
    I. Title.
    PS3561.0843C47   1991
    813'.54—dc20   90-25019
                                                                              CIP

ISBN 0-517-57466-7

10 9 8 7 6 5 4 3 2 1

First Edition

This book is dedicated to
my mother and father, Janet and Lewis Kostoff;
Melanie and our son, Jeremy;
Marian Young, a fine agent and friend;
all my friends, in particular Scott Gagel, Jerry Jerman, and
my brother Ron Kostoff, for their support and encouragement
over the long haul;
and finally, to the memory of my brother Randall Kostoff,
1959–1989.

I was unsound! Ah! But it was something to have at least a choice of nightmares.

—*Heart of Darkness*

□ □ □

There are only the pursued, the pursuing, the busy, and the tired.

—*The Great Gatsby*

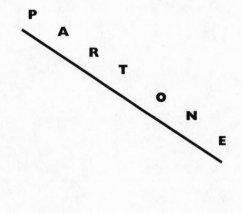

PART ONE

Robert
Staples
Kept
Trying to
Explain

ROBERT STAPLES KEPT TRYING TO EXPLAIN why he'd thrown Heidi in the alligator pit.

That was difficult enough, but Russell Tills made it even harder by moving around. Half the time Robert was talking to his back or his lurching profile. The neon-blue carpet was deep enough to hold footprints, and Russell's Italian loafers had left the floor of his office looking like instructions for a complicated dance step.

"You had a headache?"

"Right. You see—"

"Jesus. That's what I thought you said." Russell fired up another Vantage and moved away. Robert watched Russell's image surface in the window across the room. He was a *Gentlemen's Quarterly* version of Frankenstein's monster, a collection of mismatched parts, long arms and legs with tiny feet and hands, a slim waist with wide, bony hips, a large head with small wet eyes, and a mouth with lips thick as thumbs and tiny yellow teeth. Russell, however, knew how to dress and used the pastel slacks and blazer, the blue silk shirt and orange knitted tie, and the Gucci shoes to stitch together a physique that otherwise looked as if it were going to fly apart every time he moved.

"The *Herald* ran your little incident on the first page. They found out I'm representing you, I know it, and they're playing with me. I've got some enemies there. I mean, Christ, the police find three more bodies in a canal up near Opa-Locka yesterday, and the *Herald* runs you and the Glades End Mall thing on page one. It's personal."

Russell flicked an ash as long as a fingernail into a seashell ashtray and asked, "What, you never heard of aspirin, Rob? They make them extra strength now, capsules or tablets, time-released, easy on the stomach, and what I'm wondering is why this headache. Medical breakthroughs and you don't take advantage of them. It raises questions in my mind here."

"It just happened. I'm sorry. It's not what you think."

"It better not be. I hope you're not that stupid."

Robert knew Russell still didn't believe him and had chalked up yesterday at Glades End Mall as a cheap publicity stunt, and it was that probably more than the alligators that upset him. Russell Tills couldn't tolerate the idea of being upstaged. If throwing Heidi in the alligator pit had been his idea, instead of an accident, Robert probably wouldn't be sitting here right now.

"The Glades End Mall account was important, Rob. I'd been nursing it since the beginning. In fact, it was me who came up with the idea of the alligator pit. At no point in time did I think it would land me page one of the *Herald*. I've been on the phone with the mall backers, and they're upset. Four-Star Upset. What could I say? That you're sorry? The Glades End people don't understand *sorry*, Rob." Russell moved away from the window and left Robert looking at a blue rectangle of South Florida sky.

Russell roamed the office, retracing the pattern of steps he'd left in the carpet, finding each as instinctively as a migratory bird. He held a cigarette in his left hand, the right flying up to test the condition of his new forty-five dollar haircut, its sharp dyed lines shiny, almost more blue than black, under the new wet look he sported.

"I took you on as a favor, you know that, Rob? Martin Broom called me up right after Worldwide Studios went under and asked if I'd represent you. You weren't exactly a six-figure movie star at the time either. I had my doubts, but I went ahead. I owed Martin. He asked, I said okay, but with doubts."

Russell circled around the desk and stopped. "I understand debts, Robert, the what and who and how of them, but I'm not sure you do. I continue to have doubts there."

Russell abruptly gestured behind him, toward the wall and the two photographs that flanked his shoulders.

"Flagler and Fisher understood debts, Rob. Do you understand what I'm saying? They *knew* and made sure everyone else did too."

The secretary interrupted with a call for Russell before he could go on with Robert's history lesson. Not that it was necessary. Robert had seen the photographs before. For some reason he'd never quite understood, Russell maintained three offices in the greater Miami area—the one here on South Collins, another on Brickell, and one on Mimosa in Coconut Grove—but no matter how different the décor or location, Russell had the same photographs of Carl Fisher and Henry Flagler hung in each.

Russell had raised Fisher and Flagler to the level of deities and, depending on his mood or circumstances, assigned himself the role of high priest or holy ghost. Sometimes he claimed his grandfather and father had worked closely with them and at others that he was a blood relative of Fisher or Flagler. No one that Robert knew cared to dispute the claims.

Robert remembered the first time he'd met with Russell Tills in the Coconut Grove office, not long after Worldwide Studios went bankrupt and his marriage was already a memory. At that meeting, Russell claimed his grandfather had been with Flagler when he got the idea of buying bankrupt railroads and laying claims and track from Jacksonville to Key West and then building hotels at each of the major stops. Russell's father, on the other hand, had supposedly been out in the speedboat with Fisher when he was "inspired" by the development potential of Miami Beach and bought it off a Quaker named Collins, whose most tangible gain from the deal, Robert supposed, was having the oceanfront street below the window of the office named after him.

Russell, true to his heritage or legacy, saw himself not as an agent or manager but in true South Florida fashion as a "creative consultant," and in true Russell Tills fashion he'd lived up to his billing, extending and bending the definition of both words, creatively consulting his way into publicity, politics, television and film, real estate, business, and banking. Fisher and Flagler would have loved him, all three of them sharing the visionary power of prophets and the ethics of dogs in heat.

Russell had been uncharacteristically quiet since he'd picked up the phone. Robert watched him, studying the face inclining toward the receiver cradled on his shoulder while the hands fumbled for another cigarette and lighter. He had a face that worked on its expressions, whose forehead, eyes, and mouth had put in overtime, a lot of it, so that now they registered not the niceties and nuances of mood but blunt pleasure or displeasure. From where Robert sat, Russell didn't look any more pleased with the caller's news than he'd been with Robert's.

"So you've been looking and Swolt is not in Little Haiti. You can't find him, and he's not there. That's wonderful news, Manuel." Russell's knuckles were white on the receiver. "Correct me here if necessary. He's white, right? You two do know who you're following? Good. So tell me what the fuck you're doing in Little Haiti because I'm having some serious problems with your methods, why exactly you are where you are and why you keep losing him. It's not as if the guy's invisible. How can you and Miguel miss somebody who looks the way Swolt does? What exactly am I paying you for anyway? Castro threw you and Miguel out when, 1980? I figured by now you'd know what you were doing. I didn't figure you'd be calling me from Little Haiti to tell me something as obvious as the weather." He paused. "Sure. You'll get back to me. I can hardly wait to find out where else he isn't."

After the phone call, Russell made drinks, two large and hasty gin and tonics with pale lemon slices floating in them. Robert, in a slowly growing panic, downed his too easily. He'd finished it before Russell was even half done with his and had to sit there pretending to sip from it while they picked up from where they'd left off.

Robert began with some serious groveling, trying to convince Russell that he did in fact understand the nature of debts and appreciated what he'd done for him, telling Russell it wasn't so much the money but the work, the fact that it was different from what they'd discussed in their first meeting. "I guess I was counting on too much, Russell, but I thought by now I'd be doing films again. Doing promotional work for you was supposed to be temporary." Robert rested the sweating glass against his temple, the ice cubes rattling and sliding across the bottom.

For Robert, the greater part of the last year had been a blur of grand openings and groundbreakings, charities and benefits, endorsements and presentations, any South Florida hustle that required an "appearance." With a large enough amount of hype and a few stills from Robert's Worldwide films, Russell could market Robert as a "personality." The fact that it was doubtful anyone had ever seen Robert's films, or remembered them if he had, didn't really matter. Robert knew he functioned as a sort of generic-brand celebrity, fitting a slot on a promoter's program like some all-purpose green or yellow vegetable on a menu. It wasn't exactly Robert's idea of a comeback.

Russell held a lemon slice between two fingers and squeezed. "I've been working on some Lauderdale money. A couple of investors, they've never done any films, but they're interested. Nibbles. That's all at this point. But interested. Tugs on the line." He studied the trail of juice that had run down his finger and dropped on the desk.

"Now, though, I'm not so sure. And can you blame them, Rob? What, they read the papers, are they going to think? I'll tell you. They're thinking about your famous headache. They're thinking about Russell Tills's word and you working in one of their films that they've backed with some very hard cash, and they're wondering what if the star there, Mr. Robert Staples, has another headache? What then? They're thinking something worse than Heidi and alligators next time. And can you blame them?"

Robert wondered if Russell had ever intended to do more for him than he had. He'd heard the line about the Lauderdale money on two previous occasions, and nothing had ever come of it. Right now, he was afraid that Russell's debt to Worldwide's executive producer, Martin Broom, could be covered by the small change of his connections and that Russell was thinking of closing the account.

So Robert tried again to explain what happened yesterday, after he'd driven across the state to the Gulf and the chunk of reconstituted swamp near Naples for the Memorial Day grand opening of the Glades

End Mall and stood on the platform with the rest of the "personalities"—the lieutenant governor, the high-school essay winner, Miss Tamiami Trail, and the president of the Gulf Coast Golden Agers—in the bone-bending heat with clouds of bugs only slightly less oppressive than the crowd pressing around them. The headache was the closest thing he could come up with for an explanation that would appease Russell. Robert wasn't sure he knew exactly what had happened out there.

Russell began rattling the ice cubes in his glass before Robert was even halfway through with his explanation. "Do you know what it's like dealing with the Miami Humane Society, Rob?" Russell leaned forward and held his cigarette like a pointer.

"Russell, my head felt like it was going to cave in or explode. It was horrible."

"They're Nazis. I spent almost one and a half hours on the phone this morning with some brown shirt named Jamison. He's pressing, definitely, on this one."

"A head full of firecrackers, that's what it felt like."

"I don't have any leverage with the Humane Society. The need never came up before. No ready-made connections there. I'll find some, sure, but see, I'm having to work at it. Having to spend time that could be used more profitably in other areas. A *personal* stake is what I'm talking about here."

Robert let out his breath and shook his head. "I appreciate that, Russell, and I'm sorry, really. It just happened. The damn dog bit me. It had been growling and snapping all through that high-school girl's essay, and that Tritt woman wasn't doing anything to stop it, and then when Miss Tamiami Trail stepped up to do her number, it got me on the arm. All those bugs, the heat, the headache, I didn't think, Russell. I *couldn't* think. I reacted, that's all. Blind reflex."

Heidi's landing had been an accident, but Robert had known with a sickening clarity the moment he let go of her that he was going to pay for this one. She growled and bit, he grabbed and threw, and Heidi made a perfect trajectory over Miss Tamiami Trail lip-syncing her way through "Girls Just Want to Have Fun" and landed in the alligator pit. Its three occupants had been sluggish if not outright catatonic up to that point in the grand-opening ceremonies, but that changed with Heidi's appearance. There was a lot of churning, and suddenly it was puréed schnauzer.

Russell crossed the room without Rob noticing and tapped him on the shoulder. "Do you remember what you were doing when we landed on the moon?"

"What?"

Russell swirled his drink, the ice cubes clicking like dice, and Robert looked at his empty glass.

"I do, Robert. I know exactly what I was doing. Closing a deal with Coconut Frank's hamburger chain. Promotional saturation from South Carolina to California. The moment Neil Armstrong was giving his 'small step' spiel, Coconut Frank's signing the bottom line, and I'm grossing two hundred thousand just on hamburgers before the year's out. Believe me, hamburgers and history, there's a lesson in each."

With a short nod, Russell indicated for Rob to get up and follow him to the window. He pointed down at Collins Avenue, its midday congestion and confusion. Russell's office existed in a sort of real-estate purgatory, sharing the worn and battered elegance of hotels like the San Souci, Versailles, and Cadillac, all built during the 1940s and '50s, but now besieged by blocks of porno and hock shops, secondhand stores and Cuban cafés, suspended between the condos to the north and the art deco restorations farther south on Collins and Ocean Springs.

Russell leaned forward and tapped the glass instead of Rob this time. "Stop any pedestrian down there. Any of them. Ask him to name the crew on the moon flight. Then ask why Coconut Frank wears an eyepatch. Which one will he know? I lay odds on Frank. Ask and you'll hear, 'When I say my hamburgers are a feast for the eye, Mate, believe it.' That should tell you something, Robert."

Russell handed Rob a drink and went on. "There's a moon landing every day."

Robert felt the beginnings of another headache and nodded for want of any other response. It seemed to irritate Russell. The second drink disappeared as quickly as the first.

Russell grabbed Robert's arm. "You're not listening. And you're not hungry. Not enough by far."

Robert started to protest, but Russell interrupted. "Hungry men don't throw old ladies' dogs into alligator pits. Desperate men do."

"Shit, Russell, what do you mean? Why do you think I've been doing all this bullshit for the last ten months? Glad-handing at all those time-sharing resorts. Signing autographs at the fifth anniversary celebration of Bird World. Emceeing anything from Miss Orange Blossom to Miss Aqua-Lung pageants. Sitting through jaycee and Chamber of Commerce banquets. Telethons for five different diseases. The Cuban talk shows, for Christ's sake. The Miami Is Beautiful ads and the television spots. All of it."

Russell studied the end of his cigarette and waited until Robert had finished. He didn't look up when he said, "'All this bullshit.' An interesting choice of words there. It confirms what I've been saying."

Robert felt the bugs and heat and Heidi all over again. The feeling of something inside becoming unhinged, slipping, starting to loosen and rattle, threatening to break away and fly out of control. More than a headache or simply losing your temper. More complex and terrifying than that. Like meeting a deformed version of yourself in a dream and trying to kill it and all the while it smiles and drools and prods you with fat stiff fingers.

"All it reveals, Russell, is that I want to work. Believe me. In *film*, though." Robert tried for conviction, but his voice was wavering like a poorly tuned radio station.

Russell's wasn't. "That's what I gave you."

"What? Are we talking about the same thing here?"

"Exactly the same thing. Maybe you're finally learning. It's not 'All This Bullshit' over here, Rob, and 'Film' over there. It's *all* bullshit. If you're hungry, you know that. In fact, you love it. You hustle Coconut Frank franchises while we leave our footprints on the moon because you know in the end hamburgers and history are the same."

Robert told himself to calm down. After all, he'd been in tighter places than this before. Russell was wrong. Robert understood hunger, knew how it grew and what it demanded and the cost of feeding it, and how if you were unlucky, what it fed on was you. He wanted to believe he was still lucky, but when he lowered his head and closed his eyes against the sparks of pain arcing across his temples, all he saw was Heidi frozen at the top of her trajectory, a furry comet stopped in midflight above Miss Tamiami Trail and her PG bathing suit, and himself some fifteen feet away, surrounded by a soft gray nimbus of mosquitoes and no-see-ums, with his arm extended and hand empty, as if he'd just made or asked for an offering.

Florida had been the second chance, a conspiracy of possibility that let him believe he'd find what he wanted as easily as picking up shells from a beach. It was only a matter of time, and time didn't seem to matter down here. Under the South Florida sun, everything bloomed and dazzled, and you grew new skin.

The nights were different.

Then the projector stopped and the ceiling of his apartment at the Miramar Arms became a blank screen and he lay sweating while the air conditioner raged and he felt as if his life had become enclosed in a giant set of parentheses that each day moved a little closer together.

And Robert felt those parentheses now in Russell's office, tensed, and tried not to shudder when Russell moved from his desk and stopped behind him, dropping his hand onto Robert's shoulder. He left it lying there, like something moist and pulpy that had crawled out of the ocean to rest on a warm rock.

"I think we can work something out," Russell said. "For now, we need to keep you out of the public eye until this thing blows out to sea. In the meantime, I got a couple things you can give me a hand with."

Robert turned his head slightly and nodded, catching at the corner of his vision the fat gold ring inlaid with a sneeze of rubies on Russell's third finger.

They could work something out, yes.

And right then, with Russell's hand gripping his shoulder, Robert understood how Heidi must have felt just before he let go.

I T WAS THE END OF MEMORIAL DAY WEEKEND, and the
Miami International Airport's terminal was crowded. Robert looked
out the window of the lounge and kept trying to convince himself that
the smile on the travel poster hanging on the opposite wall of the
concourse had once belonged to him.

It was an empty, sunstruck smile and fit too well the flesh and bones
that surrounded it, that of a man in his early thirties who embodied
the Ponce de León myth that America nurtured—a man with all his
hair, a compact and tanned frame, smooth skin, and dark clear eyes,
a man who looked as if he'd never been sick and never would be,
who'd been excused from all large and small misfortunes so he could
have fun and be charming. A real fun guy, yes, who understood wine
lists and sports cars and G-Spots, and who stood on the beach against
the backdrop of the condos on North Collins in a pair of tight white
swimming trunks and a dazzling empty white smile.

Robert only had to shift his gaze slightly to find his reflection in the
window and see the discrepancy between it and the image on the
poster. Robert wasn't sure which upset him more: the fact that at one
time he'd been able to capture the unrelenting idiocy of the cliché on
the travel poster or the fact that there was nothing in his reflection he
recognized either.

The poster had been Russell Tills's coup, part of the Miami Is
Beautiful campaign, an attempt to convince the citizenry that its fair
city was more than the sum of its mutilations and murders and a
monthly body count that often was higher than the daily temperature.

Robert had done three versions of the beach shot. Russell and the mayor were pleased with the promotion. Things looked okay. At the time, Robert still believed he had a real shot at working in films again and that schnauzers would not end up in alligator pits.

Rob raised his glass, and the waitress crossed the cocktail lounge with another drink. He tried to forget the poster and concentrate instead on what he now faced. Russell had called it R&R, but Robert wasn't so sure. Russell had thought it in *their* best interest to let him take care of the Heidi situation and for Rob to get out of Miami for a while. He had arranged a place for Robert to stay in Key West and said he might have something for Rob later in the summer if his "headaches" were better by then.

So it was more waiting. Robert should have been used to the weight of time by now, but it felt as if each day pressed in like a finger on a vein.

In addition, there was the small favor, as Russell had called it: Robert was to meet the Bogotá flight, hand over a thick manila envelope to someone named Lauter, and then drive on to Key West. Nothing much to it. Nothing more than the other favors Rob had done and not asked questions about. But then the flight had been delayed, and Robert had been stuck waiting for an extra hour and a half.

He picked up the envelope Russell had given him and weighed it in his hand. It had the size and bulk of a script. He tried to ignore the Muzak falling around him. An actor friend of his had once told him that whenever he was developing a role, he would haunt airports and study the gestures and expressions of people leaving or returning from a flight. P&B, he told Robert. Pathos and bathos. It was all there, in the stream of people ten feet away on the concourse.

The clock behind the bar had stopped, and whenever Robert looked in its direction, he felt slightly anxious. The hands had become frozen at three fifteen and reminded him of a trap that had sprung shut. He began to play with his bar napkin, tearing it into thin strips, while he looked around the lounge.

A contingent of businessmen in crisp summer-weight suits sat at the bar munching peanuts and padding their expense accounts. Two soldiers sat at a table with their duffle bags at their feet. To their right was a Cuban couple, holding hands. At another table, a thin man in a blue tanktop and madras shorts tried to perfect a combination smile and leer for the waitress. A blind man and his seeing-eye dog took a window seat. A priest sat in the far corner reading a newspaper. A heavyset man in a rumpled green suit came in and took a table next to the priest and immediately began mopping his face with a handkerchief.

Then a pregnant woman sat down at the table next to Robert's and smiled.

Robert wanted to blame his instant unease on his nerves, the time of day, Russell turning him into an errand boy, the Muzak, his watery drinks, or the delayed flight from Bogotá, but all he had to do was look to his left.

There was something smug and arrogant in the way pregnant women occupied space. The room changed whenever one entered it. Everyone was suddenly displaced, that distended abdomen pulling everything around it with the inevitability of an eclipse.

"Excuse me," she asked, "do you have the time?"

Robert told her, and she gave him a smile that seemed both quick and slow, and before he could excuse himself, she began talking, her voice and the hands lightly resting on her swelling belly holding him hostage, trapping him in what should have been a commonplace situation: the polite conversation of two strangers passing time at an airport. Still, something about the woman bothered him, and he was just beginning to sense what it was.

He reluctantly accepted the invitation to join her. She pushed a small battered and brown suitcase with a faded decal on its side from Buffalo, New York, out of the way. The woman told Robert her luggage had already been checked through, but the suitcase was a concession to her mother, who had insisted she carry it with her. Her mother's one brush with airline baggage handlers had marked her for life when all her luggage except the brown suitcase had been lost on her honeymoon.

The woman then started talking about her husband, whose name Robert didn't catch, who was an architect, and of his struggles to make a name for himself during their ten years together in Florida, how he had worked on everything from roadside souvenir chains, health spas, video arcades, and bank branches, to restaurants, marinas, condos, country clubs, and finally malls, which were his big break, his reputation having enough clout so that he could leave Florida and start his own firm in Denver, where he'd been born, the hometown boy made good.

It had been a long struggle, she went on, and for years, she'd been his combination secretary-assistant-receptionist, and they'd had to make a lot of sacrifices, but it was all worth it. She'd been staying with her mother for the last two months until her husband found them a place, and now she was flying out to join him.

"My mother worries about the air out West," she added, laughing, "and if it will affect my labor and delivery. She doesn't think there's enough air in Denver. It's thin but pure, I told her."

Robert had not intended to lie when he said he had a sister in Denver who said the same thing. The words had followed one another automatically. He couldn't stop himself when he went on to add that his sister was recently widowed. He wanted to hide from and hurt the woman in the understated designer maternity clothes who now offered her condolences. He thought he'd be all right if he could just freeze her into a stereotype. She was kind. She was friendly. An upwardly mobile young mother who'd beaten the biological clock. At ease with the world and herself and her architect husband.

"That's the hardest part about pregnancy," the woman said after the waitress brought her another club soda and Robert a gin and tonic. "Having to deny yourself. No junk food. No colas or liquor. I never drank much, but I do miss those evening glasses of white wine."

Robert agreed that it was important to take care of yourself, and she went on to talk about the baby, Robert missing most of what she said because he was trying to convince himself that the woman sitting across from him with the narrow, finely sculpted face and the long dark hair, widely spaced eyes, and pale unlined skin lightly dusted with freckles did not resemble his ex-wife.

It was not an exact match, nothing like two sisters, more along the lines of a distant relative, a second cousin, but enough echoes of his ex-wife's features were in the woman's face to bother him. It was a coincidence, he told himself, but one he did not need right now.

"And what about you?" the woman suddenly asked. "All I've talked about is me and the baby and my husband. I haven't given you the chance to say anything."

The lies again came easily, Robert saying he was a free-lance photographer, how he enjoyed the luxury of being his own boss, going on to talk about the aesthetics of his profession and how Florida was the perfect place to practice them because Florida was the one state in the union that didn't exist except as a state of mind, a place of dreams and schemes where history was revised or erased on a daily basis and the everyday was turned into icons. Florida was alligators, oranges, rockets, Mickey Mouse, flamingos, palm trees, white beaches, bikinied women, sunshine. Florida disappeared, Robert told the woman, the moment he pressed the shutter on his camera, and that's why it was the only worthwhile subject for a serious photographer. Florida was the national mirage.

Robert didn't notice when the lies began to boomerang on him because it was suddenly easy to forget himself with the woman, and as he talked, it was like old times with Kathleen, his ex-wife, when they lay in bed with glasses of wine resting on their stomachs and made plans, when his career and marriage had been connected in some elemental way, like the pull of the moon on the tides, bound by a complicated geometry of love, promise, and desire.

And the lies slowly became the truth after the woman asked him about marriage and children, and Robert began talking about his divorce. The problems of the free-lance photographer merged with his own, and the story he told her paralleled how he had spent years chasing his break, paying his dues at Worldwide Pictures and doing whatever pickup work was around, the stray TV commercial or bit part in a series, a long hustle he was sure would eventually pay off, but the *eventually* got in the way of his wife's desire for a family. At the time, Kathleen was in her early thirties and didn't want to wait. Robert did. He'd just signed on to what he was sure would be his breakthrough film, *The Evictor*. Kathleen continued to press him about children. They had long, bitter arguments. Robert's answer to them ended the marriage.

"A little more time," Robert told the woman. "That's all I needed.

I was close. It wasn't like she didn't understand. She did. I just couldn't make her believe."

"So she left you?" The woman set down her glass and rested one hand on top of the other, leaning slightly in toward Robert and tilting her head.

It was difficult to meet the woman's eyes. "After the appointment with the doctor, she did. Yes." A Rothko print had hung in the waiting room, and Robert had sat beneath it and filled out forms for insurance and his medical history. As it turned out, two hours in the doctor's office had ended five years of marriage.

Robert could sense the woman trying to puzzle out the reference to the doctor before she said anything else, running through various possibilities—pregnancy, hysterectomy, infertility, abortion, a host of debilitating illnesses, any of which could wreck a troubled marriage. But Robert could tell by the way she still leaned toward him that she, like his ex-wife, had not thought of another possibility. In its way, the most obvious one.

Robert started to balk at finishing the story. It was crazy, he told himself, to be sitting across from this woman and talking to her about any of this. For a moment, he could not even remember her name. Susan or Sarah. What? Carnes, that was it. Sarah Carnes. Who looked just enough like his ex-wife to unlock something in him. And he wasn't even sure what that was. Regret? Guilt? Rage? Why didn't he excuse himself or just walk away? Maybe it was simply because he didn't have an answer to that question. When Kathleen left, Robert had started a long slow fall from the only grace he'd ever been sure of, and during the last year, in the blur of grand openings, sale-a-thons, and groundbreakings that had become as identical and jumbled as a pocketful of pennies, even then Robert had expected that one day he'd find Kathleen in the crowd, and everything would be okay again. All he'd found instead was the ghost of that desire sitting across from him in the form of Sarah Carnes, a stranger six months pregnant and happily married. If he looked away, all he ran into was the map of the U.S. crosshatched with red lines and the Miami Is Beautiful poster.

"Listen," she said, reaching over and touching his wrist.

"At the time, I didn't feel like I had any other choice." Her cool fingers on his wrist encouraged him. Perhaps he could make this woman understand that the visit to the doctor had not been a betrayal, but a chance, a different kind for Kathleen and him.

He remembered having come to the decision late on a Friday night, bathed in the light of "Chiller Theater" and the rapidly dwindling contents of a bottle of wine, Kathleen already in bed, while he watched the original version of *Invasion of the Body Snatchers*, Kevin McCarthy standing in a greenhouse and watching a large pod split open and spit out a torso whose head held his own face.

After the visit to the doctor, all Robert had felt was a vast release, as if he'd finally been excused or absolved from some long-standing and complicated debt. He'd seen the vasectomy as a start, not an ending. He'd tried to explain that to Kathleen.

It wasn't until the woman in the airport lounge started to slide back her chair that Robert realized that her touch had not been a gesture of comfort or understanding. She had been checking the time. He watched her slowly struggle to stand.

"I'm sorry I have to interrupt our talk," she said, "but I have to leave for my flight. It sounds like things are a little messy for you right now, but you have to remember that's natural for what you're going through. I'm sure everything will turn out for the best."

Robert repeated the phrase to himself while she smiled and reached for the small, battered suitcase. She'd lifted it as far as her thighs when its latch slipped. She let out a small cry as its contents emptied onto the floor.

The next few minutes were confusing, Robert getting up to help and ending up at her feet, everyone in the lounge watching them as he gathered the scattered bottles of lotion, a pair of slippers, a vanity mirror that had cracked in the fall, vials of perfume and tubes of lipstick, a book for expectant mothers and a fat paperback romance entitled *Midnight Passion*, earrings and a thin silver bracelet, the woman's voice but not her words registering, Robert looking up only to see that huge, swollen belly, and then someone stopping to offer help, a pair of dark brown shoes stopping at Robert's fingertips, and Robert saying more loudly than necessary that he would take care of everything, blood pounding in his ears and his hands shaking as he got to the woman's underclothes, the bras and the pastel rainbow of panties, all of them sheer and delicate and slippery beneath his fingers, then the unopened tube of K-Y Jelly for Denver where the air was thin but pure, and Robert heard the words "I'm sorry" repeated over and over but didn't realize they were his until the woman said it was an accident, that's all, an accident. Nothing more.

Robert ended up carrying the suitcase for her, and it wasn't until she joined the line at the boarding gate and turned and waved good-bye that Robert got a last glimpse of her profiled against a cloudless, powder-blue sky and realized he'd forgotten about the envelope Russell Tills had given him to deliver.

T HE ENVELOPE HAD NOT TURNED UP in Robert's frenzied search of the lounge. Nobody he'd asked had seen it, and their courtesy had given way to irritation and outright hostility under Robert's insistent questioning and inability to even identify its contents. Robert had met Franklin Benjamin Lauter empty-handed. On their way back to the lounge, they were joined by a man named Barry From West Palm.

Robert and Lauter sat at a corner table, and Barry From West Palm went over to talk to the bartender. Lauter's neutral expression unnerved Robert. He kept expecting Lauter to explode, but his face had not changed since he deboarded from the Bogotá flight. The soft gray expensively cut suit, the handmade shirt, the sharp-lined coolly colored striped tie, the slender hand-tooled attaché case—all made Lauter take on almost archetypal qualities. He was not an executive, but *the* executive. The man, himself, was hidden even while he drew attention to himself. Everything, from the dark hair carefully sprayed in place, the light blue eyes, and sculpted jawline to the tanned, smooth-shaven cheeks, fit perfectly.

Lauter took a small notebook from his suit pocket, glanced at Rob, then over at Barry From West Palm, who was working on improving the bartender's memory. Barry From West Palm was thin and rangy, but he evidently knew enough tricks to handle a man twice his size. The bartender was trying to pull away, but Barry had grabbed his wrist and was bending and twisting it so that his forearm was perpendicular to the bartop. Barry From West Palm then picked up a swizzle stick and began inching it under the bartender's index fingernail. Robert remembered the viselike feel of those fingers when Barry From West

Palm frisked him in the men's room after they returned to the lounge. Barry From West Palm had been looking for weapons or a wire and seemed disappointed when Robert came up clean.

"I hope you appreciate the position you've put me in," Lauter said. "If not, you will soon." He went back to jotting in his notebook.

A few minutes later, Barry From West Palm joined them at the table. He unzipped an aqua-blue windbreaker and scratched at an insect bite just above the frayed collar of the white shirt he wore underneath. "Working at this place," he said, "the bartender, he's seen more than enough, but nothing we want to look at." Lauter looked over at Rob again, then signaled the waitress for a round of drinks.

"What are we going to do with Mr. Delivery here?" Barry From West Palm asked. "Won't they be expecting the material when you get up to D.C.?"

"I'm thinking about it," Lauter said. He looked pointedly at Robert as he addressed Barry From West Palm. "In the meantime, give me an update. What's the status of acetone at the moment?"

"I'm hearing, you're looking for hydrochloric acid or ether; it's around, not a lot, but there." Barry looked at Robert, too, and adjusted the brim of his cap. Its sides were yellow mesh, and tiny brown squares of hair poked through. Its front was an advertisement for Ed's Salvage Shop in Key Largo. "Acetone's another story. Some people, I've been talking to them, and they say they might be able to get their hands on thirty thousand gallons soon, but they were talking markup, anywhere twenty-five to forty percent. Customs is looking around and monitoring orders, making it hard, anything looks irregular."

This shouldn't be happening, Robert thought. It didn't make any sense, Lauter and Barry openly talking business in front of him. There had to be a catch somewhere.

Lauter set down his pen. "Thirty thousand would still put us short of demand. The Colombians and Brazilians have had to slow down production. Three major shipments of chemicals have been intercepted in the last two months, and the black market has been unreliable. The Colombians are willing to pay above the market price, so that will compensate for the markup, and I imagine the Brazilians will go along too. They're having to make do with what they have, and it's affecting product quality. I'd like more than thirty thousand gallons, but even that's leverage right now. Things are pretty mixed up down there."

Robert had the uneasy feeling that Lauter and Barry From West Palm were performing for him. He sat and ran through various explanations that might excuse losing the envelope, but he knew that pleading a headache wouldn't muster this time. He had fucked up. That basically covered it. He didn't know if it was enough to let him off the hook, though.

"What about Carlos Ramierz?" Lauter asked. "Is he still threatening to testify?"

When Barry From West Palm smiled, Rob realized he had no chin. His face held a faint suggestion of one at other times, but when he smiled, any trace of chin disappeared. It was as if his face had run out of energy and quit when it got to his bottom lip.

"Oh, Carlos, he's threatening a lot of things, but none of them mean much. He had a convenient attack of honor, the Miami police accidentally busted his brother Hector. Carlos felt violated. Those were his very words, honest to God. I love it, Carlos feeling violated." Barry From West Palm paused to flick the ash on his cigarette. "The upshot, he won't talk to the Customs people because they were supposed to put the word out, leave little brother alone."

"Wait a minute. I thought Ramierz was testifying for the FBI."

"They gave him to Customs. A little gift. The FBI was afraid that some of Carlos's testimony would boomerang on their credibility. Seems Carlos only told half the truth when the FBI first got a hold of him. They don't like what they're hearing now."

"So Carlos is with Customs."

"For the time being. I've heard Customs is thinking about pushing him off on the DEA. Every time Carlos opens his mouth, he threatens one of the agencies. He had his hands in everybody's pants, and they're all afraid he's going to kiss and tell. Even the IRS won't touch him. Carlos has been granted immunity so many times from so many agencies, what he could do is blow up St. Pete tomorrow and walk the next day. No way Carlos is going to cause us any problems."

Which left them the problem Rob had caused them. Barry From West Palm looked a little too eager to solve it. He reached over, took Rob's hand, and with a barely perceptible flick of his wrist, cracked all four knuckles. The loud pop was more disconcerting than the pain. Robert sat back and told Lauter again what had happened in the lounge. Lauter kept nodding.

When Rob finished, Lauter said, "Why don't you and Barry take a walk? I need some time to think things over."

After leaving the lounge, Robert and Barry moved leisurely through the concourse and the crowds hurrying to meet or catch flights. Rob could not anticipate where Barry and he were headed, and for a while he wanted to believe that Lauter had literally meant a walk, but Barry From West Palm's smile was about as reassuring as a cloudy chest x-ray, so Robert slipped his hands in his pockets and kept his mouth shut. All that talk of FBI, DEA, and Customs had done its job and scared him silent.

Around them was the ritual, endlessly played out, of reunion and separation, people kissing, crying, grabbing, and holding each other, arrivals and departures blurring, Robert feeling even more disoriented when he couldn't tell the difference anymore between a hello and good-bye.

They stopped at a kiosk so Barry could buy a pack of gum. A red balloon suddenly broke free from a clot of people to their left, rose quickly to the ceiling, and became caught in the gusts from the air-conditioner ducts. A child began screaming. Barry argued with the proprietor, claiming he was a nickel short in change. Robert saw two security guards approaching and started to turn in their direction when Barry's hand fell over his shoulder.

"My opinion, tap the brakes on that idea." Barry leaned over and offered Rob a stick of Juicy Fruit. Above them, a string of people was paged, first in English, then in Spanish. They started walking again.

When they came to a video arcade, Barry paused at the entrance and said, "We can play it any number of ways is the point we're at here."

Robert shook his head and raised both hands. "The whole thing was an accident. I'm not any real part of this."

"You stepped in it. It's still on your shoe."

"I don't even know what was in the envelope. I already told you and Lauter what happened."

"I know. Now you have to convince me."

The smell inside the arcade reminded Robert of a faltering refrigerator whose contents were on the verge of spoiling—a deep confused odor, both sweet and sour. Barry From West Palm bought five dollars worth of tokens from a clerk in a dirty sleeveless shirt and a tattoo on his right biceps reading ROCK TILL I DIE. The light in the arcade had the murky quality of an old movie theater but none of its reassurance.

Robert blindly followed Barry up and down the aisles. They were surrounded by the sound of tires screeching, rockets blasting off, screams, sirens, explosions, gunfire, sonar blips, cave-ins, and roars. Dark figures hunched over the machines in rapt, murderous postures. The air crackled in a Crayola lightning storm. Most of the games carried various versions of Armageddon, imprisoned maidens, menageries of monsters, alien invasion forces, and labors that would have given Hercules second thoughts. Robert felt like he was in the midst of some huge primal therapy session. Instinct and technology held hands here and produced affordable nightmares.

Robert watched Barry play Sitting Ducks, Task Force XT-9, Screamer, Rock Pile, and Kamikaze Run, Barry expertly maneuvering through the mechanics of each game while simultaneously asking him questions about what had happened in the lounge. Robert repeated what he'd told Barry and Lauter earlier, everything that he'd noticed before and after the pregnant woman appeared, adding an odd detail here and there as it occurred to him but nothing that significantly altered the original story in any way that he could see. Barry nodded and kept up the questions, his bony profile washed in colored lights.

Barry walked down to Man Overboard and slipped in a token. "Your turn," he said. Rob bent over the machine and attempted to guide a rescue ship through treacherous waters to a host of floundering survivors. By the time *Game's Over* flashed on the screen, Rob had piloted five abortive missions.

"You're a real piece of work," Barry From West Palm said.

Things didn't go much better with Lab Accident, even though Barry leaned in over Rob's shoulder and delivered advice between more questions about the lounge and envelope. Robert struggled to keep the electronic virus confined to the laboratory and answer Barry at the same time. The virus's greenish-yellow smear found an open window, a cracked door, and a set of air-conditioning vents, and Robert recounted once again who'd been sitting closest to the bartender, who flirted with the waitresses, what clothes were distinctive, who left for the bathroom or used the phone. Once the virus got outside, it destroyed or caused mutations in plants, people, animals, and cities. Barry's voice followed each of Rob's failures to stop it. By the time *The End of the World as You Know It* came up on the screen, Rob was drenched in sweat.

"One more."

Things and Robert fell apart less than a quarter of the way through Lone Assassin. Barry's questions and the electronic obstacles became inseparable after Robert missed the generically rendered politician riding in a motorcade and found himself the object of a massive retaliatory assault by police and government agents. Barry stepped up his questions, pressing him, barely giving him a chance to answer one before starting another. The lounge and arcade collapsed into each other. The pregnant woman leaned over and touched his wrist, and Barry began punching. Flashes of color and pain and the smell of her perfume washed over Robert. The suitcase burst open. Robert fired and answered. Barry leaned closer, as if giving encouragement, timing and placing the punches so that Robert was never sure when or where they would land. Barry's voice was constant and insistent, the questions following a relentless pattern of repetition and variation, and Robert's explanation collapsed too, the sequence of events in the lounge fragmenting into a jumble of details that poured out of him like his sweat.

"What else, the shoes?"

"Brown. I told you."

"What else?"

"Tassels. Loafers. They were scuffed."

"Not enough."

"I can't. No. Gray. Gray socks."

"Getting there."

Barry began to slacken the punches after he was sure Rob could go no further than the green pants cuffs that had appeared along with the brown shoes of the man who'd offered help when Rob had been picking up the things that had fallen from the woman's suitcase. Robert opened his eyes against the pain in time to see the game ending with the lone assassin caught in crossfire. Then the screen went blank.

Barry dropped the roll of quarters he'd wrapped in his fist into the pocket of the windbreaker. He took Rob by the arm and led him out of the arcade, putting on a polite smile to disarm whatever attention they drew from passersby in the concourse. He was helping out a sick or upset friend. They eventually detoured into a public restroom so Rob could clean up.

Barry stood behind Robert at the sink, took off his cap, and combed his hair. Robert could barely work the taps. His body was a department store of pain. He let the water trickle into his palms and carefully raised them to his face. Most of the water spilled between his fingers.

"Hurry it up. Lauter's waiting."

"I think some of my ribs are broken."

Barry gave the comb one last flick through his hair and then checked for dandruff. "No way that. I know what I'm doing. What you're looking at, bruised ribs, four places. A side-order of kidney. Next day or so, you piss a little blood, don't worry about it."

Lauter watched them walk back into the lounge. Robert slid into his seat and picked up his drink. The first long swallow did nothing to alleviate his pain. Neither did the second. He carefully raised his arm and signaled the waitress for another. Any movement left his ribs feeling as if they were about to splinter into tiny pieces.

Barry From West Palm dropped into a chair across from Lauter and spread his palms. "He's telling the truth or close enough. This guy would probably fuck up opening a door you give him the chance."

Lauter nodded and tapped his notebook with the tip of a gold fountain pen.

"How bad will losing the package affect us?" Barry From West Palm asked.

"It depends on who has it. Whether it's one of the agencies, a freelancer, or a representative of the *coqueros.*" Lauter slipped the pen and notebook back into his suit. "Things are very unstable in South America right now. My meetings with the *coqueros* were unproductive. The old cartel people still insist on conducting business as usual and refuse to acknowledge the realities of a new marketplace. The joint antidrug efforts of the U.S. and Colombian governments haven't helped things either. The *coqueros'* answer to that problem is bullets and bombs. That response is oversimplistic and completely misses the complexity of the situation. It's counterproductive for everyone concerned."

"So you think we can work with this new guy?" Barry From West Palm asked. "What's his name, Camar Tavares?"

Lauter nodded. "Mr. Tavares possesses a considerably more enlightened attitude than some of his colleagues."

Barry From West Palm pulled at the collar of his windbreaker and went at the raised insect bite again. "We going to be able, I'm wondering here, to shut down what we started at the Derrota Newsstand? The *coqueros* just going to roll over after six years of doing business?"

"That's one of the things I'm going to work on in D.C.," Lauter said. "I'm meeting with people in and out of the agencies."

When Lauter turned in Rob's direction and gave him a long, appraising look, Robert suddenly felt the catch of the hook. The blunt talk of drug running had not been carelessness or a performance. Lauter was making sure Robert knew what he'd stepped into. Robert had been paying just enough attention to know it was about as appealing as another session in the video arcade with Barry. He sat back in his chair and restraightened his shirt.

"Right now," Lauter said, "I'm inclined to see the missing material as potentially a solution rather than a problem. However, we're going to require your assistance to keep it that way, Robert."

"Look," Robert said, picking up his drink, "I screwed up today. I admit it. But I don't think I want to be involved any further in what's going on."

"You're already involved," Lauter said. "It started the moment you turned up at the boarding gate empty-handed. Now what we have to clarify is your role in what will follow."

Barry From West Palm coughed and frowned. "Hey Franklin, you kind of lost me there. You say losing the package is okay? I'm not seeing it."

"Who's going to be hurt most from what happened?" Lauter asked.

Barry tipped the yellow mesh cap back on his head and looked at Robert, then back at Lauter. Suddenly, his frown and chin disappeared, and he smiled and shook his head in admiration. "Russell Tills. Christ, that's beautiful."

"I need to work out the details," Lauter said, "and a lot of them are contingent on who has the package and how they'll try to use it. In the meantime, however, Robert has provided us with an opportunity to rein in Russell's ego. I'm more than a little tired of Russell's grandstanding. He doesn't want to let go of the Derrota arrangements. Maybe it's time to remind Russell Tills about his place in the scheme of things."

"And Robert here is going to help us do that," Barry From West Palm said.

Lauter nodded and signaled the bartender to bring over a phone, and Robert sat and listened to Lauter explain to somebody named Hannibal Binder what had happened. Rob could tell from Lauter's frequent pauses and backtracks that Hannibal Binder didn't necessarily share Lauter's belief that the missing material presented more opportunities than problems, but Lauter persisted, his voice disarmingly neutral, placating Hannibal Binder with the same sort of tone you would use on an unfriendly dog.

When he was done, Lauter leaned back in the booth and tilted his head in Robert's direction. "Russell is slipping, and you're just the sort of fool he'd entrust a job like this to." He reached over and took away Rob's gin and tonic. "But there's something we need to establish here. I'm not a Russell Tills. It's extremely important you understand that."

Before Lauter could go on, Barry From West Palm interrupted, leaning forward and punching Robert's arm. "Hey, that's you, Rob, isn't it, on that poster over there?" Barry got up from the table and wandered out of the lounge.

Lauter glanced briefly out the window. "You're a model?"

"Actor. The Miami Is Beautiful campaign was pickup work. Something temporary."

"Have you done any films?"

"Ten."

"Any that I might have seen?"

Rob told him that he doubted it, and Lauter seemed more than willing to believe him.

Lauter made a steeple of his fingers and rested it on his chin. "What I want you to do, Robert, is go on to Key West. As far as you're concerned, you delivered the package. When you talk to Russell Tills, tell him there were no problems."

"That's it?"

"For now," Lauter said, coming down hard on the *now*. "Look at this as an acting job. There were no problems with the delivery, and you're in Key West for a little 'vacation' just as Russell wanted you to be. Play it like that."

Lauter took a sip of his drink and asked Rob where he'd be staying. Rob said that Russell had arranged for him to stay in a house on Simonton belonging to someone named Lennie Ash.

"Ah yes, the T-Shirt King." Lauter smiled and finished his drink. "For the time being, I want you to give Lennie Ash the same story as Russell. Lennie's distracted at the moment anyway. He's got troubles with the IRS and a string of lawsuits for copyright violations. I'll fill Lennie in later."

"I don't like any of this," Robert said. "If problems start coming up because I lost whatever was in that package, what am I supposed to say to Russell Tills? I don't understand what's going on here."

"Follow the script I've given you, Robert. You're an actor. A veteran of ten films. Make Russell believe you." Lauter straightened his tie and adjusted the lapels of his gray suit. "I'm going to take care of things in Washington. As you heard earlier, I talked to Hannibal Binder, an associate of mine in Key West, and he will pass on any new instructions or information you may need for your part."

Lauter stood up and, seemingly as an afterthought, offered Rob his hand. "You're in my movie now, Robert, not Russell's. *My* movie.

Remember that. I assure you that Barry and I will." Lauter picked up his attaché case and walked out of the lounge.

Robert leaned against the edge of the table and finished his drink standing up. Barry From West Palm was across the concourse in front of the Miami Is Beautiful poster. A couple of seconds later, Barry stepped back, spotted Rob and waved, and then went on to join Lauter, pocketing the felt-tipped marker he'd used on the poster to draw the smile face on the sun shining above the condos on Collins Avenue and to blacken out each of the teeth in Robert's wide, formerly dazzling, smile.

OUTSIDE THE TERMINAL, the parking lot floated in the heat, the lines of cars melting into wavering blots of primary color. Robert was light-headed by the time he found his rental and sat behind the wheel waiting for the air conditioner to cut through at least a little of the heat before he left, but the blast coming through the vents was tepid and smelled slightly burnt.

He sat there waiting for the panic to hit, but it never quite materialized. You are in trouble, he told himself. Real trouble. He was afraid, but it didn't have the edge he expected. It felt as diffuse and soft as the air blowing around him.

Robert wanted panic.

He wanted those moments with teeth, those times when his body and brain burned in a lightning storm of adrenaline, when everything he did had consequence because he knew there was something to lose. It was what he had felt in the middle of the vasectomy when the possibility of losing Kathleen was set side by side with the possibility of another life for the two of them, one that was outside the borders of convention, a world only the two of them could complete.

And he wanted the panic he had lived on after she left, when Robert thought he could still find that world by filling a screen with an image as real as the people who sat in the dark and watched it.

He was stuck with fear, and fear was cheap. Fear left you trapped in your skin, and that was the last place Robert wanted to be right now.

He listened to the thundercloud rumble and the buzz-saw whine of a jet taking off and watched it slowly rise against the backdrop of pure blue and move across the windshield of the rental car. After the jet disappeared, he realized he'd been hitting the car horn. The heel of his hand was bright red and tender.

Robert got on U.S. 1 and left Miami, stopped briefly in Florida City to get burgers at a drive-through window and to gas the car, then drove along the empty eastern edge of the Everglades toward Barnes Sound and Key Largo, gorging himself on junk food and blocking out his thoughts by tuning in to an A.M. rock station whose D.J. sounded as if he were on fire. The greasy burgers and wall of noise were as effective as anesthesia, and he drove with his mind on hold.

Just outside Tavernier Key, the air conditioner began to emit stutterlike bursts of air and then quit altogether. Robert opened the window, and when he leaned back in the seat, the point of a knife touched the back of his ear and then jumped to his jawline.

In the rearview mirror was a skinny kid, fourteen, maybe fifteen, with dirty brown hair, an acre of acne, and a shaky hand. Robert attempted a smile and felt a prick of pain, sharp as an insect bite, run along his jaw. The wind roared through the car.

"Eyes on the road, man. Think safety." Rob looked away from the rearview mirror, and the kid climbed over the seat.

The kid wore a baggy pair of jeans covered with what looked like spaghetti stains and a dark green pocket T-shirt with a large hole under the left armpit. His neck was ringed with dirt lines, and his face, small and narrow and sharp-boned, was bright red and pink, damp as damaged fruit.

"You know you talk to yourself?"

"What I want to know is what you're doing in my car."

"Easy, Dad," the kid said, dropping the hamburger bags on the floor and leaning back in the seat. "I'm just catching a ride, that's all. I was in a hurry, and you were convenient."

Robert quickly pulled the car off the road and started to tell the kid to get out when he found the knife out again, this time against his bruised ribs, and the kid explaining he wasn't too keen on hitchhiking right now, he needed to get to Key West and away from Miami for a while, and he'd appreciate it if Rob put the car back in gear and on the road.

A half hour later, they passed an immense billboard for NEPTUNE PHIL'S SALVAGE SHOP with a drawing of a shirtless man in jeans and a yachting cap and IF IT'S BEEN THROWN OUT, CAST OFF, OR LOST, IT'S PROBABLY HERE. SPECIALIZING IN REBUILT ENGINES SINCE 1972 written below. The traffic was heavier when they crossed into the city limits of Islamorada. They passed Leon's Seashell Museum, a Coconut Frank's Hamburger Haven, The Rite Price Shoe Mart, Tropical Aerobics, and the Barracuda Inn. Chevron, Shell, and Pit Stop gas stations. The Sea Winds Trailer Park. The Mangrove Lounge. Trudy's Used Furniture. Gulf Stream Haircutters. The World of Wicker. McKelvy's Bait House.

Robert kept hoping to ditch the kid along this stretch. The Upper Keys seemed like his kind of landscape. The tourists were wandering around just waiting to be taken, and there were plenty of places to hang or hide out. Lots of fast deals here, quick money, small schemes that turned on easy ambitions and mean instincts. He thought the kid would fit right in.

But throughout it all, the kid delivered a monologue, rambling on about Orlando: his divorced mother who had a healthy appetite for young Cuban males and Seconals; three stepfathers, two of whom were serving time in Raiford; a stepbrother who had made a fortune at the dog track and blown it trying to establish a string of Haitian massage parlors a few months before the AIDS scare broke out; a sister who was the traveling companion of a retired Air Force general-turned-real-estate-broker in St. Pete; and the security system at Disney World.

"I mean," he said, "there I was, standing outside the Enchanted Isles pavilion and having a good day, four wallets and it's not even eleven o'clock, and then I get collared by this guy in a dog suit. You know, Goofy, the big ears, stupid grin? I'm being careful, watching for the plainclothes, and I get nailed by a dog. Those Disney people mean business, too. The one in the dog suit kept smacking me around."

The kid spotted the police car in the parking lot of the Davy Jones Donut Shoppe at the same time Rob did. He reached over and held the steering wheel straight. "I wouldn't do that, Dad. You see, I took out some insurance."

"What do you mean?"

"I sprinkled a few crack vials all over the backseat and floor. Here I am, a poor, defenseless kid that doesn't know better about accepting rides from strangers. Then before—"

"Okay." Robert drove past the shop. "Why'd you pick me anyway?"

"Like I said, you were convenient. Though I was a little worried back at the airport when you started pounding on the horn. I was thinking *Psycho* 3, but then you cooled out. I figured you couldn't be any worse than the guy in the Goofy suit."

The kid slid over, and before Robert realized what he was doing, began running his hand along the inside of Rob's thigh.

When Rob pushed him away, the kid said, "Okay, Dad, okay. Just checking. I like to know who I'm riding with. A blow job's no big deal anyway. You'd be surprised the ones who want them, and they're not fags either."

While the kid talked, Robert tried to ease his wallet out of his back pocket and slide it in between the cushions of the front seat. He knew the kid would get around to it sooner or later and hoped to distract him by playing with the radio, shifting lanes, and varying his speed, but the little shit was on to him. He started laughing just as Robert got the wallet tucked away. Robert took it out and tossed it over to him.

An orange and blue gas truck passed them. The kid tucked his legs under him Indian-style, then lowered his head and flipped through the wallet, engrossed as a dog before a dish of food. The afternoon haze had leached the gulf of its brilliance, and the sun was a fuzzy circle in a sky running to the line of the horizon like a sheet of dirty glass.

"There's nothing in there besides a couple credit cards and some cash."

"Take it easy, uh, Robert. I'm just getting to know you." He paused. "Hey, you go by Rob or Robert or Bob?" He leaned back, and Robert noticed the kid was wearing pink jelly shoes, at least one size too small. His dirty bare feet bulged through the sides of the shoes like burnt waffles.

"My name's Walter Fields, but everybody calls me False Walter."

"Charmed to make your acquaintance."

"My mom started calling me that, False Walter, I think on account of my dad, him skipping out. I'm named after him. Anyway, that's what I go by now."

While the kid talked, he kept rifling the wallet, and Robert finally had to ask him not to rip it up. His ex-wife, Kathleen, had given it to him, and it had been old when she bought it at a secondhand shop in the French Quarter of New Orleans. The leather was delicate, seamed with cracks but still beautiful, with scrollwork ivy along the edges and on its face a raised cluster of roses which, when you looked at it in a certain way, became the profile of a woman. Robert could still remember the smell of the wallet when Kathleen gave it to him, the rich mixture of dust, leather, and her perfume.

"You know what, Rob? You ought to grow your mustache back. You look better on your license. A mustache, yes, that's it. It fits."

"How about taking the cash and giving me back the rest? I can do without the fashion tips."

"You ever notice that when most people grow mustaches they end up looking like Cubans or Englishmen? It's always one or the other."

What Robert noticed was the kid was about three days past rank. He was going to have to clean up some before he could make the sunset scene at Mallory Dock and scare up a little panhandling. Key West tourists liked their urchins a little less raw and more on the picturesque side.

The kid sat back and cupped Robert's driver's license like a poker card. "Birthdate: twelve/twenty nine/fifty-eight. Height: five-eleven. Weight: one-sixty. Eyes: Brown. Hair: Brown. Glasses: No. License number: three two five six one four. Address: Miramar Arms, L-2, Miami Beach." Frowning slightly, the kid looked back over at Robert. "I can't pin it down," he said.

"What now?"

The kid shifted in the seat and tilted his head. "Your hair's shorter and the way you got it combed back now makes it look different from your license. And without the mustache, your face looks fuller. But I keep getting the feeling I know you from somewhere."

Robert shrugged, but the kid's scrutiny had left him uneasy. There was something a little too insistent about it. Robert kept his eyes on the road. The sun, over three-quarters of the way to the horizon, was a soft, cataracted yellow and would have already set by the time they reached Key West. On the radio a D.J. with an old voice played new songs.

For a long time, the kid was so still that Robert thought he'd fallen asleep, but he was hunched over, studying something else in the wallet. When the kid looked up, Rob saw it was a photograph.

"Who's this?"

"An old friend."

The kid shook his head. "Come on, don't give me that. Right here on the back—'Love You Forever. K.' Why won't you tell me?" He held up the photo.

It was one Rob had taken in New Orleans of Kathleen, off-guard and half-turned on the balcony overlooking the courtyard of their hotel, one hand on the wrought-iron railing and the other on the way to her mouth to hide the wide, surprised smile there, the movement lifting her hair so it floated, long and black, like a curtain, over the bromeliads and orchids blooming in a long wooden planter. It was that moment of frozen surprise Robert loved, when Kathleen was balanced on one bare foot in a blue dress on a balcony exploding with flowers and light.

When Rob told the kid who was in the photograph, he nodded as if he'd known who it was all along but just hadn't been able to re-member her name. That gesture and the sight of him cupping the photograph as he had Robert's license suddenly made Robert angry enough to want to slap him. When the kid again read aloud what Kathleen had written on the back, Robert told him to shut up.

"Hey, my mom always said the same thing each time she married one of the three R's. Ricardo, Raphael, and Rene. Ricardo and Rene are the ones doing time in Raiford. Raphael runs a beauty shop."

"She's not your mother," Rob said, nodding at the photograph as he changed lanes. They were coming up on the Seven Mile Bridge. The ocean intruded on both sides, an overbearing blue.

"Man, don't I know it. But she's not your wife either." He held up his hand. "I noticed. No ring."

"Not all married men wear rings."

"If you were married to her, you would. Just one look, you can tell she's a class act. You'd want people to know." The kid went back to the wallet. After he found Robert's union card and asked what it was, Robert did the best he could to ignore him but finally gave up.

"You can read."

"This isn't some sort of joke?"

When Robert told him no, the kid still didn't believe him and kept pressing Robert to name some of the films he'd worked in. Robert mentioned the first one that came to mind.

"You were in *Ninjas from Neptune*? I saw it. The one with the judo robots, right? Who'd you play?"

"The young archaeologist. I was—"

"I know. The one who convinced the old wise man to unlock the box in the temple with the Ninja secrets in it and teach them to the regular Ninjas so they could beat the robots. Man, that was some fight scene, all that blood and sparks." He frowned. "I don't remember what happened to you though."

"I died trying to get the old wise man to safety. After he gave up the secrets, he wouldn't fight."

"You didn't marry the Ninja warrior girl at the end? I thought that was you."

"No, that was the American mercenary. I died."

The kid kept after Rob about the other films as they crossed the Seven Mile Bridge and into Ohio and Bahia Honda keys, past the rows of campers and the families picnicking at the state park under the smudged sun.

"Man, I must of seen just about everything you did, Rob. When things would get too weird, I'd hit a Cinema Six or Eight and hang out, sneak into all the movies. They were a good place to hide out."

Robert felt more and more depressed while the kid gushed on about the films, talking about his favorite scenes in *Hell Mall* and *Young Vampires on Wheels*, the women in *Escape from Women's Psychiatric Prison* and *Dairy Queen Massacre*, the carnage in *Kill Daddy Good-bye* and *Cross My Heart and Hope to Die*, and the creatures in *Vegetable* and *It Won't Die*.

The kid knew them all, and Robert could barely remember doing some of them. At the time, they'd been work, but that's all. Work at

Worldwide followed its own peculiar logic. The studio specialized in saturating the market with low-budget extravaganzas, recouping its losses and building profits by concentrating on quantity, doing two to four variations on the same film and then dropping them in the theaters like a litter of puppies.

For Robert, the films had meant some quick bucks and, more importantly, exposure, a ticket to something better. He did what he had to and waited for an opening, putting up with the grueling shooting schedules, the shoestring budgets, the scripts that were often no more than two-page outlines, playing anything he was asked to—the insipid leading man or standard-brand psychotic or malevolent alien inherent in any Worldwide picture—yet always working hard to inject something into each role that played off the cliché.

And it had almost paid off. Martin Broom had noticed him and put him in *The Evictor*. It should have been the perfect opportunity; Martin would use his leverage as an executive producer to make a small serious film, one that would consolidate his reputation and let him step outside Worldwide's usual orbit, and Robert would go along with him. *The Evictor* would be a breakthrough for both of them.

Except the breakthrough became a breakdown, the film just over a quarter completed when Worldwide went bankrupt, the whole project left in limbo, lost to the studio's lawyers and the seemingly endless rounds of proceedings. Martin Broom had decided to completely cut his losses and left producing and directing altogether, taking a teaching position at Florida State University in film and popular culture. Before leaving, Martin Broom had done what he could for Robert, putting in a call to Russell Tills, who had managed other actors and actresses that Broom knew. As it turned out, Robert was left trapped by *almost*, by all the torments and tiny consolations the word evoked, having to live with an approximation of who and what he saw himself as.

The kid's jabbering was an annoying reminder of everything that had gotten away from him, and Robert, more abruptly and loudly than he'd intended, told him to shut up.

"What's the problem?"

"You." Robert loosened his grip on the steering wheel and turned up the radio. In the west, the sky ran into the sea, the sun and horizon covered by a curtain of thick gray clouds.

"You, kid. You're the problem."

"I got a name, you know." The kid still had Rob's wallet and its contents spread across his lap, and he continued to pick through them, tentatively, as if they were something soft and leaking, like a package of thawing meat that unexpectedly gives under your fingers when you pick it up. Later, near Summerland Key, the kid fell asleep holding Kathleen's picture.

The thunderstorm broke a few miles outside Key West, hard and sudden enough that Robert had to pull off the road. Irritated by the delay and exhausted, Robert leaned back in his seat, watching and listening as the wipers lost out to the rain exploding against the windshield.

He suddenly remembered the crack vials the kid had planted in the backseat, but when he turned and checked, it was clean. The kid had been bluffing his way through the whole afternoon, and Robert could have ditched him at any point.

Why he didn't go ahead and do it now bothered him. It would be a relief to be rid of him. The kid acted as if Robert had completely forgotten how he'd ended up in the car in the first place. But Robert knew that wasn't the real problem. Robert's sore ribs were a painful reminder that he was evading the issue. False Walter wasn't his concern. The kid hadn't killed a grandmother's dog or lost a package at the Miami International Airport. Robert had managed that all by himself, and he was going to have to find some way out of the trouble he'd landed in. Robert might be in Franklin Benjamin Lauter's movie now, but Russell Tills still owned the theater.

The rain thudded around the car, and the radio blurred with static. Rob carefully massaged his ribs and let the kid sleep. False Walter lay curled tightly around himself, his head pulled into his chest and his fingers bunched at his lips. Every so often he jerked and made small noises, as if he'd been jabbed with something sharp.

My audience, Robert thought.

The storm stopped as suddenly as it had begun, but it had grown dark enough for Robert to need his lights. The western horizon was a deep red gash, and everything leaked steam—the palm trees, the pavement, the ground, the hood of the car. Robert pulled off the berm and drove on in.

On the other side of Stock Island, less than a mile from Key West, the kid started screaming in his sleep.

He thrashed himself awake, but Robert couldn't get him calmed down. He kept throwing himself at Robert, and Robert pulled over as soon as he could and grabbed him. The kid looked spooked enough to pull the knife again.

"You can't do that. You can't."

"Okay, Walter. Calm down. You were dreaming, that's all, dreaming." Rob kept him pinned until he felt the tension leave the kid's arms and shoulders.

When U.S. 1 became Roosevelt Boulevard, the traffic was heavier, and Rob had to slow down. The northwestern side of Key West was as ugly as the Upper Keys, a congested commercial strip of motels, bad restaurants, souvenir shops, gas stations, department stores, and shopping centers. It looked especially lurid this evening after the rain, the asphalt wet and hissing from passing cars and a sick rainbow of neon bleeding into the gauzy patches of fog floating everywhere. Robert asked if the kid was all right, but False Walter only nodded, staring straight ahead into the wet and light.

When Robert had to brake suddenly for a light, the kid reached over, jammed something in Rob's pocket, opened the door, and ran awkwardly across the other two lanes of traffic in his jelly shoes. Before he disappeared into the parking lot of Searstown, he waved the wallet and the photograph of Kathleen at Robert.

Robert considered going after him, but the traffic was jamming up, and he finally drove on, following Roosevelt until it turned into Truman and then swinging right onto Simonton, where he searched down the address for the place Russell Tills had arranged with Lennie Ash for him to stay. It wasn't until he shut off the car and sat back that he checked his pocket. His credit cards were there, along with the union card and an empty keychain from Disney World holding a profile of Goofy.

Robert closed his eyes and listened to the car's engine tick in the damp and heat. The car provided a small, easy sanctuary. The rain dripped from the leaves of the dark trees lining Simonton, and the warm air carried the voices and laughter of the couples walking toward Duval and the bars. Robert glanced in the rearview mirror, then leaned over and dropped the keychain in the ashtray and pushed it shut.

The exhaustion he'd felt earlier, the utter and absolute weight of all his mistakes, slowly shifted, and he felt both calm and reckless, as if the moon, appearing from behind the clouds, were a hole he'd punched in the sky and the light streaming through cleansed and changed everything it touched.

If there was to be a second chance, Robert hoped it was here in Key West, that it was waiting for him, perhaps had already started, because as he sat in the car, his hands loose and easy on the steering wheel, he was surprised to discover that he felt relief, not loss, over the fact the kid had run off with the wallet and photograph of Kathleen.

"He Sounded Like Bing Crosby"

H E SOUNDED LIKE BING CROSBY," the woman said and folded her hands in her lap. The talk-show host stepped back and raised his famous eyebrows, which were as bushy and dark as his equally famous mustache. He wore suspenders over a blue-and-white striped shirt. His hair resembled elaborate whorls of chocolate frosting. He placed his index finger in the small V between his brows. "Bing Crosby?" he repeated.

"Exactly like," the woman said. "I'd know that Irish tenor anywhere."

Robert wandered around the living room with a cup of coffee, getting a feel for the house. He'd yet to meet his host, Lennie Ash. Last night Robert found an envelope with his name on it in the mailbox, and inside had been a key and a scrawled note that Robert couldn't read. He had let himself in, showered, and gone straight to bed, his exhaustion keeping Heidi, Russell Tills, Franklin Benjamin Lauter, and the missing package mercifully out of his dreams. This morning, however, his bruised ribs had woken him when he turned in his sleep, and Robert started the day as he had so many others in the Miramar Arms: lying among damp sheets and thinking about the parentheses and how they held him like cold, clammy hands.

Robert walked past the television to the front window. Two large banyan trees flanked the yard, their limbs arching over a riot of blooming vegetation that spilled over most of the lawn. Robert named what flowers and shrubs he could recognize and then walked to the kitchen for more coffee, the voice of the next talk-show guest following him.

"He sounded like the Skipper on 'Gilligan's Island'," a man said.

"You know, going, 'Little Buddy' one minute and getting mad the next?"

The kitchen, like the rest of the house, had been renovated to conform to the basic lines of the original shotgun house, but the bulk of the interior-design changes produced a different effect. The house was like a child dressed in adult's clothes. It had even been moved from its original location on the eastern side of the island and dropped among its older, more affluent neighbors. A plaque on the living-room wall gave the dates when it had been built, moved, and renovated. The house was a long, narrow rectangle, the rooms running straight into each other: living room, kitchen, bathroom, and bedroom, along with front and back porches.

According to the plaque the house, along with hundreds of others, had originally been built to house the employees of the Cuban cigar industry that had once thrived in Key West. Robert doubted the ghosts of the employees of the cigar factories would recognize the place now. It was full of wicker and rattan and chrome and glass furniture, expensive rugs, soft-toned abstract prints, and a mahogany entertainment center housing two video recorders, a CD player, stereo, color television, and video-game accessories. The kitchen was a cornucopia of appliances. Still, the house didn't feel cramped. It had been built for large families, and even relentless gentrification couldn't eclipse the open, airy ease the rooms offered.

"Like a president," a woman said from the living room. "Not one president in particular. He just sounded like presidents do when they go on TV." Another voice piped in, "Maybe. But when I heard him he was speaking a foreign language. I think it was French."

The phone started ringing. Robert walked over but hesitated before picking it up. It was probably Russell Tills. Robert had already talked to him last night after he got in. As Lauter had instructed, Robert had lied about losing the package and made it a convincing performance, throwing in casual and offhand remarks about the trip down and the house, assuring Russell along the way that Lauter had taken the envelope with him to whomever needed such things in D.C.

Now Robert could hear the first pack of cigarettes in Russell's voice. "I let it ring eight times. Where were you?"

"I was in the back. I got to it as soon as I could."

"You know what happened when I answered my phone this morning, I think it was on the third ring? I get Jamison again, the guy from the Humane Society with the big heart for all God's creatures that you have the habit of throwing to the alligators. The guy's still upset. I told him I'm doing everything I can, but he's not satisfied with that. He tells me he's going to have lunch later today with his cousin who's a reporter for the *Herald*."

Across the room, a balding, middle-aged man said, "He sounded like Orson Welles."

"It reminded me of being at the dentist's," another woman said. "You know, when he asks you a question and you can't answer it because of the drill?"

Robert shifted the receiver to the other ear and told Russell that, yes, he had paper and pens. Stamps too.

"Excellent. Now what you do with them is you sit down and write a letter of apology to the grandmother about the dog. I don't care what you put in it as long as it comes off you being a sincere fucker. Wring her heart. Tell her you got a brain tumor causes you to do things like that. Or you're a Vietnam vet with problems adjusting to society. I want some sincere lies. Send the letter to my office, so I can read it. I promised Jamison I'd get back to him later in the week, and I want to hand deliver the letter to him and his cousin. In the meantime, I'm working on a couple other angles."

After hanging up, Robert found some paper and sat down at the kitchen table to work. He could still see the television where the talk-show host walked back and forth chin in hand and then turned to the camera to tell any of the viewing audience across America who might have tuned in late the subject of today's show. It was people who'd been visited and spoken to by God.

Like many of his friends trying to break into the game, Rob had done some TV work early in his career. The talk shows were good for a little quick cash. They were always turning up a guest short, and Robert had gone on three in various guises: he'd been the manager of an escort service, husband of an anorexic wife, and a slum landlord. In each case, Robert had served up the requisite amount of depravity, patience, and greed and tried not to think too hard about what he was doing, seeing the performances as paying dues, a survival tactic, like having to sign up for food stamps.

Robert leaned on his elbow and watched the talk-show host mug for the camera, wrapping it up, sincere in his hype as the letter Russell wanted Robert to write, but there was a buried wink in his expression too, as if he knew, like most of the viewing audience, that it was all a joke, but the problem was nobody knew on whom.

"Thank you and see you tomorrow," the host said, "when we'll be exploring the secret lives of podiatrists and the fetishes you face each time you put your foot in their hands. Until then, watch your step!"

Dear Mrs. Tritt, Robert wrote, *I never knew my grandmother, but that has never kept me from cherishing the memories of her passed on through the family . . .*

Dear Mrs. Tritt, when it comes time to tuck my son in at night, I wish you could see his eager face after we've said our prayers and I read him a bedtime story. His favorite is Heidi. There's nothing in the world like . . .

Dear Mrs. Tritt, after my wife failed to respond to chemotherapy, I found, like all of us, that I had to come to terms with my mortality . . .

Dear Mrs. Tritt, as the son of a veterinarian . . .

Dear Mrs. Tritt, for my tenth birthday, my father bought me a stuffed alligator and . . .

The morning leached away under Robert's false starts. He was beginning another letter detailing how Heidi's demise had dramatically embodied the spirit of Memorial Day when someone knocked on the door.

The guy was in the middle of the living room before Robert could get out of his chair. "I'm Lennie Ash, your host," he said, pumping Robert's hand hard enough to reactivate the pain in his ribs. Robert winced and nodded and introduced himself.

Lennie Ash was barely five feet tall. He wore cowboy boots and jeans and a yellow T-shirt with NO DEPOSIT, NO RETURN emblazoned across its front. With his splatter of freckles, jug ears, and defiant carrot-colored cowlick, he reminded Robert of a bloated Howdy Doody.

Lennie Ash thrust a package into Robert's hands and walked to the kitchen for a beer. "Hope it fits," he called over his shoulder.

Robert pulled out a white T-shirt. CANCEL MY SUBSCRIPTION was scrawled on its front, the lettering slanted and jagged.

"A little P.R.," Lennie said, thrusting a beer into Robert's hand in the same way he had the shirt. "Today's the big day. The opening of the two-hundredth Lennie's Famous T-Shirt Shoppe. I've saturated Florida."

Robert could believe it. It seemed every time he turned around in Miami he'd bumped into one of the shops or seen one of the ads jumping out along the interstate. Lennie was a very energetic advertiser.

"At night, I have dreams of everyone in Florida wearing one of my T-shirts. Twelve million pulling one over their heads at the same time."

"Your shops are the ones that look like a Dairy Queen with a steeple, right? Your face on the revolving sign in front?"

"You got it. You have any idea how many T-shirts the average American owns? Four-point-five. I defy any red-blooded American to drive through Florida without buying one of mine."

Lennie set down the beer and walked over to Robert, framing Robert's face with his hands. "Could you resist? Tell me honestly. I got the equipment to do it mirror-perfect. Lasers, that's the secret. A big outlay but worth it in the long run. You want your picture on a T-shirt, you want it clear, right? Hey, you're talking to the world. You go to one of my competitors, your face is a gray smudge. I got the equipment to give you your real face."

Lennie plopped down on the couch, and Rob got his first good look at his eyes. Bennies, whites, dexies, crossroads, black beauties, meth, greenies, copilots, or sky rockets—which fueled Lennie? His face was as animated as a pinball machine.

"The way to work it," Lennie said, tapping the side of his beer, "is not to worry about trying to give people what they want. That's a waste of time because they don't know. What you do instead is just make them want and take it from there. Today you don't wear T-shirts; you live them. 'T-shirts are a reason to be,' that's my slogan."

Robert fingered the sleeve of the CANCEL MY SUBSCRIPTION shirt and remembered Franklin Benjamin Lauter telling him to play it carefully around Lennie. With his ties to Russell Tills, Lennie Ash was still an unknown quantity in whatever Lauter was setting up. Robert looked over the couch at a print with horizontal bars of soft gray disappearing into each other and told Lennie he appreciated the use of the house.

"A lot of glass in here. The decorator said it was the going ticket. Did you know I had the whole place moved?"

"I read the plaque."

"Upscale now. A better neighborhood." Lennie swung his arm, taking in the room. "Russell called, said you needed a place. I was glad to provide."

Robert toasted him with his beer. "Friends and favors. You can never have enough of either."

"No argument there," Lennie said. "Did you know Russell helped me bankroll the T-shirt chain? He gave me the chance I'd been waiting for. When I met him, I was married to this Cuban girl named Estelle. I had some hustles, but they weren't taking me where I wanted to go. Estelle should have been my ticket, but her family hated that she married an Anglo. Estelle's whole family was connected, had ties clear back to the nineteen thirties and forties in Havana with all those Italian and Jewish gangsters like Luciano and Trafficante and Lansky. A lot of dope, booze, and gambling running through those bloodlines. When Castro spoiled the party, Estelle's family jumped to Miami and carved out a spot in Little Havana and started over again."

It sounded like the speed was telling the story as much as Lennie. Robert watched him roll the cold beer bottle over his forehead and listened to him go on about Estelle's family, but his mind kept wandering to his own problems, in particular, how long it would take before Russell Tills realized something had gone wrong with the delivery at the airport and what he would then do about it. Robert's ribs ached, and having to shift for a comfortable position in the chair evidently convinced Lennie he was paying attention because he continued to run through his rendition of transplanted Cuban gangsters and their bearing on his fate.

"So there I was," Lennie said, "married into one of the right families, and it's my fault I got red hair and freckles and my name's not Juan or Carlos? I get stuck managing this dump in Calle Ocho on Southwest Eighth Street, the Derrota Newsstand. The only real action is in the back room where Estelle's father and his cronies hang out and plan their next million. Me, I'm out front, selling Cuban newspapers, Bolita numbers, serving coffee and sandwiches, watching the local studs play pinball and pool. It was just nickel action. I can't even include the 'and dime'."

"Let me guess," Robert said, hoping to help the story along. "Then you met Russell Tills." Robert crossed his legs at the ankle and leaned back in his chair. He dropped his hand when he realized, like Lennie, he'd begun to roll the cold beer across his forehead.

"Russell had dealings with Estelle's father and all those exiled fat cats in the back room," Lennie said, "and he'd stop and bullshit with me at the front counter whenever he came around. Russell could see I was wasting my talent. I kept hoping Estelle's old man and his pals would eventually let me in on something significant, but Russell nailed it for me one day when he said, 'In families, there is no such thing as affirmative action.' Russell saw my potential and gave me a chance. I took it. By that time, my marriage was shaky anyway. Estelle was a real firecracker, and I loved her, but it wasn't going to work out, not with the way her family poisoned the air. So I did a walk on her and the Derrota Newsstand and threw in with Russell. Hey, six years later I'm opening the two-hundredth Lennie's Famous T-Shirt Shoppe."

"At what price though?" Robert leaned forward and pointed the beer bottle at Lennie. "Debts to Russell Tills never quite disappear. They may change shape and appear smaller for a while, but I don't think they're ever gone."

Lennie stretched his arms across the back of the couch and then looked at the ceiling. "You're worried about the Glades End Mall mess, right? Killing the old lady's dog. Russell told me about it."

Lennie's head bobbed back into place. "I'm not saying he won't make you pay for that, but Russell will eventually come through with what he promises. Russell's not the easiest guy to work for. I found that out when he rang up the tab on getting me out of the Derrota Newsstand, but I did what he asked and he delivered. He'll do the same for you, but he'll do it when he's ready."

Lennie got up and crossed the living room to the phone. "Ride it out, Robert," he said and began punching buttons. "Right now you're feeling like you got handed the short end of the stick and it's covered in shit. Sooner or later though someone will come along you can pass it off to, and the shit will rub off if you shake enough hands."

Robert listened to Lennie double-check with someone at Key West caterers about the details for a party he was throwing to celebrate the opening of Shoppe number 200. The only problem with Lennie's advice was he didn't know that Robert had lost the package at the airport. That left the short end of the stick even shorter, and if Franklin Benjamin Lauter had his way, Russell Tills would probably end up holding it after Robert. As for the shit, it felt so thick that Robert wasn't sure the world had enough hands or handshakes for his own to ever be clean again.

ROBERT ENDED UP GOING TO LENNIE'S PARTY after another half-dozen abortive attempts at apologizing to Dolores Tritt and three successful attempts to down some very strong gin and tonics. He knew it was time to get out among people when he noticed the doodling in the margins of the letters more and more resembled sets of parentheses.

Lennie's house was on the lower end of Truman Avenue, a few blocks away from the Hemingway house and the Key West lighthouse. The house, like most of the older ones in Key West, was a mix of architectural styles, a jumble of the simple and ornate with four columns across its front, a porch for each of its three stories, dormers, turrets, widow's walks, wrought-iron trellises, bay windows, and gingerbread trim along the eaves. Every light in the house was on. The front door was massive and baronial, but its effect was undermined by a panel of leaded glass holding the same caricature of Lennie's face that graced the revolving signs in front of his T-shirt shops.

The downstairs rooms were wall-to-wall people and blasting rock and roll. It took Rob fifteen minutes to make his way to the backyard and another crowd. The moon was visible over the tops of the trees, but its glow was lost in the four mercury lights on either end of the lawn. Robert spotted Lennie working the crowd, wearing wrap-around sunglasses and a smile fueled by black beauties. It looked like he'd attempted to mousse down his cowlick, but a number of orange-red strands had already jumped up and broken free. Robert waved and went for a drink.

The caterers had set up buffet tables and two bars along either side of the pool. Lennie caught up with him just as Robert had taken the first sip of his gin and tonic.

"I drew up the guest list myself," Lennie said. "Fifty people. Friends and associates. I should have known something like this would happen. I hired a couple locals for security, you know, check invitations, invite people in, stuff like that, but the guys were dopeheads, real mellow fellows. By eleven o'clock, they let in half the island. An invasion." Lennie dolefully swung his arm so it took in the backyard and shook his head as if he were witnessing the sack of Rome. He told Rob to enjoy himself and headed toward the house.

It was after his second or third trip to the bar that Robert heard someone yelling and screaming. A small group had formed in a semi-circle on the far side of the lawn close to the back of the house. Robert walked over.

The lawn was mottled with shadows from the trees and head-high shrubbery. A thin man in black chinos and one of Lennie's T-shirts with CHARACTER IS FATE on it was trying to drag someone out of the bushes. After a while, the small crowd began to lose interest and drift away, but the man yelled at them to wait.

"This is the one, right? Some of you were inside and saw him before he slipped out here. He's been ripping everyone off all night." The man hauled False Walter up to a standing position. "This is the little fuck who took my coke."

"You're crazy, man," False Walter said. He didn't look much better than he had when he jumped out of Robert's car. The dark hair still hung in his eyes, and the shrubs had left small scratches on his cheeks competing with the acne.

"I turn my back for a second," the man said, "and it's gone. I ought to kill you. It's within my rights. You better tell me what you did with it."

"I don't know what you're talking about. You're seriously confused, mister."

Robert watched False Walter toss back his hair and subtly adjust his posture, leaning in to test the strength of the man's grasp and shifting the position of his feet.

"I saw you earlier in the front room going through purses."

False Walter slid into a practiced whine. "You're hurting me."

"I have a knife. You want to see it? Think that will help your memory?"

The object lesson was lost on False Walter. When the thin man reached into his pocket, he loosened his grip on False Walter's upper arm, and the kid broke free. The others went after him, but most of them were too drunk or stoned to do any good. The kid ran wildly, zigzagging among them. He was almost clear by the time he cut in Robert's direction and tripped over an ice chest.

The thin man was closing in with the knife, and Robert timed his leap so that it appeared he was trying to help. They went down together, and for form's sake Robert made some energetic grabs for False Walter's leg. The kid was long gone by the time Robert and the man were on their feet.

"Sorry. I thought I had him," Robert said. The man looked at Robert and then at the knife. By the time he'd folded it up and put it back in his pocket, the anger in his narrow face had drained away. He looked at Robert without seeing him and began rubbing his left cheek over and over again. "Oh my God. It's gone," he said in a voice reserved for funerals of close friends, and then he walked away.

Robert noticed a small piece of folded paper among the ice cubes scattered across the grass from the cooler False Walter had tripped over. Robert quietly palmed it and went over to the bar for another drink.

He walked around smiling for the next half hour, knowing what nestled in his pocket. It had been quite a while since he'd been able to afford coke. His ex-wife's lawyer had parlayed a significant divorce settlement by playing off Robert's visit to Dr. Cawls, deftly tying, against all dictates of logic, the vasectomy to the abortion issue and fetal rights, something the judge as a mother of three had strong feelings about. Robert's lawyer was competent at best and raised enough objections so that Robert's status in the eyes of the court was raised from that of a crypto-Nazi to that of a simple moral degenerate. Tight finances later forced Robert into the Miramar Arms, a converted hotel in the Deco District of South Miami Beach whose squalid charms had yet to be appreciated by the restoration branch of the historical society or investors. Robert had been getting by, and just barely, on what the promotional circuit brought in. Now, with Heidi's demise, even that would dry up. Unless something changed, Robert figured he had enough in savings to last two months in the Miramar Arms before he was evicted. He was counting on the time in Key West giving him the chance to work something out.

Right now though it was enough to be pleasantly drunk on a warm night with the smell of the ocean and flowers and the sound of voices in the air. Or almost enough. Robert debated whether to try a little of the coke. He looked around for the thin man in the black chinos but didn't see him. Around him was a swirl of voices, people talking about Batman and Spengler, fast food and hysterectomies, Spielberg and nuclear disarmament, Mexico and multiple orgasms, condos and cancer, money markets and hair transplants, aerobic dancing, God, foreign car transmissions, computer software, bonefish, AIDS, receding hairlines, the water table, personal space, ballet, the DEA, Nicaragua, the Miami Dolphins, jogging, tax shelters, Madonna, child support, new wave, and endangered species.

Robert finally went into the house and found a vacant upstairs bathroom. The shower curtains were covered with rows of tiny greyhounds, and the bathmats were designed to resemble racetracks. After locking the door, Robert opened the packet. He estimated there was around a gram, worth around $150–175 on the street right now. Maybe more if it was as pure as the guy had said.

It was.

Robert had forgotten just how good good could be. Humming to himself, he carefully refolded the packet and slipped it back in his pocket. His synapses were clapping. All was right with the etc. The bank had cleared the check. When you fell from grace, you landed on your feet. There was no almost. Promise and promises held.

Robert rubbed his nose and walked over to the bathroom window. Below him, the pool was covered in flowers, hundreds of gardenias, lilies, orchids, and poincianas, its entire surface a bed of red, yellow, purple, white, and pink that shimmered like an immense impressionist painting.

Standing on the lip of the pool was a striking blond woman. She must have arrived since he'd been in the house because even with the crowd, he couldn't believe that he would not have noticed her earlier. She stood, straight blond hair falling in careless elegance, in a pink dress slit to mid-thigh and leaving one tanned shoulder bare. Her face was a series of sensuous angles, a strong jawline and high sculpted cheekbones, a thin straight nose, and a full mouth. Robert knew, without knowing how, that her eyes were green.

Standing next to her was a large man in a light blue summer-weight suit. He was about Robert's age. His face was strong-boned but slightly heavy, with thick dark hair brushed smoothly back except for one dark lock breaking across the wide forehead. The man's most arresting feature was his left eyebrow. It was pure white. At first Robert thought it was a trick of the light. The man leaned over and whispered something to the woman, then raised his glass in her direction.

The woman slapped him.

She stood on the lip of the pool and waited for the man's reaction. He slowly reached up and touched his cheek, then gave her a small nod, but he did not move from where he stood.

The woman's hair tumbled across her face when she bent to take off her sandals. Then she straightened and, without looking at the man, slowly pulled the pink dress over her head.

Her breasts were small and firm, like a model's in their symmetry, the areolas and nipples dark and definite even against her tan. Robert watched her hook her thumbs in the waistband of the lavender panties. He waited for a moment of hesitation that never materialized, and he watched them fall to the tiles and join the pink dress and sandals.

Just before diving into the pool, the woman looked up, and while Robert couldn't be sure, he wanted to believe that she'd seen him framed in the window, the moment holding the two of them before she slipped into the pool without a splash to surface some seconds later among the flowers, slowly swimming to its opposite end, arms and legs moving in easy syncopation, her flesh shimmering when the flowers parted at each stroke.

The woman's movement through the colors reminded Robert of a fragment from an old, half-remembered dream. He absently massaged his sore ribs and saw Lennie Ash come scurrying up to the lip of the pool and offer the man with the white eyebrow a drink. The man waved both Lennie and the drink away, looked once more into the pool, then bent and picked up the woman's lavender panties. He slipped them into the pocket of his blue suit, said something to Lennie, and walked away. Lennie hurried after him.

The woman turned at the far side of the pool and started swimming back. Flowers bobbed and burst and swirled in her wake. The air and water were bathed in silver light. When the woman pulled herself out of the pool, orchid petals clung to her legs and arms and breasts. She shook out her water-darkened hair, looked briefly at the bathroom window, and began to dress.

Robert fumbled with the lock on the bathroom door, cursing under his breath, and then ran down the stairs. He had to fend off three drunken challenges to fight as he squirmed through the crush of dancing bodies. He lost valuable time when two women simultaneously grabbed and hugged him, mistaking him for a dealer who had been out of the country for the last six months.

By the time he made the backyard, she was gone. He looked but couldn't find her anywhere.

He got contradictory answers from everyone he asked who might have seen her. Lennie Ash and the man with the white eyebrow were gone too. Robert decided to check the first floor of the house and went back into the crush of bodies and wall of sound but had no luck locating the woman. It was as if she'd vaporized in the silver air.

By the time Robert returned to the backyard, the coke was ebbing out of his system, faintly popping, like damp firecrackers, along his spine. He needed a drink. He slowly threaded his way through the crowd to the bar. He kept seeing the blond woman swimming through the pool of trembling flowers.

The man talking to the bartender was easily over six and a half feet tall. He was in his mid-to-late fifties and dressed in black, his thick gray hair pulled into a ponytail. His biceps were the size of grapefruits, and below them, the glass of rum he held was swallowed in his hand. His laugh was deep and choked, like a malfunctioning bellows. When he turned, Robert caught his full profile against the moon and the mercury lights. The midsection of the man's nose was virtually flat. It looked like part of his face had been chewed away.

"She did?" he said.

"Yes sir, Mr. Binder," the bartender said. "Swam the length of the pool and back naked."

"Sorry I missed it. Guess that's what I get for being fashionably late." He handed his glass back for a refill. Robert heard him ask if the bartender had seen Lennie and someone named Winde.

Robert stepped up and tapped the ponytailed man on the shoulder. It was solid as a door. Robert asked if he knew the name of the woman who'd been in the pool.

"I might," he said, tipping back his glass. "But I don't know you."

"It's important that I find out her name."

"That's not my problem." The man started to turn away and scan the crowd.

Robert decided to try one more time. "Look, let's start over here. My name's Robert Staples." He held out his hand.

Nothing prepared Robert for the look in the man's eyes when he turned around. They held an impossible mix of anger, contempt, and amusement. Before Robert could withdraw his hand, the man had it trapped between his. The handshake was a squeeze away from assault, the man leaning in and saying, "I'm Hannibal Binder. And if you're Robert Staples, I was wrong. You're very much my problem."

Hannibal Binder ordered more drinks, and Robert reluctantly followed him to two poolside chairs and sat down. The crowd was starting to thin out. Moths and bats tumbled and whirled around the mercury lights. The man's name had finally clicked into place. Robert stared into the pool of flowers, conscious of Binder sitting to his right scrutinizing him.

"So you know who I am?"

Robert nodded. "Your name came up when I met with Lauter and Barry From West Palm at the airport."

"Yours has come up, too, over the last few days. In fact, you're the reason I was late to the party. I was talking to Lauter in D.C. He believes we can turn your losing the material at the airport to our advantage. I'm still skeptical." Binder took a sip of his drink. "What does Lennie know about what's happened?"

"Nothing. At least from me. Lauter told me to give Lennie and Russell Tills the same story. As far as they know, the package got delivered." Robert glanced over at Hannibal. The pool chair could barely support his immense bulk. Robert still didn't know what to make of the face, the way the mangled mass of scar tissue redrew the relationship of every other feature, like something from a cubist painting.

"At least you've done one thing right," Hannibal said. "When Lennie needs to know anything, I'll tell him. Now fill me in on what happened here tonight."

Robert had just started to explain what he'd earlier seen from the upstairs window when Lennie Ash and the woman walked around the corner of the house and into the backyard. Hannibal got out of his chair and went over to meet them. Robert waited a few seconds, then followed.

Hannibal Binder and the woman had moved off to a quiet corner near the shrubs and their shadows where False Walter had tried to hide earlier in the evening. The woman's pink dress was a soft smudge in the darkness. Lennie stood next to Rob and shook his head. He looked tired and sweaty. Robert asked him what what was going on.

"The same thing that happens every time James Winde comes down to the Keys and runs into Denice Shell," Lennie said. "They had something going once, and he never learned to let go. Denice enjoys playing him, and everyone else ends up with headaches." Lennie patted down his cowlick. "I know Hannibal's pissed. He was supposed to meet with Winde tonight, but he took off after Denice's little pool number. Hannibal will probably blame me because it happened at my party."

Robert tried to make sense of the conversation in the corner of the yard. At one point he thought he heard his name mentioned. Most of the time the woman's words were lost in Hannibal's insistent interruptions. Only once did her voice break through, and Robert still wasn't able to catch what she said. It sounded like, "Nothing that you said is true" or "You know what I told you" or "I didn't know what else to do."

The woman's voice evoked the same sensation as her swim through the flowers: it seemed like a fragment from an old dream. Robert wanted to coax that dream to life, to pull the voice and the pink dress out of the darkness and find the woman who fit them. He looked around and spotted Lennie at the bar along the pool and walked over.

"I want you to do me a favor, Lennie," Robert said, "and introduce me to someone."

I T WAS WHAT BING CROSBY WAS SINGING ABOUT, and Robert Staples knew, when Denice Shell locked her hands behind his neck and began to slowly pull him down to the two powdery lines she'd laid between her breasts, that Irving Berlin was right about what everybody had been dreaming about, because it was white and like Christmas, and it had arrived by way of Matura, a speck of a village near Cliza in Bolivia on the eastern foothills of the Andes, where the light green coca leaves, the size and shape of shoehorns, were picked and packed in fifty-kilo bales and sent on to the *fabriqueta* in a neighboring village, and the leaves were then sun-dried, soaked in water and kerosene and stomped into a paste, the cream-colored coca base then transported to an airstrip where it was flown to a refinery outside Medellín, Colombia, owned and run by the *coqueros*, the old Colombian cocaine families, who then put in a call to Franklin Benjamin Lauter in Washington, D.C.

Robert knelt over Denice and moved toward those lines the *coqueros' fabriquetas* had processed and which had been moved by boat from Barranquilla, past Jamaica, and through the Bahamas and up into the Gulf through the Ten Thousand Islands to Hannibal Binder, who arranged the pickup, moving the coke to a holding station near Collier Seminole State Park and cutting it with quinine, lactose, and baby laxative, then packaging and shipping it to warehouses operated under one of Russell Tills's holding companies, Russell overseeing the Stateside distribution through his contacts as creative consultant.

That was the version of business as usual that Robert had cajoled from Denice as she chopped the cocaine and then stretched back on the bed and laid the two white lines between her breasts. Her voice was soft and musical, holding the cadences of a litany or fairy tale, but as he leaned over Denice, Robert suspected the lines went in other directions that suggested business was not usual. He remembered the name Camar Tavares coming up in the conversation of Franklin Benjamin Lauter at the Miami International Airport.

But for now, the only arrangement Robert wanted to worry about was the amount of time he could spend with Denice. They had spent every second of the last four days together. Once she'd stepped into his life, he didn't want to let go of her. Things had happened quickly between them, but Robert knew on some basic level they could never happen fast enough. *Enough* was a word that didn't apply to Denice or what he felt about her. South Florida was full of women striking enough to stop hearts, but Denice eclipsed any that Robert had met. There was something as elemental as genetic coding in the way Denice moved and wore her beauty, and Robert had seen it acknowledged in the sharp quick glances of other women and the stares from men whenever Denice and he were out in Key West.

This evening Denice's fingers were gentle and insistent, lightly touching the back of his neck. Her tan left her dark against the sheets and the coke between her breasts white and luminous. Robert held himself suspended above her, his hands on the pillows and the blond hair spilling over them, and watched the light from the bedroom window play across the features of Denice's face. The light had the same erotic pull as Robert's discovery that he'd known Denice before ever meeting her: the dozens of images from magazines, ads, billboards, and television commercials coalesced into the woman who'd suddenly become part of his days.

Robert watched a muscle jump near Denice's navel, its tremor rippling across her rib cage. He bent to kiss her, but a hand slipped from his neck and pressed into his chest. He could feel his heart beating against her palm. He saw himself twinned in the center of her light green eyes.

"Not yet," she said. "Slowly."

Robert leaned toward the warm space between the curves of her breasts, and the closer he got to the white lines lying there, the less sharp and straight they became, and what was left was just the white and the phantom odor of orchids, and Robert saw how everything and everyone came together in those lines and how his own life had become attached to them.

Robert's arms began to tremble. The room suddenly felt crowded. Hannibal Binder, Lennie Ash, Franklin Benjamin Lauter, Russell Tills, Barry From West Palm, even Heidi, the pregnant woman at the airport, and False Walter, they were all part of the white, and Robert wanted to sift through it, separating everybody but Denice and him until only two clean lines remained.

"Close your eyes," Denice said, dropping her hand from his chest, moving it down, holding and guiding him, her other hand still pressed to his neck, wanting him to find her and the coke at exactly the same time. She arched her back when Robert was almost at her breast and hooked her legs behind his knees. The sunset coated the bedroom window of the shotgun house in pink light. Robert bent his head and slid into Denice.

"Close your eyes," she repeated.

Then it was Christmas all over again, a blizzard of warm, wet flakes blowing through their brains, their spinal columns crooning like Bing, and everything was white and soft and wet, and they moved as if their veins themselves had joined.

ROBERT AND DENICE were on an afternoon walk near the West Martello Tower and the Monroe County Beach when it began to rain. They ran for the broad-leafed shelter of a banyan tree while the front line of the storm quickly moved across Key West for the Gulf. They leaned against the trunk, their shoulders touching. The wind lifted and flipped the banyan leaves, and small fast torrents of rain fell between the gaps, drenching them anyway. Denice laughed and said it felt like they were riding steerage in a leaky boat. Robert leaned over and kissed her, the wind as well as his fingers moving through her hair. The air was full of a waxy refracted light the color of empty shrimp hulls.

They left the tree when the brunt of the storm passed, walking down Seminola in a soft, steady rain. After a couple of blocks, Denice paused in front of a small pink bungalow and took off her sandals, tying the thongs together and draping them over her shoulder. Wisps of steam rose from the sidewalk along her bare calves. The rain had loosened the braid in her hair. She wore a pair of green pleated shorts and a red blouse with small pearl buttons.

Denice patted the shoulder of the blouse, then raised a bright pink palm at Robert. "The color's running everywhere," she said. "I'll have to scrub it off when we get back to the house." She pulled back the neck of the blouse and peered down. "It looks like I've bathed in blood."

"Sounds like the title of a Worldwide film," Robert said and winked. It felt good to be able to laugh again. That, too, was part of what he'd found with Denice. She had a way of making everything around her feel new, and Robert had been able to talk to her about his stalled career in film without the usual accompanying side orders of bitterness, frustration, and—he admitted it—self-pity. In the last week Robert felt a resurgence of his old confidence and some tendrils of hope creeping back into his life. He wasn't banging his head against the closed door of his desires anymore. Denice had pulled it wide open. With her, anything seemed possible.

Last night, Rob and Denice had stopped at Key West Videos and rented one of his favorite contemporary films, *Paris, Texas*. No matter how many times he'd seen it, the effect was the same. The film was an elegy on American space and the absolute loneliness of each drawn breath. Robert believed that only a foreign director, like Wim Wenders, could so unflinchingly capture what America sought to hide from itself. But Robert loved the film for other, more personal reasons. Wenders hadn't gone with the bankable, big-name pretty boys for the leads. Harry Dean Stanton with his pinched, craggy features and dark barroom voice and Dean Stockwell, whose round man-boy face seemed perpetually bewildered, had magnificently delivered on that choice.

After they'd watched the film, Robert had explained to Denice that he'd be satisfied with a career like Stanton's or Stockwell's. Any idealistic daydreams about suddenly looming in the public's eye as a major star had been discarded by the time he'd finished *It Won't Die*, his fifth film. From then on, Robert had worked for the work's sake, wanting to garner enough exposure to keep the roles coming in, whatever their size, and accepting in advance that the quality of the films would be uneven at best, but he had hoped with luck and perseverance that he'd develop into a solid character actor with cross-over potential. Robert wanted another shot at it. He'd worked too hard and sacrificed too much to let all of it get away from him.

Robert and Denice walked in the direction of Truman Avenue and Duval. A light rain continued to fall. Robert could smell the starch leaking from the folds of his white shirt, and his canvas deck shoes and jeans had turned dark and soggy, but it felt good to be walking with Denice, wrapped in the rain as they passed some of the older homes on the Key. Robert had always loved the tension in the architecture on the island, the mix of the Bahamian and Victorian, the conflicting pull of the plain and the ornate, as if Key West could accommodate any possibility. Denice spotted a blue-and-yellow parrot wearing a tiny paper cap, perched on the wrought-iron trellis of a third-story widow's walk. Next door, in the yard of a two-story frame house with enough severe right angles to make any puritan's day, a mammoth satellite dish nestled among the frangipani and mimosa.

They stopped at a small Cuban diner for espresso. Robert wiped the condensation off the window and used it for a mirror, finger-combing the hair that was plastered to his head. Denice pulled hers back and wrung it into a napkin. Her bare foot touched his ankle. Robert kept one hand wrapped around the small porcelain cup and reached over to touch Denice's wrist with the other.

"You've been a little quiet this afternoon," he said.

"I know."

"Is something wrong?"

"I don't know, Robert," Denice lifted her cup and blew across its surface. "A lot of that depends on you." She tucked a wet strand of hair behind her ear. "Have you talked to Hannibal in the last couple of days?"

"I didn't realize we were running that low. I'll call him as soon as we get back to the house. I was sure we had three or four grams left."

"I'm not talking about buying more recreation, Robert." Denice set down her cup and looked out the window. "I've been thinking about what you lost at the airport. It's created some problems and opportunities that are going to have to be dealt with. Not eventually. Soon."

Robert fingered the napkin under his cup, tearing its outer edges into thin strips. "I told you what happened. And I've done everything Lauter asked. I lied to Russell about making the delivery, and I've played it that way every time I've talked to him. As far as Russell knows, I'm down here until the Heidi mess blows over or is resolved. Lennie Ash thinks the same thing." Robert wadded the napkin and dropped it in the center of the table. "You know, Denice, I've got things at stake here too. If Russell Tills ever finds out I lost that package, my career wouldn't be stalled. It would be absolutely dead."

Denice dropped and softened her voice. "It's not your career that I'm worried will end up dead, Rob. I don't think you fully understand what you stepped into."

"I know I don't, and it doesn't matter. I just want to get out from under losing the package. The rest of it doesn't concern me. I'm not any real part of whatever's going on between Russell and Lauter."

"It's not that simple, not anymore. And besides," Denice said, picking up her cup and holding it at chin-level, "what would you do if I told you it concerns *me*? Because, Robert, I'm a very real part of what's going on."

Robert slumped back in the booth and squeezed the bridge of his nose. To his right, the window had fogged up again, and the sound of the rain was indistinguishable from the sizzle of the burgers on the grill across the room. "I can't believe this is happening. I didn't even know what was in the package, for Christ's sake."

Denice finished her coffee and stood up. "Problems and opportunities, Robert. There's not much difference between them if you look closely enough." Before Robert could say anything, Denice was across the diner and out the door.

Robert caught up with her a couple of blocks later. The air was still full of rain and tropical warmth. Robert felt the muddy coffee and something else burning his insides when he grabbed Denice's arm to slow her down. He stopped to catch his breath and then asked where she was going.

"Back to my place. I've got things to do. Things that you made very clear you want no part of. I understand, Rob, I really do, but you have to understand that we leave it here." Denice kept her gaze straight ahead.

"What's 'it'?"

Denice paused and turned. "Us."

Robert couldn't tell if her eyes were full of tears or rain. The burning in his stomach increased. He took Denice's arm and shook his head no. He couldn't find his voice. It was as if the rain dissolved his words before he could utter them, and he was left with a mime's version of pain, incredulity, anguish, longing, and desperation. When he tried to pull Denice close to him, the dye from the red blouse seeped between his fingers. He leaned in, pressing his forehead against hers, and again shook his head no.

"Well, then," Denice said softly.

They began walking again, Robert leaning in close, trying to recapture what the afternoon had held earlier, but everything had begun to shift with Denice's last phrase: *well, then* was the fulcrum his desire followed.

"Camar Tavares," Denice said, "has established a rival faction that's seriously challenging the *coqueros*. Lauter's met with Tavares a number of times, and Tavares is making some very attractive offers. Lauter thinks they're worth consideration. Russell doesn't."

They paused on the sidewalk under a dripping traveler palm. The rain had begun to slacken. Down the street, tourists lined up in front of the Audubon House. Beyond it was the old Key West Customs House, dark against the faint gray lines of rain. The wind carried the sounds of Duval Street coming back to life. Robert lightly touched his burning stomach.

"Is there any chance I can get out of this without Russell Tills finding out I was involved?"

Denice fingered the sleeve of the wet red blouse. "I want you to think about stepping in, not out, Robert. Lauter and Hannibal are working on a plan to use the missing package against Russell. When the time comes to implement it, you just play along. Something can be worked out, you'll see."

Robert and Denice turned left on Greene and walked toward the house on Simonton. Above them, the sky was cut by a long pale rainbow and a small single engine plane heading for the Gulf of Mexico. Robert listened to the stutter of its engine and took Denice's stained hand in his.

HANNIBAL BINDER called the *Blue Circus* his "boat," but the noun was more than a little misleading, the equivalent of referring to a Rolls as transportation. The *Blue Circus* was over a hundred and fifty feet long, its hull indigo with midnight-black trim. Below deck were five staterooms done in teak, a spacious and well-stocked galley, and a walk-in engine room. Robert had been given the grand tour.

Binder had hired a local Conch nicknamed Mohammed Jones to pilot the *Blue Circus*, and they'd left Garrison Bight Marina late in the afternoon, making a long easy loop through the National Wildlife Refuge south of Key West, staying east of Crawfish Key, then west of Man and Woman keys, moving into the intercoastal waterway, eventually passing Fort Jefferson National Monument, huge and hexagonal, built with sand-colored bricks and once housing Dr. Samuel Mudd, who'd been sent there for setting the broken leg of John Wilkes Booth. They eventually turned westward and sailed through the Dry Tortugas into the absolute space of the Gulf.

Robert and Hannibal Binder stood on the upper deck, leaning into the rail. The wind ran through the sky in great warm sheets, scattering what few clouds clung low on the horizon and carrying the smell of the ocean, sharp as iodine. When Robert looked up, the stars seemed impossibly small and far away, as if the wind had blown them like pieces of paper deep into the night.

Hannibal Binder pointed over the railing. "In the pilothouse there are maps neatly charting all that out. Longitudes and latitudes. Tidal movements. Everything out there accounted for. Why are you at the railing? What are you looking at? I'll tell you. It's not the world that's old, only our ways of looking at it. I'd say there's no difference between Ponce de León standing at the helm and you at the rail. You're looking at the same thing. The maps and charts don't mean a thing."

Hannibal turned so that his massive back was to the rail. He faced Robert. "Do you know what the first Spanish explorers called Key West? Cayo Heuso. The Isle of Bones. The beaches were covered with them. The bones came from the original settlers, the Seminole and Calusa Indians, who kept chasing each other key by key, pushing until they ran out of land. The Seminoles wiped out most of the Calusas in Key West and left their bodies on the beach, and along come our Spanish friends looking for riches, and what do they find? Bones. They claimed it all for Philip II anyway.

"Later, who comes along, but Ponce de León looking for his fountain and what does he call Key West? Los Mártires. No bones this time, just oddly shaped rock formations along the beaches. Ponce looks at them, and what does he see? Not rocks, no. He sees men pierced by stakes. Los Mártires. That's always been the problem."

Hannibal paused, walking across the deck to make each of them a drink. Beside the bottle of rum and pitcher of pineapple juice lay a glass waterpipe and a small plastic bag filled with crystal granules. Robert had watched Hannibal set them out earlier. He took some deep, even breaths and looked back over the railing.

He wished Denice were here with him, but she was in Miami meeting with Russell Tills. "Taking his temperature," Franklin Benjamin Lauter had called it in his phone call from D.C. Lauter had begun to turn up the heat under Russell. Denice, under the pretense of discussing a modeling job, had driven to Miami earlier in the afternoon to check out firsthand how Russell was doing.

Hannibal came back with the drinks and gestured toward the sky and stars as if they were something he'd placed or scattered himself. "New worlds require new people and new perspectives," he said. "What did Ponce de León and the others discover? Nothing. Or at best, what they already knew. Death and God, that's all they found. They dragged both along with them from Europe. They weren't faithful to what they wanted. It was all here, the riches, the fountain, but they couldn't see it. None of them ever saw the New World because none of them made themselves new."

Robert nodded, careful at this point not to commit himself to any opinion. Throughout the evening, Robert had not been able to shake the feeling that Hannibal was closely watching, gauging all his reactions to whatever had been said.

During the early part of the cruise, after they'd left Garrison Bight and Key West, Robert had listened to Hannibal reminisce, shining a spotlight on his past by telling Robert the string of anecdotes that formed the basis of the Binder legend: how Hannibal had sent twelve dwarfs masquerading as a Boy Scout troop to Bogotá on a coke run; how he'd managed one of the largest intercontinental shipments of the early 1980s when he remembered that cows had multiple stomachs and masterminded a body-packing scheme on a grand scale by shipping three hundred head of coke-filled Herefords to Denver; how Binder had bankrolled a line of discount service stations in South America, using the franchises to store and move huge quantities of acetone, ether, and hydrochloric acid to processing plants in Colombia, Ecuador, and Brazil; how before his fiftieth birthday, Hannibal had acquired his trademark nose, the cocaine causing the cartilage to collapse and requiring its insides to be rebuilt three times by stretching and weaving mucous membranes and taking tissue from the roof of the mouth to plug the holes in the septum; and how Hannibal had been around long enough so that he could tell you a few interesting things about both the Bay of Pigs and Watergate.

Robert had nodded, smiled, or laughed in all the right places, but he couldn't quell the case of nerves that lay on his stomach like day-old coffee. Robert knew how abrupt Hannibal's mood shifts could be. Even when he was casual and relaxed, Hannibal was imposing. It was difficult to ignore the oil-barrel bulk attached to a six-and-a-half-foot frame, the mangled nose, the ponytailed salt-and-pepper mane, or the voice deep and hoarse enough to be something out of special effects.

At the railing, Hannibal leaned in and asked, "What do you see when you look out there, Rob? Can you see it for what it is, or do you need the charts?"

"I don't know if it's that clear or simple." Robert knocked back his drink and wished they were across the deck at the table fixing up the waterpipe. That wasn't clear or simple either, but it was infinitely preferable to the view from the railing.

"Franklin Benjamin Lauter would say that it was both," Hannibal said. "Everything's clear and simple for him. Lauter worships efficiency. I don't know if he has ever even tried blow. The man moves hundreds of kilos a year, but you take away his analysis kit, and I bet you Lauter couldn't tell the difference between prime Colombian and quinine. To him, the coke's just a product you move from point A to point B. Something you factor and put on a graph."

Robert rolled the empty glass between his palms and wished he could think of something to say or do to divert Hannibal and change the subject. The growing intensity in Hannibal's voice left Rob feeling like he was riding in a car whose brakes had suddenly begun to go soft.

"Russell Tills is his own story," Hannibal said, not looking at Rob. "I've known him for a long time. I love the plastic surgery, the dyed hair, the flashy clothes. I love that denial, but it's denial for all the wrong reasons. Russell isn't denying old age or death because he's afraid of it. No, he's denying it because he's greedy, that's all."

Hannibal thumped the railing. "Your friend Lauter is merely efficient, and your friend Russell is merely greedy, and me, well, I'm what the other two are lacking. For a few years we struck an interesting balance, but that's in the process of changing. You losing the phonebook at the airport has helped to speed that change up considerably."

The rail under Rob's hand turned moist and slippery. Last night, while they were in bed, Denice had finally told him what had been in the package he lost. A phonebook. Or rather, a facsimile of one, containing an update on Russell Tills's distribution system. Within the phonebook were addresses for safe houses and warehouses; the names of known informants; laundering rates; bank account numbers; pay-off schedules and scales for friends within the agencies and local law enforcement; the names and addresses of the regular clientele and the front-and-middle-men Russell used when the coke got closer to street level; the poundage each buyer usually took. The doctored information had been integrated within the contents of a regular phone-book, making the information difficult to locate unless someone knew what he was looking for, but the value of the contents definitely making it worth the trouble to find out.

Hannibal tapped Rob on the shoulder and reached over for his empty glass, but the hand suddenly became a fist, and Robert slammed into the railing, his glass flying across the deck. The left side of his face was numb. Robert attempted to steady his breathing and tasted blood.

Hannibal slowly lifted him one-handed by the front of the shirt and pinned him to the railing. Robert tried to will his legs and feet into doing their job, and he was terrified to discover they couldn't because Hannibal had lifted him free of the deck, leaving Rob seesawing on the top bar of the railing.

"We know what your friends Franklin Benjamin Lauter and Russell Tills are," Hannibal shouted, "but what about you, Rob? What are you?" Hannibal kept one hand wrapped around Rob's shirtfront, the massive forearm of the other pressed against Rob's upper chest.

"I'm afraid, Hannibal. That's all. Afraid." The warm sea air blew around them, and the blood ran to Robert's head. If he turned in either direction, all he saw was the black waters of the Gulf, the waves streaked with silver phosphorescence from the *Blue Circus's* move-ment.

"That's a start, Rob." Hannibal shifted the position of his forearm so Rob was leaning further back. "Now tell me exactly what your angle is in all this or I let go."

"It happened," Robert gasped. "That's all. Just like I told Lauter. No angle."

"I'm supposed to believe an actor, someone who makes his living pretending to be other people? All you had to do was deliver a package."

"I fucked up, Hannibal. Honest. Nothing more." Robert slowly lifted a hand. "Pull me up now, okay? It's the truth."

"I don't believe in innocence or bystanders." Hannibal thumped Rob's chest hard. "Do you know what I think? I think your career's on the skids in a major way and you're stuck doing Russell's odd jobs, and you have to go along with whatever he says to stay on what passes for his good side. It's your only chance to get back into movies, and you want that badly enough to do anything Russell wants. You wouldn't even have to lose the phonebook. You just pretend you had and tell Lauter. It adds up to a nice little scam. Maybe the phonebook's still in Russell's office, and the ranting he's doing all over Miami is smoke. It's a buyer's market right now for that book. Maybe you're sitting on it and driving up the price. Or maybe you're helping Russell set up some people. I'm afraid I'd have to include myself in that crowd. And I don't like the company."

"Jesus, Hannibal, I don't know how to make you believe me." Robert's words spilled over the dark rushing waters below.

"Belief is an awkward construct, difficult in the best of times." Hannibal pressed his forearm harder against Rob's chest. "See, Rob, from my perspective, it's *you* who's got me dangling over the edge. If you lost the phonebook, it hasn't turned up yet, and we don't know who has it or how it will be used. Now Lauter has come up with a way to compensate for its disappearance and still teach Russell a little object lesson along the way, and I'm left in a very difficult position. I have to *believe* what I'm being told by you, Russell, and Lauter, and I like *knowing* what's going on. Lauter has used this whole mess to gain a little more control and power than I feel comfortable with."

Robert slowly and painfully lifted his head a few inches until he could just make out the full moon, the color of a grapefruit, hanging above Hannibal's shoulder. The skin along the middle of Robert's spine had been rubbed raw. His arms clutched air. He had moved to something beyond fear. His bones felt hollow.

"What's to stop me from just letting go, Rob? You see, I know the charts don't do any good out here. Who would know? Who would even bother to look for you? Russell? Lauter? You think Denice?"

"I told you the truth, Hannibal. Let me up, okay? I don't want to die."

"Nobody does. That's nothing special." Hannibal shifted his grip downward on Robert's shirtfront, and in Robert's panic all reference points disappeared. He was dangling over an ocean that was filled with stars and a sky that was as vast and dark as the waters. The *Blue Circus* could have been sailing through either.

Hannibal's voice sounded as if it came from a great careening distance. "I almost believe what you told me, Robert. You're afraid, and that's what your friend Hannibal Binder trusts. Lauter has started putting the squeeze on Russell Tills, and I'm going along with it. You better not have lied about losing the phonebook and you'd better do what you're told or I promise I'll show you what fear truly is."

Hannibal swiftly jerked up his arm, and the sky and waters parted, leaving Robert back on deck.

WHEN DENICE RETURNED FROM MIAMI, Robert was bent over the coffee table in the living room of the shotgun house on Simonton doing what he told himself was the absolutely last line of coke for the night. It was the fourth absolutely last line he remembered chopping over the last hour or so. He was in the same clothes he'd worn on the *Blue Circus* earlier in the evening, but like him, they were slightly the worse for wear, his shirtfront a mass of wrinkles and missing buttons, his pants twisted and bunched around his waist, and the whole outfit holding a disconcerting mix of odors: sea air, Hannibal's cologne, and Robert's sweat. A couple of glances in the mirror lying on the coffee table held all the attraction of a morgue shot. Fear seemed permanently etched into his face.

But it was a sudden upsurge of rage that brought him to his feet. He was screaming at Denice before he was even aware he'd started. She remained standing just inside the door while he roamed the living room, waving his arms, bumping into or knocking over whatever got in his way.

"It's nice to see you again," he shouted. "Or rather it's very nice to be able to see you or anything else at all after my little boat ride with your friend Hannibal Binder. How was Miami by the way? Russell Tills doing okay? No, he'd be doing okay if he wasn't. That's how we're playing it, right? What did Lauter call it over the phone? 'Taking Russell's temperature'? It's wonderful to have such concerned friends. Did Russell take you out to dinner after you'd discussed the new ad shots? Did you encourage him to open up? You're good at that, Denice. I can see you reassuring him, those green eyes full of concern and understanding. There's nothing more comforting than a beautiful woman. I read that somewhere. I don't remember where exactly, but I'm sure it's written down."

Robert lurched into an endtable, spilling magazines. His pulse felt like an overturned anthill. He ran his hands through his hair and swung his head around the room. Denice was in the same spot by the door. He looked at his watch, paused, and checked again. Three A.M. Robert massaged his forehead. The veins in his temples felt as thick as earthworms. He quickly walked over and turned off the television.

"Remember 'The Outer Limits'?" he asked, pointing at the blank screen. "I was waiting for you to get back, and I turned on the television, and they were showing reruns. It must have been one thirty, two o'clock, around there. You know what, Denice? I was scared. A goddamn television show set off the panics. There was nothing I could do to stop them. You weren't here. The episode was about a baby's birthday party, but you never saw the baby or the parents until right at the end. You just heard the baby making baby sounds and the parents' voices off-screen talking about the celebration. The camerawork was just interior shots of a typical middle-class home and repeated cuts back to a big pile of presents in the living room. That was the whole show, just a series of interiors and the sounds of happy parents talking and a baby babbling."

Robert moved behind the couch and began pacing its length, running his hand back and forth on the material covering its back, feeling the static build under his fingertips. "Here's the clincher, Denice. In the final shots, we see mommy's hands as she gives the kid a present, the camera then panning in on the kid's hands as he rips it open, paper tearing and flying everywhere. Then a close-up of what's in the box. And you know what's in it, Denice? Us. It's the earth. The camera pulls back in the last shot, and we see this family of monsters in their living room, these terrible looking creatures smiling while this hideous looking baby coos and tosses the earth up in the air, playing catch with it like a ball."

"Okay," Denice said, and slipped the canvas bag from her shoulder and let it drop to the floor. It was the first thing she'd said since coming through the door.

"'Okay,' what?" Robert yelled, wheeling in her direction. "What does that mean, you saying okay?"

"As in enough." Denice started across the living room. "Most of what you're saying is the coke talking, Robert. You're upset. I can see that." Denice went to the sideboard and made herself a drink.

"Goddamn right, I'm upset. I had a novel view of the Gulf this evening. Upside-down and a breath away from being dumped in it."

Denice took a sip of bourbon and crossed her arms on her chest. "I didn't think Hannibal would take it that far."

Robert started toward Denice, then abruptly stopped. The air in the room seemed to vanish. "Are you saying that you knew Hannibal might pull something like that on me? You kissed me good-bye and drove on to Miami and just let me walk into it blind?" Robert didn't know what to do with his hands.

"I knew it was a possibility because I know Hannibal. I told him you were okay, but he had to find out for himself." Denice freshened her drink and then leaned against the edge of the sideboard. "If I'd said anything to you before you met with Hannibal, it would have put you on guard, and you'd have ended up confirming his suspicions. Everyone's on edge with the way this deal's going. I figured it was best to let things work themselves out with Hannibal."

"Didn't you hear what I said?" Rob yelled. "The son of a bitch almost killed me. He had me dangling over the railing, and I could feel how badly he wanted to let go. And you figured things would just work themselves out? Just what the fuck are you doing with my life, Denice?"

Robert realized he was yelling at an empty room. Denice's drink was on the sideboard. He heard bathwater running. He quickly walked over and picked up Denice's drink but had only taken a few steps toward the back of the house when he stepped on an unopened bag of potato chips he'd knocked to the floor earlier. The sudden pop of cellophane and the brittle crackling of the broken chips echoed something in him, and he stopped and slumped into the nearest chair. His breathing was still fast and uneven, but every muscle in his body felt twisted and drained of energy. He closed his eyes and listened to the sound of running water.

Then Denice's hands were on his shoulders, her breath in his ear. "Come on, I have a bath ready for you. It'll help you relax. You must be sweating half the Andes out of your system."

Robert followed her into the bathroom and leaned against the sink while Denice undressed him. It wasn't until he eased into the tub that he got a good look at her. Until now, she'd just been a wavering image in the sights of his rage. But with the warm water lapping his chest and base of the neck, Robert slowed down and looked at her in the doorway. She was wearing a tight peach-colored T-shirt dress and sand-colored sandals that laced to her ankles. Her hair was down, flowing over her shoulders, and she'd tucked a large purple and white orchid behind her left ear. She wore a tiny seashell necklace and a bracelet threaded with thin gold chains.

"I'll be back in a minute," she said, "but I want you to think about something. A little while ago, you were screaming about what I'd done to your life. I'd like you to consider what you'd done with it before you met me. I'm not the one who killed a grandmother's dog or lost the package at the airport, Rob."

Denice turned and walked into the kitchen. Robert heard the refrigerator door open and close. He didn't need to think too hard about Denice's request. He slid lower in the tub, letting the warm water envelop him.

Denice came back, stopped by the edge of the tub, and dropped a large container of ice cubes into the water. "Not enough to give you a heart attack," she said, "but enough to give your system some equilibrium." She tossed the container on the floor and sat on the edge of the tub, crossing her legs. Within a few seconds, Robert felt the first icy rivulets touch his skin.

"You were partially right," Denice said. "Russell didn't exactly cry on my shoulder tonight, but he was worried. He knows something is not quite right, but he doesn't know why. Before he does, things are going to get a lot worse." Denice paused, tilting her head, and looked straight at Robert. "They don't have to be worse for you, though."

The ice cubes bobbed and clustered along the edges of his body, and Rob picked one up and rubbed it across his forehead and then rested it on his neck as he listened to Denice talk about Lauter's and

Hannibal's plan to unravel the network of clients Russell Tills maintained as a creative consultant. It was basically a diversionary action, an attempt to keep Russell busy while Lauter worked out the arrangements in D.C. for bankrolling the deal with Camar Tavares. Russell's clients were about to have their professional and personal lives disrupted in a variety of ways, and each one would come running to Russell to fix it. Hannibal and Lauter thought the scheme would work better if it appeared arbitrary. Russell would not be able to anticipate where the next problem came from or who was behind it. The rest of June and a good portion of July would be one long headache for Russell Tills.

"Do you think Lauter and Hannibal can keep Russell from finding out who's behind the whole thing?" Robert asked. "What's left of my career is still in Russell's hands."

"The odds are good Russell won't find out, but there are no guarantees, Rob. There's still a chance someone snatched the book and didn't understand its value and dumped it. We've been lucky so far because the phonebook hasn't surfaced." Denice leaned closer to the tub, caught an ice cube, and slowly rubbed it along the inside of Robert's thigh. "If things go as planned, Russell's credibility is going to be seriously undermined, and his bargaining power in the partnership compromised so that he'll have to go along with the new arrangement with Camar Tavares. It'll be a little object lesson in humility for Russell, and it just might end up benefitting you too. By that point, Russell will be vulnerable. Very vulnerable."

"It's still going to be tricky keeping Russell from figuring out how deeply involved I was in all this," Robert said. "I'm going to need a better grade of luck than I've had lately."

Denice slid the ice cube under Robert's scrotum, tucking and holding it in the smooth hollow with her long fingers. "Maybe it's already changed. That's what I want you to consider."

Denice's fingers slowly moved the ice cube lower. Robert gasped and shut his eyes. Denice's voice washed over him. "It doesn't have to stop here, Rob. You're already in this, and there will be room for you if you decide to stay in. It's an opportunity to prove yourself, a shot at getting what you want. All you have to do is take it. The new arrangements Lauter's working out in D.C. can work for you too." Denice let go of the ice cube, and it bobbed to the surface.

Robert tried to pull Denice to him, but she stood up and moved to the commode, setting a foot on its top and untying her sandal, the peach-colored dress riding up her brown thigh.

"Right now, I'm stuck having to go along with what Hannibal and Lauter are setting up at Russell's expense," Robert said, "but beyond that, I don't have anything to add to it besides the mistake at the airport."

Denice untied the other sandal and let it drop to the floor. "Not from what you told me about your parents' property in Minnesota and what it's worth."

Robert was not ready to discuss that. Not tonight. He watched Denice as she moved to the doorway.

"Think about it," she said. "In the meantime, give me five minutes."

The house was dark by the time the tub drained and Robert toweled himself off. He groped his way through the kitchen to the bedroom doorway. Denice had closed both the shutters and blinds, and the room was a solid wall of black. Robert leaned against the doorframe, trying to let his eyes adjust to the darkness, but he couldn't make anything out clearly. For a second, Robert felt like he was back on the *Blue Circus*, staring out over the Gulf, while Hannibal leaned in and talked about what could and couldn't be charted.

A kitchen match flared and held, and Robert saw Denice's long silhouette on the bed. She lifted an arm and lit a bedside candle, creating a small pocket of light. All the covers had been kicked to the bottom of the bed. Denice turned on her side, facing him, already undressed. She had no tan lines, and her body was one unbroken brown plane in the candlelight. She had left the orchid tucked behind her ear.

Robert slid into bed and put his hand on the rounded curve of her hip and leaned in to kiss her. "Not yet," she said. "I want it dark." She blew out the candle, and the room again disappeared. For a few seconds, a faint afterimage from the candle's flame remained, and then it disappeared. Denice's hand moved across his thigh and found him.

"I thought so," Denice whispered. "You like the dark too." She guided his hand and then his head to her breasts.

It was both unsettling and exciting to make love in a room so dark that it made no real difference whether Rob's eyes were open or closed. All the usual frames of reference vanished, including the self. Anything seemed possible. At times, Robert couldn't tell where his body ended and Denice's began. There, in the dark, they were left with just the fact of flesh, its tastes, smells, and textures. Nothing else meant.

Robert felt the first stirrings of orgasm, a gathering heat and tremors running just under the surface of his skin, but out of the darkness, one of Denice's hands found his cheek and the other his shoulder and pressed, slowing him down. "Not yet," she whispered. "More." She shifted position, sliding out from under him, and Robert momentarily lost contact with her. All he was conscious of was the beating of his heart. He slowly sat up. To his left was a faint rustle, and then something smooth and velvety moved across his rib cage. In a low voice, Denice urged him to follow it.

Robert bent and put his lips to Denice's warm stomach, lightly kissed her navel, and then moved lower, opening her legs and finding her warmth and wetness and something else with his mouth. Something cool and bitter and soft. Denice's hand was on the back of his neck. "Don't stop," she said.

Robert couldn't and didn't. He slipped one hand under her ass and lifted her to him, tracing Denice out of the darkness with his tongue and discovering the orchid she'd taken from her hair and crushed between her legs, Robert feeding on both, soft petals and warm skin spilling around him, and when he heard Denice's voice begin to break, Robert quickly rose and covered her, slipping inside and meeting her thrusts with his own, pushing through flowers and flesh until their cries filled the darkness.

TWO DAYS AFTER being dangled over the Gulf by Hannibal Binder, Robert stood in Russell Tills's office on Collins Avenue in South Miami Beach and smiled into the camera of a reporter from the *Miami Herald*. Robert had played the whole thing conservatively, wearing a pale gray suit with even paler white pinstripes, a soft blue shirt, and dark tie. He had a new haircut, and his shoes were shined. He was trying his best to resurrect the smile he'd used in the Miami Is Beautiful ad campaign.

"A little closer," the photographer said, "and smile at her, not me. You've got a good profile. Work that."

Robert turned and held out a large shoebox-shaped package to Dolores Tritt. She looked like she was dressed for a senior citizens' square dance, her dress full of red polka-dots against a starchy white background, the sleeves and neckline an intricate riot of lace, cheeks rouged a shade lighter than the dots below them, and her hair newly rinsed the color of mentholated cough drops.

"No, Mrs. Tritt," the photographer said. "I don't want you to take the package. Not yet. This shot's to capture the moment where Mr. Staples offers and you accept the gift. We're going for heartwarming here. Open up that girlish smile."

Robert held his pose and smiled. Dolores Tritt extended her liver-spotted hands and let the package rest on her fingertips.

"Fine," the photographer said. "Now I need a couple of Mrs. Tritt opening it. That's it for you, Mr. Staples, right now."

Robert joined Russell Tills and Ken Jamison, who stood on the other side of the office. Jamison, the head of the greater Miami Humane Society, was heavyset and dour and dressed in a mud-colored suit. "Not bad, Staples," he said when Robert walked up.

"What do you mean?" Russell Tills broke in. "It was perfect. Absolutely perfect. I had tears in my eyes."

"Can the shit, Tills," Jamison said, fiddling with the knot of his brown tie. "Just make sure the check's signed."

Russell turned to check himself out in the deco mirror behind him. He compensated for his mismatched features by giving each individual and undivided attention, and Robert watched him evaluate the net result of the eye tucks, facelifts, tanning beds, nose straightening, Retin-A and vitamin E doses, and custom dye jobs and hair styling. As usual, Russell's outfit had all the subtlety of a neon sign. Today it was a collision of pastel pink and black.

"That's right," the photographer said, "slowly. Open it slowly. Forget about me. Pretend you're about to open a door and see someone who's been away a long time. Anticipation and joy, that's the ticket here."

Robert, Jamison, and Russell watched Dolores Tritt open the package.

"Jesus Christ," Jamison said.

"Take it easy, okay?" Russell jumped in. "I asked around and got the best. In the business he's known as a virtual artist. A very solid reputation. Anyway, you have to admit he didn't have a lot left to work with in the first place. Like I said, with an artist, you got to expect a certain degree of license with the materials."

Robert didn't know where Russell had dug up the taxidermist, but it was more than a little obvious that when the taxidermist started to reconstruct Heidi that he only had a general notion of what a schnauzer looked like. It appeared he'd taken a Norway rat and a squirrel as his models.

Russell Tills signaled the photographer, and they rushed through the last shot, all of them in a semicircle, Russell next to Jamison and munificently brandishing a three-thousand-dollar check to the Humane Society, Robert looking down on the resurrected Heidi cradled against Dolores Tritt's polka-dotted chest, and Dolores Tritt choked up and in tears. By the time the photographer finished up, no one, including Jamison as he pocketed the check, cared whether they were tears of joy or outrage. Russell Tills leaned in and gave Tritt a quick kiss on the cheek and quickly ushered her and the stiff tangled mass of fur she held in her arms out of the office.

Russell then plopped into the chair behind his desk and lit a cigarette. After the photographer had gathered his equipment and left, Russell told Robert to fix each of them a drink. When Robert returned with the gin and tonics, Russell was leaning back in his chair, feet on the edge of the desk, and staring at the photos of Henry Flagler and Carl Fisher on the opposite wall.

"Do you know what Henry Flagler said as a selling point about Florida when he was working out his development and investment schemes, Robert? I'm quoting directly here. 'The gates of death are farther removed in Florida than any other state.'" Russell flicked the cigarette with his thumb, its ash spilling into a seashell on the edge of the desk. "Today we proved him right."

Robert nodded. The other thing he figured the day would prove was the extent of his debt to Russell. Now that the Heidi business was finished, Robert could already see the rest of the summer spooling out in an endless roster of promotional work. The thought of leaving Key West, the shotgun house, and Denice slammed into him like a door on a finger. Almost two and a half weeks ago, right after Memorial Day, Robert had stood in the same spot in Russell's office, and now it seemed like the whole cycle of debts was starting over. What made it worse this time was he wouldn't be able to see as much of Denice, and on top of that, the missing phonebook was hanging over him. Robert still had that scenario to ride out at Russell's expense.

Russell Tills put out his cigarette and immediately lit another. "Rob, I'm thinking I want you to stay in Key West a while longer."

Robert couldn't believe what he'd just heard. He'd been steeling himself for a round of appearances at places like Bird World, the Tampa Flower Club, and Sea-Breeze Condos, and suddenly Russell was offering him Key West. Robert leaned in closer and asked why.

"Because a number of my clients, people who count on and trust me, are calling up with problems they shouldn't be having, and I don't know why."

"What's that got to do with me and Key West?"

"Maybe nothing." Russell exhaled a thin stream of smoke the color of Robert's suit. "Probably nothing. I can't be sure though."

"Russell, if you're trying to confuse me, you're succeeding." Robert sat in the leather chair opposite the desk and took a sip of his drink. He couldn't quite bring himself to meet Russell's eyes.

"My associates," Russell said, "people I've worked with for a long time, are suddenly calling me up and telling me about anonymous threats, strange cars parked in front of their homes at odd hours of the day, and threatening letters from the IRS. These people are prominent Floridians. They count on me protecting their privacy and interests, and I've always been able to do that. They expect me to know what's going on and take care of it. They pay me very handsomely for that service. I've never had complaints. Something needs done, they call Russell, and it is." Russell tapped his left temple with the hand holding the cigarette, and a tendril of smoke curled over his forehead. "By all accounts, June should have been quiet. It's summer, vacation time for everybody, right? I thought I had everything under control. Except now, every time I blink, the phone's ringing with another problem."

Robert took another sip of his drink. "What does this have to do with me staying in Key West? I'll tell you up front I don't mind doing it, but I still don't understand why."

"Since you've been down there, you've met Lennie Ash, Hannibal Binder, and Denice Shell, right?"

"And Franklin Benjamin Lauter and Barry From West Palm at the airport."

"That's good. You know the principals." Russell set the cigarette on the edge of the ashtray, hooked his hands behind his head, and leaned back, looking at the ceiling of the office.

Robert seized the opportunity to score some safe points. He self-consciously cleared his throat and toyed with his drink. "I better tell you something, Russell. With Denice, it's a little more involved than just meeting her."

Russell lowered his head and smiled. "I appreciate the information. Not because you told me something I didn't already know. Instead, you showed me I wasn't wrong in trusting you. I wanted to know that trust was in place before you went back to Key West." Russell stood up and leaned over the desk in Robert's direction. "I need an extra set of eyes and ears, Rob. Nothing more. I'll call you, and you tell me what you've seen and heard. I'll draw my own conclusions."

Robert feigned exasperation. "About what? I can tell you anything I know now."

Russell held out his hand like a traffic cop. Smoke drifted from between his index and middle fingers. "I'm not asking you to interpret, just report, Rob. I don't care how large or small the detail is. You just get back to me. Imitate a railroad crossing: Look and Listen. That's all I'm asking you to do."

Robert raised and lowered his hands. "That's easy enough."

"It's probably nothing," Russell said. "But I want to know for sure. Someone's fucking with me. I don't think it's Hannibal Binder or any of the Key West crowd, but I can't afford not to be careful. I'm due to close an important business deal with Lauter sometime in July, and Hannibal and the others are partners in the thing. I can't tell you anything more about it, Rob. It's business and confidential."

Robert nodded. "I understand. Enough said."

Russell rummaged through his desk for another pack of cigarettes and shook one out. The tanning beds had left his skin the color of peanut butter. "Something else here, Rob. If you see a heavyset guy around Key West that sweats a lot and has thinning hair and a monogram, HS, on him somewhere, you call me right away, all right? Henry Swolt. That would tell me something. The same goes for a guy about your age and size, a classy dresser, with one white eyebrow. His name's James Winde. You see anybody that comes close to either description, you call me."

Robert polished off his drink. "I'll do what I can, Russell."

"So will I. You have my word on that." Russell gestured in the direction of the photos of Fisher and Flagler. "This is the way the world works, Rob. You help me, I reciprocate."

"I'd like to hear you say it. For the record."

"You're learning, Rob." Russell lit his cigarette. "Okay, you help me out with this thing, I forget the whole Heidi mess. Then once I get a finger on what's happening to my clients, I'll get you back in movies. We're talking contracts. Dotted lines."

Robert stood up and started to raise his hand. "One more thing. What if I can't find out anything in Key West that's any help to you?"

"The deal's still on." Russell took Rob's hand and shook. "In fact, what I'm hoping is you don't find out anything. That would be a good sign. Because if Hannibal or Lauter or any of the others are mixed up in this, things are going to turn out very bad for everyone, believe me."

ROBERT LOOKED INTO THE FACE OF THE DAY but couldn't read its expression. A spoon rattled among the haphazardly stacked dishes in the sink. The sun had just begun to crest the tops of the surrounding houses and trees lining Simonton, and the yard was bathed in the shade of yellow Robert had always associated with traffic lights. He leaned against the sink and waited for the long hiss and slow drip of the coffee brewer that signaled the end of its cycle. Outside the window, the yard was an advertisement for the elemental. The morning was color, light, and heat. Everything reduced but not simplified.

The spoon rattled again, and Robert rummaged around in the sink and found a scorpion, the size of a child's thumb, resting on the lip of a spoon. He carefully tipped the scorpion into the garbage disposal, then rinsed out a mug for coffee.

Sidestepping the two sagging bags of trash he'd forgotten to take out the night before, he carried his coffee into the living room and checked the locks on the windows and front door, a newly acquired habit ever since he'd found False Walter sitting there one night watching television with the sound off, a cold beer in one hand and a brown paper bag holding loose change, Robert's watch, a carton of Denice's cigarettes, a loaf of bread, and a *Vogue*. Robert had given him ten dollars, let him keep what was in the bag, and then kicked him out.

Robert had been running into the kid around the island and had usually managed to avoid him or brush him off, but when Denice and he had been to a party on the *Blue Circus*, the kid had popped up again, newly resurrected after having finally made some contact with soap and water, wearing a bright yellow T-shirt, baggy shorts with surfers careening all over them, and dark blue high-tops. He'd even gotten his hair cut. The kid had been carrying a large tray and serving drinks. He told Robert that Hannibal Binder had made him first mate on the *Blue Circus*. Robert had tried to steer clear of him on each subsequent visit. And begun locking the windows and doors.

For the third time since getting up, Robert walked to the bedroom to check if Denice had awakened yet. He stopped and leaned against the doorframe. Denice had tossed the pillows and kicked the sheets off the bed and lay in its middle like a dark starfish, her breathing easy and deep in the close air that still held the scent of last night's love-making. Robert stared at Denice, trying to will her awake, but all that surfaced were fragments of his early morning dreams—mouths sprouting in the palms of hands; burning clouds; a beach littered with hundreds of translucent jellyfish; a small plane running into a mountain.

Robert was more and more uncomfortable the longer he stood in the doorway. Across the room, Denice was naked and asleep, completely vulnerable, but it was Robert who felt exposed and scrutinized.

He carried Denice's image back with him into the kitchen. When he lifted the cup to his lips, he saw his own eye reflected on the black surface of the coffee and set down the mug and added another spoonful of sugar, wondering if it might not be better simply to go back to bed and try to find another entrance into the day.

That had been the problem for each day the last half of June brought, the nights broken by insomnia and bad dreams, then a short respite of deep sleep, followed by Robert up at sunrise and prowling the house until Denice woke. It was during these interludes that certain phrases, more tired than he was, took on new meaning—*at loose ends; what you don't know won't hurt you; at the end of your rope; six of one, a half dozen of the other; a stitch in time; it was fun while it lasted*—tormenting him like the messages in fortune cookies that turn out to be both inane and eerily accurate. The house felt empty and Robert utterly alone. Each day, it had taken Denice finally getting up and joining him or doing a couple of lines, often both, before he could jump-start his sense of well-being.

Robert set down his coffee cup and fingered a bulky white envelope with an Anston, Minnesota, postmark. The envelope contained the solution to his financial problems, but not without exacting its own price along the way.

His late parents' home in Minnesota had been the one asset that had survived Robert's divorce. As angry as she'd been about the vasectomy, his ex-wife had still instructed her lawyer to leave the estate out of the proceedings. It had been a parting gesture, a way of enabling Kathleen to make a clean break from their life together. She let Robert keep what he had been.

And Robert had just cashed in what he'd been at the going rate.

He had yet to tell Denice about the bill of sale or the money his father's attorney had transferred to a Miami bank. Ever since Robert had mentioned the property in Minnesota, Denice had been quietly but persistently questioning him about why he hadn't sold it. Robert had tried to change the subject each time, not wanting to articulate, even for himself, why he wanted to leave the property intact.

Things, however, had gotten a little out of hand since Robert had been in Key West. In the past, he adjusted his life-style to fit whatever the promotional work for Russell Tills brought in, and he had always found a way to get by. Time with Denice, though, carried its own price tag. The days were measured in grams, and Hannibal Binder was the clock he and Denice told time by. For Robert, it seemed like there was always enough cocaine or enough Denice to fill each passing hour. With the money, it was a different story: there was never enough. He had quickly run through his savings and started borrowing money from Denice. The three-thousand-dollar retainer Russell Tills had fronted him for returning to Key West to watch Hannibal Binder and the others had covered the debt to Denice but not what each new day cost. So Robert had waited until Denice was out of the house and picked up the phone and made a call to his father's attorney and sold his past.

It was worth more than he'd ever believed: $175,000. Robert tried to hold on to the feeling that each of the six figures carried its own version of the future, and he wanted to see the sum as a sign that his luck was changing. Robert knew he would have gotten less than a quarter of the $175,000 from the sale if it had not been for the fact that his childhood home sat on the corner of a four-way intersection in Anston. It was property the representatives of the Sunshine Convenience Store franchise found very attractive.

Robert had never been in a hurry to sell the house and lot. He liked the idea that they were always there, a potential safety net for whatever falls his luck brought him while he was trying to break out of Worldwide Studios into something bigger or better. Even though Robert hadn't returned to Minnesota since he had buried his father six years ago and had no real plans to ever move back, the idea of home, however abstract and idealized, gave him emotional ballast in a place like South Florida where the concept of *native* seemed a contradiction in terms and the face of the landscape changed on a daily basis while the weather didn't.

Now Robert tried to see the $175,000 as a fact that fit his days and avoided thinking about the franchise's smiling-sun logo, the lines of unleaded gas pumps, the boldface window ads for Grape Slurpees and Potato Chips, the racks of hot dogs slowly turning under heat lamps, or the counter displays of novelty cigarette lighters, candy bars, and road maps occupying the space he'd always seen as home.

Anyway, according to Hannibal Binder, Robert had other things to think about.

Robert got up from the table and put the envelope containing the bill of sale in the inside pocket of one of his jackets in the bedroom closet. Denice was still sleeping. Robert returned to the kitchen and started to clean up, but kept getting sidetracked as he moved from sink to counter to stove. Over his shoulder, the windows poured light. Robert took the dishcloth he'd been kneading in his right hand and dabbed at his forehead.

Whatever's necessary, Hannibal Binder had said. And that meant doing whatever Hannibal, Franklin Benjamin Lauter, and Denice thought would put the screws to Russell Tills in the deal with Camar Tavares and bring Russell back in line.

So far, Robert had been able to handle anything that had been asked of him, though afterward he was often left with the same queasy feeling that selling his parents' home had produced. It was ethical terrain

Robert didn't particularly enjoy navigating. He'd been put or put himself—Robert wasn't sure which—in a position where every one of his actions resulted in betrayal. He spent his time helping Hannibal, Lauter, and Denice to smear people he didn't know and lying to Russell Tills when he called for an update on the Key West situation. Robert had come to rely not on his conscience but on what he wanted as a compass to chart his moves. He did what he was asked because he wanted Denice and another chance to work in films, and he didn't want to settle for anything less. Anything less was the twin arms of the parentheses that had already enclosed too many of his days.

Robert grabbed a handful of trash bags from under the sink and went through the kitchen and living room, filling the bags with the accumulated clutter of the last week, dropping them when they were full, and then moving on. It was in the midst of the cleaning that another phrase came to him, one that was as old and worn-out as any of the others that had broken unbidden into his mornings, but this one dragged something else with it. It carried an Anston, Minnesota, postmark.

Matters of the heart.

It was the phrase his father had always used while Robert was growing up to explain what he thought Robert was too young to understand or to cover up what he didn't want Robert to know. It was an all-purpose euphemism he wrapped tightly as a blanket around any difficult subject. *Matters of the heart* covered anything from sex to theology to neighborhood gossip, anything secret or dangerous Robert's questions might unearth.

It was the phrase his father had used when Robert asked why his mother had left. All Robert could remember was a dark shape hovering over his bed in the middle of the night, the clean smell of shampoo and perfume as she leaned down, the taste of her lipstick when she lightly kissed him, and the seashell roar her absence left in the house the next morning when he came downstairs and found his father eating breakfast alone in the kitchen.

It was a phrase that Robert tried throughout his childhood to decipher in the aftermath of his mother's absence, turning it over and over in his mind, while his aunt moved in to help raise him, and his father continued being his father, leaving for work and returning home at the same time each day, mowing the lawn with a precision that Euclid would have admired, treating him to Saturday matinees and sundaes, tutoring him in math, and tucking him into bed. *Matters of the heart*, though, remained impenetrable to Robert, a phrase that evoked hosts of shadows and dampness, long drops and suffocation, its words as painful and troublesome as loose teeth.

The phrase remained wedged between his father and him, and Robert was never able to dislodge it. His mother had been a beautiful woman, and Robert was sure his father must have suffered deeply over losing her. Robert had imagined that they kept up a secret correspondence, a series of letters and midnight phone calls full of passionate yearnings and pledges of undying love. He imagined chance encounters for them and wild tearful reunions. Robert wanted to believe his father's life was more than the one he saw unfolding around him. It seemed impossible that anyone could settle for as little as his father had. Robert looked for signs of secret drinking or illicit affairs, anything that would serve as a clandestine subtext for *matters of the heart*, but saw nothing but the man he'd always seen. What changes he did see were all the more painful because of their superficiality and predictability—the hair that grew thinner and grayer each year, the waistline that quietly thickened.

When his father died, Robert remembered standing in the funeral home and scanning the crowd of friends, associates, and neighbors for a face he imagined would be both familiar and unfamiliar, but his mother and her version of *matters of the heart* never materialized, and Robert was left with a dead father and the generic platitudes and pieties from people who knew him as well as Robert did. His father was kind, decent, loyal, fair, and hard-working.

And dead, Robert remembered wanting to yell. Stone cold fucking dead.

What mattered and didn't about the heart followed Robert during the three trips he made carrying the trash bags to the curb. Across the street, a woman in a halter top and cutoffs was washing a red convertible, a bucket of soapy water next to her bare legs and a stretch of green hose snaking across the driveway to a spigot at the side of the house. Robert smiled and waved, and she returned his greeting with the hand holding the hose, sending an arc of water pulsing into the morning light and creating a small, quick rainbow.

When Robert started back for the house, he heard the phone ringing through the open door. He checked his watch. It was time for Russell Tills's call from Miami and more lies.

IT WAS A GOOD IDEA, getting out of Key West for the day," Robert said. He hit the gas and shipped Denice's Porsche around a dawddling Winnebago. "I had another one of those mornings. Things not quite in sync, a little tense. Russell's phone call didn't help either."

The sun spilled through the windshield into their laps, and the open windows pulled in the clean perfume of the ocean. For once, the stretch of A1A in the lower Keys wasn't being repaired, and Robert enjoyed the unencumbered ease and power of the car.

Denice leaned forward and took a pack of cigarettes out of the glove compartment and waited, the cigarette dangling between her fingers, until Robert punched the lighter and held it for her. "You can use a place up if you're not careful," she said. "Key West is better than most because it never quite takes itself seriously. No matter how they condo or boutique it up, the island refuses to let itself be pinned down. It keeps reinventing itself."

Denice held the cigarette between her index and middle fingers and watched the pattern of its burning. "Still," she said, "you have to be careful. You can use a place up, but sometimes it can do the same to you."

Denice searched the radio for a station but didn't find one she liked. They passed through Big Pine Key and by a series of historical markers. Outside Bahia Honda State Park, Robert swerved too late and hit a turtle that had almost made it to the median strip. Denice didn't seem to notice. When he glanced in the rearview mirror, all he saw was a dark jagged blot.

Denice shifted in the seat and stretched, hooking her arms behind the headrest, her white skirt riding up her bare thighs and her nipples pressing against the white designer tanktop. Her bare shoulders were the color of café au lait, and she had French-braided her hair. It fell the length of her slender neck to her shoulderblades in a thick blond coil. Denice continued to hold the pose, and it took Robert longer than it should have to realize what Denice was doing. It was a little game they played. Around the house or when they were out, Denice would suddenly focus on an object and strike a pose, parodying a commercial or ad shot. Robert would often join in and do the voice-over. Today, when he laughed and said, "I'll buy," Denice dropped her arms and smiled.

"You didn't finish telling me about Russell's call," she said.

"Well, you'll have to take at least part of the blame for that. I mean, I'd barely hung up and there you were, still wet from the shower, leaning in and biting at my neck. It's understandable, wouldn't you say, that I ended up a little distracted?"

Denice fingered her braid. "You looked upset. So among other things, I thought I'd try to lift your spirits."

"My other things thank you, too."

"They're welcome. Now what about Russell?"

Robert hated to break the mood of the day and ride but went on to tell Denice about the call. It had started like most of them had, with Russell spooked and going on the attack, springing an anecdote about a Miami Beach investment consultant, a long-standing satisfied client of Russell's, who'd decided to take a business associate out for tarpon yesterday afternoon, only to discover his boat had been impounded. Russell had gone on and recounted the fates of a half dozen other clients whose private or professional lives had been turned inside out and put on public display.

"That doesn't sound different from any other call of Russell's since the setup began," Denice said. "You've been fielding calls like that for the whole last part of June. What was different about this morning's? As soon as I got out of the shower, I could see something was wrong." Denice took out another cigarette, lighting it for herself this time.

She tilted her head back and exhaled, the smoke momentarily hanging in the air before it whipped out the window in a white stream. "The film work? Did Russell threaten to cut you out again? You were spooked about something. What?"

"It wasn't film. In fact, Russell's working on a package deal with one of the networks for roles in a mini-series and two made-for-television films. It sounds good to me. That's the kind of exposure I could use to engineer a very real comeback."

"You're leaving out one thing," Denice said. "*If.*"

Robert slowly nodded and passed a rental van, cutting in a little too closely so that he had to wait until the driver quit pounding the horn to answer. "If I can give him anything that will help him figure out or fix what's happening to his clients." Robert glanced at Denice, then back at the road. "Russell made the offer the time I went to Miami for the photo shoot of the grandmother and the stuffed dog."

"I didn't know for sure, but I suspected Russell would try something along those lines." Denice tilted her head and studied Robert. "How much are you leaking to Russell? I don't want to see you get hurt, Rob, and if you cross Hannibal and Lauter, you will."

Robert reached over and stroked Denice's arm. "Nothing. Or at least nothing significant. I haven't done anything to jeopardize what Lauter and Hannibal or any of the rest of us are doing. I give Russell innuendo. Not even half-truths. He doesn't expect anything more from me. I don't think he believes I'm really in a position to learn anything important. I give him status quo reports, and he's satisfied." Robert let go of Denice's arm and put both hands on the steering wheel again. "Remember, it's in my best interest to keep things going as they are too. I need to string Russell along until I can get out from under the mess of losing the phonebook at the airport."

"Good. I was hoping you weren't trying anything foolish." Denice leaned over and kissed his cheek, her hand on Robert's thigh for support. "I don't know how much I could help you with Hannibal or Lauter if you were, especially right now."

A little timing and luck, Robert thought, and he wouldn't need anyone's help. Robert intended to wait until Franklin Benjamin Lauter and the others had accomplished what they'd set out to do at Russell's expense, and then Robert would call Russell and warn him when it was too late to do any good but still leave him appearing loyal and trustworthy. By that time, Rob figured Lauter would be too busy with the new deal to worry or care how Robert had made his comeback. The whole mess with the missing phonebook would be over. Russell would have to accept the new terms of the partnership. Robert would appear to have done all he could for Russell. And Robert would end up back on location, in charge of his life once more.

"The call?" Denice asked.

"Sorry. I was thinking about something else."

"You never explained what was bothering you this morning."

Robert shook his head and dropped one hand from the steering wheel. "I can't believe I'm saying this, but I actually felt sorry for Russell. I mean, he was doing his usual number, all the bravado and ranting, but along the way, it was like something began to give and tear in his voice. He sounded scared and lost when he told me about the shooting in Palm Beach. I guess some plastic surgeon wanted a little recreational coke for a party this weekend. It was supposed to be a routine sale, but Russell's delivery boy got shot down on the sidewalk in front of the surgeon's house. Russell eventually went back to his old mode, screaming that someone was cutting into his territory and what he was going to do about it, but I couldn't forget what his voice sounded like when he first started telling the story."

When Denice didn't say anything, Robert shook his head and went on. "I figured the shooter had to be something Hannibal arranged, but I can't see where it was necessary to bring in guns. Why take it that far? I mean, given how Russell is already being set up, isn't that enough of a lesson?"

Denice flicked her cigarette out the window. "Some people are slow learners, Robert." She leaned back and closed her eyes. "Wake me up when we get outside Miami."

Despite the traffic, Denice fell asleep almost immediately. Robert had always been amazed at her capacity, no matter what the circumstances, to slip easily and directly into sleep. Each night, he had lain next to her and wrestled with the insomnia that had been going on since he'd had to move into the Miramar Arms, and each night, as he did now in the Porsche sitting next to her, Robert studied her in sleep and was never sure what he saw.

None of the women he'd known before had prepared him for Denice. She was straightforwardly blunt and enigmatic at the same time, a puzzle because she refused to be seen as one. Denice seemed to follow one basic impulse, and that was to do what she wanted, but the catch was when she did, she felt no need to explain the reasons behind it. All Rob ever saw were the results of her decisions and desires. She'd also set up some puzzling ground rules for their relationship. She didn't want to hear she was beautiful or that he loved her. And anytime Rob asked about anything connected with her past, she shut him down almost immediately. The past was the past was the past, she'd say if he persisted.

So spending time with Denice was like negotiating a slippery floor. She frequently contradicted or mixed up details when she talked about herself and yet showed perfect and instant recall whenever they talked about anything or anyone else. They stayed at Lennie's shotgun house on Simonton. Robert had never seen the inside of her place, and Denice couldn't understand why he'd want to and felt no inclination to indulge his curiosity. It was a place she went when she wasn't somewhere else, that's all, she'd said.

And he still wasn't sure what he thought about the mass of tawdry material she called her scrapbooks and journals. Denice had been keeping them for ten years. Robert had never had the chance to look at them firsthand. Denice brought them to the house only long enough to decide what was needed to hurt Russell's clients and then Robert would make calls to the *Miami Herald* and leave anonymous tips or type up threatening letters to the principals themselves. Denice had a highly developed ear for nuance and the uncanny ability to get people to open up to her. People told her things. She welcomed and drew out any and every confession, but it went no further than that because Denice didn't deny absolution so much as seem amused by it. The scrapbooks and journals and the damage they caused Russell's clients testified to that.

Still, he'd be lying if he didn't admit that what was puzzling or troubling about Denice was also in its own way exciting. There were worse things than not knowing exactly where you stood. It was not standing but moving that mattered. Things felt new when he was with her, sometimes almost unbearably new, but he'd also known too many days when he could hear mortality in the whine of a mosquito and each passing second drew blood.

Conventional wisdom said there was a difference between sex and love, but conventional wisdom did not wake up in warm tropical buttery sunlight to find a beautiful blond woman straddling his morning erection so that he entered the day and her at the same time, his body coming fully and exquisitely awake while his brain still floated in last night's dreams. Conventional, whether applied to wisdom or Denice, simply didn't hold up in Key West.

They'd crossed into south Dade county when Denice woke and stretched, her arms slowly fanning above her head. Then she leaned over and kissed Rob, nuzzling his neck and slipping her hand between his legs. "Where are we?"

Robert said they'd passed the Kendall Drive exit a while back. Denice lit a cigarette and said she wanted to go shopping but wasn't sure where. Robert shifted lanes, passed three cars, and drifted back in the original lane again. Around them, the sky was an eye-aching blue. He felt Miami in his stomach, the same sensation he experienced each time he entered the city, like he was in an immense classroom about to take an important test and though he was prepared, he bent under the pressure and bought a set of cribbed answers only to discover that while the answers were correct they did not match the order of the questions on the test. He kept forgetting that in Miami it was not the answers but the questions that mattered.

"What about the Bakery Centre?" Rob asked. "We're not far from the Sunset Drive exit."

"If we're going to do Coral Gables, let's do it all the way. Plunge right in. The Miracle Mile."

Robert took Granada Boulevard, the first exit after the University of Miami, and they drove into the heart of Coral Gables, the feverish brainchild George Merrick had birthed in the early 1920s. Eclectic, opulent, and ostentatious didn't quite capture Coral Gables. It was all that and more. Coral Gables could have been the result of a collaboration between Louis XIV and Walt Disney. Its streets were wide and shaded and carefully laid out among a bewildering variety of international architectural styles, drawing inspiration from Singapore, Paris, Madrid, Venice, and Istanbul. The touch Robert loved most was the series of canals Merrick had constructed around the Biltmore Hotel and had once stocked with gondolas.

Robert left the Porsche in a parking garage that resembled a Spanish fortress, and they walked downtown to the four blocks of shops that made up the Miracle Mile.

"I can't make up my mind," Denice said, slipping her arm into his. "Number three hundred or number one hundred."

"What are you talking about?"

"Every shop has a number, Rob. The higher the number the more exclusive. They stop at number three ninety-nine. I don't know if we should work our way up or down." She stopped and pulled on his arm. "I know. What's your birthday?"

"What does that have to do with anything?"

"Just tell me."

"December 29, 1958."

"Twelve–twenty-nine–fifty-eight. That adds up to ninety-nine. We'll start there."

"And go up or down?"

"We'll just have to wait and see."

In less than an hour, Denice had spent over three thousand dollars. She seemed to forget Robert was with her. He followed and watched her as she went into shop after shop. She was alternately discriminating and frivolous, and sometimes both, toward whatever the salespeople showed her, disdainfully rejecting what she'd been assured was the newest and most exclusive in a line of Parisian swimsuits and then a few minutes later casually buying eight pairs of Italian shoes without bothering to try one pair on. She arbitrarily treated the salespeople as if they were slow children or gurus privy to eternal mysteries. Robert tried to find a pattern to her behavior, but none emerged. He was left floundering in the wake of her purchases. His sense of dislocation increased because she charged everything and made arrangements to have it shipped to Key West. No cash was exchanged, and they left the shops empty-handed. Robert was dazed by it all. He could barely remember half of what Denice had purchased.

Two shops later, he finally grabbed Denice's arm and said, "Hey, slow down."

"Why?"

Her cheeks had a faint rose flush, and the skin on her forearm was warm. She lightly ran her tongue over her lips, moistening them, before she smiled at him. The problem was it was the same smile he'd seen her give a dozen salesclerks.

"What's wrong, Rob?" she asked finally.

"It's just," he faltered.

"It's just shopping. It's what people do. Is there a problem with that?"

"Jesus, Denice, how much of all that do you need?"

"What's need got to do with it?" Denice walked away without waiting for the answer Robert didn't have.

Nothing he could come up with could justify the existence of Miracle Mile. It completely filled its name. There was no need to turn water into wine here; all that was necessary was the right container to hold it, and water became significant, an object of value in itself. One shop window held a monogrammed keychain for $400, another a pair of light gray lizard-skin boots for $850. Perfume at $275 an ounce. A yellow silk scarf for $200. Sunglasses starting at $150. People stood in line for a sidewalk vendor selling four ounces of orange juice for eight dollars, carefully holding the small bright orange cups and lifting them to their lips with a studied reverence.

He spotted Denice ahead, moving slowly in the white skirt, the blond braid swinging across her bare shoulders, and thought of her, once again, surfacing in the swimming pool of freshly cut flowers. Denice disappeared into a doorway, and he followed.

Robert was almost halfway across the store before he noticed it was a men's shop. He resisted at first, but Denice seemed to take an immense and genuine pleasure in picking out clothes for him, debating styles and color, flattering him or girlishly wrinkling her nose when he tried something on. After a while, Robert started laughing too.

He'd begun to gauge her reaction in advance, and there was pleasure in that as there was in the ritual of trying on the clothes. It shared the same intensity and anticipation he'd always found in makeup or wardrobe when he'd been working in films. He was a different person each time he stepped out of the dressing room and stood in front of the mirrors and Denice's eyes. It was easy to let himself go here, especially if he forgot about things like the Sunshine Convenience Store franchise and concentrated instead on the sudden power and magic of $175,000 in a bank account in his name.

Robert smiled as he listened to Denice confer with the tailor, making minute adjustments to the fall of cuff or sleeve or the fit of a collar. He was measured and remeasured, the alterations set in quiet motion.

They made one more stop, at a boutique in the upper 300s. Denice said she'd been saving it. The dressing room was behind the center mirror on the wall opposite from where he sat, and Robert was never ready for what happened each time Denice pushed open the mirror and stepped out to model something for him.

He could take all of Denice in at a glance. Front, back, and sides frozen for a moment, and then as she began to move, the reflections multiplied and swept around him, Denice pulling the room's light to her, trapping it, each of her gestures a starburst that ran through the mirrors.

"Tell me what you see," she said. "Tell me what you want." Denice disappearing behind the mirror and reappearing in something demure or provocative, an ivory-colored silk pegnoir or a black garter belt and tissue-thin bra, letting him touch her only with eyes and words, Denice giving shape to desire and that desire filling the mirrors and spilling around Robert until even the smallest gesture on her part, Denice tossing back her hair or her finger grazing the small polished pearl buttons on a robe, plunged Robert into two nights ago when they'd swum out from Southern Beach and made love in the ocean, when they had matched the rhythm of the waves surging around them and disappeared into each other, unable to tell where their bodies began or left off, all reference points lost under the immense sky and in the warm sweep of the sea.

When they left the lingerie shop, Miracle Mile itself felt like an extension of the dressing room, each side of the four-block stretch a half mile long and mirroring each other in the regularity of the numbered doorways and the symmetrical arrangement of flowerbeds and the palm trees along its sidewalks pointing like long, manicured fingers at an impossibly blue sky. Robert felt both diminished and enlarged in its presence.

"It's like throwing pennies in the ocean," Robert said when they left and drove to Kennedy Park. "A bottomless wishing well. That's what this whole day feels like."

They found a place in the shade and stretched out together on the grass. Denice kicked off her shoes and rested her head on Robert's shoulder. He ran a finger down her bare damp neck and then put it to his lips, tasting salt and smelling perfume. Through the trees below them, he could see jade pieces of Biscayne Bay.

It was exciting to feel Denice lying next to him and then close his eyes and think of one of her commercials, to feel suspended between the warmth of her flesh and the power of her image. Last night he'd seen, once again, the commercial that successfully launched a new diet soft drink: Denice's bikinied torso slowly rising taut and tanned from a green sea bounded by a white beach and moving closer and closer to a can of soda sunk in the sand at a Tower of Pisa angle, the long, slender fingers closing around it and slowly lifting it past navel and barely covered breasts toward the pair of full, slightly parted lips. She was known in the business as the woman with the beautiful parts.

He called Denice's name out softly, and when she didn't respond, he eased his shoulder from under her head and rolled onto his side, supporting himself with his elbow. He could tell from the small smile drifting across her lips that she wasn't asleep and leaned over and lightly kissed her. He started to say that he loved her, but only got the first two words out before Denice's hand covered his mouth.

"What's wrong?" he asked after her hand fell away.

Denice sat the rest of the way up and began to put on her shoes. "Like you said earlier, Rob, it's been a special day. Don't spoil it by bringing up love, okay?" She got up and walked back to the Porsche.

She already had the car started by the time he caught up with her. She revved the engine and said, "Let's go," and Robert thought she meant back to Key West, but she headed in the direction of South Bay Shore Drive and Miami proper.

They raced up the coastline in the slowly gathering dusk. Neither of them spoke. Robert nursed his anger and hurt, waiting for the chance to vent them. He figured Denice was headed for a club, and after they got there, he'd try to get her to talk about what had gone on between them in the park. It wasn't the first time something like that had happened. Robert just didn't see any real need for her ground rules, no matter what Denice did or did not say.

He came out of his revery—he'd been rehearsing his lines and imagining Denice's capitulation—when Denice pulled onto the MacArthur Causeway, which connected Miami and South Miami Beach. He asked where they were going.

"A secret." She smiled, but there was nothing behind it that Robert recognized.

In every low-budget horror film there is the stock scene of the hero or heroine moving slowly through the dark toward a closed door. In violation of all rationality and common sense, he or she will open it. Whatever is discovered behind it is immaterial. The terror comes from anticipation, the hand reaching out in the darkness to touch and slowly turn the knob.

The same scene was being played out in the front seat of the Porsche. Denice got off the causeway, drove across South Miami Beach, and turned onto Fourth Street, headed, Robert was now sure, to where it intersected with Euclid Street. Where they would turn the knob and find themselves in the Miramar Arms.

"Why?" Robert asked when they'd parked.

"I want to. Give me the keys."

"Let's just forget the park and this and go back to Key West."

Denice kept her hand extended.

"Give me the keys and fifteen minutes," she said. "Then you come up."

He'd been in the car a little over five minutes before he saw the light in the front room come on. Not even the protective coloration of twilight could hide the fact that the better days the Miramar Arms had seen had disappeared with the Eisenhower administration. Robert leaned back in the seat.

The neighborhood was a semirespectable ghetto, holding an uneasy mix of people, mostly retirees on fixed incomes on their way down and a host of Haitians, Nicaraguans, Salvadoreans, and Hondurans struggling to move up. The neighborhood had been overlooked or ignored by private investors and the historical preservation societies so that, unlike the homes and buildings to the east on Fifth Street or Ocean Drive where deco flourished in a self-conscious resurrection, all Robert saw from the windows of Denice's car was a dinosaur bone-yard: not vibrant pastels but smudges of yellow, green, blue, and pink, scalloped and fluted moldings that resembled melted icing, collapsing cantilevered sunshades, balconies that could barely support the weight of the furniture on them, the ornate motifs of peacocks, nymphs, sunbursts, and cresting waves stuck on the facades like stamps on an envelope marked insufficient postage.

Robert checked his watch and got out of the car, slamming its door and looking up again at the light in the front window. The thought of Denice in the apartment left him both angry and ap-prehensive. The day should not have ended here, and Robert had no real idea how to fix or change what had happened. Stepping back into the Miramar Arms had all the appeal of plunging his hand into a backed-up sink.

The door to the apartment was ajar. He called Denice's name softly, then a little louder, but got no answer. There's no reason for any of this, Robert thought, and then wasn't even sure what he'd meant by it. The apartment had the sour smell of a refrigerator that needed cleaning out. He followed the trail of Denice's clothes into the bed-room.

The bedside lamp was on, the shade tilted so that half the room was in shadow. Denice had stripped the bed of its sheets and lay in the middle of the bare mattress.

"Come here," she said.

Robert stood in the middle of the room and tried to explain how the parentheses had haunted him here. How he'd return from a day of grand openings and groundbreakings that left him feeling as worn-out and anonymous as a piece of chalk and he'd lie in this same bed and listen to the stutter of the air conditioner and feel his life slowly close around him. Dues. Everyone said he had to pay them. And he had. Until, he told Denice, he was left in this room with the parentheses and his hunger.

"Come here," Denice said again, stretching on the mattress.

Robert undressed and rediscovered the hunger, following it from lips, breasts, navel, to a second set of lips, full and moist and pungent as pieces of tangerine. Denice curled around him, finding him too with her mouth.

After a while, they broke apart, and he followed the hunger into thrust and counterthrust, Denice's hands in his hair, her legs locked around his knees, as he pressed toward her center.

He followed the hunger until it began to follow him.

Denice slid her legs up around his waist. "Say it," she said.

"I love you."

"No."

"What?"

"Her name."

"No."

"Now."

"I won't."

"I'll stop."

"No."

"Her name. Now."

"Don't. Please."

"Her name."

"Denice."

"No. Say it."

"Oh God."

"No."

"Listen."

"I'm her."

"I don't."

"I'm Kathleen."

"But."

"I'm her. Now."

"Okay."

"I'm Kathleen."

"Yes."

"Say it."

Robert did.

THE SUN HADN'T BEEN UP for more than a couple hours when Robert found himself sitting at a wooden picnic table in Kennedy Park at the upper end of Coconut Grove. Though the table was shaded by a tall eucalyptus and Denice and he sat facing Biscayne Bay and the steady salt-filled wind blowing across it, Robert could already feel the heat rising from the earth, gathering everything to it. Now that it was the end of June, the heat would do nothing but get worse, the clockwork morning and afternoon showers just adding to the density of the air until you were conscious of the weight of each breath.

"Which one is yours?" Denice asked, opening a Coconut Frank's bag and setting out two sandwiches, a wad of napkins, and coffee in Styrofoam cups. "Did you order the Tropical Breakfast Biscuit or the Gold Coast Eye-Opener?"

"What I can't believe is I ordered coffee in this heat." Robert took the biscuit. The powdered creamers were in containers shaped like miniature coconuts, and he cracked two of them open and dumped them into his coffee. Next to his elbow, someone had carved *Tom Loves Rachael* and *Who Cares?* into the table. Robert covered both up with a napkin.

"Heat or not, I'm hungry," Denice said and started in on the Gold Coast. She was wearing the same clothes from the day before, the white skirt and tanktop, both wrinkled and smudged from where she'd dropped them on the floor of his room in the Miramar Arms. After showering this morning, Denice had not bothered with makeup, and her face looked fuller, almost girlish, without it. Her hair was tangled from the wind and still damp from the shower.

Robert took a bite of his biscuit. Denice's choice of breakfast spots had been the right idea, he thought. Surrounded by carefully tended beds of roses, azaleas, and poinsettias and stands of banyan, ficus, and traveler palms, the mirrored blue of sea and sky, and the sun pouring endless light, the day became a clean slate, and Denice and he could sit and eat in comfortable silence.

Almost. Robert kept sliding back to the night before and morning in the Miramar Arms. He didn't know how the woman who dove into a swimming pool of flowers fit the one who had lain in the middle of a bare mattress in the Miramar Arms and lifted her arms to him.

Robert looked over the picnic table into the brightness of Biscayne Bay and then over at Denice and wanted to see the Miramar Arms simply for what it was, a run-down deco apartment house in Miami Beach, something that with the money from the sale of his parents' home and the possibility of getting another chance to work in film, he could leave behind once and for all. Robert would leave everything that had happened, or not happened, in the room behind, too.

"It was a good idea, coming out here," Robert said.

Denice turned her head so that she was looking directly at him. She nodded. "It's a good place to put things into perspective."

Denice had already finished her sandwich and leaned in to take a bite of Robert's. She sat back and pointed at the table, its top covered with carved lovers' vows and obscenities. "Got anything to add?" she asked, tucking a blond tangle of hair behind her ear. "You could at least immortalize us with the traditional initials enclosed by a heart. There's some room left over in the far corner."

"It's a little hard to leave your mark on the future when this is what you have at hand," Robert said, holding up a small white plastic knife that had been lying next to the wad of napkins.

Robert then suggested going for a walk, but Denice said she wanted to sit a while longer and finish her coffee. They watched sailboats tacking across the Bay. The park and beach were still relatively quiet, just starting to fill with people. A yellow truck dropped off a couple of groundskeepers. People jogged or walked along the beach. Off to the left behind a tangle of mangroves were the high-pitched rise and fall of children's voices.

"Good day for a shoot," Robert said.

"I'm sure someone will be setting up soon. Most of the ad agencies get a lot of mileage from Kennedy Park. Nice settings, good light, and low overhead. I did work for the Masterson Sunglasses and Preview Hair Care accounts out here. Now the video people have discovered the place too."

"We tried some takes for the Miami Is Beautiful campaign here. A couple shots I thought looked pretty good, but Russell wanted something more upscale and uptown for the poster. We ended up using Brickell and Collins as a backdrop."

Denice glanced in the direction of the parking lot. A tall, broad-shouldered man got out of a light gray Mercedes. His hair and jogging suit were color-coordinated with the car. He began an elaborate series of stretching exercises. Robert was sure he'd seen him somewhere before.

"I'll be back in a minute," Denice said, getting up from the table. She walked to the parking lot, passing the man in the gray sweatsuit without a glance, though Robert saw him swivel in a not so subtle appraisal of her ass and legs as she got into her Porsche. The man finished stretching and then started down the lane for the beach. From the angle the sun hit and reflected off the Porsche's windows, Robert wasn't sure if Denice was looking for something in the glove compartment or using the cellular phone. In either case, she wasn't in the car more than a couple of minutes. On the beach, the man in the gray sweatsuit retied his shoes and then started jogging south in the direction of the Biscayne Bay Yacht Club.

"That guy looked familiar," Robert said when Denice joined him again.

"He should. We've been eating his food," Denice said and began gathering the trash. "That was Tony Ross, owner of the Coconut Frank chain."

"Okay. I remember him now. I met him once in Russell's office. And Russell brought up his name when I got in trouble with the dog thing. Russell kept going on about the moon landing and dotted lines and Coconut Frank. 'Hamburgers and history, there's a lesson in each.' Something like that."

"One also in using your fast-food chain to launder cash for Russell Tills." Denice finished gathering up the trash and dropped it in a wire basket by a drinking fountain. She glanced at her watch, walked down the middle of the lane, and stopped, looking north along the beach.

"How did you know that?" Robert asked, joining her.

"Process of elimination. With the new banking laws, washing cash isn't as easy as it once was. No more pulling up to a bank, walking in with four shopping bags of bills, and picking up a cashier's check while the bank manager whistles his way past the currency-reporting regulations. Lauter figured Russell was using one or more of his clients' accounts to launder the cash. He just didn't know which one." Denice paused and again looked to the north. A tall man in a hooded navy-blue sweatshirt came into view. He ran along the beach in an awkward, stiff-legged gait, his arms pumping mechanically as if he were slowly beating a drum.

"It took a while to uncover who Russell was using." Denice smiled. "Remember the loan applications, Rob?"

Robert wasn't sure if he wanted to know where this was heading. One of the things among others in the plan to bring Russell Tills back in line had been the bank runs. There had been nothing much to it. One afternoon Rob had driven to Miami and visited six banks. In each case, he'd gone in under the guise of applying for a loan and left with a packet of application material. Sandwiched in the material was an unmarked brown envelope. Robert drove back to Key West and gave the envelopes to Hannibal. That was it. He didn't ask questions or see it leading to anything beyond one afternoon in his life.

Below them, the man in the navy-blue sweatshirt jogged determinedly along, heading south. There was nothing smooth or natural to his movement. The wind off the Bay caught the corner of his hood and flipped it back. Etched against the sunlight and sand, the profile was unmistakable: high forehead, sharp nose, no chin. Robert remembered it all too clearly from the video arcade at the Miami International Airport.

"Jesus Christ, Denice. That's Barry From West Palm. What's he doing here?"

Denice glanced at her watch and then started up the lane. "Tony

Ross should have made the yacht club by now. He'll turn around and start back."

Robert watched Barry follow the curve of the beach until he was out of sight. Then he joined Denice in the parking lot. She stood next to the white Porsche, her hand on the door handle.

"I asked you, Denice. What's going on here?"

From the south, there were two loud pops in quick succession.

"Time to go home, Rob," Denice said, opening the door and sliding behind the wheel.

THE MERIDIAN was basically an overflow bar, a couple of blocks off Duval on Front Street. It caught what clientele missed or didn't fit into the traditional tourist bars like Sloppy Joe's or Captain Tony's. The Meridian's décor made a halfhearted effort at evoking the Pirate in the Tropics riff, but it held a lot of swash and no real buckling. It was dark though and nearly empty, and the bartender had no interest in how many trips Robert made to the restroom or his subsequent runny nose. The ceiling fans squeaked, a large macaw in a cage above the cash register squawked, every once in a while someone fed the jukebox, and the margaritas were strong and cold and on time.

Robert sat near the back of the bar near the public phone. He'd used it a half hour ago to call Hannibal Binder, insisting that he needed to talk, but not on the *Blue Circus* or in the shotgun house on Simonton. Robert wanted neutral territory, and Hannibal finally agreed to meet him at the Meridian.

It had been over four days since the shooting at Kennedy Park, but after Denice and he returned to Key West, the only problem had been the absence of problems. Denice acted as if nothing, or at least nothing significant, had happened. She simply went on being Denice, leaving Robert caught in an accustomed contradiction: she was maddeningly elusive and at the same time the center of his life.

But Kennedy Park kept intruding on the Key West scenario Denice had created for them, insinuating itself into the midnight walks and swims, the restaurant and bar hopping, the movies they rented, the lines of coke they did up, even their lovemaking. Denice might have simply gone on being Denice, but Barry From West Palm jogged through too many of Robert's dreams for anything to be simple anymore.

Robert supposed the insomnia, sweats, shallow breathing, and the tic that occasionally haunted the outside corner of his left eye added up to an attack of conscience. Conscience, though, had become a rather slippery concept, like trying to visualize the national debt. With what had happened to him since the Memorial Day weekend when he killed the dog, the line between right and wrong tended to disappear as easily as a line of cocaine, leaving Robert bent over a small square of mirror and faced with his reflection.

It wasn't conscience but Franklin Benjamin Lauter's proclamation at the Miami International Airport that defined Robert's predicament: *Remember, you're in my movie now.* Robert kept telling himself he'd trained as an actor and should have been able to pull off the necessary moves in compensating for the missing phonebook and setting up Russell Tills, but the Kennedy Park shooting had revealed to Robert what he'd known all along. He wasn't acting. He was Robert Staples and nobody else. The rest of the world had become a movie.

Hannibal Binder showed up at the Meridian after Robert had finished his second margarita and trip to the men's room. Hannibal's six-and-a-half-foot frame filled the doorway as he turned his head and surveyed the handful of patrons scattered among the tables before he slowly sauntered over to Robert's.

"If you're going to skip shaving for a day, Rob, you need to be a little more careful about what gets caught on the stubble." Hannibal ran a finger under what was left of his nose and sat down. He wore a lightweight pullover that was the same navy-blue shade as the jogging suit Barry From West Palm had worn at Kennedy Park. Hannibal took in the bar's décor, smiled as he fingered his ponytail, and ordered rum.

"So talk," Hannibal said.

"I need to know some things about Denice."

"Why are you coming to me then? Ask her yourself."

"Because it's not like she lies to me exactly. Most of the time I can't get her to talk about herself at all, but when she does, the details don't feel right, and it ends up sounding like she's talking about someone else's life. She'll be in the middle of an anecdote, and I'll get the feeling she's borrowed it. Or that she'll tell me something because she thinks that's what I want to hear."

Hannibal was silent for a moment. "Are you sure you don't want that? It keeps things simple."

Robert shook his head. "I want to understand Denice and her ground rules and why she acts like she does. Being with her is like trying to tell time with a watch that only has a second hand."

Hannibal leaned back in his chair and folded his arms behind his neck, his biceps straining against the sleeves of the pullover. The eyes beneath the powdery gray brows were flat and lusterless. "I'm not sure I like where this question-and-answer session might lead us." Hannibal dropped his arms back to the table. "And you might not either, Rob. I think I'll pass. See you around the Gulf."

Hannibal started to get up, and Robert grabbed his arm. "This has nothing to do with Franklin Benjamin Lauter or you or what you're doing to Russell Tills. This has to do with Denice and me, that's all. I'm in love with a woman I don't understand. I want you to tell me what you know about her."

Hannibal knocked Rob's hand off his arm. "Why should I tell you anything?"

"I told you. I love her."

Hannibal's laugh filled the whole bar. "Jesus Christ, you probably do." Hannibal put his hands on the edge of the table and leaned in toward Robert. "Tell me something. Does it come naturally, or do you have to work at cornering the market on being misguided? You won't be able to keep up with her. Believe me, I've seen a lot try."

"Let me worry about that." Rob knocked back the rest of his margarita and signaled for another. "I want to know about Denice. And I have something to trade."

"You may, but I doubt it's something I need to hear."

"It's about Lennie Ash."

Hannibal lifted his empty glass in the direction of the bartender and sat back down. "You'd better not be jerking me around here. I know all about Lennie. He owes Russell for helping bankroll all those T-shirt shops, but in the end, Lennie doesn't care what side of the bread the butter's on as long as there's plenty of it. Lennie will come around. He's overextended himself right now with the T-shirt chain, and there's a major crimp in his cash flow. The IRS has begun nosing around his books, and Lennie's got five outstanding lawsuits for copyright infringement because he wasn't overly careful about what he slapped on some of those T-shirts. Lennie's plenty nervous, but I've been watching him."

Robert waited until the bartender sent over their drinks before he asked Hannibal if he knew Lennie had a meeting set up with Russell Tills tomorrow afternoon. Hannibal pressed his hands together, intertwining the fingers, and carefully placed them before him on the table. The hands remained still, but Robert could see the white tension lines along either side of the knuckles. Hannibal asked him if he knew who had arranged the meeting, and Robert shook his head no.

"I'd like to know who picked up the phone first," Hannibal said.

"I can't tell you that, but Russell's definitely on the edge. I could tell that the Kennedy Park shooting really got to him. I don't know how much he suspects, but Russell insisted on a face-to-face meeting. I put him off, but Russell was practically screaming, claiming he'd have some answers soon. In the midst of all his rant, he let it slip about his meeting with Lennie Ash."

Hannibal slowly unfolded his hands and shook his head. "I'll check it out," he said finally.

"That's my part of the bargain. Now what about Denice?"

Hannibal leaned back in his chair. "You and Lennie might as well be flip sides of the same coin. Neither of you ever learn. You want Denice? Okay."

Robert listened, and the drinks kept coming, and he tried to hide his disappointment and impatience over what he should have known would happen: Hannibal characteristically making himself the center of any story he told. Still, Robert was able to at least get a glimpse of what Denice's life had been like.

According to Hannibal, Denice had been a CIA brat whose father, Allen Shell, operated under the conveniently nebulous designation of "special adviser" and spent most of his time between his Arlington and Palm Beach homes entertaining very diverse groups of people. Allen

Shell's parties were private. A lot of Washington officials counted on that. Hannibal had been put on the guest list in nineteen sixty, a few months after Denice had been born and over a year after Batista had been forced to flee Cuba when Castro seized power. Hannibal's father had been a rum runner in the thirties, and Hannibal had been raised on the ocean. He knew the Gulf like someone else would his front lawn.

In 1960, a lot of people at the parties were interested in Hannibal's sailing stories.

Hannibal had attended Denice's first birthday party on April 17, 1961. He gave her a baby shark's tooth on a thin gold chain. There were numerous champagne toasts. Denice's mother proclaimed the event an unqualified success. It was, compared to the other event that was unfolding that evening: the Bay of Pigs Invasion.

Hannibal became a frequent visitor at Allen Shell's house after April 17, 1961. Hannibal watched Denice grow up while her father and he discussed the monster America had created: the hordes of angry Cuban exiles waiting to reclaim their homeland, all of them fueled on the promises of money and arms from Washington after what had happened at the Bay of Pigs. Allen Shell's job was to keep the Cuban exiles from figuring out that the promises were empty.

He specialized in devising ways to splinter the Cuban exile groups, then kept them busy by having them inform on each other, all the while encouraging each group with support and funding. Periodically Allen Shell authorized the FBI to go in and bust some of the groups, and then he turned around and granted them immunity, funneling them through witness protection programs that put them right back on the street where the plans for the next imaginary invasion of Cuba were almost immediately hatched, and the process started all over again.

It was an old routine with a twist, Hannibal said. Not only did the right hand not know what the left was doing but also the right and left were pulling their own separate sleight-of-hands. Hannibal was happy to lend his hand to any number of projects, and Allen Shell's D.C. friends avoided eyestrain by looking the other way when Hannibal expanded his drug trade routes.

Each year, Hannibal gave Denice another shark's tooth for her birthday.

Watching her grow up, Hannibal saw what Allen Shell didn't. Denice was staging her own private Bay of Pigs Invasion. On the surface she was Daddy's Girl, taking and delivering on all the cues given her, but playing them out quietly on her own terms until she left her father with exactly what he'd given the Cubans: a truckload of promises on flat tires. Then she ran away.

Hannibal told Rob it had taken a little over three years and a dead husband before Denice found her way to him. Hannibal had never doubted she would. He'd recognized the look in her eyes every April 17 when she opened his birthday present to her. Denice had thrown in with Hannibal, Lauter, and Russell six years ago and never looked back.

"As far as ground rules, Denice had more than her share dumped on her growing up and in her marriage," Hannibal said. "Maybe she figures it's her turn to lay some down. You'll have to decide if you want to live with them or not."

"One more thing," Rob said when Hannibal stood up to leave. "How did Denice's husband die?"

Hannibal let go of the back of the chair, surveyed the inside of the Meridian once more, and dropped a crumpled twenty-dollar bill on the table. "I imagine like most people do, Rob. Unwillingly."

WE'RE HAVING SUNCH," Denice told the waitress at Bagatelle's, who smiled, pegging them for honeymooners, but probably wanted to roll her eyes instead.

"We just invented it," Denice went on, "right on this spot. It's an historic moment."

"That's right," Rob added. "We're going to be famous."

"Rich. You can be famous, Robert. I'll take rich." Denice leaned toward the waitress, parodying confidentiality. "Robert wanted to call it 'dunch,' but I told him it wouldn't work out because it sounded too close to 'dunce.'"

"I still think 'sunch' sounds like a fish. The sunch are running. A school of sunch." Robert put his hands together and made awkward swimming motions.

The waitress smiled as if she were posing for a high-school yearbook photo and explained that Bagatelle's served lunch *and* supper from eleven to midnight.

Robert sat back and watched Denice feign outrage. "Lunch at noon I understand. Lunch at midnight, I don't. Or in the middle of the afternoon for that matter. If Robert, here, had been on time, it wouldn't have been necessary to invent a new meal. But if we can have brunch, why not a sunch? I don't want lunch or supper. Three thirty demands its own meal."

The waitress pointed helplessly at the menus.

"Oh, all right," Denice said. "I'll have the stuffed yellowtail snapper."

"I'll have the escargots Martinque."

The waitress was relieved that Denice and Robert hadn't found time to invent new drinks, settling instead for gin and tonics.

Denice pointed over the balcony. "Did you know we're sitting at one end of the longest street in the U.S.A.? Check *Ripley's Believe It or Not*. It's the only street that runs from the Gulf of Mexico to the Atlantic Ocean."

The waitress brought their drinks and quickly left. Lifting his, Robert smiled and toasted Denice. When he'd set up the talk with Hannibal Binder at the Meridian Bar, Robert had forgotten about promising to meet Denice at Bagatelle's. He'd shown up almost an hour late, expecting her to have left, but he found her at a corner table on the veranda, smoking a cigarette and staring off into space. She smiled when he walked up, and Robert had been more than a little surprised. Denice didn't like to wait for anything, and she usually let everyone know that. Robert was glad to be able to shelve the elaborate apology he'd constructed on the way over.

Denice slid a package across the table. "Go on, open it." She rummaged in a bag on her lap and pulled out a large plastic royal poinciana, a pair of novelty sunglasses, and some cheap plastic barrettes. Robert's package contained a straw hat and a Hawaiian shirt.

At Denice's prompting, Robert went into the men's room and changed. He was tempted to do a quick pick-me-up line, but finally decided against it. His nose was still a little runny and tender from the lines he'd done at the Meridian.

When he got back, Denice had waylaid an elderly tourist couple with an Instamatic. The veranda at Bagatelle's overlooked Duval, and Robert and Denice leaned against its railing with the blue Gulf sky and the thin bright masts of the shrimpers' boats moored at Land's End as backdrop. Robert and Denice leaned into each other and smiled at the camera.

The picture developed as they ate. Denice kicked off one of her sandals and ran her foot along Rob's calf. The waitress kept the drinks coming. Appearing suddenly, as if they'd been squeezed out of the afternoon light or had bloomed from the jasmine, oleander, and aloe lining the railing, a swarm of yellow-and-white butterflies whirled and tumbled in the blue air. Denice set down her drink and smiled. Her lipstick left a bright red half-moon on the rim of her glass.

She picked up the photo. It looked like the quintessential honeymoon shot: Denice in a lavender wrap-around skirt and khaki-colored blouse unbuttoned to the middle of her chest, the plastic poinciana pinned above her left breast, her hair swept back and held by the pair of traveler-palm barrettes, her eyes hidden behind a pair of red sunglasses with leaping marlin at the top of the frames. Robert in a straw hat with a green visor built into its brim and a shirt loud enough to restore hearing to the deaf: bright yellow and exploding with flamingos, coconuts, alligators, thatched huts, and seashells.

Denice took the photo from Robert's hands and ripped it, not in half, but just below the lines of their necks. When she dropped the top piece in front of Rob, the sight of the detached heads with the large smiles lying among the remains of their meal made his stomach lurch.

"Vacation's over, Rob."

Robert waved for a drink, but the waitress was on the far side of the veranda, her back to them. He was sweating, and when he looked up at Denice, the incongruity between the impassive set of her lips and the novelty sunglasses made him think of False Walter's anecdote about getting smacked around by Goofy after he'd been caught lifting wallets at Disney World.

"What do you mean?" he finally managed to ask.

"That depends."

"On what?"

"You. You've been fucking me and tooting up. Playing at some little fantasy in the tropics. Robert Staples having a good time pretending to be a bad little boy. I like fantasies and play too, Rob, but I take both very seriously."

"I don't understand what you're getting at."

"It's very simple, Robert. You're going to have to make a choice. I've talked to you again and again about coming in on the deal Lauter's working out, but you always evade answering or making any kind of commitment. There was always coke or my cunt to hide in." Denice leaned back and signaled the waitress for another round.

Robert was too confused by Denice's mood swing to be angry. Instead, he explained to her what seemed obvious: he was not in the position to be part of the deal in any real way.

"I think you'd better find or make some time to rethink things, Rob," Denice said. The waitress brought their drinks. A few tables over, a young couple, who appeared to be genuine honeymooners, stood up to leave. Both of them were wearing Lennie's T-shirts, the man's reading GET OFF MY CLOUD, the woman's LET THEM EAT BURGERS. They walked off, arm in arm.

The sight of the T-shirts left Robert feeling queasy, reminding him of how he'd betrayed Lennie Ash to Hannibal Binder in the Meridian Bar in order to uncover what he could about Denice. He took a healthy swallow of his drink, then tilted back the straw hat and rubbed his forehead.

"Aren't you tired of waiting, Rob? I'm curious. You seem to have made a career of it."

"You're taking it for granted that what you want is always there. It doesn't always happen that way, Denice."

"If you're willing to take risks, it is."

"What do you call what I did at Worldwide? I risked everything for a break in films and lost my wife and what we'd saved and most of my self-respect and confidence. I didn't quit, though. I hung on even if it meant doing all that schlocky promotional work for Russell. When I met you, I'd hit bottom, but I was there from taking those risks." Robert realized he'd spoken more loudly than he'd intended. He sat back in his chair, cradling the gin and tonic to his chest.

"Oh, yes," Denice said. "Your precious film career. You can't let go of that, can you? Tell me, just how were you planning to work it so Russell Tills would deliver on his promise to get you back in?"

Robert hesitated before answering and looked out over the veranda at the impossibly blue South Florida sky. "I was going to wait until Hannibal and Lauter were satisfied the setup of Russell's clients was complete and then call Russell to warn him when it was too late for him to do anything about it. I'd still end up looking like I was trying to help Russell, and I hoped by the time the smoke cleared, I'd be back on location."

Denice lit a cigarette and smiled. "Not bad. It might have worked."

"Why won't it?" Robert asked, readjusting the verb tense as he would a notch on a belt that had been pulled too tight. "Russell's been taught his lesson. Among his clients, his credibility and reputation are seriously compromised, and that's what Hannibal and Lauter and everybody wanted, isn't it? From the way Russell sounded on the phone the last time I talked to him, I don't think he's going to fight the changes Lauter's proposing. Russell's spooked."

"He's more than that," Denice said, sipping her drink and looking directly at Robert. "He's out."

A mistake, Robert thought. He couldn't have heard Denice correctly. But why did his stomach suddenly feel hollow and cold? It was a typically hot Key West afternoon. It didn't make sense to feel cold. Denice was sitting across from him saying something about chances and taking advantage of the obvious. When Rob began rubbing his arms, she paused and asked him what was wrong.

"I thought you said Russell was out. That can't be true." Robert leaned over the table in Denice's direction, but her eyes were hidden by the red sunglasses. "The whole point of the plan was to check his ego and bring him back in line within the partnership. That's what Hannibal and Lauter and you said. It wasn't supposed to be anything more than that. A one-time thing."

"I told you before, Robert, there's a fine line between problems and opportunities." Denice lit a cigarette and exhaled. "The same goes for risks and betrayals. You see, something became apparent while Russell was being set up. He wasn't as useful as everyone originally thought. At one time, yes. But not in terms of Lauter's deal with Camar Tavares. Russell's power, like his reputation, is overinflated in that area. With some adjustments, the deal can be run without him. It's that simple, Robert."

Robert stared at the remains of the meal. The torn photo was propped against a small white segmented bowl of salt and sugar packets. "My god," he said, finally. "Do you know where that leaves me?"

"Yes. Do you?"

Robert asked Denice about the missing phonebook and how it fit the new developments. According to Denice, the biggest problem was the fact the book hadn't surfaced yet. As far as anyone could tell, nothing had been done with the information it contained. At this point, Hannibal and Lauter decided to continue with a wait-and-see attitude, but figured it wouldn't hurt if Barry From West Palm did some asking around too.

"You're hedging though, Rob," Denice said. "The phonebook's a problem, but not the one we need to discuss. You have a choice. You can still call Russell Tills and pretend to warn him about what's happened, and if your luck holds out, Russell might deliver on his promise and get you back in film. You can try it, Rob. If that's what you really want. I won't say anything to Lauter or Hannibal. I'll do that much for you."

Denice paused, putting out her cigarette, and let Rob think about her offer for a few moments. "Or," she went on, "you can do what you've been doing all summer: trying to convince yourself you're nothing more than a bystander in everything that's happened. You can go on waiting for some magical moment that will transform your whole life. There's enough cocaine around to keep that idea alive for a long time. Key West is full of people with the same kind of pipe dreams. You'd fit right in."

Then Denice summed up his last choice. He could take Denice up on her offer and become part of Lauter's deal.

"I can't see Lauter or Hannibal welcoming that opportunity," Robert said. "Neither of them trusts me."

"They will if I say so. But I need to hear it from you. What do you want?"

"Jesus, Denice. It's not that simple. This isn't just something you step into."

"Wrong. That's exactly what you do. The opportunity's there. Lauter closed with the new backers in D.C. The money's solid. Camar Tavares has his *fabriquetas* retooled to produce bulk. All he needs is the chemicals, and Lauter is working on that. Tavares will be able to ship by late July or early August. With the current agency crackdown and interference, the *coqueros* are fighting among themselves, trying to reestablish a power base. The market's wide open."

Robert sat back and shook his head. Things were happening too fast. He was still trying to take in the fact that Russell Tills was out of the picture. He couldn't quite make himself believe it. He signaled the waitress for another drink. That made as much sense as anything else right now.

"Just how deep are you in all this, Denice? I mean, you sit there and tell me I can step into the deal on your say-so."

"I didn't say it would be easy, but Hannibal and Lauter will agree to it. We have areas of shared interest." Denice fingered the red plastic poinciana she'd pinned to her blouse. "But that's really not your concern, Robert. My status in the deal isn't in question. Yours is. I'm in."

Denice got up and walked across the veranda to the cigarette machine. Robert stared at the debris on the table. The sight of the torn photograph hit him like a kick, and he covered its pieces with his napkin. The waitress appeared and started to clean off the table, but Robert told her not to worry about it.

After getting her cigarettes, Denice moved to a pay phone a few feet from the machine. She talked for a couple minutes, hung up, then looked at Rob. He couldn't get a fix on her expression. Denice opened her purse, took out a quarter, and made another call, the second shorter than the first, and then rejoined Rob at the table.

"It appears you've been a busy boy this afternoon," she said, opening the cigarettes. "Did you have a nice talk with Hannibal at the Meridian? He said you were full of questions. Mostly about me."

Robert quickly raised his hand, but Denice went on. "The questions are empty," she said. "Why do you want to pin me down with names, dates, and places? What do you have when you're done? Nothing. Or at least nothing that matters. What counts is now. Everything else is fossils and fairy tales."

"Maybe you're right. But what's wrong with saying I love you?"

Denice shook her head. "Okay, Rob. This is for you. Something to pin me down."

As soon as she started talking, Robert knew he didn't want to hear what was to follow.

"At eighteen, I was a Miss Florida finalist. I ended up there because I'd always done what everybody expected me to. I was just a step away from being crowned Miss Florida with a very good chance at being Miss America. And you know what that good little girl did, the one who had taken years of dance, piano, and voice lessons? Who knew everything there was to know about makeup by the time she was ten? Who at twelve understood the looks the husbands of her parents' friends furtively gave her and why the wives were so uncomfortable around her? Who at fifteen had her first modeling job? And who at eighteen was properly engaged to the requisite young, good-looking, and very ambitious protégé of her father? You know what she did? She threw it all away. The night before the finals she ran off and got married. And that killed any chance of being Miss Florida or Miss America.

"She married for love. And not the man her father had given his seal of approval to. Worse, in her parents' eyes, was that she married her fiancé's friend. He was not requisitely good-looking or ambitious. Her new husband was a man who believed in things and had principles. A man with a definite sense of right and wrong. The man and girl didn't have much money, but it didn't matter because they were in love. They had their own little house. The girl's parents disowned her, and the girl accepted that, too, because of love. The good man and girl eventually decided they wanted to start a family. They'd been married three years by then. The girl got pregnant. Two months later the good man was dead. The girl discovered that good men are often fools because they put their principles before anything else. After her husband died, the girl was left with nothing. She would not go back to her parents, so she had to take care of herself. The girl talked to some friends, and the friends introduced her to some people who could help her to do just that. The girl saw her chance and never looked back."

Robert thought Denice was going to stop there, but she lit a cigarette, sat back, and continued. She told Robert about Cartagena, Colombia, where she'd made her fourth run in as many months as a mule. The frequency of the visits had been her mistake because she'd been recognized or tipped off to the police. She'd worn a different colored wig and style of clothes each time, but her pregnancy had ceased to be protective coloration. The automatic deference she'd been given on the other runs suddenly hadn't been there.

She had liked making the runs. She was free of good men who were fools and little girls who did what was expected of them. The danger was real and exact in a way that had been absent in her Stateside life and past. There was also something undeniably sexual in body-packing, in the way the dozens of oil-coated and coke-filled condoms fit her vagina and rectum or nestled in her stomach. The danger and sexuality blurred into each other, and she felt as if she were on the verge of an oceanic orgasm for the entire duration of each run.

On the last, preparing to board the Miami flight, she'd been detained by a curious or suspicious customs agent and locked in a bare room the color of filing cabinets for almost twelve hours. During that time, one or more of the condoms burst from her stomach acid, and she started hemorrhaging. On the way to the hospital to have her stomach pumped, she miscarried. There was a series of emergency transfusions and visits from the Cartagena chief of police, who thought the young American woman needed a lesson in the proper uses of genitalia. He appeared one morning at her bedside to present the woman with a sprig of bougainvillea and a glass jar filled with the fetus of her child floating in a colorless liquid.

During her months of incarceration, the chief and a host of his subordinate officers and friends regularly visited Denice lest she forget her lesson, all of them vigorously trying to outdo each other in the manner with which they delivered it.

Hannibal Binder finally got her out of Cartagena after her friends in D.C. and Florida, who were afraid of being implicated or involved, talked him into sailing down. Denice's release was secured when a Washington bureaucrat decided that despite demographic findings and predictions that suggested otherwise, a new airport *was* needed further inland among the foothills along the Andes. The chief of police personally helped choose the site because it gave him the chance to road-test the new black chrome-lined Chrysler Newport that had been delivered two days earlier. Denice went back to Key West with Hannibal.

"Jesus, Denice," Robert said. He tried to take her hand.

Denice put out her cigarette. "You're wasting all that precious empathy and sorrow, Robert, because I don't want or need it. I gave you what you wanted, but it doesn't change anything. And you'd be a fool to believe it does."

Denice slowly reached over and touched his cheek, letting her hand linger there, her fingers cool and gentle. "Any more questions, Robert, about love or anything else? Or did the glimpse I gave you into my tormented soul satisfy you?"

Denice's smile burned through him. Robert's voice broke when he tried to speak. "Wait a minute. You made that up, didn't you? The whole story."

"Is that what you think?"

"I don't know. Right now, I really don't."

"It's as true as it needs to be. How's that?"

"Why, Denice? Why are you doing this to me?"

"Like I said earlier, vacation's over, Rob." Denice took off the sunglasses, the palm-tree barrettes, and the plastic poinciana and set them on the table. She stood up to leave, then paused to open her purse. She dropped the bill of sale to his parents' home in Minnesota in the center of the table.

"You're not too imaginative at hiding things, Rob," she said, "but we all need our little secrets, don't we? You'll have to decide what's holding you back from coming into the deal." Denice walked across the veranda and down the stairway.

Robert was left staring at the cold scraps of food congealing on the plates, Denice's overflowing ashtray, the wadded napkins, and the empty gin-and-tonic glasses. He reached over and picked up the bill of sale. Underneath was the top portion of the photo holding Robert's and Denice's faces and their wide happy smiles under the South Florida sun.

ROBERT REMAINED AT BAGATELLE'S and continued to drink, trying to erase what he had seen when he'd looked over the railing of the veranda: Denice slipping into the passenger seat of a green Triumph while James Winde held the door open for her. Robert couldn't shake the image of Denice deftly swiveling her long brown legs into the car's small interior or of Winde with his white eyebrow and thick black hair, carefully pressed polo shirt and tan pleated pants, swinging the door shut, circling around the front of the car, and climbing into the driver's seat.

Robert thought, too, of Lennie Ash's party and the first time he saw Winde, Denice slapping him and undressing to dive into the bright water bursting with flowers. The two scenes replayed themselves over and over again in Robert's mind. He didn't have to guess who Denice made the second call to earlier from the restaurant. But he did wonder what kind of choices Denice had given Winde. Or if it was the other way around and Winde had something on her. Whatever it was, the connection didn't matter as much as the sight of the empty seat across from him.

After he paid the bill and stumbled out of Bagatelle's, what was left of the afternoon slipped through Robert's fingers and broke. On the sidewalk, Robert remembered old binges and hangovers and the odd sense of clarity that often accompanied them, when excess had a purpose and its own logic. Today was different. He'd moved beyond the limits of logic, American citizenship, Christian charity, common sense, and decency right into a monumental confusion.

Robert started back to the shotgun house, Denice's words dogging each footstep. Nothing halfway, she'd said. She was offering him a chance to get clear. She hadn't minimized the risks or the profit if he decided to go in on the deal. Both were considerable. Robert knew if he backed out, he'd lose her. She would simply move on. There was the possibility she already had.

But if he went through with it and put up the money—or even a portion of it—from the sale of his parents' house, Robert could at minimum end up tripling his investment. The deal became his own personal Manifest Destiny, the chance that erased the need for second or third ones.

What was holding him back then? He was afraid, but who wouldn't be? Was it conscience? That he would profit from someone's need or pain? The demand for the coke was there. If not Robert, someone else would satisfy it. The demand wouldn't go away. In the face of that, conscience was something you could live with.

It was something more than fear or conscience that made him hesitate. It was ambition and desire. He had spent a good-size portion of his life single-mindedly pursuing a career in film. He had sacrificed and paid dues. He hadn't quit. He had lived for that moment when his image filled the screen in a darkened theater, a moment of pure transcendence when the cliché *larger than life* came to life. He would be everything his father had not been. The blank screen held enough room for them both.

The shotgun house was too quiet and empty. Robert could not stop sweating. A shower and change of clothes didn't help. Robert had tried calling Denice more times than he could count. If Denice had intended to intimidate him with her absence, it had worked. Being alone in Lennie's house went beyond the oppressive. Robert roamed from room to room, trying to sober up. His chest was constricted, and it felt like he was breathing through sand. Not even a couple of lines of coke could alleviate the weight of her absence. Every molecule of air carried part of her.

Robert came up with an idea that clumsily resolved itself into a plan, and a half hour later he was standing in front of the entrance to the Santa Maria Condominium Complex talking to Mr. Norman Le Coste, whose crisp white shirt, red coat with gold piping along the sleeves and shoulders, and matching red cap left him looking more like a movie usher than chief of security. Robert was working hard to carefully enunciate each word while Norman Le Coste eyed Robert and the cluster of bright balloons bobbing above his head.

"It's against the rules," Le Coste repeated.

"I can appreciate that," Robert said, "but surely you can see the position I'm in. Without your help, the whole thing will end up a disaster." Robert lifted a white bag stuffed with crepe paper and streamers and tried to put on the expression of a boy holding a fifteen-cent candy bar in one hand and fourteen cents in the other.

"I wasn't notified," Le Coste said. "There's regulations. They're a part of the package when you buy into the Santa Maria."

"But Ms. Shell couldn't notify you. If she did, that would mean she knew, and then there'd be no surprise. That's what all her friends are trying to do. Surprise her. It's my job to put the decorations up."

Le Coste turned away to survey the bank of closed-circuit televisions monitoring the grounds, the private parking area for residents, and the lobby of the Santa Maria. Robert smiled and patiently watched with him, but his stomach and smile tightened when the camera scanned the parking area and panned Denice's white Porsche. Three slots below it in the same row was the green Triumph.

Robert halfheartedly followed through with the charade. "Her car's here. She's home, so I'd better try to come back later. If she knows I'm here, it'll spoil everything."

"Suit yourself," Le Coste said, sitting back in his swivel chair. "But the rules are still going to be here when you come back. You want in, you're going to have to figure some way around them." Le Coste rubbed his thumb and index finger together and then touched the shiny black bill of his cap.

Robert turned and headed in the direction of Mallory Square. Earlier he had managed to find something resembling hope in the number of unanswered phone calls he'd made to Denice. As long as Denice and Winde weren't at her place, Robert could revise the circumstances surrounding Winde's appearance along less painful lines, say, nothing more than Winde happening to be in town and wanting to meet Denice for a drink and Denice taking advantage of the opportunity to make

Robert jealous. Robert then came up with the idea for the bogus surprise party to confirm what he wanted to believe. He intended to bluff his way into her place so he would know conclusively she wasn't there, and then he'd wait for her to get back, confronting Winde if necessary.

But the sight of the white Porsche and green Triumph on the closed-circuit screen put a new gloss on the unanswered calls. Robert couldn't come up with a scenario that didn't hold something happening at his expense. On the night he'd met Denice at Lennie's party, Lennie had told him that at one time Winde and Denice had been involved, but that Denice had eventually broken it off even though Winde was someone used to getting his own way. He kept trying to force his way into Denice's life, and while she never quite stopped him, she never let him get a secure foothold either. Lennie had not elaborated on the on-again-off-again relationship except to say there was usually trouble whenever Denice and Winde got together. Lennie didn't clarify for whom and dropped the subject completely when Rob asked what Winde did in D.C.

Key West had the reputation of possessing an unusually high tolerance for eccentrics, but the side glances and guarded looks Rob got when he reached Mallory Square told him he wasn't counted among their number. There was nothing charming or amusing about an unshaven, scowling man with reddened eyes and a sweat-soaked shirt carrying a bag full of party favors and a half dozen helium-filled heart-shaped foil balloons moving at large among the citizenry.

Robert ditched the party stuff the first chance he got and tried to melt unobtrusively into the crowd of locals and tourists gathering at Mallory Dock for the daily ritual of watching the sun set. Close to a hundred people were already there. Robert slowly worked his way to the edge of the dock.

The horizon looked like an enormous accident. The light leaked through a collison of metal-colored clouds, trickling and pooling in reds and yellows onto the flat dark waters of the Gulf. Robert wandered the long slab of concrete that comprised Mallory Dock as the day gaudily extinguished itself and panhandlers circulated, couples leaned into each other, a magician pulled brightly colored scarves from the bikinied cleavage of his assistant, bodybuilders struck poses, children ran and hollered, dogs did tricks, bikers leaned against their machines, old ladies in flowered dresses huddled together, teenagers strutted with jamblasters riding their shoulders, Midwestern tourists snapped photos, gay men camped or held hands, ponytailed locals passed joints, girls flirted with college boys drinking beer, fervent souls stood behind makeshift pulpits and preached on last things, a woman with a curtain of long black hair serenely nursed an infant, and the air burst with color and the sound of guitars, pennywhistles, and tambourines. Robert smiled and nodded but couldn't lose his rage or frustration. They shadowed every step he took.

He found a pay phone at the end of the dock. He took the card holding Russell Tills's private number from his wallet, dropped in a handful of quarters, and was furiously punching buttons before he fully thought about what he was doing. The lines hummed, the contacts clicked, and Russell's phone began to ring. All he had to do was tell Russell what Hannibal and Lauter had planned to do at his expense and Rob still had a shot at salvaging his film career. He knew, if he had to, he could do a convincing job of minimizing his part in the whole thing. If necessary, he would lie about losing the package in the first place and push all the blame for Russell's troubles off on Lauter, Hannibal, and Denice.

Russell picked up the phone and said hello.

Robert thought about Denice swimming through the pool of flowers.

"Hello," Russell said. "Hello?"

Robert thought of Denice laying the lines of coke between her breasts and lifting her arms.

"Hello, hello," Russell yelled. "Who is this?"

Robert hung up. He wasn't sure he could answer that question anymore.

Robert walked back to the edge of the dock. To the west the sky burned like fire on metal. Beyond the colors, the horizon was immense and blank. The sheer amount of space didn't let him forget. Try as he might, he could lose nothing in it.

He had run out of country. That was both the charm and curse of Key West. America dreamed and denied itself there, throwing itself against the horizon that would forever elude it, like a hopelessly ugly bridesmaid who catches the bridal bouquet. Key West was the place where everything ran out.

Robert stopped walking and looked past the woman nursing the baby to another woman dancing at the edge of the dock. Her dress was the blue of new ice, of stained glass, or mirrors held to summer skies. Her body whirled. Her hair flew. She held her arms above her head and dropped them. They were ringed with silver bracelets. Her feet were bare, and her legs long and tanned as the loose blue dress splashed with movement.

Her frenzied dance gave shape to the ritual unfolding on the dock. The sky behind her burned red and yellow. She was dancing for Robert and the others, for everyone who had been drawn to Mallory Dock to live out their lives in the face of something final, in this case, a sky closing down in an explosion of color.

WHEN ROBERT GOT BACK to the house on Simonton after leaving Mallory Dock, he found the front door partially open. He paused on the top step and heard the television, a faint stirring of voices like the low hum of insects. Right then, Robert couldn't separate relief from anger, and when he opened the door and stepped into the house, he didn't know what Denice would see in his face or he in hers.

What he found instead was False Walter slouched on the living-room couch with the remote control to the television resting on his stomach. The kid quickly jumped up when he spotted Robert and put the couch between them.

"Before you say anything, the door was unlocked, so don't start the break-and-enter riff again, okay? No way, this time. I figured it was just easier waiting for you inside instead of on the porch." The kid took a few steps toward the kitchen. "I had some deliveries to make, and you were the last stop."

Robert eased himself down onto the couch and tried to remember if he'd ordered any coke from Hannibal, but the day crashed in on him again, every hour unspooling with its own disaster and each passing minute undoing him a little more.

The kid handed him a beer and then moved to the nearest chair. He was wearing orange flip-flops, a Lennie's T-shirt with CONCH POWER across its front, and a pair of black-and-white striped shorts. His hair had been cut a quarter-inch short of the concentration camp look.

"I left the delivery on the kitchen table," False Walter said, sitting back and opening the beer he'd brought in for himself. "Thought I'd have a cool one for the road if you don't mind," he added.

Robert remained stretched out on the couch and spoke to the ceiling. "I do mind. You made your delivery, so go. I've told you again and again I don't want you hanging around here."

"Is it so bad, me stopping by once in a while? I only do it when you and Denice aren't here. It's quiet and a nice place to hang out. I don't bother anything. Mostly I just watch television."

Robert lay on the couch, ignoring the kid the best he could, letting him talk himself out, until a few of False Walter's words broke in on him. Robert tried to pull himself too quickly into a sitting position, and the muscles in his back and chest screamed. He had sobered up just enough from all the drinks and coke to get a preview of the hangover that was on its way. He remained hunched, face toward the floor, while his breathing evened, then asked False Walter to repeat what he'd said.

"I just said I wasn't in any hurry to get back to the *Blue Circus*. Things have been tense, and I was glad to get off the boat for a while."

"No. Before that. You mentioned something about James Winde."

"He was out on the boat today, that's all."

"Was Denice with him?"

"Let's press rewind, then erase, okay?" False Walter started running his hand over the brown stubble covering his head. "After I signed on as first mate, Hannibal explained what he'd do to me if I ever repeated what I heard or saw on board. He wasn't kidding around either. The man has a way of making what he says happen."

"I'll keep anything you say between us. Just answer a couple questions."

"I don't know, man. I better get another beer and think it over."

Robert could see what was coming when the kid returned with two beers, setting one in front of Robert, and then moving back to the chair and crossing his legs at the ankles. False Walter furrowed his brows in what amounted to a caricature of someone coming to a difficult decision. Robert already knew what the terms would be and let the kid run through his routine, simply nodding when False Walter said he'd tell Rob what he wanted to know if he could stop by the house whenever he wanted.

"I'm not talking about every day or anything like that," he said. "Just once in a while, you know, when I need to get away. Like I said, you don't even have to be here."

Robert nodded again. The kid took a long swallow of beer, then said that James Winde had been out on the *Blue Circus* to meet with Hannibal around ten that morning. Winde had been upset, and nothing Hannibal said could calm him down. Winde kept bringing up Rob's name and something about a phonebook and the airport and yelling about what could happen to Winde's career if the book wasn't located soon.

"The guy's not exactly a big fan of yours, Rob," False Walter said. He then went on and talked about another meeting, this one late afternoon, between Hannibal and Lennie Ash, Hannibal doing all the yelling and accusing this time and Lennie unsuccessfully trying to calm him down. Lennie kept saying he was meeting with Russell Tills about money problems, nothing more, but Hannibal hadn't bought that, telling Lennie that he'd end up wearing one of his T-shirts for a shroud if he wasn't careful.

"Hannibal sent me off to make deliveries right after that," the kid said, "and that's when I ran into Denice and Winde. They were at the bus station. See, I was supposed to drop off two grams to a guy that's paranoid about me coming to his house, so we meet there during bus changes when it's crowded. Winde was in his car outside the station and Denice took some stuff out of one of the lockers. Neither of them noticed me."

"What kind of stuff?"

False Walter shrugged. "A bunch of manila envelopes. You know, like you use to mail things? She carried three or four of them out with her, then got back in the car with Winde, and they drove off." False Walter told Robert he couldn't remember the exact location of Denice's locker, only that it was somewhere in the middle of row A or B near the top.

False Walter sipped at his beer and looked around the room with a new proprietary interest while Rob tried to make sense of what he'd heard. He figured that the envelopes contained Denice's scrapbooks and journals, but he didn't have any idea to what use they were being put, especially now that Russell Tills was out of the picture. It was still a toss-up whether Denice had something on Winde or he on her. Perhaps neither. Some connection was there, however. What puzzled Robert was the fact Denice hadn't tried to hide it. She'd climbed into Winde's car right in front of Bagatelle's, virtually throwing it in Rob's face. Yet she'd still left open the option for Rob to become part of the deal Lauter was working out with Camar Tavares. Nothing quite fit. All Rob knew for sure was Denice had disappeared as abruptly as she'd appeared in his life, and each felt like forever.

Rob got up from the couch, crossed the room to the video recorder, lifted it, and slid out a white envelope that had been lying underneath. He tossed it into False Walter's lap.

"What's this for?" the kid asked, holding the envelope as if it were hot or biting him, shifting it quickly from hand to hand.

"You don't have to lift my wallet this time. The money in there is yours."

False Walter rifled the envelope, a blur of green between his fingers. "What's the story?"

"None. It's yours. Like I said."

False Walter averted his eyes. "What do I have to do?"

"Just get out of Key West. Leave and don't look back. You don't belong here. Sooner or later you'll end up getting in trouble with Hannibal. I know that much about you. Take the money and use it as a stake toward a new start."

"Hannibal thinks I have potential. He told me so himself."

"He's got you on a long leash, that's all."

"Hey, I've been on shorter ones." False Walter shook the envelope at Rob. "Hannibal is okay to work for most of the time. Once in a while he gets a little high-strung and likes to break things. He just doesn't pay attention to who's around when he does."

Robert lowered and shook his head. "Are you telling me he hurts you?"

"He's a big guy. He doesn't mean to, but sometimes he gets carried away. Like I said, he's high-strung. It's nothing I can't handle."

"Why don't you take the money and leave? There's close to a thousand dollars in the envelope. It's yours. No strings attached."

"I can make that much every three weeks or so doing coke deliveries for Hannibal. I don't need your money." False Walter flicked off the television and got out of the chair. He tilted up the beer and turned toward the front windows, saying something Robert couldn't catch. When Robert asked him to repeat it, False Walter threw the envelope at him.

"You ever think about where, man?" he yelled.

"I don't know what you mean," Rob said. "If you need more money, I can get it."

False Walter stood with his fists clenched and leaned toward Rob. The light hollowed out his features, leaving him looking even more gaunt than usual. "I'll tell you what," False Walter said. "I'll take the money and leave if you'll answer one question. Where am I supposed to go? Back to Orlando and dear old Mom and her Seconals and Cuban boyfriends? Or maybe Miami and get my old job as a spotter at a crack house back? Swell opportunities there if you can move fast enough and enjoy target practice. Why do you think I ended up here? So tell me, man, even if I wanted to leave, where would I go that's any different? Just answer me where."

Robert studied the palms of his hands. He didn't look up until he heard the front door close.

IT HADN'T BEEN a standard coke delivery after all. After False Walter left, Robert found a rectangular package on the kitchen table. Taped to its top was a small white envelope and inside it, a cream-colored card of heavy embossed paper, the kind used for formal invitations. The card was blank except for a ticket stub with ADMIT ONE stamped in its center. It had been paperclipped to the card's top edge. Below it, in Denice's handwriting was: *I Dare You.*

Robert got a beer and took the package back into the living room and opened it. Inside was a video of *Hell Mall*, the sixth film he'd done for Worldwide Pictures and the first one on which he got top billing. He looked at Denice's message again and then slipped the film into the video recorder. While the credits rolled, he did a line of coke and then sat back with the beer, hoping that they would corral his hangover.

The opening shot was of a mall's main concourse and of the huge fountain dominating its center. The fountain's jets pulsed in elaborate and graceful arcs around and above knots of busy shoppers. After a while, the fountain's hiss and the background music begin to increase in volume. At first the shoppers don't notice, but soon they're pausing, then stopping to look around in confusion as the hiss turns into a tidal roar and the Muzak breaks down into thundering bass notes that echo like the accelerated beats of a heart. The fountain's waters take on a slightly pinkish cast, then gradually darken. The camera cuts to a woman's terrified face and her long scream. Then to the crowd running and ducking for cover as the fountain erupts in a ceiling-high geyser of blood.

Which stops when Robert's character jerks awake at his desk and looks up to see his strawberry-blond girlfriend in the doorway of his office. He is the mall manager, and she runs a small greeting card shop. "The dreams again?" she asks and then crosses the room to rub his shoulders.

Robert leaned back against the couch and tried to remember how the film ended. In *Ninjas from Neptune, Kill Daddy Good-bye, Vegetable, It Won't Die*, and *Dairy Queen Massacre*, he got the girl. In *Cross My Heart and Hope to Die, Young Vampires on Wheels, Escape from Women's Psychiatric Prison*, and *Meat Me*, he died, but he drew a blank on *Hell Mall*.

Robert kept nursing his beer and watching the film, but he found himself glancing down again and again at the coffee table and the card with Denice's message.

On the screen, his character struggled with his recurring bad dreams and his slowly growing belief that the merchants in the mall he managed were members of a Satanic cult; his suspicions heightened when he checked library and county records and discovered the mall had been built on the site of an old graveyard and that twelve of the merchants were descendants of sixteenth-century devil worshipers burnt and originally buried there; his fears eventually confirmed and then the frenzied attempts to find and warn his girlfriend of the danger she and the others were in, only to discover she was missing and the probable sacrificial victim for the darker designs behind the mall's Midnight Madness Sale; his discovery of a secret doorway and his desperate scrambling through the bowels of the mall where she'd been imprisoned; her rescue and their impassioned reunion; and finally, in the guise of escape, his girlfriend leading him through a labyrinthine passageway that eventually brought them out in the center of the mall where twelve hooded figures stood in a circle around the fountain, waiting for their high priestess to don her black robe; the final shot freezing Robert's character opening his mouth for a scream that never came.

Robert didn't feel the beer bottle slip through his fingers or hear it when it hit and rolled across the floor. It took a while for him to figure out who was laughing and to realize that the laughter was coming from him. He understood Denice's dare now.

He knew the film was bad. Nothing more than standard Worldwide fare—ass and tits, gore, predictable plots, all packaged with a slickness and open cynicism that were was familiar as fast food. What he had not known was just how bad his performance had turned out to be. At best, he was utterly forgettable.

He'd accepted, just like everyone else working in a Worldwide film, that the scripts inevitably contained cardboard characters whose motivation, when discernible, grew out of only a very primitive notion of psychology. The challenge, as Robert saw it, was to accept the fact that the characters were one-dimensional but to then get inside and play the stereotype against itself.

And the trick to doing that was to perfect the details. A pair of rolled or unrolled cuffs. The vaguely overdue haircut. The movement of fingers extracting a wallet. The barely suppressed yawn. The missing button. A slouch. The small unexpected modulations in the way he delivered his lines. The degree of eye contact. Robert had tried to incorporate into his roles the small details or gestures that would give new life to the cliché. If he played the cliché well enough, it ceased to be one.

Not a bad strategy for an ambitious young actor paying his dues in low-budget extravaganzas. It was a fine strategy, in fact, if the actor could pull it off.

Robert hadn't.

If he'd seen that before, he hadn't admitted it to himself. Until tonight. The little touches he prided himself on in his characters were no more than crumbs that he had mistaken for a cake.

On one level, it was almost funny. Maybe that's why he couldn't stop laughing.

ROBERT WAS DRIFTING between sleep and waking when Denice appeared in the doorway, and at first he mistook her for something from his dreams. Moonlight pooled and ran like melted frosting around them. Denice leaned against the doorframe and placed a hand on her hip, her dark blue dress barely distinguishable from the room's shadows. Three silver bracelets encircled her left wrist. When she tilted her head, her hair ran with moonlight and tumbled around her shoulders, a wide pale sheath falling over her forehead and covering one eye.

"What do you want me to say?" Denice asked softly. "That I'm sorry? I don't think that quite covers it, but I'll say it if you want."

Robert didn't know if she was talking about his performance in *Hell Mall* or about James Winde or both.

"I came back," Denice said, again quietly. "That should tell you something." Her arm lifted and her hand flew open, the bracelets shimmering. A small white packet landed on the sheets. Robert reached down and picked it up. Denice continued to stand in the doorway.

"It's a little piece of what's possible," Denice said, "compliments of Camar Tavares. A sample of what he can do." Denice shifted her position in the doorway. Robert heard the long slow hiss of a zipper. The blue dress fell around Denice's ankles, disappearing into shadow.

"What do you want, Robert? You still haven't said anything." Denice unhooked her bra and dropped it to the floor. "Is it Winde that's bothering you? What do you want to know? Come on, ask me what you have to. Maybe it'll mean something to you."

"No. It doesn't matter," Robert said. The day had emptied him of everything but this moment in the moonlight.

"Are you sure?"

"All that matters is that you're back. I don't care about anything else." He watched Denice lean over to unsnap her hose and peel them off. Robert opened the bedstand drawer and took out a hand mirror. When he looked up, Denice stood naked in the doorway, her body banded in shadow and light.

"Come here," Robert said, answering at the same time the question Denice had asked earlier in the afternoon at Bagatelle's. He was stepping into the deal, ready now to follow what was necessary into whatever was possible. After watching *Hell Mall* tonight, he knew there was nothing to hold him back anymore.

Denice slid into bed next to him. Robert balanced the mirror on her stomach and chopped two lines. The moonlight spilled over the mirror so that the cocaine appeared inseparable from either. Robert put his hand on Denice's thigh for support and leaned over.

It was the closest thing to pure he'd ever done, a completely different species, nothing like the coke they'd found in Key West and Miami so far this summer. Robert lay back and felt his exhaustion and confusion drain away. The coke rush was a transfusion. No, he thought, better than that. More along the lines of a resurrection. It felt like every one of his nerve endings had rolled away its own little rock.

In the silver air, when Robert moved into Denice, everything else disappeared. The night broke from its axis, and their bones refused to hold them. Flesh splitting and fitting, they moved, thrust and counterthrust until even that disappeared, dissolved in the churning of their bodies, as they forced it back to the sea, a heaving and rolling, a sinking through silvered depths and tidal pulls, until they became creatures of the deep, strangely jointed, extra-eyed, and oddly colored, feeding in the depths and the dark on simple things.

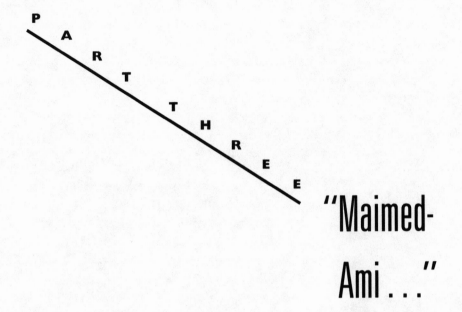

PART THREE

"Maimed-Ami..."

MAIMED-AMI, that's what they'll have to change the name to," Lennie Ash said, "when this deal with Camar Tavares hits street level. The old Colombian *coqueros* aren't going to stand around and let Camar Tavares move into their Stateside territory. Franklin Benjamin Lauter can sit up in D.C. and talk all he wants about the Big Picture and Transitions, but on the streets it'll be an all-out war." Lennie kept the Bronco moving at a workmanlike seventy-five as they passed through the lower Keys and approached the Bahia Honda Bridge. Robert leaned back in his seat and let Lennie talk. Listening to him was easier than thinking about why they were on their way to Miami.

"In my opinion," Lennie said, "this new arrangement came together too fast. Tavares splinters from the *coqueros* and starts talking big. Lauter's suddenly hopping planes between Medellín and D.C. and acting like he and Tavares are lifelong *compadres*."

"His product's good," Robert said. "You have to admit that. Tavares seems to know what he's doing."

Lennie assaulted rather than shifted gears. The Bronco careened through the light late-morning traffic. "Yeah, but can he do it?" Lennie asked. "That's the question. Without the chemicals, all Tavares can do is talk. The usual black-market sources have dried up. Unless Hannibal can scare up enough acetone, ether, and hydrochloric acid, all Tavares's new processing plants and his offer of bargain-basement prices on top of the line goods don't mean a thing."

Lennie leaned over and knocked open the glove compartment, rummaging around with his free hand until he found an amber prescription bottle. He flicked off the lid and popped two tablets. "You want a

Crossroads?" he asked. Robert shook his head no, and Lennie tossed the bottle back into the glove compartment.

"Don't get me wrong," Lennie said, drumming his fingers on the steering wheel. "I want this deal to work out. I won't say the money isn't good. With my cut, I can get the IRS and all those copyright lawyers off my back and still have a bank account with a view. I'm tired of having to Scotch-tape the whole T-shirt operation together, so you won't hear any arguments from me about the money. I just hope Lauter knows what he's getting us into with the new backers, that's all. The *coqueros* aren't going to take this deal lying down."

Lennie was quiet for the next few miles, keeping his eyes on the road and not on Rob. He continually cut in and out of traffic to avoid downshifting and fiddled with the stems of his sunglasses and the radio dial. A thin film of sweat covered his face, darkening the skin around his freckles so that it looked like he was suffering from heat rash. The pale red cowlick sprang straight up from his forehead. Lennie was wearing, he'd told Rob earlier, the T-shirt that had helped launch his original line of shops. The shirt held a map of the continental United States, but with a Dadaist's sense of proportion. The country's outline remained the same, but the state of Florida swallowed over three-quarters of the land mass, the other forty-seven states packed into the space left over. The effect of the map's image was even more disconcerting when it had to accommodate the lines of Lennie's squat torso.

Robert wasn't sure if Lennie had figured out Robert had betrayed him to Hannibal Binder a week ago at the Meridian Bar, but he did know that Lennie didn't want him in the new deal. Lennie had made that very plain last night when they'd met with Hannibal on the *Blue Circus*. Robert had been sitting right in front of him while Lennie tried to talk Hannibal out of letting Robert in. Lennie's objections hadn't carried much weight though since he was basically in the same position as Robert. Two wild cards, Hannibal had called them. Both Lennie and Rob had close ties to Russell Tills. Since Hannibal and Lauter were planning to run the show without Russell, they figured it was time to run a credit check on Robert's and Lennie's loyalties. That's why they were on the way to Miami this morning.

Lennie flicked off the radio and began rubbing the back of his neck.

"Do you feel bad about this meeting? I do. I mean, Russell was the one to give me my first break. I couldn't have bankrolled the T-shirts without him. Anything else, I'd be on it faster than a fly on shit, but this, well, I just wish Lauter and Hannibal had come up with something else for us to do."

Lennie abruptly switched lanes and said the problem with Russell Tills was he could never see that he was a relic. He got his style from the spaghetti-eaters and bagel-boys who moved into Miami during the thirties, forties, and early fifties, a time when Cuban and Colombian only brought to mind cigars and coffee beans. Russell was still functioning in the world of Meyer Lansky and Capone, the politics of rum-running and gambling, cutting deals on moonlit terraces over Cuba Libres with New York and Chicago gangsters wearing brown felt fedoras and breaking in their new suntans in the land of art deco, adjusting to a different kind of heat from the one they fled up North. Russell saw himself as some sort of descendant, ready to carve up Florida like a birthday cake. What he didn't see was he was living in his own doomed little republic.

At any other time, Lennie told Rob, Russell's connections would be impressive. Even Lauter admitted that. Russell's network was wide and diverse enough to include bankers and oral surgeons, television evangelists and astronauts, tennis stars and restaurant owners. And that, according to Lauter, was precisely the problem: it made coordinating any serious distribution of coke almost impossible. Too many people involved. Too much nickel and diming. Too much time and too many directions for moving the product. Russell Tills was an institution that had outlived its purpose and utility, an old-fashioned general store of connections hopelessly struggling to compete with the new streamlined efficiency of Lauter's mall.

"And I'm not looking forward to us delivering the foreclosure notice," Lennie said. "Russell's old, but he's not harmless." Lennie mopped his brow, then lip, with the edge of his hand. "I just hope he leaves his two bodyguards at home. They're pure *escoria.*"

"*Escoria?*"

"Scum," Lennie said. "That's what the Cubans called anybody who landed in Mariel Prison. The lowest of the low. Charlie Manson's a puppy compared to most of them. Castro tossed them in with the rest of the regular refugees when Carter offered asylum here in 1980. Russell used his Immigration Agency connections to get 1-94 forms for two of them and hired them as his bodyguards. Manuel Contiga and Miguel Evelito, those two could make a snake cringe, believe me."

Lennie patted his stomach, gave Rob a sickly smile, and lifted his T-shirt. Tucked into the waistband of his jeans was a Smith & Wesson .38 Airweight. "Yours is under the seat," he said.

"Wait a minute, Lennie. Nobody said anything about guns."

Lennie hit the horn and then turned and glared at Robert. "That's exactly why I was so pissed about you coming into the deal. You don't have any idea how things work. I've been in this since the beginning, six years ago, in Calle Ocho when Russell, Hannibal, and Lauter set up the Derrota Newsstand shootings and opened the door for the *coqueros* to come in and set up shop. What do you think Russell's going to do when we tell him the Derrota Newsstand partnership is null and void and he doesn't have a place in the new one?"

Robert leaned back in the seat and looked at the ceiling. "I don't know," he slowly said.

"Neither do I. That's why the guns, Rob." Lennie took out a stick of gum from his shirt pocket and folded it into his mouth. To the north, the skyline of Miami gradually started to fill the windshield. Lennie popped his gum and shook his head. "There's something I still don't understand, Rob. Why are you in this? I got lawsuits and IRS troubles. I need the money. But why you?"

You could lose yourself waiting, Robert said, but sooner or later there was a moment that showed you what your life held. Robert was learning. He was making distinctions. You searched out the lowest common denominator and started from there. You didn't make the mistake of ignoring the obvious because it was always the obvious that blinded or crushed you.

For example: Denice was not Kathleen. That was obvious.

Robert's career had not gone where he'd expected it to. That, too, was obvious.

This was obvious too: if you knew what you wanted or how to get it, then the waiting was over.

Robert now knew what he wanted.

There was the money the deal would bring. And Denice. But there was something else too, more basic, the bottom line of all the confusion, the messes, and mistakes he'd made of himself and his life. His wanting came down to one thing.

Robert Staples did not want to be ordinary.

More than anything else, he wanted an escape hatch from that, to step outside the ordinary and all its built-in disappointments and demands, all the days and ways that ground you down and left a pencil stub of an existence. He did not want the promises of God or Country or Family. Nor a life filled with newspapers, microwaves, children, insurance premiums, pets, Touch-Tone phones, get-togethers, computer software, radial tires, business lunches, grocery lists, second mortgages, lawn mowers, or digital clocks.

He wanted out of the whole package deal. He did not want to be seen as the Good Son, Dutiful Husband, Industrious Employee, Happy Daddy, or Model Citizen.

He wanted out.

Though he hadn't seen it at the time, the vasectomy had been the first step. He'd been trying to get out, not out of a marriage, but out of the tricks that biology played on humanity, the vast conspiracy of the species to perpetuate itself, its insistence on a common destiny. The vasectomy had been a purposeful disruption of that destiny, a refusal not only to play by the rules of the game but also a defiant break from the game itself.

He was free now. Free to reinvent the game and make up new rules. Denice had shown him that. He didn't need the old words, the talk of love and beauty. Like history, they were so many garbage bags, bulky and misshapen, full of misplaced hopes. You could root through them forever and never recover what you'd lost.

Robert explained to Lennie that he'd taken out the trash.

CALL ME MORAL SUPPORT," Barry From West Palm said, suddenly stepping up to their table at the Club Toledo. Robert hadn't seen his approach and doubted that Lennie or Russell had either. Not that it would have been difficult to find them. Russell had not exactly been taking the news stoically. He'd already broken a round of drink glasses, overturned an ashtray, and delivered an intimate and detailed curse on both Lennie's and Robert's bloodlines. But as the meeting went on, Russell's bravado had begun to wear a little thin around the edges. He was spooked. Robert knew the feeling. While Russell sat through the explanation of how he'd been set up and then cut out of the new deal with Camar Tavares, Rob couldn't help thinking about what it had been like to watch *Hell Mall*, when suddenly the underpinnings to your whole world gave way and collapsed.

The patrons of the Club Toledo continued to ignore them. Russell Tills, for one thing, owned a controlling interest in the place, having gotten in early on the South Beach restoration move, when deco was suddenly seen as an endangered species, one whose preservation would produce no small amount of cash. The clientele of the club reflected that too, conveniently dividing itself into two types, the elderly wealthy retirees who wanted to protect their initial property investments and the upwardly mobile, the young businessmen and -women who were trying to boutique, café, and condo their way into any available space. Russell had known how to play the interests of the Restoration Committee off those of the other two groups so that all three were dependent on his favor. Nobody, therefore, was about to comment on Russell's behavior, no matter how outrageous.

Barry From West Palm put his hands on Russell's shoulders and squeezed, then leaned forward so that his face was upside down and right in front of Russell's.

"You going to ask me to join you? Here, I come all this way, catch your retirement party, stop by personally on behalf of Mr. Franklin Benjamin Lauter to thank you for all your years of distinguished service, etcetera, provide some moral support here, not only to you, Russell, but to Lennie and Roberto there, who for all I know are grade-A fuck-ups, I thought I'd drop in, have a drink, make sure everything's clear and acceptable."

"It's not." Russell made the mistake of trying to shrug off Barry From West Palm's hands, which then slowly tightened along the lapels of Russell's apricot sports jacket. Russell's eyes started to well. Barry let go and pulled up a chair. Robert and Lennie gave him ample room.

"Which is it? Not clear? Or acceptable? Robert and Lennie not do what they were asked?"

"The two messenger boys explained the situation very clearly," Russell said.

Barry From West Palm wore an aqua windbreaker, jeans, white shirt, and a cap the color of new cash with JAKE'S CRAB HOUSE across its front. Two sets of claws doubled as quotation marks.

"So I'm to assume not acceptable here." Barry fingered the bill of the cap and leaned back in his seat. He and Russell stared at each other. Lennie signaled for a new round of drinks. Robert looked around the room for the two Cuban bodyguards. They hadn't shown up with Russell, but he was afraid they might yet.

The interior of the Club Toledo, formerly the Hotel Del Ray, was a confusing clash of geometry and romance, a battle between Depression Moderne and Tropical Deco, a 1930s version of Buck Rogers visits the tropics, with its bright walls outlined in neon piping and cut in quarters by bright blue bands, the sets of escalator-style stairs and curved chrome handrails, the doors festooned with peacocks, nymphs, borzois, flamingos, and sunbursts, the terrazzo floor with its polished pastel mosaics, and the high domed ceiling ringed with concentric recessed circles of pink and green. Everything here had been designed to suggest a way out, an escape from a world that had crashed with the stock market. Machinery and Moonlight. Speed and Sunlight. Rocket Ships and Swaying Palms. Ways out that were a lot more attractive than some of the ones Robert heard Barry From West Palm outlining for Russell.

"You know what they call the strip of I-95 between Miami and Fort Lauderdale now, Russell? The Meat Market Express. No shit. That is one very weird piece of asphalt. The cops try, they can't control it. Carloads of maniacs is what we're talking about here. Joyriding with a twist. You got these guys cruising there enjoying doing things to people with knives and guns. No reason behind it, they don't discriminate, just pick somebody and run them off the road and kill them. What say you and me tool out there some night, and I drop you off, let you get acquainted? You and them could talk about what's not and is acceptable."

"We laid it out, Barry," Lennie said, slurring his words. "Absolutely."

Across the room, a group of eight started a happy birthday to Ray. In the center of the table was a chocolate cake with pink candles. The waitress wheeled in a cart full of packages wrapped in silver paper.

"I could make trouble," Russell said. He lit up another in a long line of Vantages. "You know I could."

"No question there," Barry From West Palm said. "Except at this point, I'd say it would be mostly for yourself."

"Mr. Franklin Benjamin Lauter's not the only one who knows people in D.C. I could make things pretty uncomfortable. Lauter should know that."

Barry didn't respond right away. He ignored the drink Lennie pushed in his direction. He had managed, though Robert didn't know how, to grab Russell's wrist without seeming to move at all. A vein began to pulse in Barry's neck, but when he finally spoke, it was in the matter-of-fact tone of somebody ordering a pizza over the phone.

"You talk to anybody in D.C. lately? Give some of your friends a buzz. See who returns your call. The word's out on you, Russell. You're tainted meat."

Barry bent Russell's wrist upward until the tip of his cigarette began to burn a hole in the sleeve of his sports jacket. The apricot material darkened, frayed, then disappeared, leaving a hole slightly larger than a penny. Barry From West Palm maintained the pressure, and eventually there was the smell of singed hair. All the color from his tanning-bed sessions leached out of Russell's face.

Barry From West Palm slowly released his grip. Russell tried to move his chair away, but Barry hooked it with his foot. "People are laughing, Russell. At you, man. Right in your face, they're laughing at that dyed hair, those clothes too, the color combo you got there, you looking like a walking pack of Life Savers. They're laughing at the way you *live*, man. You're finished here."

Russell smoothed the front of his yellow shirt and adjusted the knot in his tie. "Maybe I'll take it to the DEA and cop immunity. How would Lauter like that? I wouldn't even have to go far. Henry Swolt has been seriously tagging me all summer. I'm sure he'd love to get together, have a talk."

Barry smiled at the name Henry Swolt and lifted his hands so that they framed Russell's head. When he nodded, Russell asked why.

"Just measuring, that's all. Rough estimate. I wasn't sure about the size."

"Of what?"

"Of the box I'm going to need after I cut your fucking head off, Russell. You got a funny-shaped head, going to have to choose carefully to find the right fit. Don't want to mess up that hairstyle. Lots of things to consider here. The post office won't deliver unless everything's just right, and if you want to meet with your DEA friends, I want to make sure you get there okay."

"Do you think that's the first time I've ever been threatened?" Russell asked.

"No, I'm thinking it's your last."

Lennie Ash, weaving in his seat, began to shake his head. "This is just Calle Ocho and the Derrota Newsstand all over again. It never really stopped. Russell said Swolt, right?"

Barry turned and grabbed Rob instead of Lennie. "Why you let him do that, all the drinks? The Derrota Newsstand, Jesus. We got work to do after the party here. How much good he going to be, huh? Maybe I should have hired a babysitter, watch you two, make sure you behave yourself."

Barry's fingers were wrapped around Robert's forearm like tape, and he was afraid when Barry released his grip that the skin would peel away too. "Russell was a half hour late for the meeting," Robert said quickly, "and I didn't notice how much Lennie was drinking until it was too late to do anything about it." Robert tried to pull his arm away. "I'll watch him now. I'm doing all right."

"I bet you are, all those trips to the bathroom you made. Think I didn't know that? You got a bladder problem, Rob, or maybe you looking to relieve yourself along different *lines*?"

"I told you. I'm fine."

Barry's fingers changed from tape to spider's legs. "You're telling me you're steady, Rob, I can count on you, that what I'm hearing? I'm not to worry like I got to about our pal Lennie?"

"That's what you're hearing, Barry." A couple lines, Rob thought, to keep things in perspective, that's all it was. The idea of carrying a gun had taken some getting used to.

Barry let go of Rob's arm and reached over and caged the bourbon in front of Lennie. Lennie lowered and rested his head on the tabletop. Russell had run out of cigarettes and signaled the waiter for more. In the meantime, his fingers began a nervous inventory of his chin, jawline, eyebrows, temples, and earlobes, finally stopping at his side-burns. "No matter what you say, Barry, we're tied, all of us, to each other," Russell said. "Lauter's making a mistake. You just can't pretend you can undo the Derrota."

"From what I see, Russell, Lauter doesn't pretend much of any-thing." Barry went on and flipped up the bill of his Jake's Crab House cap in imitation of an expired parking meter. "You're history."

The waiter brought the cigarettes, and Barry helped himself to one, then offered to light Russell's. "I hear Switzerland's a nice place. Very low crime rate, someone moving there wouldn't have to worry much. You'd be a big hit there too, I bet, what with those clothes, make a definite impression, those people used to whites and browns, and then you, Mr. Rainbow. I'd say, something to consider. Seriously."

"And what if I don't like snow?"

Barry waited half a dozen heartbeats before answering. "How you feel about dirt? I'm thinking of approximately six feet of it here. Making the worm scene." Barry got up abruptly and walked across the room.

Russell turned to Rob. "Nobody does this to me. Nobody."

"I think they already have." Robert pushed his empty glass into the middle of the table. "I don't know if it matters much at this point, Russell, or if you believe me or not, but I'm sorry for the way things turned out."

Russell leaned back and folded his arms. "Oh, it matters, Rob. Count on that. You and a few others might be surprised at just how much it does."

Lennie was suddenly sitting straight up in his chair, the improvement in his posture resulting from the fact that Barry From West Palm had unexpectedly returned and jerked him up by his hair.

"Don't want you to miss Russell opening his retirement present, Lennie. Sober up." In Barry's right hand was a package wrapped in silver paper. Robert leaned over and looked across the room where Ray and the members of the birthday party huddled around their plates of cake, studiously avoiding any glances in their direction.

"Go on, Russell," Barry said, leaning over. "Open it. I picked it out for you myself."

AFTER LEAVING THE CLUB TOLEDO, Robert spent the afternoon driving around Miami in Barry From West Palm's cherry-red Camaro. Barry had handed him the keys and told him it was time to go to work. Lennie had been supposed to accompany him, but Barry had taken Lennie along with him to sober up. Robert was going solo on this one.

As he left South Miami Beach and crossed the McArthur Causeway for Biscayne Boulevard, Robert wondered why he was driving the Camaro instead of Lennie's Bronco. It made more sense for Barry to keep his own car, but he'd insisted that Rob take it. Insisted a little too forcefully, Robert thought, but by now he had pretty much given up trying to figure out Barry From West Palm.

After the first half hour, Robert began to understand the point behind the Camaro. Every streetcorner-and-curb hustle artist recognized it. There was nothing subtle about the car, its paint job buffed to the sheen of a newly minted coin, the monstrous chrome headers erupting from the twin slots in the hood, the windows tinted hearse black, and the Glass-pac exhaust system rumbling like a portable volcano.

Driving the car was like riding around inside of Barry's head. The seat covers were hot pink and dotted with a number of irregularly shaped stains that Robert had no inclination to inspect. A cardboard car deodorizer hung from the rearview mirror, its face holding a photo of a bare-chested woman named Cherry sitting astride an alligator. The dash was covered in thick white fur except for a rectangular swath in its center that had been clipped. In the bare patch were three plastic statues of Jesus, each with outstretched arms and the heads missing.

One of the heads had been glued to the tuner of the radio, another to the top of the stick shift, and the last to the lighter in the dashboard.

When Robert went down into Liberty City and Overtown, sites of some of Miami's finest race riots, to complete the drops and pickups, the Camaro's singular presence protected him. There among the burnt shells and dilapidated tenements and shops the city council was continually promising to renovate were young blacks who in any other circumstance would have liked nothing more than to hand Robert his white ass back on a platter, but who when they spotted the car, became instant brothers, crowding around and announcing, "New man driving Barry car; man here on business," and escorting Robert to his contacts.

It was the same everywhere he went, no matter how different the locale. In Little Havana, with its crowded cafés, black beans, mud-dark coffee, bolito games, and anti-Castro rhetoric. In Coral Gables where old money confused homes with shrines, and in Coconut Grove where the newly rich color-coordinated their Mercedes and jogging outfits. In Hialeah, at the track. In Opa-Locka, with its subdivisions, the houses identical and evenly spaced as cans on a shelf in a grocery store.

Everywhere it was the same. Robert handed someone an envelope and got one in return. He dropped each one in a small duffle bag that matched Barry's windbreaker and then drove on to the next place. The procedure never varied.

By the end of the afternoon, Robert was amazed that he was still alive or possessed all his limbs. He didn't realize how scared he'd been. Things should not have been that routine. Not in Miami. And especially not now. You just didn't spend an afternoon meeting the types of people he had without running into some very serious threats or problems. Robert didn't have to be told who he had been dealing with. After the first couple of drops, it was evident he was meeting the representatives of some major coke distributors, many of them who must have had ties to the Colombian *coqueros*. Robert wondered what Mr. Franklin Benjamin Lauter had done, or was in the process of doing while the deal was being worked out, that had convinced them to cooperate. Robert knew that Barry was only indirectly responsible for the deference shown to him this afternoon. Being psychopathic didn't make Barry unique or safe in Miami. It was the fact that Barry From West Palm was a representative for Lauter that made the difference.

Leaving Hialeah, Robert followed Okeechobee until it turned into North River Drive, paralleling the Miami River as it angled through the southern portion of the city from its origin at the port off Dodge Island. Robert had one more stop to make. To his right the Miami River was a dirty green, the wind giving its surface the texture of crumpled cash. The car ate a half block each time he shifted. He was moving, and it suddenly felt good. A tug churning up the river whirred by like an insect. The houseboats moored along the shore were flashes of white, no different from the ones that disappeared under the left tires of the Camaro.

He was in and moving now. Lennie had choked today. Robert hadn't. Pickup, drop, and move on. This was his second chance, and Robert had pulled it off. This wasn't the Miami International Airport. Not this time.

Palmetto trunks and telephone poles blurred by, indistinguishable from each other. Lennie and not Rob had screwed up. The Camaro's gas pedal fit Rob's foot like a glass slipper. One more stop, that's all. Rob was in. The South Florida sun was a golden egg. The Camaro raced the river to the ocean. The boy in Rob's conscience had cried wolf once too often. Robert smiled to himself. The secret that had been kept from everybody was that Humpty Dumpty never fell. The Camaro felt airborne. So fuck all the king's horses and men.

Robert followed North River Drive until it intersected with Flagler. As he was approaching the turnoff for the lower portion of Biscayne Boulevard, he had to brake suddenly for a red light, and when he looked up, there was Denice.

She was silhouetted against the skyline of the city, her image stretched across a billboard the size of a theater screen. Denice floated among the white right angles of downtown Miami, she and the buildings set against a postcard-blue sky. Denice lay on her side in a tight one-piece swimsuit banded like a bright rainbow.

The light changed, but Robert waited, ignoring the honking behind him, as he took one last look at Denice stretched before him, a hundred square feet of flesh rising out of the city, wrapped in unearthly colors, floating above it all, blond as the sun and suspended in her own piece of sky.

IT WAS BUCCANEER DAYS in Miami Beach at the Lincoln Road Mall, and while Robert sat on the terrace of a coffee shop on the edge of the crowded concourse, scanning faces for Barry From West Palm and wondering why, with the Club Toledo less than twenty minutes away in South Beach, Barry had chosen the mall for the drop-off, a heavyset man wearing a suit the color and texture of wilted lettuce dropped into the chair across from him.

"Ever have trouble sleeping, Robert?" he asked and dabbed at his face as if at something spilled. As he folded and refolded the white linen handkerchief, the monogram HS appeared and disappeared.

Robert tried to place him. Except perhaps for the sweating, the guy was ordinary and anonymous looking as a peeled potato.

"The name's Henry Swolt, and I'd say close to fifty hours for me." He stopped a waitress and ordered a glass of ice water and a slice of Key lime pie and, as an afterthought, a refill on Rob's coffee.

"You look like you need the caffeine. Me, ice water's fine. Fifty hours, wide awake, a quirky metabolism, it's just something you learn to live with. You, though, I'd say you have no problem with sleep. A few nightmares maybe, but otherwise no problem. With me, it's not so much a problem as a condition. The tan Chevrolet following you all afternoon, that was me."

Robert kept his mouth shut and his eyes on the crowd for Barry From West Palm. Below the terrace in the center of the mall was a large fountain and next to it a float in the form of a papier-mâché pirate ship. Buccaneers were singing and waving cardboard swords.

"You didn't know that," Swolt said. "I picked you up off the causeway and stayed with you all afternoon. It confirms what I was thinking, you having no trouble sleeping. Of course, I was sure of that at the end of May at Miami International when I lifted the envelope with the phonebook in it you were to pass on to Lauter."

It can't be, Robert thought. It can't. But Swolt's lopsided smile told him it was.

The waitress who brought their order was a thin brunette with pale skin. She wore a pair of tight black pants, blue shoes with absurdly high heels, and a pirate's hat. Someone had pen-and-inked a skull and crossbones on her left cheek. After passing out the order, she left Rob and Swolt with an "Ahoy mates" delivered with all the enthusiasm of someone picking a scab, and walked away, wobbling on her heels as if the floor were the deck of a pitching ship.

"Still," Swolt said, when Robert wouldn't respond, "I'd say you've come a long way since Miami International. Watching you today, I knew Mr. Robert Staples had stepped into the game. I'd say, too, you're going to find it a little difficult to step out of it, especially when you're going to have to explain to your friends how you lost another delivery. It's going to raise some serious doubts on their parts about you." Swolt sat back and steepled his fingertips. "Unless."

Unless. Robert let the word roll by him. Where the hell was Barry? Robert kept his face expressionless and looked across the table at Swolt. It seemed impossible, given the mall's air conditioning, but the man was still sweating. His wide bland face glistened, and the armpits of the pale green suit coat were dark.

"A little talk is what I'm proposing," Swolt said.

"We don't have anything to talk about."

"I think we do, yes."

"No. You're wrong there."

Swolt pulled on his earlobe and tilted his head. "You know about sleep, don't you, Rob? Sleep's a gift from the gods. It keeps the world from eating us up. We're reborn each morning. But it's a gift with a catch. If you're reborn each morning, you never grow up. Sleep keeps us stupid. You discover that if you don't sleep, that sleep is as much a trick as it is a gift." Swolt leaned back and placed the glass of ice water against his temples. "I don't believe you've woken up yet, Rob."

Another float, smaller but also in the form of a ship, was being pulled up the concourse toward the first one. At its prow stood a woman with thick black hair spilling down the middle of her back. Wearing a silver swimsuit bisected by a banner reading MISS SHIVER ME TIMBERS, she was flanked by two tiny Cuban women who appeared to be twins and wore MISS FIRST MATE and MISS CABIN PERSON across their red-and-blue swimsuits. They threw handfuls of chocolate coins wrapped in gold foil at the crowd.

Swolt touched Robert's wrist. "Let's get down to business. What did you tell the FBI?"

"What are you talking about?"

"The FBI. I imagine you've heard of the organization, Rob. What I want to know is what you told them."

"Why would I talk to the FBI?"

"They're pretty sure I snatched the phonebook. They don't want the DEA to get credit."

"I haven't talked to them."

"I find that hard to believe. Honestly, I'd say that is improbable, given the circumstances. I've heard things around the office. No co-ordination. Failure to follow proper channels. Violations of procedure. The FBI acting on its own. It's not the first time. Customs and the CIA do all the time, too. Tell me what you said. Approximately."

"Approximately nothing."

"Information. Bits and pieces. You provide, and I'll put them together."

"Why don't you tell me? I don't know what's going on here."

"Did they offer you a deal? If so, well, I'm prepared also."

"I never talked to them."

The smaller float pulled up next to the larger one, and the three women boarded the ship next to the fountain. The mall manager presented a bouquet of roses to Miss Shiver Me Timbers. She took one and put it between her teeth, and more cardboard sword waving and cheers arose from the crowd.

Robert turned from the railing and leaned back in his chair. Swolt wasn't the only one sweating here. Robert knew he was keeping his features composed, but Swolt was right. There was no way he could explain losing two deliveries. Swolt's presence and the little mall show below him reminded Robert of everything he had to lose and had already lost.

"Off the record, that's the situation here. I have no particular interest in busting you." Swolt reached under the table with obvious effort and lifted the duffle bag containing Robert's afternoon pickups. "A little cooperation on your part, I forget I ever knew you. You walk."

Where, Robert thought. He was reminded of how he'd offered False Walter the money to leave Key West and the kid had asked the same thing: *where*.

"A way out," Swolt said. "That's what I'm offering you."

"I don't think so."

Swolt's fingers keyboarded up and down a gray-and-green striped tie, stopping on each trip to caress the monogram on its lower half. "You don't like hearing this, do you, Rob, I can tell, it's bothering you, the fact I'm awake and you're not, but it's a machine, Rob, a big greasy machine that makes all this happen, and you're a part, and your associates are a part, and I am too. A machine, big and black, that runs everything and doesn't distinguish between the official and unofficial."

Rob began to sense an opening. Swolt was stretching, ready to grab anything that passed for an explanation or connection. Robert felt a strange, momentary empathy. He had been there too. Ask Heidi.

"Why do you need me if you have the duffle bag? Or, for that matter, if you snatched the phonebook?"

"Significance depends on how you define the circumstances surrounding it. It's a connect-the-dots picture." Swolt waved to the waitress for more ice water. He still hadn't touched his pie. "Nothing is quite unofficial anymore. That's the problem I keep running into with this investigation. The unofficial has a way of overlapping with the official. There used to be clearly drawn lines. Now I have to draw them myself."

"And where are they supposed to lead?"

"Toward something major at the end of summer. A lot of the lines run from Lauter, and I can't connect them all, but I know they do. I have the phonebook from the airport and this duffle bag that will help me figure that out. And you."

Robert decided to take a chance. It was a hunch, that's all, but it felt right. "I just realized something, Swolt. You're mavericking it, aren't you? The DEA doesn't know what their boy is doing. And you don't know shit. You're working on your own here."

Swolt held up the bag again and attempted a smile that never quite came off. "Evidence, Rob, right here. All I need."

"I don't think so. If it was, you wouldn't need me. You're fishing, Swolt. You don't understand what was in the phonebook you lifted, and you won't understand what's in the bag."

Swolt put the bag back on the floor. "I understand hair implants, Rob, and I understand what I have in my possession makes a lot of people nervous. I'm figuring out the why and how here, but I'm the one who has to do it. The agency bigwigs have another name for it. Occupational stress syndrome they call it and graciously arrange a short leave of absence. But they did it because I was awake and wasn't tricked by sleep anymore."

Swolt appeared reduced to a handful of gestures and expressions. His face was as flushed and shiny as a waxed apple. "Stanley Rose thought he could trick me right after I snatched the phonebook. Stanley, my boss, is an agreeable and funny man. He collects Puerto Rican and Cuban jokes. Over three thousand of them. He keeps them on his desk on index cards in little metal file boxes. Has them cross-referenced too. Always a joke to put you at ease. 'What do you call a Cuban in a pink Cadillac with a flat tire and no spare?' You know, stuff like that."

Swolt pulled out his handkerchief and went through his mopping routine. It didn't appear to do much good. "I've known Stanley for going on seven years. He did his job, not much more, but the point is he did his job. What I'm saying is I *knew* Stanley.

"Then I go into his office, he wants an update on my progress with Lauter, and the funny thing is Stanley's head is wrapped in bandages. Hair implants. Now, Stanley is a middle-range supervisor at the agency. He's basically inconspicuous but has access to a certain amount of information. I understand hair implants are expensive. When I think of hair implants, I think of Frank Sinatra, people like that, not Stanley Rose. But as I said, Stanley is an agreeable and accommodating fellow. Concerned too. He was the one that recommended the leave of absence."

Swolt was all faulty wiring. There was still a good chance of getting the duffle bag back. Robert decided to see if he could push the right button. "Calle Ocho. You were there, weren't you, Swolt? The Derrota Newsstand. You've been a part of this all along."

Swolt seemed simultaneously pleased and pained by the reference. He loosened his tie and sat up straighter. "The Derrota Newsstand in Little Havana, yes. That's where a lot of the Cuban drug people met, not the pushers, but the movers, the old ones, they'd meet there, drink coffee, tell Batista stories, talk about the old days, and set up drug deals.

"My partner, Carl Lamm, and me, that March we'd been staking the place out the best we could because we knew something major was going down very soon. It was Carl who brought his brother Seymour into the agency. He pulled strings, a lot of them, but got him in."

Swolt paused, waiting for a reaction. When the one Robert produced didn't satisfy him, he repeated, "Seymour Lamm."

"I don't know a Seymour Lamm."

Swolt cut into the Key lime pie before him but left the fork embedded in the wedge. "I'm disappointed, Rob. You said 'Calle Ocho,' and I therefore thought you understood."

"I did too," Rob lied. He was trying to surreptitiously stretch his leg and hook the bag on Swolt's side of the table, but he stopped at what Swolt said next. It was too much to believe.

"Seymour Lamm is the brother of Carl Lamm, my former partner. Seymour Lamm is Barry From West Palm."

"What?" Robert's mouth went dry. "I don't understand. Barry was agency? That's impossible."

Swolt shook his head and then took a drink of ice water. "Barry

From West Palm came after Calle Ocho. Think about it. He was billing himself as a designated hitter. You want somebody dead, you going to call up someone named Seymour Lamm?"

"I see what you mean."

"Maybe." Swolt looked as if he were undergoing apoplexy. The front of his shirt was soaked through, and his face was two shades beyond livid. He began to pull repeatedly on his coat sleeves. "Carl and I had the Derrota covered. A well-placed informant, everything. We were ready to move."

Rob was able, just barely, to piece the rest of the incident together. Swolt rambled and babbled, his speech rushed and repetitive, bordering at times on the incoherent, the details of the bust like a bag of marbles dropped on a slippery floor.

A lot of it had to do with his partner, Carl Lamm, the quality of his work and friendship, and how hard they'd worked to put together the Derrota Newsstand bust and what it would mean to both of them, the promotions, raises, commendations, as well as the professional pleasure of being able to put away some of the old Cuban drug kingpins.

Everything, Swolt said over and over, had been set, a reliable informant, Carl Lamm able to pass himself off as a buyer, the Cubans ready to deal, everything going as it should, they're ready to move in, and then the backup turns out to be Barry From West Palm, née Seymour Lamm, the backup being standard procedure, but his time, Swolt said, it didn't feel right. And he didn't remember until it was too late that Barry wasn't the backup who'd been assigned to the Derrota.

Everything went right: They made the buy, Swolt brought in the money, the Cubans laid out the coke, Carl and he were ready to bring out their badges, and then Barry From West Palm stepped through the door, looked around, and started shooting.

He killed everybody in the room. Or almost everybody. Swolt survived. Seymour Lamm picked up the money and coke, walked out of the Derrota Newsstand, and became Barry From West Palm.

Then Robert made the mistake of asking Swolt why he hadn't busted Barry. He was an eyewitness, after all, and had the wounds to prove it.

"You don't understand, do you, Robert, you said 'Calle Ocho,' but you don't understand, you're still asleep. I just bust Barry, right, the man who set us up, killed his own brother. I mean, I was there, I finger him, justice is served. Except by the time I'm well enough to testify, Barry claims he wasn't the backup at the Derrota, was nowhere near it, he and his partner were working Hialeah, tracking down some leads on a marijuana deal, his partner corroborates the story, they have witnesses, never mind what kind, the witnesses can place Barry and his partner at the track at the time of the Derrota shooting, suddenly there's no case, only a back room in a newsstand full of dead bodies, the agency's money missing, and people are asking *me* questions about procedure, because now the backup, a man named James Winde, who was supposed to be there, is claiming he called my partner and me, told us he'd be late and to wait for him, saying Carl and I violated procedure by going in without him, claiming by the time he got to the Derrota, it was all over, everybody shot, the money and coke gone, so Barry ends up walking, he's clean, and I lose everything, my partner, my promotion, the case officially closed, or as Stanley Rose, my boss, is famous for saying between Puerto Rican and Cuban jokes, 'Big cases, big problems, small cases, small problems, no . . .'"

Swolt slumped in his chair and gulped ice water. Out of the morass of details in Swolt's account, Robert kept coming back to one: James Winde was DEA and was supposed to be the backup for the Derrota Newsstand operation. That explained what Denice had on Winde. She had come into the Derrota through her connection with Hannibal Binder. Hannibal had filled in that piece of the puzzle when they'd talked in the Meridian Bar about Denice's relationship with her father and how she'd run off, gotten married, lost her husband, and then hooked up with Hannibal and his friends. Robert figured that's when Denice must have met and become involved with James Winde. Denice had also been filling her scrapbooks and keeping her journals the whole time, and they probably accounted for the on-again-off-again quality of Denice and Winde's relationship. Winde couldn't press too hard or Denice would expose him. It also explained why it would be in Winde's best interests to keep tabs on Denice.

"It's time to go. We have to finish this," Swolt said.

"I can't help, not like you think," Rob said after Swolt explained they were going back to his house and then through the contents of the duffle bag and phonebook.

"I'm not talking about a choice anymore, Rob."

"You're misreading the situation."

"I don't think so. No. I saw you at Miami International with Lauter, and I can tie you to Russell Tills and Hannibal Binder. You're driving Barry's car and fucking Denice Shell. You're the dot that will help me connect them all. You'll help me make a picture that'll make Stanley Rose's hair implants stand on end."

Robert kept trying to explain, but nothing he said could erase the half smile or odd combination of smugness and desperation playing across Swolt's face. He started in again, trying another angle, but Swolt interrupted.

Swolt brought in Calle Ocho once more, what had started there, Barry From West Palm not acting on his own, the hit instead bankrolled by Lauter, the opening it created, the point all those dead Cuban coke kings made, Lauter fronting for the Colombians, expanding their market and cutting himself, Tills, and Binder a big piece of it too, the Derrota Newsstand the beginning of it all, the opening Lauter had made for himself, and how Robert was going to help Swolt close it once and for all.

"Fifty hours or six years, Rob, at times they're the same." Swolt got up from the table and looked at his untouched piece of pie as if he didn't recognize what it was. Then he did something that Robert hadn't counted on. Swolt handcuffed the duffle bag to his wrist.

In the center of the mall, Buccaneer Days was reaching its finale. Miss Shiver Me Timbers in the silver swimsuit was making the mall manager as well as the owners of other shops and stores walk the plank. The Cuban twins were helping by applying black blindfolds. Miss Shiver Me Timbers shook the men's hands before they walked out on the diving board that had been rigged to the side of the float and off into the fountain whose waters were filled with dozens of plastic toy sharks. The Dade County Community College Marching Band was playing a medley of Jimmy Buffett tunes.

Outside, in the parking lot, the light was bright and intense. Robert fumbled for his sunglasses. Swolt couldn't locate his car. They wandered up and down the rows, Swolt growing more and more frustrated in the heat and his exhaustion. From the back, his suitcoat looked like a wet and wrinkled dollar bill.

Then Barry From West Palm stepped out from behind a black van and said, "Henry, that piece of shit you drive, you looking for it, it's over there, section T, row five." Barry gestured with his free hand toward the lower edge of the lot. "Henry, what say you and Robert walk down there, nice and casual, and we'll all go for a ride?"

The duffle bag handcuffed to his wrist made Swolt awkward. His hand had barely made it beneath the lapels of his coat before Barry From West Palm shot him twice in the face.

R OBERT ASKED WHERE THEY WERE GOING. He addressed
the words to the back of Barry From West Palm's head. Barry was
driving, and he had a head. Lennie Ash was sitting next to Barry, and
he had a head. Robert was in the backseat, and he had one. Swolt
was in the backseat, too, and he didn't. Or not much of one.

"We got to make a pit stop," Barry said, "and then I think it's a
good idea we take Swolt home. He's had a long day." Barry pulled
into a self-serve Sav-Mor and gave Lennie some cash, telling him to
buy two five-gallon gas containers and then fill them up.

Barry leaned over the seat and tapped Rob on the shoulder. "What
you think about the Camaro? I bet you never been in a machine
handles like that. I do all the work on her myself. Wash and wax too,
once a week minimum. Not like this piece of shit we're driving now.
Pure Agency. They always buy mom-and-pop cars. Four door, no
chrome, as much class as a fucking box. But the Camaro, it's a real
dream."

Robert agreed. A real dream. A numbness was settling in him that
he wasn't sure if he should fight or encourage.

Barry leaned over again. "Hey, you doing okay, Rob? You look a
little green there. You want me to tell Lennie get you a Fudgesicle?
They'll settle your stomach right away, those things. You talk to some
people, they say Tums, Rolaids, Pepto-Bismol, all that shit, but me,
I say Fudgesicles, that's the ticket."

Lennie came back with two red gas containers and wedged them
between his legs in the front seat. The lock to the trunk was jammed.
At the mall, Barry didn't want Swolt leaking all over his Camaro, so

they'd been forced to take Swolt's car and put the body in the backseat. After all, Barry had said, it was Miami. Play it like the emperor's new clothes.

The frightening thing was it had worked. Barry had shot a man in the face in a crowded mall parking lot in broad daylight. Then they put the body in the car and drove away. No high-speed chases or wailing sirens. Everything that should have happened didn't.

A few blocks from the Sav-Mor, Barry told Rob and Lennie to roll down their windows. "The air conditioning just won't cut it," he said, slipping through an intersection on a yellow light. "Every time, you can count on it. Knife, strangle, drown, or shoot them, every time they die, they shit their pants. Can you believe it? Going out with a pantsful of shit, the last thing you do? Something like that, it makes you think. You ask me, undertakers earn every cent they make."

Fifteen minutes later, they pulled up in front of Swolt's house behind a car of the same make and color. Swolt's lawn was neat and freshly mown. A line of red roses fronted the porch, and the house reminded Rob of the ones in Key West on Olivia near the cemetery. Picturesque poverty. Simple and severe, all straight lines and right angles, a squat sister to the suburban tract homes from the early fifties. There were two oversize lightning rods jutting from the roof and three pieces of metal lawn furniture on the front porch behind the border of roses.

The front door opened, and James Winde walked quickly down to the car. When he got close enough for a look in the backseat, he abruptly stopped, raised his white eyebrow, composed himself, and glanced casually around the neighborhood. Winde gave his best version of a politican's smile and leaned down to the open driver's window. "Jesus Christ, Barry", he hissed. "What's going on here? No, don't answer that. Just get the car in the fucking garage and then come into the house. We'll talk there."

The garage was connected to the house by a small closed-in walkway. Barry, Lennie, and Robert found Winde in the kitchen, standing to the side of the window and carefully checking out the street. The air conditioning was off, and while the house was stifling, Winde had yet to break into a sweat. He was a little over six feet tall and thick but not yet running to fat and knew how to dress to appear slimmer than he was. Every crease of his suit was sharp and straight, nothing wrinkled or out of place. Rob figured him for his late thirties, but the face still retained many of its boyish features, his cheeks tanned and smooth shaven and his thick black hair carefully combed except for a lock which broke across his forehead, curling above that single white eyebrow.

"I suppose you can explain," Winde said, stepping up to the kitchen table and looking at Barry.

Barry readjusted the Jake's Crab House cap on his head. "Sure, Jim. Nothing complicated about it. Swolt was going to shoot. I shot him first."

"Why not go for a disable? Why the face? Didn't it occur to you we might need Swolt alive, at least for a while longer?" Winde dropped his hands to the back of the kitchen chair and squeezed.

Barry shrugged. "Chalk it up, an off day. My aim was a little high, so what?"

"I can give you a *so what*, Barry. A large one." Winde let go of the chair and swept his arm around the room. "The phonebook's not here. I've already gone over the place twice. You and these other two stooges are going to end up costing me my appointment. The President's Commission is in the process of reviewing candidates for heading up the new task force. My name's in that goddamn phonebook. As are the names of a number of other of my colleagues in the DEA. If that book surfaces now, it could wreck my whole career. And if that happens, I promise I'm not going down alone."

Barry leaned over and tapped Rob's shoulder. "You said the book was here, right?"

Rob shook his head no. "That's what Swolt said. All I know is that we were supposed to come back to the house. He thought I could help him explain some things in the book."

"Shit." Winde banged the top of the kitchen table and walked to the sink. "That doesn't help at all. Swolt could have had the phonebook stashed somewhere else and planned to pick it up on the way in." Winde suddenly turned and pointed at Robert. "Did you have it drawn?"

"What?" Robert asked.

"You were right there with Barry and Swolt. Why didn't you draw that piece you're carrying under your shirt and cover Swolt? If you had, Swolt would be sitting here now and answering questions."

"Everything happened too fast," Robert said. "I didn't have time to think." He returned Winde's gesture, pointing at him across the room. "You weren't there, so you can't know what it was like."

"No, I wasn't," Winde agreed, "and I wasn't at the airport when you let Swolt snatch the goddamn book in the first place. It seems like every time I turn around, you're in my life, fucking it up one way or another. What Denice sees in you is beyond me."

Robert quickly stepped up and swung. By reflex, he slipped into the predictable moves that would fit an action sequence in one of the Worldwide films and remembered too late how the fights were nothing but choreography. Winde did not slam into the wall and lie still or fall across the table and break it in half. He simply absorbed Rob's punch and countered with his own, and Rob was on his knees on the kitchen floor and holding his throbbing stomach. He sensed Winde coming in for more and started to turn away, but it was Barry's hands that hooked him under the arms and lifted him to his feet. Robert moved to the table and sat down.

"I think I'll go wait in the car," Lennie Ash said. They were his first words since entering the house. He started for the door to the walkway and then stopped. "Oh, man. I forgot. Swolt's still in the backseat."

"Sure," Winde said, unclenching his fists. "That's a perfect place to stash a body. Why bother with the trunk?"

Barry From West Palm started laughing. He began twirling the car keys on his index finger. "Right under our noses," he said. "Swolt, it's just like him, doing something like that." Winde looked as if he was going to lose his temper and start swinging again until Barry explained that the trunk of Swolt's car was jammed. "Might be a good idea, what say, to check it out," he said. "Never know what we might find."

After Winde, Lennie, and Barry left for the garage, Robert wandered around Swolt's house, rubbing his stomach and trying to even his breathing. The exterior of the place might have made the requisite stabs at propriety, but the interior held, all too clearly, the signs of the single life. Dishes that were left a day too long. The notes of things to do taped to the refrigerator door. The pants and shirts draped over the living room furniture. A half-completed crossword puzzle on the floor next to a worn plaid easy chair. A dogeared *TV Guide* next to the remote control. Despite the signs of Swolt's presence, the house didn't feel lived in. It was more like something had been lived out there.

The bedroom was the worst. Swolt had covered most of the wall directly across from the bed with posterboard. On it were hundreds of names, dates, and places, all written in a tight, constipated hand and connected by lines and arrows that looked like they'd been erased and redrawn countless times. The wall resembled a cross between diagrams of football plays and strings of mathematical equations.

The bed still held Swolt's shape, the signature of his insomnia, and Robert wondered how many nights Swolt had lain there and stared at the posterboard on the wall. He wondered what Swolt had seen when he tried to connect the names, dates, and places, and what they had come to mean to him.

No. Robert knew what they had come to mean. They meant the end of a man, one with wide bland features, a set of overworked sweat glands, a predilection for monograms, and an obsession over what had started and ended in the Derrota Newsstand six years ago. They meant, as Barry From West Palm had said, going out with a pantsful of shit.

Robert heard a noise behind him and turned. Barry stood in the bedroom doorway, holding a container of gas in each hand. "Tilt on the trunk action," he said. "Nothing in there but a spare and that was leaky. Winde left but said to go on and torch the place. He'd already been over it twice and no luck. Even if he missed the book, ten gallons of unleaded ought to do the job. This place will go up easy."

Barry From West Palm started in back, at the bathroom, pouring a line down the halls along the walls, then moving into the bedroom and soaking down the mattress and box springs. He sent Rob into the kitchen to look for matches.

When Rob came back, Barry had just finished soaking down the living room. The smell of gasoline was overpowering, bringing tears to their eyes. Barry pointed to the worn plaid sofa and said, "I figured we'd leave Swolt there or on the bed, but another idea, it just hit me. Toss me those matches and then tell Lennie to pull the car out front and park. You wait with him."

Less than five minutes later, as a silent Lennie Ash kept the car idling along the curb, Robert looked over Swolt's bloodstained shoulder at Barry From West Palm crouched in the doorway. He lit the book of matches, waited until it caught and flared, and tossed it into the house. Barry walked quickly across the lawn and slid behind the wheel Lennie had vacated, and they were off. They kept the car windows down to blow out the smell of gasoline and what was left of Swolt.

THE LIGHT WAS BEGINNING TO SOFTEN when Barry turned the car onto Poinciana Drive in Coconut Grove, the Atlantic and surrounding lawns losing some of the brashness of their afternoon primary colors. Sailboats tacked toward the marinas. Barbecue grills were going. Well-groomed people, dressed in pastel sweats or bright shirts and tanktops, walked, jogged, or bicycled. Barry smiled and waved as they drove past. A few blocks later, he pulled into the driveway of a mammoth stuccoed house with a red tiled roof and a honeycomb of cool dark arches.

Barry walked in the front door without knocking and was back after a couple minutes. He told Lennie to put the car in the side drive. Rob and Lennie were then to join him out back.

Russell Tills was sitting along the pool with a pitcher of margaritas for company. Wearing a pair of Ray-Bans, a green paisley print robe, and clogs, he kept crossing and recrossing his legs when Barry pulled up a chair and motioned Rob and Lennie over. Russell Tills repeatedly rang a small silver bell next to the margaritas and looked toward the back door.

"I already told you," Barry said. "Nobody home but you, Russell."

Russell kept ringing the bell.

"Welcome to Florida," Lennie Ash said quietly over Rob's shoulder.

When Rob asked what he meant, Lennie smiled and stepped away. He seemed to have sobered up suddenly.

Russell kept ringing the bell every thirty seconds or so.

"Your arm, it's going to get tired," Barry said. "I'm telling you, your two Cuban boys, the ones you're so proud of, aren't home yet."

Russell put down the bell and picked up a margarita. "How'd you get in here?"

"The front door, Russell. I turned the knob and went in. You got a little careless, must have had your mind on other things." Barry poured himself a drink. "See, your Mariel boys ran into a little car trouble out at the Lincoln Road Mall. You know that silver El Dorado you loaned them, Russell? Well, the damnedest thing happened to it while your boys were in the mall seeing what Robert was up to. Somebody took the distributor cap and cut a bunch of the spark plug wires on the machine. Top it off, two of the tires got punctured." Barry took a sip of the drink and smacked his lips. "I'm guessing here, Russell, but I bet the reason you haven't heard from your boys, they're afraid to call or come back until they get that car fixed, on account they know how much their boss loves that Caddy."

Russell tried to leave the table, but Barry grabbed the hem of the paisley robe. Russell's attempts to get free made the whole thing look like a slapstick routine, the curvaceous blonde with her skirt caught in the elevator door, except in this case the cheesecake shot that resulted was mostly pathetic. Russell wore a red swimsuit no bigger than a handkerchief and had old-man legs, spindly, all bone and vein.

"What, you going to desert your guests, Russell? If we're talking gracious host here, I think you better brush up on your etiquette, otherwise we might feel slighted, you trying to get up and leave. We might get the impression you don't like the company, and we're not welcome here. So, come on, sit down. We can't stay long anyway."

Russell sat back down. He tried to appear composed but couldn't keep himself from checking the doors at the back of the house every so often. Barry waved Lennie over and whispered something. Lennie nodded, then motioned for Rob to follow him. They walked back to the side drive and the car. Lennie told Rob to wait and disappeared in the direction of a groundskeeping shed behind the garage. Rob heard glass break and then the creak of a door. A couple of minutes later, Lennie reappeared, pushing a red wheelbarrow. He dropped it in front of Robert and said, "You should have seen this coming."

There was no trace of alcohol or hangover in Lennie's voice. Robert again asked what was going on. Lennie kept drilling him with his smile.

"Like I told you on the drive up this morning, Rob," Lennie said, putting his hands on his hips, "you don't belong in this deal because you don't pay attention, and so you end up missing how things work."

"What are you talking about?" Rob backed against the car and crossed his arms on his chest.

"Maybe I should have talked to Russell and had him set me up in the movies instead of T-shirts," Lennie said. "After all, I didn't do too bad of a job acting at the Club Toledo today. I was a pretty convincing drunk. You bought the show."

"Why are you doing this?" Robert kept trying to get behind Lennie's smile. At Robert's back, the car engine ticked as it cooled.

"Call it *Lennie's Revenge*. It's a movie about a guy with a T-shirt chain who's got a lot of lawyer and money problems. He's just about to put the bite on another character named Russell Tills for enough money to make those problems disappear. Then this other character who's a real asshole spoils everything by telling someone named Hannibal Binder about the meeting." Lennie paused, smiling again. "Want me to tell you how it ends, Rob?"

Robert shook his head and stepped away from the car. "Look, I'm sorry, Lennie. About saying anything to Hannibal. And everything else. When I lost the phonebook, Franklin Benjamin Lauter threatened to make my life a bigger mess than it was if I said anything to you about what was going on. Lauter and Hannibal knew you had close ties to Russell and wanted Russell out of the picture before they let you in. I'm sorry, but it's just the way it was."

"Well, you're right about the *was*," Lennie said. "You see, I had a couple of my own meetings with Hannibal, and he put in some calls to Lauter. And today while you were running errands in the Camaro, Barry and I had the chance to get some things straightened out. So, Rob, things look okay for me. I'd already gotten myself in the clear before Swolt ended up dead. Hannibal and the others don't have any doubts about Lennie Ash."

Lennie smiled and pointed at the car, then the wheelbarrow. "Barry's expecting you and Swolt poolside," he said and walked off.

Robert turned and looked into the backseat. He walked away and then circled back. The tar on the drive was still soft from the day's heat and pulled on the soles of his shoes. He looked at the red wheelbarrow and then at his hands.

Everything was perspective, he told himself. First you found it; then you had to maintain it. He took the packet of coke from his front pocket and did two fat lines off the hood of the car. Then he opened the rear passenger door and climbed in.

Perhaps he could see it as one of those word problems in algebra, he thought. *There is a dead DEA agent in the backseat of a car. Most of his head is missing. A former actor in low-budget horror films has to move the body from the car to a wheelbarrow. How long will it take the former actor to get the body poolside before he has to admit the absolute monstrosity of the action?*

No matter how Robert positioned himself, Swolt kept folding in unlikely places and slipping out of his grasp. It was like trying to handle a two-hundred-pound bag of ice cubes. Robert worked with his eyes closed for a while, but that somehow made it worse. He knew it was impossible, but it felt like Swolt was still sweating. Robert crouched, getting his hands under Swolt's arms and pressing his head against Swolt's chest, then lifted and pushed. He repeated the sequence two more times, and the body flopped out of the car and into the wheelbarrow. He arranged the position of the arms and legs so that the weight was distributed more evenly and then wheeled the body into the backyard.

"Hey, look who dropped by to see you, Russell," Barry said, standing up. "Your pal, Henry Swolt, from the DEA. He probably wants to see if you have any more tips for him. He's done following up the tip you gave him after our talk at the Club Toledo. He followed that one up, just like you said to."

Russell Tills didn't attempt to deny it. He winced when Rob wheeled the body next to the table after Barry had waved him over the rest of the way. Then in a voice holding more margaritas than hope, Russell asked Barry not to kill him. The whole thing, tipping off Swolt about Rob's pickups, he said was just a judgment of error.

"One thing I'll say for you, Russell, is you got a way with words. 'A judgment of error,' I guess that's one way of looking at it. I bet you old Henry Swolt would agree with that. Especially with his 'head off fucking shot.' I'm using your lingo here, Russell, figure maybe we can understand each other better than earlier at the Club. Then, I'd say, 'your ass up your head was.'"

"Listen, tell Lauter I understand now. It was a mistake. I was angry and wanted some payback. I'll step out of the deal willingly. This isn't necessary. I'll be gone, four days at the most. I remember you mentioning Switzerland."

Barry leaned over and took Swolt's limp hand and began to pat Russell on the shoulder with it. "A lot of ocean between Switzerland and Miami, Russell, and I'm thinking, if you're up on survival techniques, the plane goes down. Some practice might be in order here." He pointed at the pool.

Barry grabbed Russell's right wrist and held it while he handcuffed it to Swolt's. Robert picked up the duffle bag where it had fallen on the pool tiles. Lennie walked over to the table and made a show of pouring himself a large drink. He lifted it in Rob's direction and smiled.

Barry tipped back his Jake's Crab House cap and told Robert to take out the Smith & Wesson Airweight. He waved, signaling Robert to hurry up. "Come on," he said, "if you're in this." Barry took two steps back and said, "Shoot him."

Robert stood at the edge of the pool and held the gun and tried to figure out *him*. He looked down and saw the front of his shirt and pants were damp and sticky. There was something he needed to say, but it slipped away each time he opened his mouth.

Connect the dots, Swolt would have said.

If you want, Denice had said. Nothing halfway.

"It was a mistake," Russell Tills said. "I see that now. Really."

"Come on, Rob," Barry From West Palm said. "He won't know the difference. I already started the job."

"You mean—Swolt?"

"Did I say Russell?"

"Why Swolt?"

"It's called 'accessory,' Rob. You say you're in this, shoot him. I want a commitment."

"But he's already dead."

"Shoot him."

"It doesn't make any sense."

"A jury'd disagree. Accessory is what we're looking at here."

"I can't."

"Think about it. But not too long."

"I can't."

"Decide."

It was like a sneeze. You didn't decide on a sneeze. It just happened. You could feel it beginning, the way the body gathered itself, and then the sudden release.

Robert shot Swolt in the chest.

Russell Tills started screaming, and Robert, still holding the duffle bag, dropped the arm holding the gun to his side. The echo of the shot continued to run through him.

Then Barry wheeled Swolt to the edge of the pool, Russell crying now, saying it was all a mistake.

"Your Cuban boys come back in time, they'll give you a hand, I'm sure. In the meantime, think Switzerland."

Barry pushed Russell and Swolt into the pool.

Russell's robe billowed, gathered water, and sank. Barry From West Palm stood on the lip of the pool and watched.

"The key to the handcuffs is in Swolt's right pocket," he said. "I wonder if Russell, he'll think of that before his Cubans get back." Barry turned away from the pool and faced Robert. "I suggest we take off. Russell's boys aren't too bright, but they're mean."

Robert handed Barry the blue duffle bag containing the afternoon pickups. Barry laughed and threw it into the pool. "Worked pretty good, didn't it?" he said. "I figured Russell, he'd tip Swolt off after the meeting at the Club Toledo. I knew Swolt would jump at anything connected with the Derrota Newsstand. He followed you all over Miami while you were picking up empty envelopes. A moving mousetrap, that's what you were, Rob. That duffle bag was just a piece of cheese that ended up helping catch Russell and Swolt." Barry loudly snapped his fingers twice and patted Robert on the shoulder.

Lennie, standing next to the table, finished off his margarita. "You should have seen this coming, Rob," he said.

THE BEDROOM WINDOW was open, and a night breeze, persistent as breath, swept down Simonton from the Gulf and filled the curtains.

Denice wore a pair of chartreuse stockings. She lay back, lifted her legs and held them, a **V** that Robert traced and retraced, his fingers following the lines of color, moving slowly, a blind man's careful touch, until he reached the point where material and flesh met, the top of the stockings dark against Denice's thighs, a borderline that he slowly approached and then crossed.

Denice wrapped her legs around Robert and squeezed.

Swolt's face exploded.

Denice touched Robert's cheek, neck, and chest.

You should have seen this coming, Lennie Ash said.

Robert buried his hands in Denice's hair.

Shoot him, Barry From West Palm said.

Denice lifted her hips.

Barry From West Palm crouched in the doorway with a book of matches.

Robert was pushing it away, all of it, the whole day, Robert could do that, there in Denice, push it away, lose everything in the supple folds and fit of her flesh, Robert pressing and plunging, Denice urging him on, Denice in the chartreuse stockings, holding him, Robert wanting to find comfort and release in that embrace, the interlocked flesh, but it was a connection that was either much too simple or complex to quell his trembling, the sudden explosion of nerves that he'd blamed on the lack of hot water when he'd returned from Miami and walked into the house on Simonton and heard Denice in the shower and joined her, stepping into the steam and spray and Denice's long tanned arms, the soap lacing her limbs, standing under the stream of hot water that touched him like Denice touched him, that covered every pore, standing there even after Denice left the shower and called to him, Robert in the shower and all that water covering him and Denice calling to him, the water suddenly and unexpectedly changing from hot to cold and Robert remaining in the shower, unable to bring himself to touch the handles that would cut it off, all that water, suddenly cold, and Denice's voice from the bedroom, and that's when the trembling started, Robert standing under a cold shower and unable to move, listening to Denice call his name, while the water went from hot to cold and numbed him and he couldn't move and he dropped the bar of soap, watched it slide toward the drain, and then the trembling, Denice calling his name and him dropping the soap and alone in the shower, all that water, suddenly cold, and the trembling, the coldness at the very roots of his nerves, and Denice in the next room, the soap sliding around the drain, and Robert stepped out of the shower, walked across the room, and found Denice, who had put on the chartreuse stockings, Denice still damp from the shower as she lay back and lifted her legs, and Robert traced their soft and lean lines, while the windows were full of the Gulf air and the wide night sky, Robert traced and trembled and found an opening that he thought would take him out of the day.

By the time they were finished, they had kicked all the covers and sheets onto the floor. Robert stood by the window, his flesh slowly drying, and watched Denice sleeping. On the other side of the curtain, the wind carried the smell of the ocean, and a new moon hung like half of a set of parentheses in the dark.

And Robert explained to Denice, who was sleeping.

You couldn't kill a man who was already dead. That was a fact. A man without a head was dead and you could shoot him, whether you wanted to or not, and it didn't matter because he was already dead, you might have pulled the trigger, but it didn't really matter because you could shoot him once or a hundred times and it wouldn't matter because he was dead.

Denice had never looked more lovely, and Robert could tell her what he couldn't at other times, because she was sleeping and the ground rules didn't matter right then, and it was just this once, just for tonight, and he wanted to hear the words, needed to speak them.

But Robert, standing by the window, got tangled in the *You're beautiful* and *I love you*.

It should have been easy and simple to say them, but it wasn't. Robert tried again and again to speak them in the stillness, to tell the sleeping woman in the chartreuse stockings something old and simple.

You couldn't, he told Denice, just once, it didn't matter, I pushed the red wheelbarrow, and you lifted your hips, because I was in the backseat, and Barry From West Palm rolled down his window and said it's true, I needed to hear something simple, but I gave him the matches and held you in the shower, and it was a heart shot and too much cold water, and tonight I just wanted another swimming pool, but it doesn't beautiful and you're matter, because, you see, you could pull the trigger but you couldn't love a dead man.

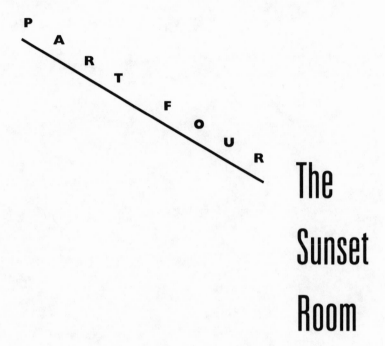

PART FOUR

The Sunset Room

THE SUNSET ROOM was a glassed-in extension of the Club Ultimate built out over the water with an unobstructed view of the Gulf. It was used for private parties of up to twenty-five people. This evening, with only Rob, Denice, Hannibal, and Barry From West Palm in it, the room was full of the forlorn feeling that comes from too few people in too large a space.

"Where's Lennie?" Hannibal asked. "He was supposed to be here a half hour ago."

"Lennie, I figure he's changing his pants again on account he keeps pissing himself every time it hits him what happened." Barry From West Palm took the complimentary book of matches from the ashtray and used its top edge to clean his fingernails. He glanced over at Robert and slowly tilted his head, as if puzzled by something. Robert had caught him doing the same thing a couple of times earlier in the evening and had avoided meeting Barry's eyes each time.

"Lennie better get here soon," Hannibal said. "We have things to talk about."

A week and a half ago, near the middle of July, Franklin Benjamin Lauter had come down from D.C., and they had all sat in this same room and had a legitimate celebration. They had arranged and successfully shipped the acetone, ether, and hydrochloric acid Camar Tavares needed to fuel his processing plants. They'd lucked out with the shipping arrangements, managing to include the chemicals within a load of toxic waste materials that a number of people felt would be better off out of sight, out of mind, and out of the country.

Lauter had also been meeting with his D.C. contacts to secure the money for the first batch of coke and had even been able to deflect some of the interagency interest in Swolt's death. With Russell Tills's departure for Switzerland, the old channels of distribution were gone, and there were a lot of hungry noses around, and if the risks with the present deal were higher and more complicated than Lauter had originally anticipated, well, that was Florida and to be expected. Things were working themselves out. At least that's how it had looked a week and a half ago when they'd sat around the banquet table in the Sunset Room and toasted each other and the deal.

Robert had done what he had to to bring about the moment those glasses were raised. He'd double-checked delivery dates, dropped off bribes to Customs and EPA officials, and helped screen the nonunion crews hired to load the chemicals. There were times when he was faced with a what-is-wrong-with-this-picture moment, when he found himself doing what the person he once was or thought he was would have balked at or refused. Denice would then remind him that wrong was a commodity whose value on the open market was grossly inflated. Robert's perspective would be a whole lot clearer, Denice said, if he took his ethics and shipped them out on the tanker with the toxic wastes and chemicals. It became a question of Robert's getting properly adjusted, and Hannibal Binder helped out by providing Robert with all the adjustment he needed. The cocaine was not a substitute or an excuse. It was there, and so was he. Things happened. Things needed to be done. The cocaine was there to help frame the picture each moment held.

Last night, Lauter had flown out of D.C. for Medellín with half the money for five hundred kilos of pure cocaine at twenty thousand per kilo from Tavares's plants. Stateside the cocaine would be worth anywhere from eighteen to twenty-four million, depending on how it was cut and the elasticity of the market. It would be worth even more if it were converted to crack, which was what Hannibal was lobbying for.

It had been difficult not to get lost in the magic of the numbers. All day, Robert, Denice, Hannibal, Lennie, and Barry From West Palm had waited for Lauter's call confirming the closing of the deal in Colombia. It had been a long wait. A six o'clock news bulletin ended it.

Robert had been in the shotgun house on Simonton and might have missed the television bulletin completely if Denice hadn't suddenly thrown her glass of wine against the living room wall.

The television had flashed pictures of the downed plane, its pieces strewn over the side of a mountain in Colombia with five body bags laid out in a small clearing.

While Robert listened to the commentator, he did some elementary arithmetic. The pilot and copilot equaled two. Senator Jason Casings, his aide, and Congresswoman Susan Billings equaled three. Three plus two did not add up to Franklin Benjamin Lauter.

Lauter was and was not supposed to have been on the plane. Senator Casings's fact-finding tour in South America had been the perfect cover for Lauter to close the deal with Camar Tavares. Courtesy of the U.S. government, Lauter had caught a ride to Colombia, prudently deciding to travel as a John Doe since as Franklin Benjamin Lauter he'd already taken enough trips over the last few months to draw some unwelcome attention. Ghosting on junkets like Casings's was a common enough practice anyway, a convenient accommodation for mistresses or business associates on unofficial business.

The pilot's log, recovered from the crash, had shown four passengers though, one more than the five in the body bags. There had been bullet holes found in the pieces of the fuselage, and the Colombian government was blaming the whole incident on the *coqueros*. The downed plane was part and parcel of their style of retaliation for U.S. government interference in the drug trade. But so far the old cocaine cartel people had not claimed responsibility. The White House was cautiously outraged, having to hold the full force of the moral fury it wanted to loose in the world press because all the bodies recovered from the crash had been burnt beyond recognition, and identification through dental records posed a slight problem since the teeth had been removed from each corpse. Ambiguity tended to take the edge off moral outrage, and D.C. bureaucrats knew better than Robert the potential messy implications of *three plus two*.

Lennie hollered from the doorway of the Sunset Room and hustled over to the table, plopping into the seat next to Barry From West Palm. He was wearing a T-shirt with HE'S NOT HEAVY, BUT HE'S A BOTHER on its front and an overdose of Sagebrush cologne.

Barry From West Palm put down the matchbook and rubbed his nose. "You smell like a Mexican whorehouse in the middle of August."

"Where've you been?" Hannibal asked.

"On the phone with the IRS."

"At eight at night?"

"Those guys never quit. They work in shifts. Always on my case. They're a pack of dogs." Lennie gulped at the draft the waitress placed in front of him. "Any more news?"

"Yeah," Barry From West Palm said, "but I hate to break it to you. You know when you were a kid, all those presents under the tree on Christmas morning? Your parents put them there, not Santa Claus."

"Well, what are we going to do?" Denice asked.

Hannibal was looking out the glass wall facing west where a half moon rode the edge of the horizon and appeared to have risen from the dark waters. Robert remembered Hannibal telling a story about water-skiing from Key West to Cuba on his eighteenth birthday.

"First," Hannibal said, "we have to find out whether Lauter's alive or dead. I called Camar Tavares earlier in the evening, and he's checking into the situation from his end, but for right now, he's as much in the dark as any of us. Nobody seems to know what happened to Lauter."

Hannibal paused and then reached over and took Denice's hand, lightly stroking its back. "We're going to need your help here, Denice. You have to go to D.C. and see your father. He's got the connections to find out what happened. Allen can put in calls to all those CIA cronies of his, and then we'll know what we're looking at."

Denice jerked her hand from Hannibal's and quickly lit a cigarette. "Is a face-to-face necessary? You know how things are between my father and me. It's been an all-out war since I turned seventeen."

"It's time for a truce," Hannibal said quietly, "or at least the appearance of one. Your father has access to what we need to know. I have Winde working on it too, but he has to tread carefully because he's still under review for the task force position. He can't afford to ask too many questions right now."

"Christ, Hannibal," Denice said, waving her cigarette. "You know how difficult my father can be. He's a smug, self-righteous bastard. He whitewashed all his years and dirty tricks for the CIA so that he could champion himself as a defender of Liberty and Justice for the anti-Fidelistas. The man's insufferable."

"But he knows things," Hannibal persisted. "And even smug, self-righteous bastards miss their daughters. You can play that angle for a while."

Denice picked up her glass and looked out the window.

"But what if it turns out Lauter's dead?" Lennie asked.

Hannibal studied Denice for a few seconds before he spoke. "We need to be prepared to make some fast readjustments. Camar Tavares is about to begin processing the coke. We're going to have to find a way to replace the front money that disappeared with Lauter and keep the original investors reassured so they don't back out. That first shipment belongs to us, and we have to make sure it stays that way."

Lennie pulled absently on the neck of his T-shirt and looked around the table. "But aren't those readjustments going to be hard to manage on short notice? What if the backers suddenly get spooked and pull out? We'd be left empty-handed."

"Glad to hear a little concern on your part, Lennie," Barry From West Palm said. "Maybe you're finally getting your attention adjusted so it's on the deal and not on those fucking copyright lawsuits and IRS guys. We've had to cut you a lot of slack lately. Rob, there, had to do half your work on getting those chemicals out because you were always running off to phone your lawyer. You wanted in the deal bad enough. It's time you started paying more attention."

"I know, I know," Lennie said. "I'm working on getting all that straightened out. Don't worry, you can count on me."

After what Rob had seen on the six o'clock news bulletin, he wondered if it was possible to count on anything. He had the taste of *almost* in his mouth again. Everything about the deal had looked fine. Tonight was supposed to be a celebration. Robert had put up half of the $175,000 from the sale of his father's house as his stake in the deal with Tavares. Now it, along with the sixth body, had disappeared in the plane crash. Denice wasn't the only one who had a difficult father to deal with. The fact that his father had died six years ago didn't make his presence any less real tonight in the Sunset Room. Robert had managed to lose in one day what it would have taken his father over half his life to earn.

The waitress stepped up and asked if they were ready to order dinner, and Robert went through the motions of studying the menu, but his mind kept wandering back to the man who'd helped bring him into the world and then raised him when Robert's mother left. His father had been a high-school history teacher, a man of belief, who studied and taught the accumulated mistakes of mankind and never saw his own. He believed in a grand pattern, a great design, into which everything fit. Man was more rational than animal. In his world, the right hand could know what the left was doing, and the sum of three plus two was never in doubt.

"I'll have the swordfish," Hannibal said.

Robert watched the waitress move around the table. She looked impossibly young, thin and gawky behind her uniform, mascara, and lipstick. Another Key West runaway. She could have been False Walter's sister.

"Tell you what," Barry From West Palm said, snapping his menu closed. "Bring me something with claws."

Robert leaned toward Denice. The room's recessed lighting framed her face. She had yet to open her menu. "Do you know what you want?" he asked.

"Yes," Denice said, tapping the rim of her glass with a bright fingernail. "But I'm not sure it's what I'm going to get."

YOU REMIND ME OF SOMEBODY DEAD," Barry From West Palm said. "It didn't register till the other night at the Ultimate when I looked over, you sitting next to Denice. A match, I was thinking, a little blast from the past."

Robert nodded, half-listening. It wasn't exactly the shakes, more like his skin was trying to move in two directions at once. He asked Barry to turn down the air conditioning.

"It's not on."

"Maybe I should have stayed home and rested. I'm not feeling so hot. Why are we going to Fort Lauderdale anyway?"

"Like I was telling you, you been holed up in that house for a day and a half, need to get out for some fresh air." Barry From West Palm pulled up at a red light, looked at Rob, and pointed across the street to a revolving bank sign displaying the time and temperature. "Ninety-eight degrees and you shaking like a fucking dog. Man, my advice, you better slow down a little. That stuff you been getting from Hannibal has been nudged but not stepped on. A little of that, is what I'm saying, will take you a long way."

"I'm maintaining," Robert said.

Barry pulled away from the red light. "A pretty song, that. I'll bet Elvis used to sing the same tune every morning in his Las Vegas shower."

Barry's opinion to the contrary, Rob would have to say he was coping. Things were just a little stressful right now with the whole deal in limbo. He could even hear it in Denice's voice when she called. They had counted on her father and his contacts to have the inside track on information about the downed plane, but so far all their sources came back with contradictory answers. Lauter was dead. Lauter was alive. He was buried in an unmarked grave outside Cliza. He'd been seen getting his shoes shined outside the police station in Bogotá. Denice was going to have to stay in D.C. until something concrete came up, and that just left a bad situation worse. Denice and Robert had already been in one long, drawn-out fight. He had assumed, incorrectly it turned out, that he'd be going with Denice to D.C. Nothing he said or did could make Denice change her mind. Her phone calls from D.C. provided no comfort or reassurance either. Long distance worked equally well to describe their emotional content.

The news from Medellín wasn't much better. Camar Tavares had expressed his concern over Lauter's mortal status but assured Hannibal that the deal was still on: they would get the first batch of coke from his plants. That was fine, but unless their luck suddenly changed, they were faced with replacing the front money that had disappeared along with Lauter.

Things were tense, but Rob was coping. He would appreciate a little more sleep from time to time, but without Denice each night was a torment. He couldn't find rest in any form.

Rob put his head against the back of the seat as Barry From West Palm pushed the Camaro through North Miami, Pembroke Park, and Hollywood, and then on into Fort Lauderdale. Barry kept fingering the radio dial, twisting the plastic Jesus head back and forth, but the radio only seemed capable of pulling in a succession of A.M. stations that filled the front seat with screaming D.J.s, jingles, public service announcements, news, commercials, weather reports, and, occasionally, music. Robert didn't even know who they were going to see. All Barry had told him was that they were going to Fort Lauderdale for a visit.

Just beyond the city limits, they took Route 84 to A1A and then to Seventeenth Street where they hooked up with A1A again as it ran along the coast. Barry became moody and distracted, breaking his silence only once when they passed the Swimming Hall of Fame Museum to tell Robert they had Tarzan's swimming trunks on display there.

The Lauderdale coastal strip held the usual Florida contradictions. The transitions between neighborhoods, business districts, and recreation areas were abrupt or nonexistent. Old buildings were torn down and replaced by new buildings designed to look old. Block after block of small businesses appeared interchangeable. The whole stretch left Rob with the uncomfortable sensation that he was viewing an immense, congested bazaar with the substance of a mirage.

Barry suddenly began pounding on the horn at two senior-citizen pedestrians trying to make it to the median strip and the row of condos two lanes beyond. They raised hands holding Revco prescription bags and waved at Barry to slow down.

He pulled up next to them and stopped. The senior citizens hesitated, smiling uncertainly when Barry leaned out the window.

"Tell you something," he said, "you wave those bags all you want, the next time I'll be taking your teeth out my tires and scraping you off the grille. Think about it. No more shuffleboard or bridge. No more watching the tube in your furnished condo. You see this car coming, wave those little bags again, your kids'll be collecting the insurance and all the cash you got squirreled away same time as I'm hosing you off this machine."

"Easy," Rob said, as Barry squealed away.

Barry one-handed the steering wheel and gestured with the other. "The thing is, they don't know when to die, that's what gets to me, when they're old and won't die, my opinion being we should be like those guys in tribes in Africa, somebody gets old, they take him out and kill him. I wouldn't mind a piece of that action."

Robert didn't doubt it. Barry suddenly pulled into a 7-Eleven, sat drumming his fingers on the steering wheel, and stared through the windshield at the advertisements for Cokes, chili dogs, and Cheez-its. He said he'd be back in a minute and was, climbing into the car with a small brown bag and an expression that said he'd made a decision. He told Robert they had to make another stop.

They went a couple blocks and then got off A1A, taking side streets that were closer to the ocean and full of small retirement homes from the late forties and fifties, small and perfectly square, hidden behind an onslaught of sea grapes, hibiscus, azaleas, and poincianas.

They abruptly left the small retirement homes, and without transition a line of condos appeared, reminding Robert of dominoes set end on end. They were back in beachfront territory, all small cul-de-sacs and white sand and concrete. Barry pulled into the parking lot of the Sand Dollar Estates.

They were halfway to the door and the bored security guard manning it when Barry remembered the bag and sent Robert back to get it. Riding the elevator, Barry inspected its contents and swore. "Strawberry, Raspberry, Banana, Orange, Citrus Mix, Grape, watch, she'll bitch because I didn't get Watermelon. I take one of fucking each off the rack but forgot the Watermelon, and which one you think she'll notice isn't there? You can bet it'll be Waterfuckingmelon."

They got off at the tenth floor and walked down a long, airy hall. The carpet, walls, and doors were all the same soft sand color and made the passageway appear seamless. Barry let himself in the next to the last door from the end of the corridor, not bothering to knock or call out when they entered.

The apartment's insides were spare and severe, all glass, chrome, and imitation wood. The only piece of furniture out of proportion with the others was the television. It swallowed the east corner of the room, the console's controls looking like the instrument panel of a jumbo jet and the screen the size of its windshield. There was also an odor that Robert couldn't immediately place, but halfway across the room, following Barry to the glass doors leading to the balcony, Robert identified it. It was an old person's smell, one he associated with grandmothers' or maiden aunts' homes, an odor of incipient decay and bath powder, both overwhelmingly thick in the effort to cancel each other out.

Barry made Robert stay inside. On the balcony sat an old woman. She slowly unfolded when she realized Barry was standing there, and the first thing Robert noticed from where he stood was the eyes, which were small, dark, and blank as a crab's. Next was the hair, yellow-white and thin, a pink patina of scalp shining through. It was the absence of a chin though that told Rob who she was: Barry's mother. Her face ended at her lower lip, abruptly collapsing like Barry's into a long thin neck.

Her clothes were also hopelessly incongruent with the standard retirement line in Florida as well as with the contemporary lines of the apartment's décor. She wore a dark blue skirt, ankle length, that, along with the stiff white blouse, suggested mourning. But even that effect was undercut by the pair of ostentatiously oversized earrings dangling from the sides of a head no bigger than a large cantaloupe.

Barry dropped the bag of bubble gum into her lap, on which already lay what looked like an eight-by-ten photograph face down. She looked up at Barry and then began scrabbling through the bubble gum, squeezing, smelling, and dropping each pack back into her lap.

"Be back in a minute, Mom," Barry From West Palm said. He led Rob into his mother's bedroom, which, like the rest of the apartment, was spare and functional. There, too, the only thing indicating someone lived there was the odor of lilac bath powder and stale flesh.

Barry began opening closets. Each of them was crammed with his mother's possessions. Barry noticed Rob's bewilderment and said, "The way she sees it is, Jesus when he comes back, Him being busy and all, He's not going to wait around for her to gather her shit, so she packs it all in here, then the angels can carry it back to Heaven for her, no sweat."

Barry tossed two boxes out onto the bedroom floor and moved deeper into the closet. "You figure it out. The woman, she's crazy and won't die. She's sitting on a fortune, and what she do? Nothing. She calls out for groceries, never leaves the place. You saw that outfit in the living room, that monster TV, it set her back over three and a half grand, and what she watch on it? I'll tell you. This TV preacher looks like a car salesman and the Road Runner. Nothing else. She tapes them every time they come on, then watches them over and over all day. That set pulls in two hundred stations minimum and what I'm saying is she watches the Road Runner and a preacher."

Barry came out of the closet with a dark blue suit, expensively cut, but at least five years out of style. He threw it on the bed and went back in the closet. Next he brought out a pair of dirty black dress shoes, a white shirt, and a dark red tie. He threw them on the bed. "Okay, here's the deal. You get changed but keep the door locked. I'll be back in a minute."

"What do you mean?"

"I mean, you put on those clothes and I'll be right back, that's what I'm saying."

"Why?"

Barry sighed. "Just do it. Save the whys for later."

"I don't know, Barry."

"What don't you know? You forget how to take off and put on clothes? I come back, you're dressed. We'll wing it from there. Listen, you do this for me, I owe you. Barry From West Palm never forgets his debts." Barry started to leave the room, then paused. "It's a joke. A little one on my mom. She loves jokes." Barry locked the door behind him.

Robert slowly began to put on the clothes that Barry had laid out on the bed. He focused on dressing, concentrating on buttons and zippers, the texture of the materials he put over his flesh.

Despite the fact they were out of style, the clothes lent his appearance a weight and stability that were completely incongruent with his life. Robert saw, in effect, whom he might have been. The mirror, like the Miami Is Beautiful poster, showed a man who was in control of his life, a man who was just short of conventionally handsome but whose features were "interesting" because they were photogenic, suggesting the male stereotype of handsome while neglecting to deliver on it. The mirror, Rob realized, held the image of the man his ex-wife had been in love with. A man who was steady in his love, his life, his work. A man who could find a simple and real pleasure in watering his lawn and tucking towheaded children into bed each night. A man who was connected to and found sustenance in the everyday and mundane, who would live a life, die, and be forgotten.

The mirror broke so easily and suddenly that Robert could not really remember throwing the lamp.

When Barry opened the door, Rob was sitting on the edge of the bed with an unsettling rigor mortis smile and his eyes closed. He had almost sweated through the white shirt.

Barry cleared his throat but didn't comment on the wreckage. He walked across the room and with a gentleness that Robert didn't believe Barry was capable of, eased him to his feet.

"I feel sick. I need to get out of these clothes." Robert started to sit back down, but Barry stopped him. Robert made a feeble attempt at waving his arms. "You don't understand, Barry. I'm sick. I want to sleep."

Barry tilted his head as if he were checking the composition for a photograph, then pulled out a plastic comb and started running it through Rob's hair, trying various styles until he found one that satisfied him. He stepped back. "Looks right parted low, it makes the top look thicker."

The suit was uncomfortable, too heavy for this time of year, and tight across the shoulders and pelvis. When Robert looked down, he saw himself spread across the bedroom floor, each shard of mirror holding a piece of him.

"Why do I have to dress like this? What's going on, Barry? I don't understand."

"Man, I already told you. It's a joke on my mom. Family-type stuff."

"I don't see what's so funny."

"Believe me, it'll kill her." Barry pulled a dingy handkerchief from his back pocket, bent over, and began, almost reverentially, to polish the dusty black shoes from the closet that Robert had put on. Robert was too stunned to move or protest. He stared at the back of Barry's head as he knelt with the gray handkerchief and moved it over and around the black shoes. The shards of mirror flashed with the movement.

Barry rose, took Rob's arm, and led him out of the bedroom back to the balcony where his mother sat, erect, perfectly still except for the jaws working on the fat wad of gum.

"Watch this," Barry From West Palm said. He leaned over and shouted, "Hi, Mom. I'm back. Want me to throw you over the balcony?"

The woman unwrapped a piece of Citrus Mix, dropped it in her mouth, and nodded.

"Like holding a conversation with a pile of sand," Barry said.

Robert turned from the furious jaw action on the Citrus Mix to the view over the balcony. It was an impressive, expensive view. The Atlantic stretched before them, immense, the color of avocados, and cut by the cul-de-sac's two beaches, one directly below, the other across a small bay.

Barry's mother unwrapped two more pieces of gum and dropped them into her mouth, her jaws busy and quick. Barry shook his head in admiration or anger.

At this point in the afternoon, the beaches were almost empty, the light yellow and diffuse, like melted butter. Robert watched a small boy playing by himself on the beach directly below. He carried a small blue pail and darted along the waterline, dodging waves, running in and out with the constant ebb and flow, and creating, intentionally or not, with his tanned quick movements the easy sentimentality of a calendar photo: the oblivious exuberance of a child at play.

Another image, indistinct at first, slowly began to form, gradually taking shape in the wavering light. It was of another child, across the narrow bay, sitting on the opposite beach. Against the white sand, the child was no more than a silhouette. After a while, Robert noticed a tiny insectlike regularity in the child's movements. The child was methodically digging in the sand, pausing only when a wave rushed in, rose to waist level, and receded. Then the child returned to the digging.

Something in the scene, the coincidental appearance of the two children, their position and movement in the sand and light and water, seemed to demand a connection that Robert was unwilling to make. He felt like he'd been ambushed, caught off guard as he'd been earlier in the summer when False Walter stuck a knife to his throat and climbed over the backseat of his car and later climbed out with his wallet and his ex-wife's picture.

Turning around, Robert discovered Barry's mother staring at him. The wad of gum distorted the shape of her face so that it seemed to crumple and return with each movement of her jaws, every one of her features in motion except the black eyes that continued to scrutinize him.

Barry laughed and flipped over the photograph in her lap. His mother's arms came to life, jerking and flailing awkwardly as if at a fat, buzzing fly. The diamond rings on her last three fingers caught the sun and flashed. In the center of her lap, surrounded by the pieces of bubble gum, was a print of Jesus Christ.

It was the standard inexpensive reproduction that Robert had seen in scores of homes when he was growing up in the Midwest, a profile shot from the shoulders up, a soft brown background, a cream-colored robe, a fuzzy nimbus highlighting the flawless complexion, the long, soft fall of hair, and the carefully trimmed beard, a pair of eyes that looked both soulful and vacant.

Written across the bottom half in a large, looping script, which Robert recognized as Barry's, were the words: TO MILDRED LAMM, ONE OF MY BIGGEST FANS. HOPE TO SEE YOU SOON. JESUS H. CHRIST.

"That picture she's holding there," Barry said, "that preacher sent it to her after she pledged five grand on one of those call-in things. I write the guy a letter, explain the old lady's crazy as hell, it was my inheritance she's spending, I ask the guy who looks like a car salesman nice to give it back on account the old lady's mind is wet matches. I tell him she'd send the Road Runner five grand they got one of those toll-free numbers at the bottom of the screen. The letter took a long time to write, and I laid it all out, and you know what I get for it? The preacher sends *me* a picture of Jesus, tells me he's praying for my mother's mind and mine."

Barry looked out over the balcony and shook his head. "I tell you, Rob, you figure it out, a mind like that. She even added the *H*."

"What?"

"The picture. I wrote on it, I signed *Jesus Christ*. She added the *H*. You know what it stands for? Howard. My old man's name, a guy smart enough to die at fifty to get away from that crazy bitch but dumb enough to leave everything in her hands."

Barry flicked the top corner of the picture. "It wasn't the old man so much as it's Carl though. When Carl died, Mom got serious about J.C. She bought this place and dug in, waiting for the rerun."

The old woman kept her head bent and busied her hands in her lap, the fingers tenacious and grasping, the piles of bubble gum and the print trembling and bouncing against the dark blue cloth covering her legs.

"Imagine a twig, you break it," Barry From West Palm said, "then you break it a couple more times, you got a picture of Mom's mind there."

Robert asked who Carl was.

"The punchline," Barry said.

He put his arm around Robert and pulled him close, then leaned down and fairly screamed in his mother's ear, "Next best thing to what you've been waiting for, Mom. J.C. couldn't make it, so I brought Carl instead." Barry pulled Rob into the old woman's field of vision.

The jaws slackened as she scrutinized Robert. Barry smiled when the old woman's hand began to twitch, then said, "Never thought I'd deliver, did you, you old bitch, but there he is, right in front of you, your favorite, your dear son Carl, come back to see you, right in front of your own fucking eyes, just like you always remembered him, your Carl's back from the dead, come to see you again, pay you a little visit."

Barry turned to Robert. "Wave hello to Mom, Carl."

Robert raised his hand, let it fall.

The old woman reached out and claimed it. Her palm was dry and hot, the fingers insistent. Robert wanted to jerk his hand away, but at a glance from Barry, let the woman have it.

"He wants you to sign the papers, Mom. He came back just for that, so you'd do it, so his brother Barry would get what's his. Carl wants that, Mom. He wants Barry to get what's his. He came all the way back from Heaven to tell you it's okay."

The woman opened her mouth, but said nothing. The wad of gum lay wedged against her lower lip. She still clutched Robert's hand tightly. Robert didn't want to think about what he was hearing. Barry was circling the balcony, his face red and distended, a mask resembling a fit of adolescent rage or religious ecstasy. The old woman's fingers were creeping higher up Robert's arm, rubbing the dark cloth of the suit, then pressing against it, seeking out the flesh beneath. Robert felt appalled and numb, as if what was happening on the balcony were both unbearably alien and yet familiar, something he distantly recognized but didn't understand.

Barry's words swirled around him. "What do you say, you crazy old bitch, is he here or not, come back from the worm scene, didn't I tell you I'd bring him back some day, ask your preacher looks like a Toyota salesman he could do that, I'm telling you I deliver, and here he is, Carl, your youngest, the one you thought was so fucking wonderful, Mr. Pretty Boy all dressed up and back from the grave, come to see his mom."

Barry paused, pointed, and shouted, "Smile at Mom, Carl."

Robert pulled his lips back across his teeth. His mouth had gone completely dry, and the undersides of his lips stuck painfully to the enamel.

The old woman's eyes, black and shiny, almost all iris, bore into his own. Her fingers had moved to his upper arm, clutching a handful of his biceps and coat. A second later, she began to tug and pull Robert down to her. Robert watched her expression change, the face struggling to fit itself to the words slowly forming on her lips. Barry stood next to them urging both on, giving Robert directions, his mother encouragement, all in the voice of an out-of-control tour guide.

Robert watched the old woman's lips birth a single sentence, delivered in a tone that was anything but what he expected, not in some old crone's hoarse hiss or rheumy growl; when this unremittingly ugly woman opened her mouth to speak the three simple words, her voice was as liquid and lilting as a girl's, and it cut through Barry's voice, the coarse net of words he threw out again and again, and her voice cut through the makeshift death-mask Robert had composed for her with his wide, fixed smile, the bland good-son demeanor.

"I know you."

The words silvery and sharp, coming from a face that had collapsed, the tissue as wrinkled and thick as a wad of gum left in the sun. Nothing in the face or the hard black eyes told Robert how he was to take the sentence. The three words had been perfectly clear but the intention behind them as opaque as three feet of ice.

"Fucking-A you know him, Mom, of course you do. Why wouldn't a mom recognize her own dead son? You know what else, I'm betting Carl enjoyed his visit a lot but he's got to get going and he's wondering if you'll sign those papers like he wants you to so his own brother could get what's his, what should have been his all along, a little favor here, Mom, for *Carl* who came back from the goddamn grave just to visit you." Barry snapped his fingers and said, "Tell you what, I'll go in and get those papers, let you and Carl say good-bye, and when I come back you can do what he wants you to, the favor I've been talking about."

Barry disappeared into the apartment before Robert could stop him. Robert wasn't sure if the old woman had heard Barry's words or not, but Robert was still hearing her three as she tugged on his arm, pulling him toward her.

As he submitted to the pressure of her fingers, Robert saw that the old woman was pulling him toward her not to study his face more closely but to kiss her dead son. He wanted to scream but his throat had closed up. The fat wad of gum had dislodged the woman's dentures, and her teeth floated in her mouth.

When Robert was just a few inches from her face, the old woman stopped her tugging even though the pressure of her fingers didn't slacken. They held their position for what seemed forever, Robert looking at the teeth that clacked and clattered and roiled about the woman's ruined mouth.

The kiss never came. The woman's free hand slowly rose from her lap, stopped, and unfolded at the edge of Robert's lower lip. In the center of the palm was a bright pink piece of bubble gum.

The woman let go of Rob's arm, but he remained where he was, as if the fingers were still holding him. The woman had the pink square between thumb and index finger and kept brushing it against Robert's lips with a motion as steady as someone winding a watch, waving, or writing.

Robert closed his eyes and opened his mouth.

The woman placed the piece of gum on his tongue.

Robert stood up and moved away. Barry came back through the sliding glass doors. Robert turned and leaned into the balcony. Over the Atlantic, the sun was a fiery yellow ball. Behind him, the woman made soft sounds that could have been either crying or laughing. A hot breeze rose and ran.

Behind Robert, Barry said, "The bottom of the page, Mom. The dotted line, that's right. Sign both places."

Robert bit into the gum, and gripped the balcony railing. The sun burned into his face, but he felt chilled.

Behind him was the sound of a pen scratching across paper.

BARRY FROM WEST PALM lifted and pointed his fork, on the end of which was a piece of irregularly cut steak, and said, "I'm telling you, those clothes, this light, you're Carl. Not like him, I'm saying. But him."

Barry popped the piece of steak into his mouth and waved the fork like it was a lit match he was trying to put out. "The other night, the Ultimate Club, when I saw you next to Denice, it hit me, you and Carl, but I never figured it would turn out this good. Far as I'm concerned, what you did today helping me out, you got a pal for life."

They were in the House of Beef, just south of Miami, where Barry From West Palm had stopped on the way back to Key West to celebrate his mother signing over the estate. Robert hadn't even taken time to change. He was still wearing Carl's clothes, his own left on the bedroom floor with the shards of broken mirror. Robert had practically run out of the condo in Lauderdale to the car, but the coke in the glove compartment hadn't been able to touch him.

He had yet to take the gum out of his mouth. It had become lodged somewhere in the vicinity of his back molars, and he couldn't bring himself to swallow it. He had developed an irrational fear that any move or decision on his part would precipitate something disastrous. That when he took off the coat, his arms would come off with it. Or that the suit had grown into his skin, grafting itself to his flesh. That if he took off the shoes, his feet would be all bone, hard and white and skeletal.

The restaurant was dark and the air vaguely moist. Robert kept looking at the placard propped near the cash register advertising the day's special. It seemed ominous in its abbreviations and misspelling, a cruel, cryptic joke played on the customers by the gnomish man in a pale green suit manning the register:

> 10 oz T Loin or R Eye
> S Bar
> B Pot FF or O Rings
> Sof D or Cof
> Veg Soup
> Desert.

Barry From West Palm spun his plate around for a better angle on the steak. He held the knife like a pencil. "You know, what with what the old lady finally coughed up today, I'm taking the money and investing it in the deal. This is my chance to be a player. I've already kicked the idea around with Hannibal. I figure, after we close the deal, I can take the profits and bankroll them into a nice little nest egg. I'm thinking down the road, it wouldn't be too bad, I open my own restaurant, a place like this, house specialty, stuff like that, you know, a place where you got to wear coats, a catchy name, something like 'Barry From West Palm's Rib Palace.'" He stopped to signal the waitress for two more drafts. "I'm not locked into ribs though. Chops is a possibility too."

Robert sat in Barry's dead brother's clothes, feeling more and more dislocated from any familiar reference points. His stomach was empty, but he didn't feel hungry. He was exhausted but knew he couldn't sleep. It was as if one by one his senses were detaching themselves from him. Meanwhile he was listening to a man who shot people in the face and threw them handcuffed to live people into swimming pools and burned down their houses talk about opening his own restaurant.

Robert mustered enough moral indignation to suggest Barry name the restaurant after Carl, but when Barry paused and seemed to give it genuine consideration, something broke loose in Robert and became a laugh that ripped through his insides and rose burning his throat until he choked it off. It was a laugh that he never wanted to hear again, the same one that had escaped from him when he'd watched

Hell Mall on Denice's dare. It was a laugh that took the paint off any belief.

"Nah, I don't think so," Barry said finally. "Carl got enough top billing when he was walking around on earth. I could maybe put a picture of him and Mom in the lobby, something like that, but not his name with the restaurant."

"I meant it as a joke, Barry. You know, like the kind you played on your mother?"

Barry set down his fork. "The way you said that, man, you even sound like him now. The one thing about Carl, he always had the answers. Or thought he did. Looking at it one way, Carl bought what he got." Barry went back to his steak, but didn't let chewing get in the way of talking. "I mean, here's a picture of the guy, he's got my old man's good looks, everybody loves him, he's decent is what I'm saying, does his job good, the guy's smart and good-looking, everything they say in the high-school yearbook come true, this guy, he's my brother I got to live with, and the thing is he lives up to what they say, he *believes* all that shit and that makes it worse because he *becomes* it.

"You got any idea what it's like, how fucking difficult it is, to grow up with someone who thinks he's decent? I mean, the son of a bitch's always trying to help out, do things for you. And all the time he's doing this stuff, you know he knows he's doing it because he's better than you. Just him doing it, it's like the whole goddamn world's pointing its finger at you and saying of course a sorry son of a bitch like you needs help from someone like him. That's Carl. Man, one level, it's like he'd been inviting those bullets since he was born."

"And you really killed him like Swolt said? Your own brother?"

Barry said when it came to the Derrota Newsstand that Swolt was there, but so were a lot of other people. He eyed Rob's untouched steak, and Rob slid it in Barry's direction. Barry speared the steak and dropped it on his plate. From where Rob sat, the T-bone resembled the continent of South America. He watched Barry begin to cut it up.

Barry took a bite and nodded. "All I'm saying is there was people in it, and there was people in it. Everybody had a reason but that didn't mean they understood the Derrota."

At the time, Barry went on, the Cubans were solidly entrenched in the coke market and had been getting quite a bit of mileage out of government and agency protection that basically gave them a free hand to deal and kill anybody who remotely got in the way as long as the Cubans continued to genuflect to Uncle Sam, mourn Batista's disposition, and plan mostly imaginary assaults on Fidel Castro. It was, according to Barry, the perfect scam. Money and mayhem with immunity.

Barry said he'd come in through some associates of Lauter's when Lauter was working as a go-between for some disgruntled Washington interests and the Colombians who were anxious to cut themselves a larger share of the Cubans' action. The Washington people were willing to give Lauter the same sort of slack as they had the Cubans if he could change the channel and they liked the picture. So Lauter worked out the Derrota Newsstand scenario.

The funny thing, Barry said, was the Washington people didn't understand that the Derrota would have happened sooner or later anyway. Lauter stepped in and rode the inevitable. The power base for moving coke and grass had been shifting to the Colombians, and the Cubans' methods for conducting business, however violent and venal, still fell short of their neighbors' farther south. Lauter's genius was in convincing the government and agency people that he was vital and instrumental in bringing about something that would have happened on its own.

Lauter brought in Russell Tills and Hannibal Binder, both of whom were already established as dealers and had convenient connections to the Cubans. It had not been particularly difficult to convince either one; with Russell, it had been simple greed, and for Hannibal, the opportunity to take some risks, shake things up. As manager of the Derrota Newsstand, Lennie had come in on Russell's coattails.

Lauter had been given carte blanche to carry out the Derrota operation, and maybe, Barry said, that had been the problem. Wiping out the Cuban coke kings had been easy. They were old and fat and careless. But Lauter's machinations had created some strange ties and connections that even now were being played out. Everybody who owned a piece of the Derrota thought that piece was the most important one and explained all. Even Lauter probably didn't understand what he set in motion.

"You make it sound like he's still alive," Robert said.

"My feeling, it's going to take more than a plane crash to kill Lauter. The timing, I'd say, was convenient. Then you got the missing teeth. You take a step back a few years, look at the Derrota, you know anything could happen. Unless you got an inside line, Rob, I wouldn't count Lauter out. Give me odds Lauter and Jesus, who comes back from the dead first, I'd say Lauter'd lose only because he saw an angle in it."

My movie, Lauter had said to Rob back at the airport. On the other hand, Robert had seen the news footage, the charred mountainside and the wreckage of the plane.

Barry had polished off half of Rob's steak before he pushed it away and leaned back and lit a cigarette. The gum Barry's mother had placed on Robert's tongue floated around the back of his mouth. It had long ago lost whatever taste it held.

"It was Winde," Barry said, "he was the one approached me. Winde had access to agency files, was looking for people what he called could be 'recalibrated,' and he liked what he saw, eventually introduced me to Lauter. It was all a job was how I was looking at it, me working for somebody either way, so why not Lauter."

"What about Denice? How did she fit into the Derrota?"

"Denice was there, a lot more than I thought. See, I had met Winde first."

"You already said that." Robert felt Carl's coat pull across his chest when he leaned forward.

"Winde was from D.C. So was Denice. They went back a long ways. Her father introduced them. See, Winde was his boy, and Denice's old man brought him along and taught him the ropes."

"I don't understand. I thought Denice came into the Derrota News-stand through Hannibal Binder."

Barry leaned back and shook his head. "Denice didn't need help. She's always known how to take care of herself. The way it worked, Carl was the one pulled some strings and got me in the DEA. Carl's regular partner was Henry Swolt, but sometimes Carl switched off, worked with Winde. Winde was the backup at the Derrota that never showed up. He never told me that Swolt and my brother would be the ones who went in. By then, I was already feeling cramped by the way the DEA did business. I'd met Lauter, and he liked me, so I figure okay with the Derrota. I walk in and start shooting. In the middle of it, I see Carl."

"You mean you didn't know? But you still stayed in? Even after Winde had set up your brother?"

Barry gestured with his cigarette. "Listen what I've been saying, Rob. It doesn't and didn't make a difference. There was nothing I could do about it, the Derrota, once it got started, it had its own rules, and that's how you played. Carl, he didn't believe it, but he was playing by them too. Everyone was. Denice wasn't any different from me. She helped Winde set up Carl and Swolt. You know the saying, 'You had to be there'? Well, you did, but that still doesn't cover the Derrota."

Barry called a waitress over and asked for the check. Robert sat back and slipped his hands into the pocket of the suit. He pulled out a wad of Kleenex, a faded pink print of a woman's lips blotted in its center. Barry was still talking, but Rob had quit listening. He was trying, unsuccessfully, to avoid imagining Denice and Winde together in D.C. Robert could still see her packing for the trip and yelling that he would only be in the way if he went along. Her father wasn't his problem, Denice had said, but if her father had introduced Winde and Denice, Robert wasn't so sure about that anymore.

"You see how it was?" Barry asked, standing up with the check. "Carl never had a chance."

Robert nodded and took the wad of gum out of his mouth and folded it in the Kleenex. Then he dropped it on his plate and followed Barry From West Palm out of the House of Beef into the warm Florida night.

THE MEETING FORMALLY BEGAN when Fred Caliber started talking about the teeth. In addition to Hannibal, Robert, and Barry From West Palm, Fred and three of his business associates were on the *Blue Circus* just off Sugarloaf Key. Lennie Ash was resting below deck, sidelined by a newly discovered ulcer. The sun had set an hour ago, and the Atlantic was dark and smooth as a blackboard.

Until Fred Caliber brought up the teeth, Robert had gone through the motions of paying attention during dinner. All he wanted was Denice back. She was due in tomorrow or the day after. Things in D.C. were still up in the air. None of her father's contacts could come up with anything conclusive about Lauter. He was still dead and alive, buried in a shallow grave outside Cliza and seen drinking rum coolers in Cartagena. Dead and alive. Until Denice returned, Robert and the world felt the same way. He could not, waking or sleeping, get the flat taste of the bubble gum out of his mouth.

Everyone turned his head when Fred loudly cleared his throat. He wanted to make sure everyone appreciated what the 176 molars, incisors, and bicuspids, and the plastic sandwich bags that held them, represented. Fred, who was originally from the Midwest, where points and principles were important, waved the bags of teeth, dropped them in the center of the deck table, and then sat down.

Rob had known Fred Caliber from when he worked with Russell Tills, and Robert was surprised to see Fred playing in this game. Fred had always struck Robert as someone who liked to work from a base of simple, easy greed, a Midwestern, no-nonsense, generic brand of avarice. No frills, just the cash please. Fred, a former Chicago city councilman who'd spent the majority of his life in someone's pocket, had retired to Florida for a little fun in the sun and had discovered that fun could also be profitable. He learned to bend his principles South Florida style and bankrolled his retirement with one hundred thousand square inches of Gulf Coast dirt.

It had been a blatantly simple scam. For a dollar, you could own one square inch of Florida, complete with a certified deed. Fred found four Haitian families willing to dig up their backyards and put the dirt in one-inch-square plastic cubes that eventually ended up as one hundred thousand pieces of bric-a-brac up North. It was a dollar-a-throw laugh, a novelty item that left a snowbound January a little less oppressive and one Fred Caliber $100,000 richer. From there, it had been a short step to working with Russell Tills, Creative Consultant.

It was, however, a very long one to Medellín, Colombia, and Camar Tavares and five hundred kilos of cocaine.

Fred's three associates slid their boardroom bodies into low-slung deck chairs and loosened ties in an attempt to let everyone know they understood it was time to *really* get down to business and that formalities didn't stand here.

None of the three, however, while listening to Fred and the smooth-toned modulations of the rhetoric he'd perfected during his twenty-eight years as a city councilman, could keep from glancing at Hannibal Binder and his dark bulk, salt-and-pepper ponytail, and mangled nose that had all the charm of an industrial accident. Hannibal was making everyone a little nervous this evening. He refused to call Fred's three business associates by their names, instead dubbing them Hear, See, and Speak No Evil. The three men in their blue three-piece suits and synonymous hairstyles all wore identical tight smiles whenever Hannibal spoke.

It was See No Evil who spoke up when Fred finished his spiel on the teeth. "The upshot," he said and adjusted his cuffs, "and correct me if I'm wrong here, of the issue Mr. Caliber, Fred rather, was raising seems to be contingent on the present status of Mr. Franklin Benjamin Lauter's mortality and how that impacts on the establishment of the original intentionality of the long-range planning while at the same time acknowledging the real possibility of readjusting priorities given the ambiguities inherent in the current data base."

"Hannibal, what I hear," Barry From West Palm said, "you got ambiguities in your data base, the best thing to do is bring somebody in to spray for them. They get into your data base, they're worse than palmetto bugs. Next thing you know, they're crawling all over your intentionalities."

"Completely unnecessary," Fred said in Barry's direction. "I did not bring Mr. McMichaels and his associates down here to listen to that. Mr. McMichaels raised a valid point and has done so many times in the past when he worked with Russell Tills who, by the way, also valued the opinions and expertise Mr. McMichaels lent to projects. His MBA in product distribution afforded access to reliable methods and techniques and as such was considered a valuable resource."

"My opinion, Fred, is you and these boys been sucking on the tits of Russell's connections too long. You're soft, been having it too easy. Correct me if I'm wrong is what I'm saying, but I look around the boat, and I don't see Russell Tills. I'm in your shoes, that would tell me something. I'd be giving Mr. Russell Tills's absence a lot of consideration before I opened my fucking mouth. That's my opinion." Barry, wearing a green paisley print shirt, blue jeans, and a baseball cap with VIRGO across its front, nodded and sat back in his deck chair.

"Hannibal," Fred said, "do we have to take this?"

"I think so. Yes."

Fred set his drink on the table. "Hannibal, please. Mr. McMichaels approached me in good faith and assured these other two gentlemen that this was a professional organization. On my part, I was delighted to set up the meeting with you so that they could see firsthand how you conducted your business, and I'd hoped that after we clarified how we were going to handle the matter of the teeth, these gentlemen would feel confident to become partners in your little project. Silent, solid partners, as it were."

"Speaking of the teeth," Hannibal said.

"My contact assures me they're genuine. Absolutely." Fred picked up his drink and gave a general toast.

Barry started whistling, then abruptly broke off. "I'm thinking your mama probably had the old man convinced she was cherry the wedding night too."

Hannibal sighed and shook his head. "You have to admit five hundred dollars a tooth is pretty steep, Fred. Especially up front."

"The contact will take them to the agency people. They'll pay, and you know it. He came to me first. In good faith. That's why I called you."

Barry leaned back in his deck chair and began laughing. "My guess, you visit Little Havana or Little Haiti, you'd meet quite a few people smiling with just their gums and all of them waiting for a visit from the tooth fairy."

Hannibal waved Barry down. "Fred," he asked, "just how well do you know the contact?"

"I talked to him. At length."

"That's not what I asked."

"The contact is trustworthy, Hannibal. We talked. I met him through Mr. McMichaels. That's who he originally contacted. McMichaels then got in touch with me right away."

"Okay, Fred," Hannibal said. "You talked. Tell me why we should buy the teeth."

"The investment will clear up once and for all if Lauter's alive. I don't have to tell you the rumors. Every day it's something else. With the teeth we know for sure. Not to mention it's basic insurance and will keep them out of the agencies' hands. They're threatening to make trouble."

"One hundred and seventy-six is five and a half sets of teeth, Fred. What if the half belongs to Lauter? What have we learned? That he's dead? Or has bought himself some dentures and is still alive? I fail to see why the teeth are important, beyond recharging your bank account."

"Consider the Stateside situation. Face it, Hannibal, you have a problem. Tavares will be ready to ship by the end of the month, you said so yourself. The original front money disappeared with Lauter. What are you going to do if neither Lauter nor the money show up? It's looking more and more doubtful either will. In the meantime, the original investors have been burned badly. You surely can't expect them to invest more, not after all the shake-ups of this summer with Russell's departure, Lauter's disappearance, and all the agency meddling starting."

Fred paused and sipped his drink before continuing. "If you're going to keep the lines of distribution open, you need to provide tangible reassurance of control. The teeth could do that. It's a gesture, I admit, but a crucial one, especially when it's coupled with the deal Mr. McMichaels and his associates are offering you."

As if on cue, McMichaels smiled from the deck chair. False Walter came up from the galley to serve drinks. Robert refused to look at him when he took his drink off the tray.

"It's something to think about, Fred." Hannibal turned in the direction of McMichaels and the others. "The drinks okay? Not too strong?" Hannibal downed his in one gulp and said, "How many more crucial gestures are we looking at after the teeth, Fred?"

"Wait a minute here, Hannibal."

"When I said it was something to think about, I meant you, not me, Fred."

Fred held up his hand. "I am simply acting as an ambassador of sorts here, bringing people together who have common interests."

"They call them ambassadors of sorts now?" Barry From West Palm asked. "That's harder to spell than pimp."

Hannibal leaned forward in his chair. "Try again, Fred. You've explained why we need to buy the teeth, but not completely. There's one more reason, and I want to hear you say it."

Fred began to shake his head as if to suggest vast reservoirs of disbelief and sorrow. The performance was not in any way convincing, and Fred dropped it after a while and sat staring into his drink.

Hear No Evil suddenly spoke up. "I think I can help out here. In certain quarters, Mr. Binder, your reputation possesses a negative impactibility in regards to the quality-control distributional characteristics of standardized operational procedures. We can help mimimalize that."

"I think it's time we call this meeting to a close," Fred said quietly to his glass.

"I wanted to hear you say it, Fred, not him."

Fred picked up his glass. "Consider it said, then. I was trying to be tactful. It seemed unnecessary to pursue the matter. I thought the purchase of the teeth would quell any serious doubts. It was simply a gesture."

McMichaels cleared his throat and balanced his drink on the knee of his crossed legs. "Mr. Binder, we came here to offer you our services, not pass judgment. We will cover the missing front money. You will take it and make the buy as planned. When the product reaches Stateside, we will supervise its distribution. Considering demand, the profit margin should be considerable enough that the original investors can be repaid and still leave you and your associates well compensated for your trouble. It's all rather straightforward."

"It's straightforward all right," Hannibal said. "It means I have to turn myself into an errand boy for a bunch of white-collar wunderkinds before we can do business. And you'll give the errand boy a nice tip if he does his job. What you seem to be forgetting is this is my deal. With Lauter gone, I'm in charge."

Fred sighed. "Without them, as you know, you can't do a thing. You need the front money and the distributional lines."

"Without me, they have nothing to move along those lines."

"Let's keep it off the playground, Hannibal. It's push and shove and doesn't accomplish anything. We're talking personality here more than anything else."

"You're wrong, Fred. Very wrong." Hannibal stood up and moved away from the table. He abruptly stopped, turned, and threw three empty deck chairs overboard. After the splash, he shouted, "We're talking about the way things are run."

Hannibal's next action fit something out of a Worldwide screenplay, a cliché brought to life. CUT TO: *the monster roaring and rising to its full height.* Hannibal became an angry piece of the night, but what was happening around them was not simply theatrics. Hannibal was seriously trashing the decks of the *Blue Circus*, breaking glasses, throwing ashtrays, smashing furniture, and making a grand show of tossing all the life preservers overboard. The rest of them sat among the wreckage, each afraid to move or say anything. Hannibal's shadow darted and swarmed over them.

The ocean, Hannibal roared, was God's swimming pool. Ponce de León invented Easter. Moses had climbed the mountain to find not a burning bush but a coca plant. Noah had built the *Blue Circus*. Abraham had killed his son and adopted Lazarus. Cain had a brain tumor. Job founded insurance companies. Columbus courted Lot's wife in the rain. Cortez wrote the Book of Revelation. Jesus and Faustus both wept. The Whore of Babylon did catalogue work for Sears Roebuck. Adam was illegitimate. Eve starred in *National Velvet*. And Pontius Pilate, Hannibal roared, had the right idea, washing those hands of his, washing them once and for all, because he understood, Hannibal roared, that God was, at best, a blind man gutting fish.

And because of that, all there was left was risk. Lucifer's legacy. You imported the Garden of Eden from the hillsides of the Andes and put it up the nose of every segment of American society. And then sat back and waited for the rerun. One sniff. One bite.

Hannibal, standing on the forecastle, shook his huge fist, not at Fred but at the star-smeared sky, and shouted, "We're talking about the way things are run."

And Robert, watching Hannibal and his shadow spilling into the Atlantic, recognized the gesture. It was one step and part of a summer away from the Miramar Arms and the parentheses, the twin halves of his days that had grown closer and closer together, leaving him trapped in his skin, imprisoned there with a brain that held a galaxy of desires. Robert also understood CUT TO: *the monster roaring*.

When Robert turned his head, he found False Walter standing behind the chair. "It'll be okay in a little while," the kid said. "He gets this way."

"How okay is any of this? Why are you still here?"

"Hey, I won't be for long," False Walter said. "I got some money stashed, and I'm just waiting for my mom to call. She and her boyfriend Raphael are moving to New Mexico. They're going to open a beauty salon. She's supposed to call in a week or so and let me know for sure what city they're moving to. She was talking about Santa Fe. That's the capital, isn't it? I'm pretty sure that's what she said. She wasn't too clear on all the details and the connection wasn't too good."

Robert shook his head and turned away from the kid. Hannibal climbed down from the forecastle and moved to the rail. Looking around, Robert noticed that Barry From West Palm and McMichaels had disappeared. Fred and Hear and See No Evil were looking into what remained of their drinks. To the south, Key West's skyline was as precise as a pointillist painting, a confluence of sharp, bright dots that pushed back the wide night sky.

Fred Caliber said, "Like it or not, Hannibal, live with it or not, you're still looking at the teeth."

Hannibal remained at the rail, quietly looking at the wide swath of moonlight coating the Atlantic. After a while, he said, "You're right of course, Fred. All this is totally unnecessary. The problem though is you can live with that. I can't."

From below deck, Barry From West Palm shouted, "Soup's on."

Lennie Ash came stumbling up the stairs, clutching his stomach. "Oh my God. I was resting, but my stomach was hurting like hell. When Barry said soup, that's what I thought he meant. Soup. I got up, thinking a bowl might do some good for the ulcer. Barry said soup. I'm sure I heard that. But, oh my God."

In the galley, Robert and the others found Barry From West Palm and McMichaels at the stove. At first glance, it looked like they were parodying a domestic scene out of Norman Rockwell, Barry the husband, home after a hard day at the office, standing behind his wife at the stove and leaning in to give her a peck on the cheek and take a peek at what was cooking for supper.

In this case, though, supper was McMichaels's hands.

A sheath of black electrical tape covered his hands from wrist to fingertips, and trapped between McMichaels's palms was a squat aerosol can of Reddi-Whip. Barry had McMichaels bent over the front burner on the stove, straining to keep the taped hands over the bright orange coils by leaning against him and holding onto his forearms. The seal on the can had broken and begun to hiss.

"Hear that?" Barry From West Palm said. "You'd better start talking or from now on, you're out tooling around in your BMW, you'll be looking for handicapped parking slots."

McMichaels twisted his head over his shoulder, face streaming tears or sweat, and between gasps, begged Fred to do something.

"Hannibal," Barry From West Palm said, "you'd better tell False Walter to find a bucket and mop. He's going to have a mess to clean up here in a few minutes."

Fred took a step back and slid his hands into his pockets. Mc-Michaels's two associates huddled near him. "That's enough," Fred said. "I don't know what you're trying to prove, but it's time to stop."

Hannibal kept his eyes on McMichaels's face. "You're forgetting something, Fred. I didn't start it. You called me."

The can began to bubble and spit along the seal. "Little metal pincers," Barry From West Palm said. "That's what you're going to end up with. Then you come up with a good idea, you go to snap your fingers, all you're hearing is *click, click* instead. Crickets will love you."

From the corner of his eye, Robert saw Lennie duck his head past the doorframe and then disappear back up the stairs. Robert didn't know what was stopping or starting here, but he'd seen enough. He'd taken False Walter by the elbow and started herding him toward the doorway when McMichaels finally broke before the seal on the aerosol can did.

"Cubans," McMichaels said. "Two of them. They brought me the teeth."

"How about some names?" Barry From West Palm asked.

"Manuel and Miguel. The one named Manuel Contiga did all the talking."

"Son of a bitch," Hannibal yelled. "Fucking Russell Tills. He's still playing. Or trying to. Manuel Contiga and Miguel Evelito are his boys."

Robert stepped back into the room. He'd heard the names before. Hannibal, as crazy and dangerous as he'd acted this evening, had been right all along. The whole deal was being sabotaged in different ways from both ends—first Colombia with the downed plane, and now Stateside, thanks to Russell, who still wanted his piece of the action as well as his revenge. McMichaels wasn't the only one faced with the threat of getting burned.

Fred's shoulders slumped under his white shirt. He looked around the galley, then lifted and dropped his arms. "You have to understand,

Hannibal. I didn't know. McMichaels and his associates looked solid. I had no idea they were fronting for Russell Tills or that it was Tills's boys that produced the teeth. The contact they introduced me to wasn't even Cuban. All I saw was the chance to bring together two parties with mutual interests and pick up a little cash along the way."

"Fred, the friendly ambassador of sorts," Hannibal said. He turned to Barry From West Palm. "Get them all out of here as soon as we dock." Hannibal lowered his head and fingered what was left of his nose. "Better yet, get them out of here now."

"No, Hannibal," Fred said. "That's not necessary. I'm not a good swimmer. This has all been a mistake."

Hannibal was already on his way out of the galley. "There are some life preservers floating around out there somewhere. And a good moon. Maybe you'll get lucky and find one."

ROBERT HEARD A CAR DOOR SLAM and lifted the blinds on the front window with the back of his hand. There was a dark gray roof of clouds, but no wind, and the rain came down hard and straight in a silvery wall. He could barely make out the white Porsche parked along the curb, the storm smoothing out its lines so that it looked like an egg resting on its side.

The blinds rattled against his hand as he watched Denice, hooded by a black umbrella, cross the lawn. The rain ripped through the banyan and jacaranda leaves, but closer to earth seemed to lose its force and definition, turning into patches of fog that resembled smoldering fires.

Denice walked slowly, the umbrella canted at an angle so that Robert was not sure if she saw him watching from the window or not. Around her the yard dissolved into pure color, the rain and fog erasing the shape of the flowers and shrubs, turning the oleander, frangipani, hibiscus, mimosa, orchids, bromeliads, and bougainvillea into floating patches of pink, green, yellow, red, and purple.

Halfway across the lawn, Denice stopped and closed the umbrella. Within seconds she was drenched. She took off a tan jacket tailored to match her skirt and dropped it on the lawn. The rain plastered the white silk blouse she wore underneath it to her skin, her tan and breasts rising through its material. Her blond hair darkened under the weight of the rain. Denice lifted her face and held it to the sky. The fog swirling around her calves was the same color as her blouse. She kicked off her shoes and walked the rest of the way across the lawn. Robert dropped the blinds as she approached the porch.

Her skin was cool and slippery and her hair held the scent of the rain even against the sheets that had not been changed since she'd left. At first their lovemaking was urgent and awkward, Robert's skin suddenly too warm against hers and the trembling that ran through him having nothing to do with the fit of their bodies. Robert clutched at Denice as if he were a man wracked with a voracious hunger, hurrying home in the rain with a sackful of groceries pressed to his chest, and who with each step felt the bag give and tear a little more under his fingers.

His orgasm broke like a fever. The trembling continued in his arms, shoulders, and legs. Denice stroked the back of his neck. He waited until his breathing evened before he lifted his face from the wet tangle of her hair and rolled onto his back. Denice kissed him lightly on the cheek and got up for the bathroom. Robert watched her walk across the room, and when he looked back to where she'd been lying, he saw Carl's suit through the open closet door, its dark, heavy folds hanging crookedly in the air. Robert closed his eyes.

He awoke afterward from a dream in which he had to erase an endless row of blackboards. Denice lay next to him and rested her hand on his stomach.

"I missed you," Robert said.

"Obviously. I'm going to be sore for the next two days." Denice smiled, and her face looked young and vulnerable without the makeup. "Answer me this. Is it better to miss someone or be the person missed?"

"Right now, I don't know if I can tell the difference."

"Maybe there isn't one."

"But then what?"

"Maybe then you're fully alive and don't have to cling to things like 'better.'"

But what, Robert asked her, was there left to cling to in the face of what he'd witnessed during the meeting with Fred Caliber on the *Blue Circus*, when people sat over drinks and discussed purchasing bags of teeth, when Hannibal's tirade over the way things were run sounded half an octave from psychosis, or when it included Barry From West Palm and his electrical tape and can of Reddi Whip? All Robert had thought about since that night was getting out. The deal was falling apart around them, the front money gone with Lauter, Russell Tills trying to set them up through McMichaels and his associates, and the attention Swolt's death and Lauter's disappearance with Senator Casing had drawn from the media and agencies. Swolt, Robert told Denice, might have been smiling in his grave if he had anything left resembling a face.

"Then why are you still here?" Denice's fingers softly traced the lines of his rib cage.

Robert pulled her close. "You. This."

Denice slid down and rested her head on Robert's chest. "It's reversible, Robert. Over ninety percent success rate in most cases."

"What are you talking about?"

"Your vasectomy. You can get it reversed and then do something really daring and risky, like steal back your wife. Then you two can buy a little house and settle down with nice little lives and when they're over, they can put you in nice little graves with the nice little worms. Everything will work out just like it's supposed to."

"I didn't say I wanted that."

Denice slowly stroked his chest. "What is it then? A chance to star in *Hell Mall Two*?"

"I'll tell you what I don't want. I don't want to end up dead or in prison. And with the way Hannibal's handling this deal, those two seem real possibilities."

"They are. They're real. And those two possibilities make anything else real too. Anything. You still want to believe you can change your life as easily as a tire. It doesn't work that way, Robert."

"How does it work then?"

Denice waited before answering, face pressed against his chest, her palm covering his heart. Her skin still held the smell of the rain. She spoke softly into his chest, and there was no goading or mockery in her voice, no false bottoms. She spoke with the infinite patience of someone explaining to a child how to tie a shoe.

"If you want to change your life, the first thing you throw out is *or*. It's not us in this room or Barry From West Palm and Hannibal on the *Blue Circus*. They can't be separated. *Or* is whistling in the dark, the lies you tell to people on their deathbeds. As long as you have *or*, you have a way out, but things only get real when you quit believing there is one. Then you can close the door on who you were. And what's left is what is right before your eyes, and that changes every second. What's left is anything, and that's all there ever is. That's why you like coke, isn't it, Robert? You don't do it so you can find a way out. Cocaine is one way of getting to anything. And to hold on to anything, you have to risk everything. That's how it works."

Robert took a deep breath and let it out slowly. "Are you saying there's a chance the deal can still go through? Even after all the complications from Swolt, Russell Tills, and Lauter?"

Denice nodded into his chest. "I stopped by the *Blue Circus* and talked to Hannibal before I came here. Right now, according to what little my dear father was able to find out, the U.S. government considers Lauter dead but won't officially say so. The CIA and the president's people are working on acceptable scenarios for why he was on the plane in the first place and will cover up or use whatever's left over to their own advantage. In the meantime, we'll follow through on the deal with Camar Tavares."

"With what?" Robert asked. "The original backers have pulled out since Hannibal took over. Even if Lennie, Barry, Hannibal, and the rest of us pool our resources, we'd still fall way short of what we need. How are we going to get the money?"

Denice slowly walked her fingers over Robert's chest. "You're forgetting what helped us with our problems before, Rob. Remember my journals and scrapbooks? How handy they were when we were harassing Russell's clients? I've talked to Hannibal about some ways we might put them to use again. A little bit of pressure in the right places, and we might just come up with the backing and front money we need."

"Or end up in deeper trouble."

Denice shook her head. "That's the beauty of using the scrapbooks and journals. There's enough material to get us immunity for three lifetimes if we ever had to use it."

"Assuming we're still alive for it to do us any good."

Denice lifted her head from Robert's chest and lightly kissed him. "It's the only kind of good there is, Robert."

They spent the rest of the day like pocket change. They showered, dressed, and lounged around the house, listening to music, sipping gin and tonics, and reading as the rain gradually slackened until there was nothing left but the tick of drops falling from the eaves and thick white waves of fog rolling across the yard and breaking against the windows.

Denice was in the kitchen and Robert in the living room chopping lines of coke when he looked up and saw James Winde on the national news. Robert dropped the razor blade on the coffee table and went over to turn up the volume. From the corner of his eye, he saw Denice look in, then turn back into the kitchen.

Winde played the press conference as if it were a premiere for his latest film. He had the moves down, instinctively knowing when to turn for a camera or question, keeping that trademark eyebrow and strong no-nonsense jawline on display. He used his hands as effectively as a boxer or minister. His light gray suit fit agency regulations but not salary. He was explaining his role as head of the president's newly commissioned task force to combat drugs.

"I'm here to tell you the task force is not another bureaucratic Band-Aid for one of our nation's gravest problems. For me, this is not so much a job as a mission and not so much a mission as it is a crusade."

Robert heard Denice come in from the kitchen. She stopped and stood behind the couch. She lightly rattled the ice cubes in her drink.

"I will not downplay the difficulty of the job before us. We are not only at war with the South American cocaine cartels but also with ourselves. Let me speak bluntly here. Drugs provide pleasure. Pleasure is a part of life. Who among us wants to live without it? It's human nature to seek pleasure, and there are a lot of ways to satisfy that search. Cocaine makes you feel good. That's what people find. How can you just say no to human nature? Too many people can't. However, they say yes at the expense of another basic lesson that human nature teaches us."

Denice delivered the next line perfectly in sync with Winde: "Too much of a good thing will kill you."

"Therefore," Winde said, "the president's task force has the crucial but unpleasant job of saving people from themselves. We are not fighting drugs so much as a time in our nation's history that has sanctioned self-interest above everything else. When we have to look in the mirror of history, will we be able to meet our own eyes without flinching or turning away?"

"Haven't you seen enough?" Denice asked.

"It's almost over," Robert said.

"The president has promised us a kinder and gentler nation, and I'm proud to say that the task force is here to help him keep that promise. The task force is a symbol of a new America, one that works with the spirit of cooperation to bring about a better life for us all. There will be no room for mavericks or hot dogs on the task force. It's a one-hundred-and-ten-percent team effort, and I consider it an honor to be heading it up."

There was a closeup of a poster that mirrored the pin on Winde's lapel, five sets of hands, like scoops of ice cream, piled on top of each other, one for each of the agencies in the task force: DEA, Customs, FBI, IRS, and state and local law enforcement. Below them was the slogan: WE'RE DOING GOOD.

Robert cut the television off in the middle of a commercial for a fast-food chain and a lucky customer's search for a McTreasure and moved back to the couch. Denice stood next to the front window in the same spot he had earlier in the day. The blinds shivered when she crossed her arms and leaned against the window frame.

Robert pointed toward the blank television screen. "Did you see him when you were in D.C.?"

Denice nodded.

Robert set down his drink. "Is that why you didn't want me along with you?"

"Winde is a friend of my father's," Denice said, shaking back her hair. "More of a protégé actually. That's what Winde does best. He meets people and ingratiates himself. He accumulates favors, and, as you just saw, those favors eventually pay off. No one can ever say that Winde isn't ambitious."

Robert let out his breath and asked, "What else isn't he, Denice?"

"That tone of voice again," Denice said, matching it. "The hungry little male ego. I didn't think any of this mattered. That's what you once told me about Winde. What made you change your mind? Simply that I saw Winde, among others, in D.C.? The press conference just now? What?"

Robert dropped his head to the back of the couch and spoke toward the ceiling. "It's just that Winde acts like he has some kind of claim on you."

"He probably thinks he does," Denice said flatly. She crossed the room and stood in front of the couch. "Does that make him any different from you? Or my father? Or Hannibal Binder with all his stories about watching me grow up?"

"It does somehow," Robert said. "It feels different."

Denice sat in front of the coffee table, picked up the razor blade, and finished chopping the lines Robert had started. "Winde is politics, Robert, nothing more than a game my father and I have been playing for years. My father drops Winde's name and introduces him to the right people, provides him with contacts he'd never be able to get on his own, and, in exchange, Winde is a go-between, keeping tabs on the wayward daughter who won't return Daddy's calls or come home."

Denice did her two lines and sat back on the floor, her hands behind her for support. "Do you see now, Rob? Can you understand why it was so hard for me to go to D.C. and see my father about Lauter? To have to step back into all that family history and whatever claims my father thinks he can make in its name? But I did it, Robert, because I want what this deal can bring. And I think you do too. It's our chance to erase everything once and for all. No more claims or price tags." Denice leaned forward, picked up Rob's drink, and downed it. "But for the deal to work, we're going to need the protection Winde can provide as head of the task force."

Denice laid down two more lines and slid the mirror across the coffee table. She was right, Robert thought. He wanted, more than he could admit right now, what the deal would bring. He'd been on the edge of asking her about the Derrota Newsstand and what Barry From West Palm had said about Winde and her setting up Swolt and Barry's brother Carl, but Robert was afraid that if he asked, he'd also have to reveal how he learned about it, and more than anything else, Robert wanted to forget what had happened when he'd gone with Barry to visit his mother. It was better to drop the whole thing. He bent over to do his lines. He didn't want to have to try to explain what it felt like to successfully impersonate a dead man.

NERVES AND INSOMNIA and a little bit of a dependency problem, Robert thought, while he rummaged in the kitchen drawer for a spoon, mostly nerves and the lack of sleep, though he had to admit a couple of lines would have helped to organize the day because he was having a little more than a hard time focusing his energy and concentration. He'd spent most of the morning attempting to pack for Sarasota, and a drawerful of black and blue socks had defeated him. No matter how hard he tried, he couldn't separate and match the colors, and in a rage he ended up emptying the whole drawer on the bedroom floor.

Things hadn't been any better when he tried to pack his shirts and pants. None of them fit anymore or at least not very well, the pants slipping off his hips and the shirts ballooning around his rib cage and waist. And every time he leaned into the closet, he had bumped into Carl's suit. Even pushing it deeper into the closet hadn't helped. Against the light walls, the dark suit looked like his shadow or one of those boardwalk backdrops with painted figures and a hole for the face.

Robert had finally given up and gone into the kitchen for lunch, but the prospect of making a sandwich seemed even more daunting than separating socks, so he'd settled for a grapefruit and a can of soda. Robert knew the signs. He might have crossed over the line of what Denice called recreational abuse, but not without help. The last week and a half had been particularly bad while Denice and Hannibal and the rest of them had scrambled to put the deal back together. Lauter was still missing, so they'd gone with an alternative plan, Denice pulling out her scrapbooks and journals and Hannibal orchestrating the extortion. So far it looked like the scheme would work, but Robert had spent too many nights wondering at what point he'd moved beyond *accessory* and too many days trying to remember something as simple as whether he'd eaten breakfast or not.

It would all be over soon, he told himself, and then he'd quit the coke cold. Hadn't Denice said they could be and do anything once the money from the deal came through? Well, a few weeks from now he didn't want to be doing what he was at the moment: sitting at the kitchen table, feeling alternately feverish and chilled, and staring down into the pink insides of grapefruit halves that reminded him of a dissected sea creature, some mutated cousin to the jellyfish pulled from the depths. He was going to have to quit soon. He'd know when, he told himself.

Robert heard the front door quietly open and close and figured Denice had finished her packing early. He dumped the grapefruit in the trash and walked into the living room. False Walter was crouched by the front window, peering through the blinds. He looked quickly over his shoulder at Robert, then back out the window. Robert asked what he was doing, and the kid got up and ran past him toward the back of the shotgun house.

Robert found him rooting around under the bed. False Walter came out with a beat-up shoebox. Robert grabbed him before he could get away and asked again what was going on. The kid said he was sort of in trouble and tried to wriggle out of Robert's grasp. False Walter's face was red and blotchy and his clothes a mess. Except for the buzz cut, the kid looked as he had when he climbed over the backseat of Robert's rental car earlier in the summer. Robert shook the kid by the arm and asked what kind of trouble he was in.

"Big," False Walter said, "but I'm going to get out of it, you'll see. I kind of need to stay here a while until things are clear though. Then I'm gone, I promise. I'll stay out of your way."

Robert was tempted to let go of False Walter and drop the whole thing. The kid was about to vacate his life, and that was fine with Robert. Robert was going to Sarasota with Denice in a few hours, and he could leave the kid and whatever trouble he was in behind.

He might have been able to do that, except the kid started crying.

Robert leaned over to check, but the tears seemed genuine. They left the kid looking younger than fourteen. Robert reached in and took the shoebox and sat on the edge of the bed.

"Oh, Christ," Robert said when he opened it and saw it was full of cash.

False Walter suddenly froze and looked toward the front of the house. He grabbed the box from Robert, mouthed *please,* and scrambled for the closet, worming into the corner and pulling Carl's dark suit farther down for cover.

Robert followed Lennie Ash's string of "heys" to the kitchen where Lennie had already opened a beer. As usual, Lennie was jumpy from his daily dosage of amphetamines. His face was covered in a sheen of sweat that left his freckles looking like a heat rash. He was wearing one of his T-shirts with ASK ME ABOUT MY DESTINY across the chest and a pair of old jeans. As Rob was afraid he would, Lennie asked if he'd seen False Walter.

"Yeah, the kid stopped by early this morning to say good-bye." Robert went to the refrigerator and got a beer for himself. "False Walter said he'd had enough of Key West and was hitting the road." Robert wondered where his lie would take him or what it would end up costing. He couldn't shake the image of False Walter huddled in the closet, his small face collapsing like a cornered animal's.

"Well, at least he got a head start," Lennie said. "I hope you wished him luck. He'll need it."

"Why?"

Lennie tipped back his beer, swallowed, and then wiped his mouth with the back of his hand. "Because he's been free-lancing. Hannibal was too busy with everything that's been happening to notice, until this morning when he discovered he was almost a kilo short. False Walter had been skimming off the top all summer and setting up his own trade. Hannibal went over the edge when he found out and called Barry From West Palm in Miami."

Robert sat down at the table and cradled his head. "You can't be serious. Barry?"

"I tried to talk Hannibal out of it," Lennie said. "I told him the kid wasn't worth this kind of trouble and to just write the kilo off and forget about it, but ever since Fred Caliber tried to sell him those teeth, Hannibal's been doing a paranoid number. It has to be his way or not at all. I can't say I actually liked False Walter, but I hope the kid has the smarts to get some distance behind him and fast." Lennie patted down his carrot-colored cowlick and looked out the kitchen window. "Barry's coming in tonight as soon as he's done with the Cubans. He finally tracked down Russell Tills's boys, Manuel Contiga and Miguel Evelito. They're holed up in South Miami Beach, not far from the place you used to live. When Barry's done, Russell's going to have a hard time getting a hold of his help if he comes up with any more ideas about payback for being cut out of the deal."

Lennie fumbled through the pockets of his jeans until he found a prescription bottle. He shook out two tablets and washed them down with a swallow of beer. "Tagamet. For the ulcer. I'm living on them now. This deal can't close too soon for me. I envy you and Denice getting to work the Gulf Coast. I have to go to Miami with Hannibal. It's not going to be much fun."

Rob concentrated on each sip of beer, trying to figure out what he was going to do about False Walter and thinking that if Lauter hadn't disappeared, they'd be in the closing stages of the old deal. Denice and he would be packing for an extended vacation in the Bahamas instead of for Sarasota, and Robert wouldn't have to worry about struggling to separate and match socks or living with the sweats and the metallic taste in his mouth or what it had felt like to include a Smith & Wesson Airweight .38 in his toiletry bag this morning. But then, if you started out the summer by throwing a grandmother's dog into a pit of alligators, just how much sense could you expect your life to make?

Lennie finished his beer, belched, and stood up. "I know we'll be looking at a lot more cash with the way the deal's been restructured, but I'm still worried. Hannibal sees this as his chance to be a cowboy again. He's working as much on the final installment of his legend as he is on moving the product. From the start, I told him we shouldn't fuck around with crack. The risks of just getting the coke Stateside are bad enough, but crack—we step into that, we're out in some very weird territory."

Robert slowly got up from the table. "I think we're already there, Lennie."

Lennie shrugged, then held the empty beer bottle up to the light and studied it as if it were a crystal ball. "I'll pass it on to Hannibal that the kid's gone. Maybe he'll drop the whole thing, and we can get on with the deal." Lennie tossed the bottle into the trash. "I left the rental van out front and dropped off the expense money with Denice earlier. She said you can pick her up at her place later this afternoon."

After Lennie pocketed his Tagamets and left, Robert picked up the living room phone and dialed information. He couldn't let himself think about what he was doing or he knew he would stop. He listened to a relentlessly chirpy recording give him the number, and he copied it on a piece of newspaper, then pressed down the receiver and dialed. Robert ran his hand through his hair and tried to remember how much of a time difference there was between Florida and Arizona. Kathleen, his ex-wife, picked up the phone on the fourth ring.

"It's me. Robert."

A slight pause, then, "This is a surprise, Rob. What's it been? Almost two years?"

"A long time, Kathleen. How are things?"

"Very good. I'm happy and busy. Phillip has landed the contract to build a new senior citizen complex outside Phoenix, and Caleb is almost a year old. I'm working part-time in a gallery and learning to appreciate and pitch Southwestern art. It's not all just horses and cowboys. There's a lot of exciting talent out here."

Robert found himself caught in a string of pedestrian responses like "that's good" and "I'm glad" while Kathleen talked about the everyday details of her life in Arizona and an even more tangled string of evasive answers when Kathleen asked about what was going on with him. He could sense equal measures of puzzlement and anger from the other end of the line. Kathleen knew him too well to accept vague references to an "important deal" and "working out some problems with the backers" at face value even if Robert couched them in terms of film work. After a particularly interminable stretch of silence, Kathleen finally forced the issue herself and asked why he'd called.

"I need some help," Robert said.

"Is it money? I can ask, but I don't think Phillip is going to be too hot on the idea of a loan."

"No, it's not for me. The help, I mean. It's for someone else. This kid I know."

"You've lost me, Robert."

"It's a little hard to explain. The kid's got himself into some trouble, and it'd be better for all concerned if he was out of Florida for a while."

"How old is he? Does he have a name? Parents? What kind of trouble? How do you know him? You're not telling me anything, Robert, least of all what you expect me to do."

"The kid's name is Walter Fields. He's a fourteen-year-old runaway who's sort of attached himself to me. And Kathleen, if there was any way I could take care of this myself, I would, but I can't just now. Believe me."

"Should I, Robert? This sudden burst of empathy for kids is a little hard to understand coming from a man who runs out for a vasectomy without telling his wife. Ex-wife, rather."

"Maybe I've changed."

"Maybe you have. That doesn't necessarily mean for the better. There's a lot you're not telling me."

"It's complicated, Kathleen."

"No, it's not. It's repetitious. You're not a bad man, Robert, but you have the knack of ending up in bad situations, and whether you intend it or not, someone always gets hurt."

"That's why I called, Kathleen. I don't want to see anything happen to the kid."

"I understand that," Kathleen said. "But just don't tell me you've changed. I don't believe it. You've never learned to let go of anything until it's too late to make any real difference or do any good. There's a sort of corrupted innocence about you, Robert, that's very dangerous. Probably most of all to yourself." Kathleen let out a long sigh. "Shit. I don't know why I even bother. You probably haven't heard anything I've said. You're just waiting for me to say it's okay to send on the boy, and you knew I'd do it, didn't you, even before you called?"

"It won't be for long. He's an okay kid. He needs a couple of breaks, and I couldn't think of a better one than you, Kathleen."

As they worked their way to good-bye, Robert remembered those small, seemingly mundane moments from their marriage—Kathleen stepping from a shower or opening a letter, pouring a drink, brushing her hair, or sitting on the sofa with her legs curled beneath her— moments that, without warning, spoke to a genuine comfort and ease, and Robert would think, My God, I'm married to a beautiful woman, and we have a lifetime of these moments ahead of us. Robert also wondered, after he hung up the phone, why those moments had never been enough. He'd run away from what most people wanted and would have been happy to find. Those moments, however, had fit him too easily, and he'd been afraid not that the moments wouldn't last but that they would end up owning him.

Robert made another call, then fixed a drink and walked to the rear of the house to find the kid. It was already after one o'clock, and he only had a couple hours to shave, shower, and finish what passed for packing. Robert opened the bedroom door and told the kid it was all right to come out. He had to repeat it two more times before the kid believed him.

"I wasn't sure," False Walter said, holding the shoebox against his chest. "I thought I heard Lennie leave, but when I cracked the door, you were still talking."

Rob told him he'd been on the phone and then bent and began to gather the socks, shirts, and pants scattered on the floor. The metallic taste in his mouth persisted, and so did the sound of Kathleen's voice when she'd said good-bye. The drink didn't help to get rid of either.

The kid circled warily around the bed, keeping some distance and clutching the shoebox. "I know you get mad at me sometimes and don't like me hanging around the house, but—" The kid paused, looking from the bedroom door to the window at his back.

" 'But' what?"

"You wouldn't call Hannibal and tell him I was here, would you?" False Walter tried to meet Rob's eyes and backed off. "I really don't think you'd do that. I really didn't. But I was just wondering."

Rob shook his head and dumped an armful of clothes on the bed. He was about to pick up his drink from the nightstand when he noticed his toiletry bag was on its side and partially unzipped. It never stops, he thought and tossed back the drink. Then he turned to False Walter, put out his hand, and told him to give back the Smith & Wesson.

"How do I know you're not setting me up?" the kid asked, moving away from the bed.

"You mean, like you did me this summer, telling me you needed a place to hang out once in a while, when all you really needed was a place to stash your cash and a phone to deal the coke you stole from Hannibal? Did you ever think of the position you were putting me in with that little stunt?"

"It wasn't just that," the kid said. "Really."

"Prove it to me then," Robert said, stopping by the corner of the bed, "and give me back the gun."

False Walter hesitated, then slipped his hand under the T-shirt, pulled out the gun, and tossed it on the bed.

"Everything else now," Rob said, picking up the gun. Christ, the safety was off.

"What do you mean?" The kid glanced at the shoebox.

"Empty your pockets. If you want me to help you, I need to know what's going on. No more games or surprises."

False Walter did as he asked and then turned his pockets inside out and stepped back and opened the lid of the box to show Rob there was nothing but cash inside. Robert picked through the contents False Walter had laid in a clear space below the pillow: a couple packs of bar matches, seventy-eight cents in change, a soiled rabbit-foot keychain, a quarter gram of coke wrapped in foil, Rob's wallet that he'd lifted on the way down from Miami, a pack of sugarless bubble gum, a ballpoint pen, and a small blunt-edged key.

Robert held up the key. "You were really pushing your luck, kid. How long have you had this?"

False Walter shrugged, looked around, and said, "Since this morning. I went through her purse and palmed it when Denice was talking to Hannibal. It goes to locker A3 at the bus station. I never had the chance to use it on account of Hannibal finding out what I did with his coke. I figured the bus station would be one of the first places he looked for me, so I hung out at the aquarium until I could get over here."

Robert slipped the key in his pocket, picked up the quarter gram of coke, and told False Walter he could have everything else. While the kid gathered up his stuff, Robert explained that False Walter could stay at his ex-wife's until his mother and her boyfriend sent for him. False Walter had two weeks to work that out, no longer, and then Rob wanted him out of Kathleen's house. The kid was to stay completely clean while he was in Phoenix. No pulling any of his customary scams or hustles. He was also not to say anything about drugs or drug deals and was not to bring up the name of anyone, including Rob, connected to either. Rob told False Walter to pass himself off as a runaway who'd had some scrapes with the Key West cops and leave it at that.

If False Walter agreed to play it that way, Rob would get him out of Key West before Barry From West Palm showed up. A bus was leaving late in the day at the same time Rob was for Sarasota, and he would drop him at the station on the way out. He'd time it so there'd be no wait.

"Is she the one with black hair?" False Walter asked. "You know, the one from the picture in your wallet that was standing on the balcony with all the flowers?" The kid shifted the shoebox to his left hand and scratched his cheek. "Do you think we'll get along okay?"

"Probably." Rob began refolding his shirts. "She has a soft spot for poor risks."

ROBERT AND DENICE DROVE WEST on the Tamiami Trail straight into the sun. It sat on the horizon like a perfect orange, waiting to be peeled. The radio was full of love songs. Denice wore a thin blue sleeveless blouse and a pair of faded cutoffs. Her hair was pulled into a ponytail and held with a thick silver comb. She had kicked off her sandals and sat with her feet on the dash. Outside the window, the Everglades arranged itself into postcard shots. A flock of egrets flying over a hammock. Miles of sawgrass stretching like a Kansas wheat field. A marina of airboats. Pink-and-white clusters of brome-liads. The Miccosukee Indian Village. Signs advertising tax-free cig-arettes and alligator wrestling.

Denice wiggled the big toe on her left foot. "This little piggy went to Bogotá and cleaned up. It went wee-wee-wee all the way home in a stretch limo."

"Provided, that is," Robert said, "the big bad wolf hadn't already huffed and puffed and blown it down."

"No way. Little Red Riding Hood had already taken care of him. She wasn't afraid of a few teeth. Besides, it's only little boys who cry wolf and carry around glass slippers."

"That's because they know what happens at the stroke of midnight."

"And it's the smart little girls who see through the glass slippers and know the next stop is the little old woman who lived in a shoe. So they watch where they step." Denice leaned forward and turned up the radio.

The Tamiami Trail was basically a straight shot from Miami through the Everglades to Naples. It was a drive with minimal distractions, and let Robert think about where it was leading. The end of the deal might fit a fairy tale, but nothing else about it did. He kept feeling something he could not give a name to. It wasn't quite fear or anticipation or anxiety, nothing he could recognize, the feeling teasing him like a dream that could be either pleasant or horrifying but which is interrupted just before the dreamer discovers how it turns out.

Robert kept running the details of the deal through his mind as if by sheer repetition he could crowd out what he was feeling. Everything hinged on whether Hannibal Binder could work the anti-Fidelista Cuban angle. The original front money had disappeared with Lauter, and Camar Tavares would send the first batch of cocaine from his processing plants to someone else unless Hannibal could come up with more cash. The D.C. people who originally put up the money for the chemicals to get those plants going again had received a very nice return on their investment and had been more than eager to plow back those profits when Lauter had offered them a piece of the follow-up action. After Lauter's disappearance, these same people in D.C., however, were not so eager to get burned twice and had balked when Hannibal had tried to reopen the deal. Hannibal also had the tendency to make people nervous. He'd been acceptable as part of the old package of Russell Tills and Franklin Benjamin Lauter, and tolerated when he'd been tied to Lauter, but by himself was considered too big a risk. When it came to bankrolling drug transactions, the D.C. crowd wanted someone a little less colorful than Hannibal running the show.

There had been more calls to Colombia, but Tavares, while still giving them first shot at the shipment, insisted that he'd move nothing less than five hundred kilos. At twenty thousand per kilo, the time and risk involved weren't worth anything less. Hannibal managed to bully one concession from Tavares and insisted the payment be made Stateside under controlled conditions. Nobody wanted another round of plane crashes and missing teeth. Tavares agreed to send an associate to Miami to verify the existence of the new front money and would take the second half upon delivery.

So everything in the initial arrangements was in place except for one thing. Without the original backers, Hannibal, Robert, Denice,

Barry From West Palm, and Lennie didn't have enough cash to bank-roll the shipment. A large percentage of their pooled resources would be swallowed covering the Stateside expenses. Robert, for his part, put up the remaining money from the sale of his father's house. Robert was all the way in this time, but even with what Hannibal, Denice, and the others had staked, they were still short almost $750,000 for the buy. Given the shake-ups in the status quo during the summer, new investors were wary, and if they took the deal closer to the street and opened their doors, the whole thing, as Lennie pointed out between doses of Tagamet, would turn into a free-for-all.

That's when Hannibal Binder started thinking about 1961. Sometimes the best way to solve a new problem was to resurrect an old one. Hannibal maintained that if anyone could understand the complications, ambiguities, and dangers implicit in the downed plane and missing cash, it would be the Cuban anti-Fidelista cells. They had seen every one of their plans nosedive with the Bay of Pigs Invasion and had to accommodate the limbo it left their lives in.

From what Robert had picked up, none of the anti-Fidelista cells were unified except in common purpose. They all fervently believed in *la lucha*, their struggle to get rid of Castro and regain their homeland. Over the years this struggle had taken on the dynamics of a soap opera plot—deals within deals with the government and agency people that led to betrayals and duplicities that produced conspiracies, both large and small, real and imaginary, often at the same time.

Hannibal was hoping to capitalize on the love-hate relationship the anti-Fidelista leaders had with D.C. The exiles nurtured a deep and bitter resentment toward the U.S. government over what they saw as its betrayal of *la lucha* with the Bay of Pigs fiasco and the government's subsequent tolerance of Castro's presence. At the same time, the exiles worked hard to curry D.C.'s favor because without government funding they would not have the finances to establish the campaigns and operations that would bring *la lucha* to fruition.

For their part, the CIA and other agencies worked with D.C.'s tacit approval—and sometimes with no approval at all—to keep the Cuban cells splintered, playing them off one another, feeding one set of egos this month and starving it the next. The anti-Fidelistas were always a useful source of information and a ready source of recruits for some of the government agencies' extracurricular activities.

The majority of the anti-Fidelista cells had marginal interest in drugs, but they did have a very definite interest in cash, which could be used to secure weapons and keep counterinsurgency operations alive. Denice had quietly done some checking through some D.C. contacts to see which of the cells were due funding, and then Hannibal started making the rounds. Three of the exiled group leaders flatly turned him down on the basis of revolutionary principles, two others kept hedging on the terms of Hannibal's proposition, and then Hannibal hooked up with the leader of Los Mártires Two, Carlos Ramierz, who was more than willing to temporarily rearrange his idealism for some capital gains.

Then they ran into their next major snag. Carlos had, in both the anti-Fidelista and government circles, a problem with credibility. The *Two* of Los Mártires Two did not refer to the second wave of martyrs to the Cuban cause but rather to the number of members in the original cell—Carlos and his brother Hector. Over the last few years, Los Mártires Two's membership had fluctuated between eight and fifteen when Carlos had managed to recruit some of his cousins and a few disenfranchised members from other groups. That D.C. agencies recognized Los Mártires Two was due primarily to the fact that Carlos and his cohorts had big ears and even larger mouths and had, therefore, achieved minor celebrity status on the informer circuit.

Carlos Ramierz's credibility skyrocketed like South Florida real-estate values when Denice gave Hannibal material from her scrapbooks and journals. The information was important and potentially damaging enough for the agencies to revise their opinion of Ramierz.

Denice had found the perfect extortion victim: her father, Allen Shell. He had a role in every significant permutation from what had started on April 17, 1961. Allen Shell had managed to keep his reputation spotless among the anti-Fidelista cells even while he orchestrated all the behind-the-scene betrayals at their expense. The Cuban community saw him as one of their own and a true patriot and champion of justice. Denice knew her father's vulnerable spots and didn't hide her satisfaction at exploiting them.

Hannibal, Denice, Robert, and the others were to be very silent partners while Ramierz contacted Allen Shell and threatened to leak his double-dealings with the anti-Fidelistas to the press. They were counting on Denice's father attempting to maintain his credibility by quickly applying pressure in the appropriate areas so that emergency allocations could be funneled to Carlos Ramierz and Los Mártires Two in the service of *la lucha*. There would be questions raised about Carlos's new status by certain D.C. parties—but not many, not from what Denice knew of her father and the roster of favors he'd developed over the years.

When the funding came through, Carlos Ramierz was to divert it to Hannibal, who would then contact Camar Tavares in Colombia. Ramierz would get his original investment plus interest back after shipment and whatever he could trade off his newly created status as king of the Cuban freedom fighters. Barry From West Palm had already had a long talk with Ramierz about the problems that would arise for him if Hannibal's, Denice's, or any other names surfaced from those trade-offs.

Which left Robert and Denice on their way to the Gulf Coast to make arrangements for when the coke hit Stateside. And which left Robert with the feeling he could not give a name to. It was the same feeling he'd had when he got the closing papers in the mail after he sold his father's house and that followed him this afternoon when he called his ex-wife and put False Walter on the bus to Arizona.

No matter how many times Robert ran the deal through his mind, he still ended up feeling like a gawky adolescent who stood over the phone and rehearsed his lines before working up the nerve to call the girl who had always seemed inaccessible. Despite the complications, the deal sounded workable as Hannibal had laid it out, but right now all Robert heard was the dial tone. He was too far in, though, to completely break the connection.

"Turn in here," Denice said.

"Jesus, Denice," Robert said over the crunch of gravel in the parking lot, "we're less than a half hour from Naples. Why don't we wait? This place is a dump. The owner can't even spell."

A tall pink-and-green neon traveler palm with OASIS topping its crown and MOTEL lying at the base of its trunk rose from the roof of the office. Closer to the road was another sign:

> Welecome
> Vancanc
> Free K-Bul.

The second *e* in "Free" was an upside-down G. Through the van's bug-splattered windshield Robert could make out a half dozen or so matchstick bungalows lost in the murk of the trees behind the office. There were two other cars in the parking lot. The air was thick with the smell of the Everglades, a swampy mix of standing water, dark rich earth, and close heavy vegetation.

"I like it," Denice said, opening her door and stepping out. "Leave the glass slipper in the van, Rob," she said over her shoulder. Above her, the neon sign crackled in the dark.

AT NOON THE NEXT DAY, Robert pulled off I-75 at a Trader Joe's convenience store outside Punta Gorda. There was a pay phone at the far corner of the store near a sign that read FREE AIR and a loop of brown hose. While Denice went in to get something for lunch, Robert called Miami.

He leaned against the cinderblock wall and its scrawled numbers and graffiti and looked across the lot to the interstate and the bright lines of traffic roaring by. Above them, the sky was a deep but distant blue.

"I'm here," Lennie Ash said from the other end.

"It's Robert. I need to talk to Hannibal."

"Things are hopping here. Fill me in and I'll pass it on."

"Hannibal said he wanted me to talk to him directly after we met with Ed French. We did, and I'm waiting, Lennie."

"Hannibal's out right now. He went to Little Havana to hold Carlos Ramierz's hand. Ramierz's having an attack of conscience over the money. His feelings are hurt because some of his anti-Fidelista cronies are calling him a traitor to the cause, but you ask me, it's all bullshit. Ramierz is just trying to put on the squeeze for a few extra points when it's pay-off time."

"You sure the money's coming through?"

"Hannibal's on top of it. Don't worry about this end. You and Denice get to the Coast and find those houses."

"What about Winde?"

"Hannibal's been talking to him about the schedule of the Miami busts. Winde's going to have the whole task force mobilized. They'll bust the major dealers, and that'll dry up the market for a while and push up demand. We should have everything in place to meet it by then. Winde's also supposed to talk to some local enforcement people in Sarasota, but he's high visibility now and doesn't want to lean too heavily and raise questions. So you and Denice take it careful there."

A light gray compact pulled up to the self-serve pumps, and immediately two screaming kids hopped out of the back and ran into the store. A moment later, a man in his early thirties with pale, boyish features and the beginnings of a paunch stepped out and stretched. A tired-looking woman with a small nose and sharp chin rolled down the window on the passenger side. From where he stood, Robert could just see the hairless crown of the baby she was nursing.

Robert gave Lennie a rundown on the meeting with Ed French earlier in the morning. French owned the salvage-and-storage operation tucked away in a small fishing village in the Ten Thousand Islands that they were going to use to warehouse and prepare the coke before they moved it up the Coast. Ed French was balding, overweight, and in his late fifties, his voice so low it was basically a growl. He kept an unfiltered Camel tucked in the corner of his mouth as if it had been stapled there while he went over the inventory with Rob and Denice, the lactose and quinine they'd use to cut the coke, the used furniture to be gutted to hide it in, the containers of distilled water and boxes of baking soda and chemicals for converting the coke to crack after they'd moved it to Sarasota in the rental trucks. Though they'd have to wait for Camar Tavares for specifics, French had gone over the basic procedures for making the drop and getting it to the warehouse.

"Your impression is that everything's copacetic then, Rob? Nothing seems funny?"

"French was strictly shipping and receiving. His brother-in-law might be another problem though."

While he explained to Lennie that French's brother-in-law, the local sheriff, wanted an additional five thousand for providing protection the night of the drop, Robert watched Denice leave the store and start across the lot. It soon became obvious that Robert wasn't the only one watching. The young father putting unleaded in the compact kept glancing from the whirling dollars-and-cents columns on the pump to Denice, obviously braless and in tight black jeans. Halfway across the lot, Denice paused, tucking the bag in the crook of her left arm and shoulder and rummaging around until she found a beer. She popped it open one-handed and licked the foam spilling over its top before she slowly leaned back and took a long swallow. Above her, a string of red and green pennants snapped in the wind. The man's wife kept her gaze directed at the front windshield, never once glancing in Denice's direction or at her husband.

"I should have figured that," Lennie said. "Everyone in the swamps is related, and French is going to have his whole fucking family on the payroll before this is over. They're worse than the Cubans about stuff like that."

"I gave French the down payment and told him I'd have to talk to Hannibal about the extra money. He didn't seem too happy about that. He said his brother-in-law likes everything laid out in advance."

Lennie Ash sighed long distance and said they'd probably have to pay it and then hung up after Rob had repeatedly assured him there was nothing else he needed to know on his end. Robert walked back to the van. The light gray compact was gone.

Denice had a chili dog, fries, and a beer set out on the dash for him. "Too bad you didn't think to include the hot dog in the little show you put on back there," Robert said, pulling out.

"I gave him what he thought he saw, that's all. Forget it."

Robert couldn't. He knew how the man in the gray compact felt. He'd felt the same thing late last night in the Oasis Motel when, after making love, Denice had dropped immediately off to sleep and his insomnia had driven him to 2 a.m. television. The Oasis's décor left Robert feeling as if he were on the set for a porno film—its furniture possessing all the aesthetic appeal and durability of cardboard, the windows hidden by two sets of burnt-orange drapes crookedly hanging from bent rods, and the floor covered in golf-course green indoor-outdoor carpeting. An uneventful seascape hung above a small glass lamp filled with discolored and broken seashells. The Book of Revelation had been scissored out of the bedside Bible. Robert had been willing to settle for any distraction, but he hadn't been ready for the soap commercial. "Turns any bath into a Feast of Flowers," the announcer had said, and there was a shot of Denice, younger-looking and with shorter hair, diving into a pool of full-petaled blossoms. The image from his first encounter with Denice that he'd always thought had arisen from a half-remembered dream turned out to be a forgotten television commercial.

"So you never actually talked to Hannibal?" Denice asked after Rob told her about the conversation at the convenience store.

"No. Just Lennie. Why?"

"It just seems like Lennie's awfully nervous this summer, especially since Lauter disappeared."

"I've never seen him any other way. With all those IRS problems, he's got a lot riding on this deal."

"We all do." Denice reached over and took a sip of Robert's beer. "At least Hannibal's there too."

"What are you getting at? Do you think Lennie needs to be watched?"

Denice shrugged. "Who doesn't, Robert?"

A half hour later they got off I-75 at Venice and took 41, which ran along the coast and through the middle of Sarasota. At the Siesta Key exit, they rented a nondescript sedan for Robert, and he followed Denice while she looked for a place to stay. Though he tried to ignore it, the feeling he could not give a name to returned and ran like a crack through the hard light of the afternoon. His hands began trembling, and his bones felt as light and porous as a bird's. A high-pitched noise needled its way through his inner ear. Robert avoided looking in the rearview mirror.

Denice got off 41 and took a short jog onto an access road that fed what had probably been a thriving commercial strip twenty years ago but which over the years had become a Darwinian casualty in the boom-and-bust cycles of Gulf Coast development. The stores and shopping centers along the strip all had the look of second or third mortgages and the feel of garage sales. There was something sad and forlorn and stubbornly hopeful about the clutter of doughnut and tire shops, video and craft stores, furniture outlets and dry cleaners that reminded Robert of an overweight woman on a crowded beach bravely smiling behind new sunglasses.

Though he'd hoped otherwise, Robert now saw where they were headed. He followed Denice into a section of old one-story motels that resembled run-down ranch houses set at right angles to each other. Most of the pools were dry though there were pieces of frayed and unraveling plastic lawn furniture leisurely arranged along their edges under faded and torn sun umbrellas. The motel entrances were usually fronted by stunted palms or sickly cacti the color of old watermelon rinds.

Robert followed Denice past the Stardust, the Cadillac, the Mermaid, the El Dorado, and the Nightcap motels into the parking lot of the Moonbeam. They registered as Mr. and Mrs. David Candle, the name of the character Robert had played in his seventh film, *It Won't Die*. The day manager wore a yellow polo shirt that was a step up from a bar rag and a soft, easy smile Robert associated with child molesters. He gave them the key to room 63 and proudly announced that all the units had been sprayed earlier in the week.

Robert didn't want to stick around the room, and since it only had one phone and there was a little less than three hours until most of the real-estate offices closed, Robert and Denice divided up the real-estate listings and he left to work out of a coffee shop he'd seen on their way in that was within walking distance of the motel.

At the edge of the parking lot was a small seashell stand run by a tall, bony man in faded jeans, white shirt, and sunglasses that looked as if they'd been pressed into his face and the skin had grown around them. Robert nodded as he went by, but the man looked right through him.

The Neptune Sandwich Shop was full of fluorescence, Formica, and poorly tinted seascapes. Robert found a corner booth near the phone and ordered coffee. He started on the real-estate office listings, calling a string of agents who all sounded like they'd taken the same assertiveness training course. Robert asked about renting mid-size two-bedroom houses that were either unfurnished or partially furnished, preferably with a range and refrigerator, and jotted down anything that sounded promising and said he'd be by tomorrow to look at them. He checked and circled some of the best possibilities on a city map but knew he wouldn't really be able to tell anything until he had the chance to see the places firsthand.

It made sense to use Sarasota as a base for the crack houses because they'd be the width of a state away when James Winde and the task force started the Miami busts, but picking the location of the houses was still tricky. Sarasota, like most of the large South Florida cities, did not quite have a handle on what it was. The city was simultaneously a retirement community, beach resort, and commercial hub. Robert and Denice were trying to find five houses and two more as backups. They wanted neighborhoods that were quiet but not too quiet and that still left them easy access to the interstate and airport if there should be trouble. They needed places that wouldn't draw attention from the transient crowd if they were there for any length of time and places where they wouldn't blend in to the point of attracting friendly and nosy neighbors.

Robert took a break from the phone and bought a paper to study the classifieds. He'd only turned a few pages before he noticed his hands were black with ink. The sweats had started again. His shirt was plastered to his back. The muscles in his chest jumped.

He knew it wasn't a good idea, but he still had an hour of phone calls in front of him, and he wasn't ready to go back to the motel. Robert looked around the shop. Next to the cash register, the waitresses compared lipstick shades. Along the counter two nondescript men sat over cheeseburger platters. In the booth opposite his were two senior citizens whose skin was as brown and creased as walnut shells. They appeared disconcertingly androgynous. Both wore tiny knitted caps, green and yellow tanktops, and blue bermuda shorts and sat across from each other like images in a mirror.

"I-49, that's what I was waiting for," the one on the left said. "He called I-51, I-48, and I-50, just like that in a row, but do you think I-49? Nobody wins with B-N-G-O. Try calling that and see what happens."

Okay, Robert said to himself and got up to hunt down the men's room. Its door was marked SKIPPERS, and it got worse when he stepped inside. Draped across the ceiling was a skein of plastic netting in which hung, not the expected shells and starfish, but dozens of pink deodorant bars like the one in the urinal. Above the sink, a clipper ship with a movable mast dispensed soap. A plaque proclaiming THAR SHE BLOWS with *You Wish* penciled underneath hung next to the forced-air drier.

Robert locked himself into the third stall, quickly tooted two lines, and sat back. After a few minutes, things evened out. In the spirit of the room's décor, he imagined a plaque hanging from his brain reading STEADY AT THE HELM. He flushed the toilet and went back to his booth.

A little after five, Robert finished up the phone calls and gathered his list, map, and paper and left the shop. He walked up the motel strip. It's started, he told himself. Things were set in motion. A process as powerful as destiny had taken over. The money would be turned into coke and then the coke became crack and the crack was turned back into money, and the money was transformed into pure possibility, and possibility owned the world and shed time. Means and ends danced on the head of a pin while the angels laughed all the way to the bank.

Robert stood on the curb and looked at the string of neon motel signs embedded in the skyline. He was reminded for a moment of Key West sunsets. He dodged his way through four lanes of rush-hour traffic and paused at the edge of the Moonbeam's parking lot to catch his breath. The air tasted of ocean and exhaust. His side hurt, and he was sweating more than the run warranted.

Robert walked past the seashell stand and a tourist couple who stood in front of it. The man in the white shirt and sunglasses regarded them impassively while they studied the tiered rows of shells. He didn't appear to have moved since Robert had last seen him.

When the couple made their selection, the man took a mechanical arm, one as long and thin as a fishing pole, at whose end were two curved metal pincers, and guided it out over the rows of shells, stopping at the one the couple pointed at, carefully lifting it from its place and dropping it in a pink plastic bag webbed like a net. Robert tucked the map and newspaper under his arm and kept walking.

At the door to the room, he glanced back over his shoulder and saw the man in the dark sunglasses hold out the mechanical arm, the shell still dangling in the bag, to the tourist couple who stood below him, ready with their money.

THE PALMS WEREN'T SWAYING, but the night held enough surf and moonlight to evoke the usual associations of a lovers' walk on the beach. The stars spilled across an indigo sky. The waves were rimmed in silver and pale green phosphoresence. The surf rolled in, following Rob and Denice and erasing their footprints, leaving the sand smooth and unbroken except for clusters of small white shells.

After dinner in a quiet restaurant on St. Armand's Key, Rob and Denice had driven along the coast until they found a deserted stretch of beach. They'd left their shoes in the car and walked in their evening clothes, Rob in an off-white linen suit, dark blue shirt, and paisley tie, Denice in dark stockings and a black dress that left her tanned shoulders bare. She wore her hair in a loose knot and a thin silver bracelet on each wrist.

The dinner had been part of an early celebration since Denice had found equally good prospects for the crack houses as Robert had. If things continued to go well, they could wrap up the Sarasota end of the deal in a couple days. They'd celebrated in style with champagne and carafe after carafe of wine between the shrimp stuffed with peppers and crabmeat, the marinated sea scallops, lobster, and mango salad. Denice had also been making some serious dents in the coke stash during the evening. Robert's nose was still sore and tender, and he'd compensated by keeping the bartender busy. Even with the drinks though, he still felt a little on edge and had envied Denice's trips to the ladies' room and the smile she brought back each time.

They held hands as they walked on the beach. The surf pulled at their ankles, and every so often Robert caught a whiff of Denice's perfume. Around them, partially embedded in the sand and coated with a thin layer of moonlight, were the translucent bodies of jellyfish.

"I couldn't resist," Denice said. "This morning I called my father to see how he was doing. I don't know which was a bigger shock—hearing from his daughter without her being bullied into it or worrying that Carlos Ramierz will expose him and reveal all his dirty tricks. It was a distinct pleasure to throw him off balance with the call. My father's a man who is used to having the advantage in whatever he does. He prides himself on that. It was nice to have the situation reversed for a change."

One of Robert's pants legs had come down, and he let go of Denice's hand and bent to roll it back up. "Do you think there's any chance your father suspects we're in with Ramierz?"

"No," Denice said. "At least not at this stage." She walked on, a couple of steps ahead of Rob. "Maybe he'll eventually make the connection. Because if I know my father, he won't let the incident rest. He's pragmatic enough to take the short-term solution and pay Ramierz off, but in the long run he won't be able to stand the idea that Ramierz had something on him, and my father will pull some of his customary strings, and Carlos Ramierz and Los Mártires Two will suddenly disappear. Before he has Ramierz killed, my father may or may not take the time to find out if Ramierz was working with anybody else. But by that point the deal will have gone through, and it won't matter much anyway."

"Except to Ramierz," Robert said.

"And me," Denice said. "I'd like him to know who was behind it. I just hope I'm there so I can see his face when he finds out."

Denice turned and shook loose her hair and gave Robert a dazzling smile fueled on coke. "Know something funny?" she asked. "My father promised me the stars as a child. Literally. On clear nights he'd take me outside on the lawn and let me pick out the ones I wanted. And I believed him." Denice leaned in and quickly kissed Robert. "And now that we're closing the deal with Tavares, I feel I'm about to finally collect on that promise." She slung her purse over her shoulder and laughed. "God, I wish we had the Porsche here instead of those rentals. I'd like to drive all night and just keep moving, make something happen, and run it all out. I don't want this night to end."

Before Rob could say anything, Denice turned and ran on ahead. He started after her, but the drinks and food left him heavy, and he wasn't able to gain much ground. Denice remained about fifty yards in front of him. The salt air burned his nostrils. He fell once when he misjudged his step and the surf caught him off balance. Denice moved easily and quickly, a lithe shadow in the moonlight. Robert momentarily lost sight of her when she disappeared around a wide curve in the beach.

On the other side of the curve, the beach broke into a series of low, rolling dunes. The white sand was too loose to hold footprints. Robert called Denice's name, but she wouldn't answer. Once he thought he heard her laugh, but when he looked in its direction, he saw a flock of gulls skimming the surf.

Robert wasn't sure how long or far he'd wandered before he finally found something resembling prints on the far side of the dunes where they'd started to flatten and taper out again. He walked around another curve in the beach and came to a construction site bounded by a high chain-link fence and a sign reading FUTURE HOME OF THE VALHALLA RESORT COMPLEX. He leaned into the fence and peered through. This time he was sure he heard Denice's laugh. He moved down the fence until he got closer to the waterline. A section of the chain-link had been twisted far enough back for someone to get through it in a crouch. Robert ducked and went under.

The immediate stretch of ground was cluttered with machinery— backhoes, Caterpillars, cranes, and earth-movers. On the other side of them were a couple of haphazardly placed trailers and piles of building supplies covered by canvas tarps. Robert saw a shadowy movement off to his right and headed in its direction. Only the superstructure of the Valhalla had been put up, and as he crossed onto its ground floor, above him were at least twelve stories of I-beams forming a thick grid against the night sky. There were lights strung in some of the corners but not enough to make a real difference in helping him negotiate his way. Robert's footsteps left flat echoes on the plywood flooring.

He might never have found Denice if she hadn't called to him. He followed her voice to the portion of the Valhalla facing the Gulf. Her breath was fast, and her kiss hard, her hands equally urgent. Even as he gave in to them, Robert knew from the tension in her shoulders and upper arms that Denice had found time to hit the coke stash again. Her purse lay partially open at their feet.

Their hands fumbled with zippers, snaps, and buttons, loosening or pulling back enough clothing to find the warm flesh beneath, and Denice's lips were on his neck and Robert supported her lower back as she tried to pull the dress far enough up to wrap her legs around him, the plywood flooring flimsy enough to leave balance precarious, Denice laughing and urging him on, Robert straining to lift his hips and find her but weaving under her weight, dizzy from the drinks and anticipation, Robert lost in one long ache and almost finding Denice when he heard footsteps and saw the quick glancing beam of a flashlight. He lowered Denice to the floor and put his hand over her mouth. She tried to bite him just as the flashlight swept over them and kept going in wide random arcs.

"I told you goddamn kids a hundred times," the guard shouted, "this is private property. You don't want to listen, fine. I'm going to haul your asses into the police station. Let Mommy and Daddy bail you spoiled little shits out of jail. I'm sick of this."

Robert looked around. He knew Denice and he couldn't negotiate their way across the ground floor of the Valhalla without getting caught, and below them, the beach was still torn up from the construction, making it too easy to sprain or break an ankle or leg if they jumped. It would be embarrassing but necessary to simply stand up and try to talk their way out of the mess. The guard was starting to sweep the flashlight back in their direction. Robert rolled over, struggling to tuck in his shirt and get it rebuttoned. Denice was rummaging through her purse and softly laughing. Robert was just untangling the zipper on his pants when Denice suddenly stood up and shot out one of the lights on the second story.

"Fuck Mommy and Daddy and you," Denice screamed. "You can't tell us what to do."

"You better stop it right there," the guard shouted back. "You're already in enough trouble. Let's keep it simple. There's no need for guns. I don't want anyone getting hurt."

Denice was still laughing. Robert started to get up.

"How about putting away the gun?" the guard asked. "We can work something out here. I promise."

"Okay," Denice called out. This time she fired in the direction of the voice. The flashlight fell and rolled across the floor.

Robert hesitated, trying to get his bearings, the gunshot and Denice's laughter still echoing in his head, and then he saw Denice crossing the ground floor of the Valhalla, headed for the chain-link fence and the cover of darkness, and he was up and running too.

ROBERT HAD HOPED FOR MORE from the shower than it delivered. He stood under a thin, tepid spray while the motel's plumbing thumped and gurgled and banged around him, and he left it feeling as sore and exhausted as when he'd stepped in. He took a long time drying off and then wrapped a towel around his waist. He wiped the condensation from the mirror over the sink and combed his hair. He brushed his teeth and wiped out the sink. He did anything he could to postpone stepping through the door into the other room. He didn't know what to say to Denice. Not after what had happened at the construction site.

As it was, Robert didn't have to say anything. Denice was in the middle of the unmade bed with her back to him, her head lowered and shoulders hunched, quietly crying. She was still in the black dress she'd worn at supper. Robert picked up the clothes he'd dropped earlier and straightened up the room. At one point he accidentally bumped the bed, and Denice lifted her arm and waved him away. Then she lowered her head again. The television was on, but the volume was turned down to a faint staticky hum. On the screen, a pair of dogs jumped around a woman's legs.

Robert let Denice cry herself out, the blond hair hiding her face, the muscles in her shoulders jumping and shuddering. He made each of them a strong gin and tonic and set them on the nightstand. He slid carefully onto the bed and moved behind her, putting his hands on her shoulders.

Denice jerked at his touch. "Wait, okay, Rob? Just wait."

"It'll be okay," Rob said. "We can check out of here tomorrow and put tonight behind us. We'll finish up the real-estate business and then get back to Key West. Things just got out of hand, but we'll work them out, you'll see." What he'd said was as much for his own benefit as Denice's. Robert wanted badly to believe it too. He leaned in and kissed her neck.

"Jesus, be careful, will you? I told you to wait. Okay? Don't be greedy."

Robert was about to ask what she meant, but as he leaned in again, he saw for himself: the small rectangle of mirror balanced on the top of her thighs, the long white line she'd cut, and the ghost of the other one she'd snorted. He'd mistaken the movements of her cutting and the sounds of her doing up for shakes and sobs.

Rob dropped back into his pillow and waited until she'd finished. He listened to the low grind and rumble of the ice machine outside their door and the slow fall of the leaky showerhead in the bathroom. On the television screen was a commercial for plastic wrap. A pair of hands deftly covered a plate of leftovers and held it up for inspection.

"Your turn now," Denice said, putting the coke and mirror on Robert's chest.

He watched Denice pick up two pieces of lemon from the drink tray and then move to the bathroom where she leaned over the sink and rinsed out her nostrils with cold water and then followed up with the lemon slices, squeezing them into her cupped palms and rinsing again. Her face was flushed and her eyes teared when she walked back in and leaned against the doorframe. "You better hurry if you're going to catch up," she said.

Robert could feel his heart beating under the mirror on his chest. Denice smiled and started to undress, but she was already disappearing into the room's décor, becoming part of the mirrors, television, and lamps bolted into place, the battered and cigarette-scarred nightstand, the faded blue drapes and thin carpet, the warped linoleum on the bathroom floor, the murky seascape on the wall above the bed. The scene and setting had been played out long ago by the hundreds of strangers who'd passed through the room, by the dozens of women who stood undressing in the doorway and the men lying on the bed who'd watched them.

"Come on, Rob," Denice said, slipping into bed. Her hand burrowed in the sheet and along the inside of his thigh. "Okay, then. You lie still, and I'll chop the lines." Denice rolled over, straddling him, and moved the mirror to the center of his chest.

When Robert looked down, the mirror threw back a distorted reflection of Denice's face, the angle catching her cheek and jawline and magnifying them, half of a lip and four teeth floating along a bright pink gumline. Over her shoulder, the television ran a commercial for rent-a-cars. A man in a loud green suit waved a handful of dollars.

Denice left the two lines on the mirror for him, slipped her thumb into the plastic bag and came out with a small conical pile of coke balanced on her nail. She then wet the index finger on the other hand with her tongue and pressed the finger to the thumbnail. She pulled back the sheet and found him and began slowly rubbing her finger and the cocaine in small circles. Robert felt himself quickly grow between her fingers and the muscles along the back of his legs begin to tense.

Denice took him briefly in her mouth, then turned back to him, smiling, and noticed he hadn't touched the coke. She leaned forward, locking Rob in a stare, and he felt the warm pressure of her thighs and saw himself floating in the green eyes, and he hesitated, then began to relent, but before he could, Denice said, "Fine," and took the mirror and coke and got out of bed, moving across the room to the desk next to the television stand. Her hands were shaking when she leaned over, but she persisted, daring Rob to say something, and when he started to, she jumped up, interrupting him.

"Ah, the Voice of Moderation, how well I know and remember it. You see, I was married to it for over two years. My good, reasonable, principled husband had that same voice. Carried it with him everywhere. Even into the bedroom. He only took reasonable risks too, Rob. And that's what killed him. The good man is now good and dead."

"It's just," Robert started in again, but Denice reached over and turned the volume of the television all the way up, a late night talk-show host's monologue exploding into the room, the sound of his voice twisted beyond anything human. Denice just as quickly turned it down.

"I don't have time for 'just,' Robert. You have to push past 'just' and 'or' and 'better' and all those other little words you love so much. They may get in your way, but not mine. It all comes down to what you can take. And I can take a lot."

Robert tried to block out the motel and just see the woman in front of him, but she wouldn't remain still long enough. Her movements had an energy that went beyond coke nerves. All Robert saw was the flash of a bare arm or leg that disappeared into a quick image from the TV screen that became the print of the ocean that hung in the cheap frame on the opposite wall. It was as if Denice pulled the whole room along with her every time she moved. He wanted to make her stop or find a way to separate her from the motel room.

The tricky thing about love was that all the clichés applied. Robert wanted to hold on to the Denice he'd known on other nights, when each moment was a constant June, an astonishment of the senses, and he could call what he felt, if he had to call it anything, love. Nights when after making love, he'd lie next to her with her hand in his, hers small and fine-boned, a pocket of warmth, and if he concentrated, he could fell the pulse tick in the center of her palm. He wanted those moments that opened like doors or windows onto something else, that suggested ways out or back in to a world full of promise and mystery, moments that simultaneously heightened and denied the fact of mortality in the same way looking at old snapshots did.

But in the Moonbeam, when he tried to find the woman whose body he'd once touched and tasted and entered, he found instead they had opened the door of the cliché and locked themselves in. They played house in the anonymous and easily illicit and turned themselves into appetite. They were fingers and mouths. They were rumpled sheets and moist openings. They were throbbing members, swollen nipples, wild moans. They were she wrapped her legs around his waist. They were nails on skin and heat. They were flesh and friction. They were. Nothing else.

*　*　*

"Christ, Denice. We're talking about a human life. You may have killed somebody tonight."

Denice leaned against the television and then tilted her head and gave Rob a small smile. "Why don't you tell me again what it was like to shoot Swolt, Rob?"

Robert sat up. "That was different. You know that."

"I'm not so sure. A trigger's a trigger." Denice pointed her index finger and then crooked it.

"Swolt was already dead."

"Is that a big enough difference to live with, Rob? The gun was in your hands. We're talking about a human life, remember?" Denice moved in front of the television, its light coating her upper thighs silver. She crossed her arms over her breasts and looked at him, waiting for his answer.

"Swolt was part of the deal and a problem. The security guard wasn't. You're twisting things." Rob picked up one of the gin and tonics from the nightstand and took a long swallow.

"No more than you're twisting things, Rob. You're still trying to believe you can explain everything and make it fit neatly. You're afraid to take risks unless they're safe and reasonable. But nothing is, Rob, whether it's what happened at the Valhalla tonight or what you did to Swolt. You still haven't learned that."

"I don't know if I want to."

Denice uncrossed her arms and moved to the edge of the bed. "People do what they want, Rob. Some want more than others."

Then there were hands on him, warm and probing, and those hands were joined to arms that wrapped around him and the arms were joined to shoulders that held the scent of perfume wrapped in sheaths of blond hair and then there were breasts and nipples, the delicate line of rib cage, the taut stomach, the wiry tangle of pubic hair, the long tanned legs sliding over and tangling with his, Denice's voice pouring over and claiming him, softly saying that what she wanted now was to finish what they'd started at the Valhalla.

But when Robert slipped into Denice and felt her tighten around him, he couldn't separate the moment when they'd stood inside the skeleton of the Valhalla, hungrily pulling at each other's clothes as their bodies strained against their limits, from the moment that followed when Denice pulled the trigger and the flashlight rolled across the floor.

He pushed deeper into Denice, wanting to find that space where the movement of flesh upon flesh was simultaneously fierce and sweet, strange and familiar, but his body betrayed him, and Robert floundered, unable to recover the rhythm of their lovemaking, Denice slipping farther and farther away as Robert struggled to catch up, his breath hammering in his lungs.

His release, when it came, was sharp, a hot twisting that caused him to duck his head and cry out.

What Robert couldn't understand was the blood.

Denice's legs were still locked around him and she was smiling and they were still moving, but there was blood too, dotting the pillowcases and Denice's cheek, and when Robert tried to speak, his throat closed up.

He could not give a name to what he saw in Denice's green eyes when she put her hand on the back of his neck and moved even harder against him. She parted her lips, and there in room 63 of the Moonbeam Motel, Robert saw the cliché they'd constructed for themselves begin to collapse. They had broken through and down into a space where something more than flesh yielded. Robert lifted his hand and touched his face. It was wet and hot, and no matter how he tried to tell himself otherwise, the nosebleed felt like it would last forever.

ROBERT SIGNED on the dotted line. From an air-conditioning vent hidden among the citations for sales, a large circular clock, and photos of properties fanning out like a display of baseball cards, a stream of cold air blew over the back of his neck. Carl "Woody" Woodell stuck a large dry hand across the desk and told Robert it had been a pleasure and that he hoped Robert would come by when he'd decided to move up from renting and was in the market to buy.

"Remember, you're never just a client at Gulf Properties, Mr. Tyndall," Woodell said, standing up. "*People* live in our houses."

Robert nodded, smiled, shook hands once more, and left. As he walked back to his car, he wondered if "Woody" Woodell would have modified his parting speech if he'd known the alias, Frank Tyndall, that Robert had used came from his fourth film, *Meat Me*, and that Frank Tyndall as a nondescript manager of a supermarket meat department had used the basement of his suburban tract home and the ranks of meat-cutting implements secreted there to turn half the population of his hometown into ground round.

It was a little after twelve, and Robert still had one more agency to call on about the property near the Sarasota-Bradenton airport. In addition to the house with Gulf Properties, Robert had closed on two backup houses with other agencies earlier in the day. He'd used a different name each time, all from his films, and he was trying to remember who he was supposed to be for the next place.

The Gulf Coast sun was not kind to anyone under it this afternoon. Its glare burned away the brightest color, whether it was on a shirt or blouse or the paint job on a car. When Robert touched the car door handle, it was like putting a finger on a lit match. Somewhere along the way he'd lost his sunglasses, and even if he squinted, the light was excruciating.

He got in the car and reread the article in the late morning edition of the paper about the shooting at the Valhalla. It barely rated six lines. As it turned out, the security guard was unharmed, but the shooting was under investigation. A police officer was quoted as saying the incident fit the pattern of a growing number of vandalism and looting cases on construction sites in the Sarasota area. Robert refolded the paper and dropped it on the seat. The relief he had hoped for never quite materialized.

On Route 41, the traffic was moderately heavy, and the ocean was bleached of color and movement by the light. It lay outside Robert's window like a large spill, the birds above it resembling paper cutouts glued on a wall.

Even in the car, Robert felt exposed. He was reminded of the scene, played and replayed in dozens of B films, when the gangster flanked by policemen and led from the halls of justice after sentencing is set upon by a mob of newsmen, the flashbulbs going off and trapping him before he can fully cover his face. The sky today had the same effect on Robert.

Denice wouldn't have bothered to try to shield her face, he thought.

But Robert knew he would. That's what he'd tried to explain to Denice last night in the Moonbeam after he'd gotten the nosebleed stopped. Robert didn't know if he'd given up or in, but he knew this: he needed excuses. Denice might be able to erase or leave them behind, but he couldn't play it that way. He would take any kind of excuse he could get, anything that would let him get his hand over his face before the light caught him. Even if it turned out Denice was the biggest excuse of all.

Robert got off 41 at the De Soto exit and drove to the real-estate office where, luckily for him, all the agents were busy and he was able to leave a deposit for a key with the receptionist and go on by himself. He didn't want company when he checked out the house again. It had been one of the better prospects from the other day, and he didn't expect to stay that long anyway.

The house was part of an early seventies subdivision that failed after the developer realized that the majority of the upwardly mobile middle class was not too excited about sinking their savings in a home that lay below a flight path to the Sarasota-Bradenton airport. The developer then decided to rebill the subdivision as a retirement community and had only slightly better luck because condos had begun to catch on. He cut his losses by putting up simple, inexpensive tract homes, but quite a few vacant lots remained on the curving palm-lined streets that still bore names more appropriate to the original conception. Robert drove past Delacroix, Mirabelle, and Hanover, turning left on Mayflower Lane and stopping in front of number 601.

The yard hadn't seen a mower in at least a month and a half, and Robert made a mental note to pick one up with the expense money, adding it to the list of things needed for the other houses, everything that would help them blend into the neighborhoods.

Number 601 Mayflower Lane looked like one of the easier ones. The house was on a curve in the street, out of range of any direct observation from neighbors. They didn't seem to pose much of a problem anyway. The lot had ample frontage, and of the closest two neighbors, according to the realtor, one was arthritic and widowed and the other was a couple who had an infant son and worked swing shifts.

Robert walked up the drive and let himself in. He left the door open behind him. The front room had the damp-cardboard smell he'd always associated with empty houses. The picture window in the living room was the only one of significant size. The stove and refrigerator in the kitchen were a bonus. They could move another range into the second bedroom when they brought the coke from Ed French's warehouse.

The backyard was something of a liability. It was small and nosedived into what Robert was sure the developer called a natural habitat, but which in reality translated into a swamp. Standing on the back stoop, Robert could clearly see where the developer's original dream or landfill contract dead-ended.

When he turned to go back inside, Robert ran into a short man wearing light blue slacks and a short-sleeved white shirt buttoned to the collar. He had a deep tan and hair the color and texture of whipped cream. He wore white canvas deck shoes without socks. His palm and fingers felt like a live eel when he took Robert's hand.

"My name's Peter Wright," he said, "but you can call me Pete. I was driving by, and I saw your car."

He moved back into the kitchen and spread his arms. "You could do better and you could do worse. That's what I told my wife, Evelyn, when we moved down here. A place in the sun is still a place in the sun. She didn't disagree. We've been married forty-four years."

The man smacked his head and smiled. "Excuse me, I get to talking and forget myself. I didn't even ask your name. Mine's Pete, like I said."

It took Robert a second to remember which one he was using. Then it came to him. Gregory Pale, the head psychiatrist of the private institution in *Vegetable.*

"You a family man, Greg?" Wright asked, leaning back against the kitchen counter. "This place'd make a nice starter home until you could work up a down payment on something bigger."

Robert began quickly organizing the details of his story, about how his wife would be coming down later in the month from Indiana, their jobs as teachers, his in a high school teaching history and civics, Denice's as a substitute in the area elementary schools until something permanent opened up, but Robert didn't have to worry about making everything fit because Wright was off and talking again before Robert got beyond the preliminary details.

"You should have seen it, the way we had the place fixed up, looked real nice. Evelyn was always good at stuff like that, same thing with the house we had in Hershey, PA. Nothing fancy, but nice. Raised four kids there. Three boys, one girl." Wright squinted at a fine crack in the ceiling plaster, frowned, and went on.

"They were all good kids. Put all four of them through college and was happy to do it. Never made it through myself. The money was a little tight at times, but the Hershey Company was good on overtime. I was foreman in the Kisses Division, you know, the little pieces of chocolate wrapped in foil? Worked my way up and I was making pretty good money by the time I retired. Want to hear something funny, though? I worked for Hershey thirty-seven years and never ate one of their Kisses or candy bars. I'm allergic to chocolate, it turns out. They told that one at my retirement party. It gave everyone a laugh, believe me."

Robert began trying to edge out of the kitchen. There was a slight roll to the floor, and each of his steps ended in a small squeak. Then he stopped. He couldn't leave just yet. Not until he got something clarified. Robert had to know why Wright had stopped by today and if he was the type to make it a habit. From what Robert had seen so far, he was. No matter how good the location was, setting up house here wouldn't work if Wright kept dropping by to reminisce. Robert supposed he could say something to the real-estate agent when he went in to sign the lease. Do it quietly and tactfully. But it was still a way of drawing attention, however small, and that was something they all wanted to avoid. He hated passing up the house because of a pesky old man.

"They still in the refrigerator?" Wright asked, and when Robert looked puzzled, Wright went over and opened it. "Left two of them kind of like a house-warming present." Wright pulled out two long-neck beers, the bottles dark green with white lettering, and went on the explain how hard it was to find Rolling Rock in Florida.

"Used to drink this all the time in PA," he said, starting to put them back in the refrigerator. Then he tilted his head around the door. "What say we crack them open now? You look like you could go for one, and I know I could."

"Okay, but it'll have to be a quick one. I have to be going."

Wright took a magnetized bottle opener in the shape of a red and green parrot from the freezer door and opened the beers. He handed one to Robert, and they clinked bottles. Robert thought of the light outside and the way it fell over the afternoon, and he welcomed the first long cold swallow.

Wright smacked his lips and then smoothed down his hair with his free hand. "Oh hell, might as well tell you." He pointed to the second drawer next to the sink. "Your wife might find it and throw it out."

A shiny new penny was taped to the bottom of the drawer. Robert and Peter Wright stood holding their beers and looking down at it. Robert had no idea what to say.

"It's not like I'm superstitious or anything," Wright said after he closed the drawer, "but I'd appreciate it if you and your wife would leave it there, at least for a while. We left one in the same place in our place back in Hershey. Evelyn asked me to do it. It's just the way she is. The same thing with the electricity. I had to leave it on even after we moved out. Evelyn doesn't like the house dark."

Robert didn't know what else to do except nod. He was already running through the other properties on the list he'd compiled. He had the feeling 601 Mayflower Lane wasn't going to work out after all.

"Like I said, Evelyn fixes up a place nice, and moving's hard on her. She gets attached. That's why the penny. She can't stand the idea that there would be nothing left of us in the house after we moved. It's also kind of like a good-luck thing for who moves in after."

Robert finished his beer in another long swallow and set the bottle in the sink. "I promise to tell my wife to leave it there. And speaking of leaving, I need to. Thanks for the beer."

Robert thought Wright was stepping in to shake his hand, but instead found his arm caught. Wright's fingers again reminded him of writhing eels. Wright said he was sorry in a way that suggested he wasn't. Robert started to back off, but Wright followed, still clutching his arm.

"I was just driving by the place today," Wright said, his voice tightening. "I do that sometimes, and I saw your car. I didn't want to intrude, but I was curious. I figured I could tell Evelyn who was moving in. Maybe it'd cheer her up a little. Especially if there was kids. Evelyn was a good mother."

Robert said he had to be going. Wright kept saying he was sorry, but wouldn't let go of his arm. He was also beginning to wave the beer bottle around a little too energetically for Robert's taste.

"A young guy like you, a nice dresser," Wright said, "I'll bet your wife, she's a real looker. Am I right?"

"She's very attractive. Look—"

"I thought so. Attractive. A looker. A knockout. I'm not surprised."

"I told you, I have to go now. How about letting go of my arm?"

Wright didn't appear to hear him. "That's something Evelyn isn't. A real looker, I mean. It's a fact. She never was, not even when I first met her. No one I know would ever describe Evelyn as a looker. But we've been married forty-four years. That's something, isn't it, I mean, sure there were times I'd see some nice-looking woman crossing the street and I'd wonder, but it never went any farther than that, I was home every night after work, Evelyn never had to worry where I was, and we were nice to each other, ups and downs sure, and maybe not as exciting as some, but we're talking about a life, and what I want to know is after all those years of working and saving and doing the best we could, don't you think we deserve a nice retirement in Florida, nothing fancy, just a nice little place where it's warm and sunny?"

"Sure. I guess so. Why not?" What else could you say to a question like that, Robert wondered.

"Evelyn always dreamed Florida, and that's what I saved for all those years. So you explain it to me."

"What? Listen, I really have to go now. I'm sorry, but I do." Robert began to pry Wright's fingers from his arm.

"We're down here six months and my wife starts getting headaches and sick to her stomach. The woman never complains, but I talk her into going to the doctor. They find lumps. Under her arm and in her breasts. They look around some more and then it's in her brain, the tumor's like a little time bomb in there, and the doctors know it's there, but can't get to it. They tell me Evelyn would be better off in a nursing home since I can't afford private care. What could I do? I put her in one and moved in too. The house didn't feel right without her."

"I'm really sorry," Robert said. Right then, he wasn't sure if he was describing himself or offering Wright condolence. Maybe both.

"I don't want sorry," Wright yelled, but his voice broke and his eyes began to well. "I want you, or someone, to explain it to me. Explain my wife and the tumor and Florida and forty-four years of marriage."

Robert bolted. He shook free of the old man's grasp and ran through the kitchen, living room, and out the front door to his car. The afternoon light caught him full-face, and without his sunglasses, his eyes had begun to water by the time he slid behind the wheel and made his getaway.

THE BONY MAN who ran the seashell stand slowly turned his head and watched Robert pull into the motel's lot. Nothing in the way he appeared had changed from the first time Robert had seen him: he still wore the white shirt, jeans, and the dark glasses that looked as if they were part of his face. By the time Robert parked, the man had turned around and was facing the street again.

Robert dropped the keys after he'd taken them out of the ignition. While reaching toward the floor, he looked up between the steering wheel and rearview mirror and saw the motel's sign floating directly above him, as if it had broken free and lodged itself in the sky. Even in the hard light, the sign glowed—a blue neon half moon meant to double as a face in profile, complete with a yellow neon eye that intermittently winked.

The room had been closed off for most of the day and smelled like a tidal flat. The maid's idea of cleaning seemed to consist of putting out fresh towels because the room appeared just as disheveled as it had been when he left this morning. Robert began to straighten up. He had to do something or he'd start hearing Peter Wright's voice again asking him to explain *why*. Denice wasn't due back from the realtors for at least two hours.

He was bent over his suitcase, trying to determine which side contained the clothes that were clean when at his back a voice said, "I already took them out. While you're at it, you might want to think about this too. Being dead. Which is what you're inviting, you leave the door open, Rob."

Barry From West Palm was dressed in pleated lime slacks and a dark blue shirt with intersecting black triangles. His sunglasses had left red indentions on either side of his nose, and his light brown hair was bunched at the top of his head from the elastic sides of a sun visor with two pelicans on its front and SAIL THE WIND printed on its brim.

Barry looked around the room, then stretched his arms and neck, sending his adam's apple careening toward where Barry's chin would have been if Barry's face hadn't decided to stop just below his lips.

"Swell digs, Rob. What, you never heard of Holiday Inn, Best Western, any of them? Me, I like the Shoney's on account they always got a restaurant right by. Thirty-two-item breakfast bar, all you can eat. They got good waffles. I can see why you pass all that up though, get to stay in a place like this. I bet you had to have reservations weeks in advance."

"What did you mean when you said you already took them out?"

Barry pushed past Rob to the bathroom. When he came back out, he stopped by Rob and said, "The gun and the coke. I didn't figure you needed to get your hands on either one right now." Barry gestured in the direction of the closet and bathroom. "Hurry up and get changed. Ditch the shirt and tie. We aren't going to be visiting any real-estate agents. We're going on a ride. Wear something dark."

"What about Denice? She isn't back yet."

Barry walked to the door, cracked it, and looked out. "She's already taken you for a ride. My turn now. Like I said, get changed."

After they'd gotten into Barry's Camaro, Barry slipped the key into the ignition, checked the rearview mirror, and turned to Robert. "All buckled up there?"

Robert nodded.

Barry From West Palm hit him in the face.

While Rob was bent over, straining against the belt and the pain breaking across his cheek, Barry leaned over and put him in a viselike headlock, bending him over farther still. Colors splashed across the back of Robert's eyelids. For a while, all that registered was the smell of Barry's cologne. Old Spice. It was the kind every one of his friends' fathers, including his own, had worn while he was growing up.

"I figure I hold you like this long enough, maybe some of that blood you got in you will move to your head, and maybe, enough gets there, your brain'll start working again. I hear you got your head up your ass, it cuts the circulation off after a while."

Robert felt a tickle in the back of his throat and was afraid his nose had begun to bleed again. A seashell roar climbed through his ears. When Barry finally let go, Robert threw his head back against the seat and gulped air.

"I hope your brain, it's all systems go now, because I'm only going to say this one more time. You're carrying a Smith & Wesson Airweight .38, you don't leave it packed in a suitcase in a motel room with a lock that looks like something out of Tinker Toys. You don't go driving all over Florida without the gun." Barry tapped the top of the steering wheel. "Those two Mariel boys, Manuel and Miguel, Russell Tills set loose on us, I shut them down, but that doesn't mean it's over. A deal like this, word gets around, you think the old Colombian coke guys, the *coqueros*, are just going to sit back and let Camar Tavares move into their territory? You run into one of the *coqueros'* boys, you won't have time to think about the gun in your suitcase. By the time you blink, you'll fit in one."

Barry From West Palm waited until Rob nodded and then started the car. They drove down the access road past the string of motels until they got to the Neon Slipper. Robert listened to the blink of the turn signal and did the same as the blood backwashed out of his brain. Barry made the turn, drove part-way across the lot, and stopped.

The small parking lot was full because the motel shared it with a cluster of adjoining businesses, a video shop, a small deli, a toy store, discount shoe outlet, pet shop, and used-record store. Barry From West Palm sat patiently behind the wheel, the Camaro's engine rumbling in the silence, and Rob watched him out of the corner of his eye, wondering how long it would take to unbuckle the seat belt and get the door open.

"You're not supposed to be looking at *me*," Barry From West Palm said. "You know where *I* am."

Then Rob saw the rental van. It was parked two slots down from the entrance to the video store. Barry From West Palm eased the Camaro farther down the center of the lot, and Robert sensed before he actually saw where they were headed. It was the kind of feeling that arose in the split second before you knew you were going to step on a loose shoelace or patch of ice.

Barry From West Palm stopped the car and kept his gaze straight ahead. Robert looked across the hood to the door to room 99 and the DO NOT DISTURB sign hanging from its knob. Parked in front of the door was a dark green Triumph convertible. An iridescent oil spill lay in the empty slot next to it.

Robert fingered his seat belt and then slipped his hand underneath it and cradled his stomach. Barry waited until Rob had the chance for a good, long look, then turned the Camaro around and drove through the lot, taking a left on the access road and heading in the direction of 41 South. He punched the button on the glove compartment, and the lid flopped open. "I got the gun here with me, under the seat, but you look in the corner of the compartment there, you'll find what you want."

Under a clumsily folded map of Florida was the stash from the Moonbeam, soft white and wrapped in a plastic sandwich bag. Robert closed the glove compartment door and sat on his hands. He wasn't sure if he'd made a choice or a gesture. Right now, it felt like a choice.

"Something that had to be done," Barry From West Palm said. "I needed you seeing it with your own eyes. I guess, sorry, that's what I could say here, but it's hard to feel sorry for a dumb shit, Rob, and you win the prize there. Not just my eyes either. Denice and Winde, they didn't even bother to go farther than three, four blocks from where you were staying. They're either careless or figure you stupid. You don't need a bookie, give you odds on which one."

Robert thought about the Neon Slipper. The door to 99. The DO NOT DISTURB sign.

What's your birthday? Denice had said.

December 29, 1958.

That adds up to ninety-nine.

So?

We're on Miracle Mile, Rob. Every shop has a number. The higher it is, the more exclusive the shop. We'll start at ninety-nine.

And go up or down?

We'll just have to wait and see.

"It makes you feel any better," Barry From West Palm said, "I'll kill Winde for you when this thing's over. I owe you one anyway, the way you helped me out, earlier there, being Carl and getting my mom to sign those papers. The thing is, right now, I can't chance you trying to take out Winde until I know what he's up to and the deal, we get it behind us."

Barry whipped into the drive-through lane of a fast-food chain and ordered a fish sandwich, cheeseburger, two fries, and large soft drinks. Barry had already eaten the fish sandwich by the time they were back on the highway. Later, when Barry raised his eyebrows at the untouched cheeseburger, Rob told him he'd lost his appetite, and Barry said too bad and speared the burger. Robert cracked the window and sat back, letting the Gulf air blow over his face, and tried to block out the sounds of Barry eating. Above the horizon, the sky was a wall of white light.

Barry slurped at his drink, then reached over and lightly punched Rob's shoulder. "A good idea, you keeping an eye on the side mirror. You're catching on, Rob."

Robert let Barry From West Palm believe what he wanted. The wind felt good on his face. Barry From West Palm kept the Camaro at just above the speed limit, and for the moment, movement was all Robert cared about. At Punta Gorda, when Barry said they were behind schedule and got off 41 for the interstate where they could make better time, all Robert did was nod. Make better time. That was fine with him.

Barry From West Palm kept glancing in the rearview mirror and over at Rob. "The attitude I'm recommending right now is see it as Denice giving you a set of horns and drop it."

"I don't think it's that simple."

"The fucking part is, but the rest of what's going on in that motel room, I know it isn't. I've been watching Winde. Nothing else we can do right now. Winde's not exactly what you call Mr. Trustworthy, especially now he's the head of the task force on drugs. Winde's always been ambitious, and this task force thing, it lets him work both sides of the fence. Hannibal's afraid Winde might try to use those new connections to rip us off legally. Wouldn't be too hard for him to set us up and then bust the whole operation, wait till things cool off, and push the confiscated weight on his own. The best we can do is anticipate, he decides to try anything funny. It wouldn't be the first time, something like that, it happened."

Barry rolled down his window and tossed out his soft drink and the wrapper from the burger. He shook his head and then pointed over his shoulder, back in the direction they'd come from. "It caught me off guard there, the thing with Winde and Denice. I don't know why I didn't figure her. I followed Winde all the way from Miami, and it didn't hit me until he turned into the motel. It made sense then. A weird kind of sense, him meeting Denice. It was like the Derrota and the whole thing starting over."

The Derrota Newsstand again. Every time he talked to someone, Rob heard another version of the Derrota. Swolt had his. So did Barry From West Palm. Russell Tills. Hannibal Binder. Denice. Lennie Ash. And Benjamin Franklin Lauter, alive or dead in Medellín or Buenaventura, probably did too. Robert listened to Barry run through it one more time, hitting its highlights: the old Cuban drug network unofficially headquartered in the Derrota Newsstand, Lauter using some D.C. interest in housecleaning the Derrota for his own ends since it gave him the chance to open the door to Miami for the Colombian *coqueros*, Lauter bringing together Russell Tills and Hannibal Binder, the three of them planning to set up their own network of production and distribution, Winde helping out from the agency angle, recruiting Barry and setting up his partners—Henry Swolt and Barry's brother Carl—so that when the shooting started, the smoke would never clear. And it hadn't for six years, until earlier in the summer when Lauter was trying to figure out how to edge Russell Tills out of the arrangement that had grown from the Derrota and Robert helped him out by accidentally losing the package he was supposed to deliver at the Miami International Airport.

"This deal with Camar Tavares has the same feel as the Derrota," Barry From West Palm said. "Things, they're moving ahead, but everyone's got a piece of action going on the side."

"What about you, Barry? What do you have on the side?"

Barry gave Rob a long stare. "Two things. One is staying alive. The other is protecting my investment. I sunk my old lady's money in the deal. I want my cut and what's coming to me. I'm going to walk out of the deal with my skin and some real change in my pockets."

"Denice said there's no such thing as a reasonable risk."

"She would." Barry From West Palm shook his head. "And you're the type that would listen to shit like that. You're as bad as my brother Carl."

"What did he ever do except get in the way of some bullets that came from your direction, Barry?"

"Oh, man. You're something, for sure. Were you listening at all, the time we paid my mom a visit and I explained about Carl? What did you think I was, just talking? I laid it out for you. I didn't figure I'd have to spell it. It was right there, you bothered to look."

"What are you trying to tell me?"

"What I shouldn't have to."

"It's pretty obvious that Denice and Winde go back a long way. What else?"

"What else is my brother Carl."

"Denice knew him?"

"Better, I'd say, than you know her. Better than Carl did, too." Barry shook his head and checked the rearview mirror. "I told you, she was in on the Derrota from the beginning. Think about why. You figure Lauter, Tills, and Hannibal going to give her a piece of the action because she smiles a lot and has a nice ass? They feel sorry for her, she ran off and got married before she could be Miss Florida? What do you think she had to trade, get in a deal like that?"

Oh my God, Robert thought. It was there, hidden under the rock of Denice's past that he'd never bothered to lift all the way because he'd been too busy trying to crawl out from under his own. He had asked enough questions. He just hadn't added up the answers.

"Fucking-A," Barry said. "Crying. You really didn't know any of this, did you?"

Robert's wet face surprised him too. He couldn't remember when he'd begun crying. It didn't seem any easier to stop either. His heart slammed against his chest like a fist belonging to a small, stupid bully, and his throat kept closing up.

"Denice and Carl were married, man," Barry said. "The whole husband-and-wife scene. Carl bought into it."

"That's enough, Barry. Okay. Enough." Robert waved his hand in front of his face and then dropped it to the door handle.

"I checked it out afterwards," Barry said. "I mean, I was the guy, after all, shot him."

"Winde must have put Denice up to it. What did he have on her?"

"The finger, man, point it the other direction. Denice set up Carl. He never saw what was going on. See, Denice was pregnant at the time, and Carl was doing his happy daddy routine." Barry hit the horn and whipped around a truck filled with watermelons. "You could flip a coin though and have the same odds who the father was, Winde or Carl. I don't think it mattered to Denice. All she wanted was in the deal. Winde wanted her, and they took it from there. Worked out fine for everyone but Carl."

Robert slowly sat back in the seat. He carefully lifted his arms and wrapped them around his middle as if he were handling an egg that had cracked but had yet to split open. Rob didn't go on to ask about the baby. He could remember all too clearly the story Denice had told him at Bagatelle's about her miscarriage.

"Why'd she marry Carl in the first place?" Rob asked. "Was it what Hannibal told me, that she wanted to get back at her father? Or away from him?"

Barry From West Palm shrugged. "Probably. I know Carl had it bad for Denice. You got to remember how Carl was, too. Good-looking and everyone liked him. Always had girls around, but Denice really threw him. Maybe it was the same for her, too, at least in the beginning. It wasn't until you were around Carl long enough you really got to know him, that you discovered what a pain in the ass he could be. Carl's problem, he acted like he invented Good. Carl had the chance to go places in the agency, if he'd looked the other way once in a while or a few favors, he'd helped out some people, but Carl liked the book, going by it and acting like he wrote it himself. No slack for anybody with Carl. He could have cut himself a piece of the Derrota. The only reason he died there was because he was Carl."

Robert remembered the pull and weight of the dark suit on his shoulders and the piece of Kleenex holding the lipstick print he'd found in its pocket. The suit had been hanging in the closet of the house on Simonton for almost a month. He wondered if Denice had ever recognized it.

"You see what you're looking at now?" Barry From West Palm said. "If Winde and Denice are working their own angle, they might figure they need another Carl. And you fit the shoe, Rob."

Barry From West Palm followed I-75 past Golden Gate and the exit for Naples, skirting the edges of the Everglades. Robert tried to avoid looking at the glove compartment. Every time he was tempted to reach for the coke, he turned the glove compartment into the door to room 99 at the Neon Slipper. That slowed down the desire to open it but didn't help much with the shakes or sweats. Or the memories.

A sign for U.S. 41 flashed by, and Rob told Barry he'd missed the turn-off for the Tamiami Trail. Barry From West Palm said he was aware of that and kept driving south toward the coast.

"I thought we were going to Miami."

"We are, but first, something else. We got to pick up the front money from Carlos Ramierz."

"But that wasn't supposed to come in for at least four or five days."

"Hannibal, he figured it wouldn't hurt, everybody thought that. Only thing I said, no way I was going into Ramierz's little guerrilla base in the Everglades to pick it up, so we did a compromise, a quiet little place along the coast here, that ought to be about five miles down the road. We pick up the cash, take it back to Miami. Hannibal already has Camar Tavares's associate booked in the Fontainebleau. Soon as he sees the cash's okay, he's on the next flight to Colombia, and Tavares ships."

Barry From West Palm followed a stretch of road bordered by wind-bent stands of scrubby palms and the undifferentiated green-and-brown sprawl of mangroves. He pulled into a gravel parking lot and stopped under a huge faded red-and-yellow sign proclaiming: WELCOME TO REPTILELAND. Another car was parked at the end of the lot, but no one was in it. Robert and Barry waited in the Camaro.

The entrance to Reptileland was a long, one-story cinderblock build-ing that had lost most of its paint. Part of the roof had collapsed, and the front door was missing. The picture windows were a memory, but a series of promotional signs still ran across the front of the building. HOME OF HARRY, THE KILLER KROKODILE. SNAKES, SPIDERS, AND LIZARDS IN THEIR NATURAL HABITAT. SOUVENIR AND SNAK SHOP. WE DARE YOU TO TRY OUR GATOR BURGERS AND MOCCASIN DOGS. FUN FOR THE ENTIRE FAMILY. TOURS EVERY HALF HOUR. SEE NATURE AT HER MOST TERRIFY-ING. FREE MAPS.

Barry honked the horn once.

There was movement just inside the doorway. Someone called out, "That you, Barry?" The accent was definitely not Cuban.

Then Lennie Ash came trotting across the parking lot, carrying a brown suitcase. He waved his free arm and was all smiles. Barry looked from Lennie to Rob to the headless plastic statues of Jesus glued to the dash. He started to unbuckle his seat belt, and Rob did the same.

"You're late," Lennie said, leaning in the window as if he were about to give Barry a quick welcoming kiss. He'd set the suitcase on the hood of the Camaro. A pair of handcuffs dangled from its handle.

"What the fuck's going on? You're not supposed to be here." Barry craned his neck and looked over Lennie's shoulder. There was no movement anywhere.

"The call came through this afternoon. A change in schedule. Ramierz showed early. I made the pickup. The money's all here. Absolutely."

"I don't like the smell here," Barry From West Palm said.

"Hey, Barry, it's me, Lennie. Okay?" He gave Robert and Barry From West Palm a wide smile and then stepped back and shot them.

IF BARRY FROM WEST PALM had been born with a chin, it would have been resting on Robert's chest. As it was, when Robert came to, he found Barry's body on top of his and Barry's head turned at a seemingly impossible angle, his cheek lying flat against Robert's chest but with his eyes directed at the ceiling of the Camaro. The brim of the sun visor Barry had been wearing was crushed and bent so that its slogan now read AIL HE WIN. Barry's mouth was frozen in a comic-book O. A busy mosquito was attached to his cheek.

Robert tried to find the purchase to get up from the floor of the Camaro, but his left arm was numb and distant, and his shoulder throbbed. He worked his legs against Barry's weight, slowly drawing them up until his knees were bent, using them to displace some of Barry's bulk, and then he put his right hand on Barry's shoulder and pushed. Barry moved a couple of inches lower. Robert went through the whole thing again and moved the body another inch or two. Robert was afraid he was going to pass out. He was covered in sweat, but managed to get through the maneuver another time before he had to stop and rest.

Robert watched the mosquito leave Barry's cheek, circle the dome light, and then settle on Robert's arm. He tried unsuccessfully to shake it off. It clung and bit.

He looked up at a knot of orange-and-white wires dangling from below the dashboard. Above it was the head of the plastic Jesus Barry had glued to the radio dial, its face averted, still holding the same easy-listening station Barry had subjected them to on the ride down. At the farthest edge of his vision, suspended against the pale light coming through the windshield, was the cardboard car deodorizer with Cherry, the airbrushed pinup girl, sitting astride an alligator and cupping her breasts. Everywhere else—the seat, floor, and the front of Robert's shirt—was blood.

Robert was about to draw his legs up for another push when he heard a car pull into the gravel lot, a door open and close, and voices, one of them Lennie's and another that sounded familiar but he could not place just then. He lay still and closed his eyes just enough to still be able to distinguish two shapes that hovered in the window on the driver's side and then melted away. Robert achingly drew his legs up and pushed again.

Barry eventually became wedged against the gearshift. Robert had moved him a little less than a foot. With his good arm, Robert reached up and grabbed the edge of the dash and pulled while he used his knees to force Barry's upper torso back far enough to slip out from underneath. For a second, from the way the body gave against his knees, Robert was afraid Barry would literally fall apart or that Robert would sink right through him.

His left shoulder throbbed as if he'd been slamming it into a door, and Rob was barely able to move his arm. He was pretty sure the bullet was still lodged in his shoulder because something ground against bone each time he moved.

I'm alive, Robert told himself and waited for some sense of joy or wonder or, at the very least, relief from the discovery, but all he was left with were the blood-soaked seats and the three gaping holes in Barry's back and the gun lying next to him and the large red-and-yellow sign at the edge of the lot floating in the hard light and everything Barry had told him about Winde, Denice, and Carl. *I'm alive.* It sounded like the title of a Worldwide film.

Robert walked through the side gate and onto the main grounds of Reptileland before he thought about what he was doing. He was away from the car. That was a start. He was carrying Barry's Llama .22 automatic. That meant something too, though he could not exactly say what. His shirt felt gritty against his skin, at least in the places where he could tell the two apart.

Robert followed the curving gravel paths past the DO NOT FEED signs and the rows and rows of wire cages banked along the walk, all of them open and empty. To his right, a tall, desiccated traveler palm, surrounded by tired tropical vegetation that had once passed for someone's idea of atmosphere, pointed at the sky like a long finger. He passed another bank of empty cages and then a picnic area. Farther on was an alcove in the vegetation bounded by a chain-link fence that held an empty, mud-caked pit sprinkled with trash. A sign above the pit proclaimed: HARRY'S HOME.

The tropical landscaping gave way to a playground, a series of collapsing concession stands, and a miniature golf course. Running along the outermost border of Reptileland was a long cement seawall. Large sections of it were spray-painted with obscenities and lovers' vows.

Robert moved through the playground, past the merry-go-round creaking slowly in the wind, the sliding board pulling free of its supports, the rusty tangle of a jungle-gym set, pausing by the see-saws to check the safety on the Llama. He thought he saw movement on the far side of the golf course.

Robert started walking again, not going out of his way to hide his approach. It wasn't that he felt careless or reckless. It was just that getting shot simplified things. When he'd crawled out of the carnage in the front seat of the Camaro, Robert discovered an odd clarity. He knew that trying to anticipate what he would do or what could happen to him wouldn't work anymore. Every plan led to the Neon Slipper and the door to room 99. What was left was Reptileland, and there were plenty of signs here to help him with anything he needed to find.

He walked behind the string of boarded-up concession stands and onto the golf course, following its fairways. The Astroturf was faded and peeling, large portions of it rubbed bare like patches of mange. Most of the ceramic menagerie dotting the course had been broken or overturned by vandals. As he walked, Robert stepped over a bright green alligator tail, the head of a red lizard, and a pink flamingo neck.

At the eighth hole, Robert found Lennie Ash lying face down in a stagnant water hazard ringed by smiling ceramic frogs.

Robert stopped at the ninth hole and the badly tilted windmill flanking it. Franklin Benjamin Lauter was bent over the suitcase, checking the cash. Robert waited until Lauter turned around to raise the gun. Lauter didn't seem surprised. Robert wondered if Lauter had ever been surprised in his life.

"A nice touch," Lauter said, "but a bit redundant, Robert. First me, now you. The next thing you'll tell me is Barry's come back from the dead, too."

"I don't think you have to worry about that."

"I wasn't."

Lauter had managed to kill Lennie without wrinkling or marring his own wardrobe. He looked like he was ready for a luncheon at a country club. A pair of sharply creased rust-colored slacks. A pale yellow knit shirt. Brown loafers. Tortoise-shell-rimmed sunglasses that adjusted to the light. A gold Rolex. Even the wind off the ocean couldn't disturb the hair perfectly combed and sprayed in place.

Robert told Lauter to throw the gun he held loosely at his side over the seawall. Lauter hesitated but finally gave in. "Your sunglasses too," Rob added. When Lauter asked why, Robert said he wanted to be able to see his eyes.

"A bit dramatic, Rob, but okay. Anything else?"

"Yes. Move back against the seawall and spread your arms across its top." The gun had begun to tremble in his hand, and Robert didn't need any sudden moves. The throbbing in his left shoulder had grown worse, and the feeling in his arm was leaving.

Lauter made an elaborate show of doing what he'd been told. Then, when he was in position at the seawall, he glanced over at his watch and said, "Let's cut the lights-camera-action stuff, Rob, and get down to business. I'll give you ten percent of what's in the suitcase, and you walk out of here. I forget I ever saw you."

Lauter looked like he was lounging against the wall, not being held prisoner. "Don't you have a few things turned around?" Rob asked. "Isn't it supposed to be me that forgets seeing you? And what about the gun? I could shoot you and take all the cash."

"Let me answer your second question first. You won't shoot me because you can't. You're not the type. Lennie or Barry would, but not you. As regards to your first question, it would be more convenient if you forgot seeing me, but it won't matter in the long run because I'm due to be formally resurrected soon. So, how does ten percent of a little over $750,000 sound now?"

Robert kept the gun steady on Lauter and remained silent. Lauter took that in, and then, a little impatiently, began to outline the reasons for Robert accepting his offer.

Lauter glanced at his watch and then at the sky and said that even if Robert tried to walk away with the money, there would still be no deal because there never had been one in the first place, at least not along the lines that had been originally worked out. He and Camar Tavares had an arrangement, and it didn't include Hannibal, Lennie, Robert, Barry, or any of the others in any significant way. Lauter had needed capital for a new project and the plane crash and disappearance with the original front money had given him the first installment. Lauter said he'd been counting on Hannibal's ego to get the second reel rolling and Hannibal hadn't disappointed him. Lauter waited until Hannibal had set up and renegotiated the deal and then put pressure on Lennie, the easiest of anyone involved to turn. Lauter had a lot of friends in the IRS, and Lennie had been more than happy to give him the time and date of pickup. Lennie just hadn't counted on Lauter personally flying Stateside to meet him. The element of surprise had helped since it turned out that Lennie had some ideas of his own about the size of his share that Lauter had been forced to disagree with. "And so," Lauter said, slapping his hands along the top of the seawall, "here I am."

Robert put every ounce of strength and concentration he had on keeping the gun steady. He remained silent and waited. He was determined to make Lauter fully explain himself. Robert remembered all too clearly what it had been like when he had lost the envelope and Lauter had sat across the table and waited for him to explain.

Lauter crossed his legs at the ankles and looked over Rob's shoulder toward the tall traveler palm rising from the center of Reptileland's main grounds. "You need to consider the anti-Fidelista Cubans, too, Rob," he said finally. "You might take the money from me, but staying out of Carlos Ramierz's way after he finds out there is no deal is not going to be easy. He and his Anti-Fidelista pals are not going to look

kindly on any laissez-faire tampering with the funds for *la lucha*."
Lauter drummed his fingers on the top of the seawall. "It's your choice,
Robert, but believe me, you're playing way over your head here."

"That's what everyone keeps telling me," Robert said finally. "Barry
From West Palm said the whole deal reminded him of the Derrota
Newsstand."

"From a certain perspective, I suppose it does."

"What about from yours?" Robert tried to keep his words from
betraying his struggle to hold the gun steady. Every one of his muscles
trembled. His shoulder burned. He felt like he was balancing a brick
on the end of his fingertips. He was going to have to make a decision
soon about what to do with Lauter. He was counting on Lauter to say
or do something to help him make it.

"You still don't see, do you?" Lauter said. "We're not talking about
addiction, pleasure, or evil. We're not talking about greed or ambition.
Or personalities or life-styles. We are talking about something very
different. Cocaine is not a drug. It's power. Nothing else. It makes
things happen. That's where its ultimate value lies. It's what the world
runs on. The Derrota was a necessary conduit for that power. It fit
the times. Excessive, extravagant, flashy, and fast. But the eighties are
over, and the nineties call for something different."

Lauter paused, and Robert was afraid that was all he was going to
get out of him, but the pause was for effect because Robert realized
that Lauter had become caught up in his own explanation. The power
that Lauter talked about ran Lauter, too.

"The first signs of that change," Lauter said, "are already here. Look
around and what do you see? A call for the return to traditional middle-
class values. Couples scrambling to beat the biological clock and starting families. The happy household as a refuge from a world that seems
out of everyone's control. People talk about cholesterol levels and the
ozone layer. They're tired and afraid of the fast lane. They want
reassurance. And providing that reassurance can produce some very
large profits."

It was hard to believe what Lauter said next or how glibly he delivered
it. In order to give people what they wanted, he was now working as
a middleman for some influential and interested parties in D.C. and

for Camar Tavares and some of his Colombian associates. The D.C. people were willing to lay out a large amount of cash for Camar Tavares to produce large quantities of low-grade coke. Lauter would help with the shipping arrangements and public-relations details. "Necessary infrastructuring of belief modules," Lauter called it. A refinement of the new diplomacy in which the wolf didn't don sheep's clothing but rather the lion's and then stretched out next to the lamb.

In the new arrangement, Lauter said, every coke shipment would culminate in a well-publicized bust by the new task force. Everybody benefitted. Camar Tavares got his money, the D.C. people came across as cavalry-to-the-rescue in the war against drugs, and the average American tuning into the national news could sit back and feel safe for another day. *My movie*, Lauter had called it at the Miami International Airport and Robert supposed it was. The war on drugs was transformed into a form of entertainment.

"The times call for a different way of packaging the coke," Lauter said, "but it doesn't diminish its power. That's why I intend to walk out of here with my cash, Robert. It's seed money for what we're working out. A sign of good faith."

"What happens to the confiscated poundage after the staged busts?"

Lauter gave him a thin smile, and as it appeared on Lauter's tanned and smooth-cheeked face, Robert started to come to his decision. A thin smile. A cliché. Denice and he had found theirs in the Moonbeam Motel. Here in Reptileland, he was looking at another. Both times, he had ended up covered in blood.

"I want to know one more thing," Robert said. "Has Winde been in on this deal from the beginning?" The smile remained on Lauter's face, but something else leaked out along its edges. Amusement or contempt. With Lauter, it was impossible to tell them apart. Robert kept the gun pointed at the center of his chest.

"That's what all this is about, isn't it? You stand there holding a gun on me, not because of what's in the suitcase but because of Denice and Winde. I offer you the ten percent and take the time to explain why it's in your best interest to accept it, and all we've really been talking about the whole time is a piece of ass."

Robert almost shot him right then.

"I can arrange it so you get Denice back," Lauter said. "That's no problem. You can keep the ten percent too. I have my own plans for Winde. He's always been useful up to a point, but Winde has the tendency to assume too much and overreach. I don't think he fully understands what he's grabbed hold of this time."

Lauter ran his hand across the top of the seawall and told Robert that heroes were also a form of reassurance, dead heroes in particular. Lauter thought it only fitting that when the first bust of the new arrangement came up that Winde as head of the newly commissioned task force be on hand to make it. It would be a bust of heroic proportions, and Winde would be justly and widely eulogized for his valiant front-line efforts.

Behind Robert's back, the miniature windmill on the ninth hole creaked slowly in the wind. When Lauter finished talking, he pushed himself away from the seawall, walked over to the suitcase, and opened it. Robert watched him count out the ten percent, not bothering to look once in Robert's direction, Lauter's posture and every one of his gestures suggesting the matter was already closed. Lauter left the money in a precise pile next to his shoe, closed the suitcase, and stood up.

"I told you we could work something out, Robert," he said.

Robert nodded. That's what they were here in Reptileland for, to work something out, and he was now beginning to see what it was. He told Lauter to pick up the money he'd left next to the suitcase and throw it over the seawall.

"What? You can't be serious."

"I told you. Pick it up and throw it over the wall. Or I'll kill you. I promise you I will."

"You crazy bastard. Why? What's this supposed to mean?"

"Do it."

Lauter hesitated, shifting his weight on the balls of his feet, his eyes searching out Robert's but finally not liking what they saw there because he did what he was told, picking up the stacks of bills and flinging them into the waters of the Gulf.

"Now open the suitcase," Robert said.

Lauter was in a semicrouch, calculating the distance between Robert and him and how quickly he could cover it, but he pulled up when

Robert said he had figured it, too, and there were time and room enough for him to get off two shots. He'd already decided on their placement: the upper chest and lower abdomen, areas of significant damage, according to Barry From West Palm. Lauter raised his hands in a gesture of placation and said that none of this was necessary. Robert agreed. Necessary or unnecessary didn't figure in what was being worked out here. He told Lauter to throw the rest of the money over the seawall.

Lauter's hands were shaking by the time he'd finished, and the back of his shirt had pulled free of his pants. His face was flushed and his hair disheveled. There had been no efficiency to any of his movements, just an unrestrained fury each time his fingers touched another tightly packed bundle of currency.

"I just threw over three-quarters of a million dollars in the goddamn ocean. I won't forget what happened here, Staples." Lauter kicked the empty suitcase.

"You weren't supposed to."

"You don't do something like this to me. Nobody does. I hope you understand that."

Robert told Lauter to pick up the suitcase and then waved him away from the wall, telling him to stop walking when he got to the water hazard at the eighth hole and Lennie's body. He made Lauter turn Lennie over and go through his pockets until he found the keys to the handcuffs on the suitcase handle. There was blood on Lauter's hands and his yellow knit shirt when he finally produced the key.

"Throw it over here," Robert said, after Lauter had unlocked and taken the cuffs from the handle. "Now handcuff yourself to Lennie. Then hold his arm and yours up so I can see they're on."

Robert tucked the gun under his arm and slowly bent over and picked up the key. He slipped to one knee, barely able to keep his balance. For a moment, he was afraid he was going to pass out. He closed his eyes and tried to hold on to whatever was starting or finishing here. He lifted his face into the wind. He thought about Denice and the door to room 99, Carl's suit hanging in the closet in the house on Simonton, Barry dead on the floor of the Camaro. He looked over at Lauter squatting next to Lennie at the water hazard and dropped the key in his pocket.

"You know none of this matters." Lauter lifted his and Lennie's arms and let them drop. "My lawyers will have every charge dropped within a half hour. If it even gets that far. So what I want to know is why. The deal between the D.C. people and Tavares had nothing to do with you. I explained that. Winde was going to be taken care of. Everything would have worked out to your advantage. You could have left here, clear and free. What have you accomplished? To make me throw your cut and all the rest into the ocean, that's either stupid or crazy."

"No," Robert said. "Neither."

"What then?"

"An almost. I wanted you to know what it felt like. Maybe you're right and none of this matters, but while you're handcuffed to a dead man and surrounded by mosquitoes and all those smiling ceramic frogs, I want you to think about that money floating around in the Gulf and how everything almost worked out. That's your why."

Robert turned and walked away, cutting across the main grounds of Reptileland. The wind and the smell of the ocean followed him. In the parking lot, he checked to make sure the keys were in Lennie's rental. Then he shot out the tires of Lauter's car and Barry's Camaro. A salty taste flooded Robert's mouth, and there was a moment, a long one, when he considered reaching through the passenger-door window and opening the glove compartment and taking the coke stash. He couldn't say what finally stopped him from doing it. He supposed there were reasons. There usually were. He just wasn't sure they mattered at Reptileland. He wasn't sure he did either.

Before he got in Lennie's car, Robert wiped down the gun and dropped it in a trash bin whose top and lip had been painted to resemble gaping alligator jaws.

ROBERT STAPLES WAS SITTING AT THE COUNTER of an all-night diner at the end of the night. From behind a narrow green metal door at the far end of the counter, someone, probably the cook, cursed in Cuban. It was followed by the clatter of pans and the vicious thump of a knife against a cutting board. The waitress, carrying a pot of coffee, paused to turn up the radio on a shelf behind her. The air conditioning was working at half capacity. Robert began to notice flies.

"You want more or what?" the waitress asked, leaning into his face. In her left hand, she held up the coffee pot. She was young, with dark shiny skin and eyes. There was a small plastic flower tucked in her black hair just above her ear.

Robert sipped at his coffee, hoping it would provide a small counterbalance to the effects of the painkillers. He knew every emergency-room doctor was required to report gunshot wounds, so after leaving Reptileland, he'd bypassed the hospitals in Naples and driven to Ed French's warehouse and salvage operation outside Marco in the Ten Thousand Islands, figuring that along with a sheriff and shrimper and general store manager, there had to be a doctor, or someone close enough to being one, who was related to French. Everyone in the community was in one way or another. French's third cousin, who was also the game warden, took the bullet out of his shoulder. A cousin to French's wife's uncle ran the pharmacy and provided the Percodan. French's wife got him some clean clothes. All for a price, but French had reluctantly agreed to add the cost of the services to the warehouse bill. Robert let him worry about collecting on it.

Robert had gotten back on the Tamiami Trail and driven across the

Everglades and back to Key West on automatic pilot. It had taken him most of the night. He had gone back to the shotgun house on Simonton and picked up some of his things and then swung by the bus station and used the key to locker A3 that he'd taken from False Walter. A little after 4 a.m., Robert pulled onto U.S. 1 and left Key West behind. He'd managed to get another hour and a half of driving in before his exhaustion forced him to stop at the diner north of Islamorada. By that point, Robert had worked out an idea that had a chance of saving what was left of his life.

The diner's pay phone was out of order, but the waitress pointed out another at the far edge of the parking lot where it intersected with the street. Robert thanked her and said he'd be back in a few minutes. He crossed the lot and shut himself in an old phone booth that was illuminated by its own small rectangle of light.

The call to the Moonbeam Motel should have been easier to make than it was. Robert tried to keep the image of the door to room 99 in the front of his mind, and he thought the distance, the fact that there were hundreds of miles separating them, would help keep him safe from the pull Denice had always been able to exert on him, but he felt it working on him the moment she picked up the receiver and spoke. Her presence had immediately flooded the phone booth, surrounding Robert as he leaned against its glass walls, Denice's voice evoking her touch, then the long tanned body, its taste and heat and tightness, and all the times Robert had been joined with it. Robert felt the same need and ache that he'd experienced when he'd returned to the parking lot at Reptileland and thought of the coke lying in the glove compartment of the Camaro, and he tightened his hold on the receiver and interrupted Denice, hearing all the promise and allure and sensuality leak into the oceanic hum of the telephone lines as he told her what had happened at Reptileland and then laid out the conditions of his proposition.

"You still haven't told me where you are," Denice said.

"That's not as important as where I've been. I found quite a few interesting items in locker A3 at the Key West bus station."

"You're bluffing. I have the key right here." The line went momentarily dead, and then Denice was back on again, her voice flat with either resignation or cold anger. "Okay, Rob. You have the key as well as my scrapbooks, journals, and the phonebook you lost at Miami International. All the dirt, and it's in your hands. You could bring half of D.C. and Miami to its knees. What are you going to do with it?"

"I want a trade-off. I need some insurance against Lauter. He's not going to let me walk away from what happened." Robert stopped and let Denice think about the next step. He knew it wouldn't take her long.

"You say Lauter's still at Reptileland?"

"Probably. He can't go far handcuffed to Lennie's body, and there's nothing for miles around the place. It's going to take him a while to find help. I took the keys to the ignition and shot out the tires of the cars left in the lot. Reptileland is below Naples off Forty-one on an old access road. You and Winde could be down there in a couple hours."

"Why didn't you just shoot Lauter yourself and save all of us the trouble?"

"Because I wanted Lauter to think about what happened there. And I want you and Winde to do the same thing on the drive down."

Robert heard a small click and then a long exhale after Denice lit a cigarette. "Okay, Robert. Let's say Lauter is eliminated. I suppose it doesn't matter if I believe you or not about the money being thrown into the Gulf because even if it wasn't and you have it, it's still out of reach for now. Unless—"

"I don't have the money," Robert interrupted. "You might as well accept that. It'll save you a lot of time trying to figure out some way of getting it back. When we restructured the deal, I kept out a little over five thousand dollars from the sale of my parents' home, and that's it. You're welcome to whatever's left floating around Reptile-land."

Denice was silent for a moment. "Why didn't you take what you put into the deal from Ramierz's money?"

"You probably won't understand this, Denice, but I didn't want it. Somewhere along the way, I lost the right to it. The money wasn't mine anymore."

"A pretty speech, Rob. Be sure to remember it down the road when you try to bankroll a future on five thousand dollars. I'm sure it'll be a comfort to you."

"My future's not the only one in jeopardy at the moment. There's still the matter of the contents of the bus locker."

Denice waited a moment, then said, "Okay, Rob. We'll take Lauter out. Winde can work it so that Reptileland is a showpiece for the new task force. He can stage a bust so that it looks like the deal went sour and all the bad dope dealers shot themselves up. It'll play well in the media and should cover most of the damage from what's happened. When things stabilize, we can renegotiate Lauter's deal with Camar Tavares. With Lauter gone, Tavares is going to need a new middleman to handle the D.C. people. That kind of protection is just too sweet for Tavares to pass up. With a little grooming, Hannibal Binder might fit the spot. Things could turn out okay for everyone concerned."

Denice waited, letting the silence work for her, before she softly added, "For you, too, Rob. You know what kind of leverage the contents of the locker gives you on Winde. He'd have to back off and give you and me some room. You and I could play it differently this time. We deserve another chance. We're more alike than you've ever wanted to admit. Winde might not like you back in the picture, but there'd be nothing he could do about it."

"That is, until he needed a star for his next staged bust," Robert said. "I've had to shoot a dead man and impersonate another one this summer. That's as close as I want to get. You and Winde can cut any kind of deal you want with Tavares. I want out."

"What are you going to do with what you took from the locker, Rob?"

"I want to know something first. How did you get your hands on the phonebook?"

Denice sighed. "Winde and I found it at Swolt's place before you, Barry, and Lennie arrived with the body. I left with the book, and Winde stuck around and made sure you and the others didn't get suspicious when the book wasn't at the house. Winde wasn't sure what Swolt had said to you. Barry saved us a lot of trouble by shooting Swolt in the parking lot of the mall because with Swolt dead, there was no one to contradict Winde's claim he couldn't find the phonebook. That's why he had Barry burn down the house. We figured it would keep anyone from looking for the book or asking too many questions until Russell Tills was out out of the partnership."

Robert leaned against the glass wall of the phone booth. The pain in his shoulder and arm was coming back, and he shook out two Percodans and swallowed them. Denice asked again what he was going to do with the contents of the locker. Robert looked back across the lot at the diner and the blue-and-yellow neon sign on its roof reading EAT HERE.

"Once I know everything's all right," Rob said, "I'll send the phonebook and your journals and scrapbooks back to you in Key West. Before I do, I'm going to make copies of each and put them in a safe deposit box along with letters to the *Washington Post* and *Miami Herald* explaining their significance. If anything should happen to me, my father's attorney will be authorized to open the box and go public. Make sure Winde understands that, or his illustrious career will be over. I don't want anything from Winde or you except to be able to walk away without having to check my back every five minutes."

"That's all you want, Rob?" Denice asked, letting the question hang between them.

Robert waited, too. He listened to the hum and faint crackle of static running through the lines and looked past the smudged fingerprints on the glass walls of the booth to the brightly lit service station across the street, empty now except for the green and red pennants flapping in the wind and the attendant who stood on the middle gas island and wiped his hands on a rag he'd pulled from his back pocket. "Yes," Robert said finally.

"Okay, then. You always did confuse risks with betrayal," Denice said. "But there's something else I want you to remember, Robert. Whatever else you thought, I never asked to be forgiven or understood."

"And I never wanted to be Carl," Robert said quietly, maybe too quietly, because he wasn't sure Denice had heard him, but when he tried to start over, the phone was dead in his hands.

Robert walked back to the diner and took his seat at the counter. He pulled some napkins from the dispenser and wiped his face. His arm and shoulder still throbbed, but the painkillers had begun to kick in. He looked up to find the waitress leaning over the counter. "You want them scrambled or fried or what?" she asked. Her lipstick was the same shade as the bottle of ketchup next to the napkin dispenser. Robert watched her play with the plastic flower tucked behind her ear and guessed that at some point he'd begun to order breakfast.

"Fried."

"How fried?" She tapped the pencil against her palm.

"Over easy. Over very easy." Robert watched her disappear behind the metal door and wondered when he'd decided he was hungry.

To Robert's right was a large plate-glass window that held his reflection and that of the other patrons—werewolves, a friend of his had once called them, all those who for one reason or another found themselves adrift in the early hours of the morning: two truckers who sat over coffee and cigarettes; three teenagers who'd been out drinking; a disgruntled tourist couple; a mechanic on break; a bored cop; two men, solitary, slightly seedy, nondescript as salt shakers; an elderly man, impeccably dressed in a three-piece suit; a nurse, just off her shift, who kept glancing at the door, as if expecting somebody.

The well-dressed old man was explaining to the waitress in carefully measured tones about Key limes. "Most people confuse Key with Tahiti limes, which are green and lemon-shaped and the ones most frequently found in supermarkets. Key limes are nothing like them. They are, in fact, yellow and the size and shape of golf balls. It is almost impossible to find them in Florida today. That is why Key lime pie is a misnomer. There are no Key limes in Key lime pie." He sounded immeasurably sad. The waitress nodded and fiddled with the radio dial.

Farther down the counter, a man in a faded red T-shirt sat hunched over his coffee. He suddenly swiveled on his seat and announced, "There are forces at work here. We are not alone. But the question is, do we want the company?" Before anyone could reply, he abruptly swung around to his coffee.

The nurse lit a cigarette and watched the door.

The placemat in front of Robert was bordered by oranges and alligators. In its center was a list:

Florida Facts

ORIGIN OF NAME: Florida, from the Spanish, meaning
"Feast of Flowers."
STATE SONG: Old Folks at Home.
STATE FLOWER: Orange Blossom.
STATE NICKNAME: Sunshine State.
STATE MOTTO: In God We Trust.
STATE BIRD: Mockingbird.

The waitress brought his breakfast, and Robert began to unwrap the silverware that had been rolled up in a white paper napkin. The whole idea of food and the act of eating it suddenly seemed foreign and unbearably strange. He was to pick up these stainless-steel objects, cut up the matter before him, spear it, then put it inside him. If he did, everything would be okay. A basic need would be satisfied.

But why, if it was so basic, did it seem so strange, so contrived and elaborate, everything from the silverware designed to fit fingers and hands to the signals from the brain, the workings of digestive juices, the network of veins, the anticipation of intestines?

Nourishment and waste, something basic. This eating was necessary to life, Robert thought, and he was alive, so he should eat the eggs, hash browns, and bacon because he was alive, and eating would keep him that way. There should be nothing strange about any of that. It's what diners were for, after all, and by coming to this one, Robert was acknowledging its purpose. That was a start of sorts.

He still didn't feel exactly hungry, but it seemed important that he speared food with his fork and put it in his mouth. Perhaps he could force himself back into whatever was necessary. Eat himself into hunger. Then, if that worked, he'd worry about taste and the other four senses. It would take work, but he was willing to try. With a little luck, he'd be back on the street in no time, a happy primate sure of himself and his needs, everything in working order.

As he was finishing his eggs, a portion of the yolk slipped off the fork into his lap. He tried scraping the egg off the pants with his fork but ended up smearing it worse.

The waitress appeared, took away his plate, and wiped the counter, all of it, it seemed, in one fluid, efficient movement. Robert asked her for the sponge, and after she indifferently handed it over, he dabbed at the stain on the pants, thinking it wasn't a question anymore of putting Humpty together again so much as simply trying to clean up after him.

The well-dressed old man made a move to leave, then thought better of it. The man in the faded red T-shirt began to count the sugar packets in the bowl before him. The nurse lit another cigarette. The waitress cocked her hip and repositioned the yellow plastic flower in her dark hair. The three teenage boys blew her wet drunken kisses from across the room. The tourist couple argued. The cop checked his watch.

Robert watched them all in the window, their reflections still there, though fainter now as the night leaked away, leaving the morning sky the color and texture of smeared blue-gray clay. Robert kept staring into the window, pushing beyond his reflection, and thought, it just kept coming up. Maybe that was the problem. The sun kept coming up. You kept pushing it down, but it kept coming up. Over and over again, it just kept happening, reminding you that you'd made more mistakes than plans, planned more than you hoped, hoped more than you loved.

When he looked away from the window and fumbled for his change, Robert Staples didn't know if that sun coming up was a risk or betrayal, but he knew it was time to find some way to live under it.